P9-DMC-493

Falling Stars

Tim Tigner

This book is a work of fiction. Names, characters, places and incidents are products of the author's imagination or are used fictitiously. Any resemblance to actual events or locales or persons, living or dead, is entirely coincidental.

Copyright © 2017 Tim Tigner

All rights reserved.

ISBN: 1979259380

ISBN-13: 978-1979259385

For more information on this novel or Tim Tigner's other thrillers, please visit timtigner.com

If something strikes you as unrealistic,
kindly consider taking another look at reality.

(Links are included after the novel to help get you started.)

This novel is dedicated to Nikita. I love you, son.

ACKNOWLEDGMENTS

Writing novels full of twists and turns is relatively easy. Doing so logically and coherently while maintaining a rapid pace is much tougher. Surprising readers without confusing them is the real art.

I draw on generous fans for guidance in achieving those goals, and for assistance in fighting my natural inclination toward typos. These are my friends, and I'm grateful to them all.

Editors: Andrea Kerr, Jana Marck and Peter Mathon.

Writing Consultants: Judy Marksteiner, Rosemary Paton and Sandy Wallace.

Technical Experts: Tim Ellwood for weapons, and Kevin Mikesell, MD for medicine.

Beta Readers: Errol Adler, Martin Baggs, Dave Berkowitz, Doug Branscombe, Kay Brooks, Anna Bruns, Diane Bryant, Pat Carella, John Chaplin, Ian Cockerel, Robert Enzenauer, Geof Ferrell, Andrew Gelsey, Emily Hagman, Susan Harju, Robert Lawrence, Margaret Lovett, Michael Martin, Ed McArdle, Joe McKinley, Phil Nichols, Bill Overton, Brian Pape, Michael Picco, Sharon Ring, Mickey Rudolph, Chris Seelbach, Todd Simpson, Ronald Spunt, and Robert Tigner.

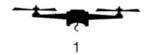

1

Raven

Versailles, France

The drone perched atop the slate roof like the big black bird for which it was named, saving battery, waiting to strike. Its minders waited nearby in a black Tesla Model X: a pilot, an engineer and the team leader.

Under normal operational security protocols, the three Russians would have hidden away, out of sight, as drone commanders usually did. But this wasn't a normal operation.

This was a test run.

A learning exercise.

All three team members needed to experience the first human capture directly.

The pilot needed confirmation that Raven's cameras were sufficient for combat operations. The engineer needed confirmation that Raven's weapons would work as designed. The team leader needed feedback, immediate and first-hand. If they unearthed any flaws, he'd have to figure out how to fix them, fast.

The house beneath the slate roof was typical old-European city-center. A centuries-old stone-block facade abutting both neighbors on a cobblestone street. The street lights were also classic. Old gas lamps turned electric, now yielding to dawn. The neighborhood was still asleep, other than the baker—and the three Russians in their silent Tesla.

"Why this particular house?" Boris asked.

Michael glanced over at the design engineer. Initially surprised to hear him speak, Michael quickly understood that the query wasn't chitchat or idle curiosity. It was a technical question from a technical man. Boris could build anything. Fix anything. Create anything. He was Leonardo DaVinci reincarnate. But like many savants, his talents ceased at humanity's edge. He was often oblivious to things beyond the mechanical realm. "It's not the house that's special. It's the occupant," Michael replied.

Boris grunted dismissively without turning from the window, his interest extinguished.

"And what's special about her?" Pavel called out from the Tesla's third row. The pilot was former military. He knew better than to ask indulgent questions. But Boris had cracked the door and curiosity had emerged.

Michael kept his eyes on the house while replying. "What makes you think it's a woman?"

"You told Boris the target weighed fifty kilos."

So he had. One point for Pavel. Michael decided to toss him a warning disguised as a bone. "Ivan has a score to settle. She interfered with one of our operations a few years back. Today, she gets what's coming."

Their employer was literally a living legend. *Ivan the Ghost* was the man to whom the wealthy turned when they needed dirty deeds done without a trace.

Or at least he used to be.

Ivan didn't take jobs anymore.

He'd given up his work-for-hire business in order to develop Raven, and the plan that went with it. If that plan worked, and Ivan's plans always worked, he would rake in billions. With a *b*. If it didn't, well, Michael chose not to think about that. Like most geniuses, Ivan had a temper. And like most pioneers, he could be ruthless with those around him when things didn't go his way.

But they would go his way.

Ivan wasn't just a genius. He was meticulous.

Before driving half the night to Versailles' city center, he had them run Raven through tests. Dozens of tests. Dogs at first. Then calves. The trial attacks were nothing short of mesmerizing.

The drone itself was impressive, if not a technological breakthrough. A scaled-up version of the quadcopter you could buy at any hobby store. They powered it using breakthrough battery technology from the lab of John Goodenough—stolen of course—and framed it with the same carbon-fiber construction used on racing bikes and tennis rackets. Boris built it to carry 250 pounds of active cargo, and hinged it to fold up for transport by SUV.

Raven's main offensive mechanism was the true marvel—both for its apparent simplicity and for its amazing action. They named it *The Claw* because it was Raven's grasping mechanism, although to Michael it looked more like a snake than a talon.

Roughly the width of a broomstick and thirty feet in length, The Claw was constructed from segments of aluminum tube, anodized black and ingeniously cut to articulate. If properly positioned, The Claw would wrap around the victim's waist with the push of a single button, automatically applying enough pressure to squeeze flesh without crushing bone. Boris insisted that the mechanics were rudimentary, but The Claw's speed and grace still stole Michael's breath every time he saw it in operation.

Of course, the trick to a clean capture was getting The Claw close enough to strike. Pets and livestock were one thing, humans were literally a different breed.

Given Raven's speed and nimble nature, Pavel was confident that he could catch anyone outdoors. The way he figured it, about a third of the victims would behave like a deer in the headlights, too frightened to react. Another third would allow curiosity to override judgment, rubbernecking until it was too late. For the final third, the warrior class, there was the taser.

Under normal circumstances, Michael was certain this particular target would require the taser. She was a fighter. But today she wouldn't get the chance. Not with Raven silently perched and The Claw ready to strike.

"How long have you worked for Ivan?" Pavel asked, breaking the silence from behind the Drone Mobile Command Unit. He was trying to make the question sound casual, but came up short.

Michael weighed his response. In fact, he'd been with Ivan since Ivan was in middle school. Michael had just won Russia's welterweight youth boxing championship when Ivan's hard-charging father had recruited him to be a companion and mentor to his son. It was Michael's first paid position, and it would be his last. After twenty years, Michael knew he was destined to be with Ivan to the end—be it abominably bitter or unbelievably sweet. "Long enough to know that he treats those who please him extremely well—and those who don't, accordingly."

A mood of grim reflection wrapped around the Tesla like a black burial shroud.

But only for a moment.

Before another word was spoken, the front door of the house opened, and Jo Monfort emerged.

2

Not a Dream

Versailles, France

Josephine Monfort stepped onto the stoop of her house and began to stretch. She'd always loved her early morning runs, but ever since moving to the posh Paris suburb of Versailles, they'd been positively blissful. This was her meditative time, her opportunity to put her body to work and her mind at ease. What better place for that than the grounds of the legendary palace built by Louis XIII? What better time than dawn—when the birds were chirping, the bread was baking, and the tourists were sleeping?

Jo braced her hands against the cool stone and leaned back into her calves. She'd dreamed of swarms of locusts, and was eager to push that pestilent thought from her mind. A good run would be perfect.

Two seconds into her stretch, she sensed an ozone disturbance off to her left, like a television coming to life in a cool, dry room. A flash of movement followed, then something brushed against her waist. Something hard. Something cold. Faster than she could flinch it wrapped itself around her, like a cattle lasso or a boa constrictor.

She seized the end of the object with both hands while sizing it up. A steel cable gripped her waist. No not a cable, a mechanical construction. And not steel, more like black aluminum. She had to be dreaming. This couldn't possibly be real.

Time slowed, just like in a dream. She became capable of calculating actions between heartbeats and planning battles between breaths, but she could not escape the feeling that this couldn't possibly be happening.

Willing herself to wake up, Jo wrapped her right hand around the loose end of the coil and her left around the lower loop. She tried pulling them apart.

The object pressed back. It felt alive.

She clawed at the mechanical creature this way and that, trying to pry it from her flesh.

It wouldn't budge. Not a millimeter. Not with everything she had.

She didn't stop.

It got worse.

A billowing hum erupted from the rooftop some twenty feet above her head. It sounded like a swarm of locusts and signaled the second stage of the assault. That explained her earlier dream but shed no light on her present inexplicable condition.

She traced the tail of the mechanical snake up to the source of the sound, a shadow of an object now emerging from atop her home. A big black UFO. No, not a UFO. A drone.

The object that ensnared her was much smaller than a military craft, but much larger than a civilian one. Roughly the size of a mattress, it was shaped like an X with propellers extending from each corner. The snaking cable descended from a spool in the center. It resembled the line dropped from a Coast Guard helicopter, although this was clearly no rescue.

Jo's hands continued to battle her bindings while her brain grappled for answers. If this was an assassination, why not use a gun? If an abduction, why not a couple of thugs and a panel van? There had to be something bigger, deeper, or broader behind the attack. Something strategic. Something sinister. Something ...

The answer struck her as swiftly and unexpectedly as the snake. Ivan! Ivan the Ghost. The grandest strategist of them all.

Jo had been part of the team that put a big black mark on Ivan's otherwise flawless record. She had long suspected that he would not forget, that he'd have his revenge, that this day would come. But Ivan had disappeared, and most believed that he was either dead or retired. Apparently he had fooled everyone, yet again.

Without relaxing her grip on the snake, Jo studied the drone hovering overhead. No doubt it had cameras. Was Ivan observing her now? Was he going to watch as the metallic snake crushed her to death?

Convinced that she couldn't overpower the metallic snake, Jo began searching for another weakness. Her focus shifted skyward and settled on the propellers humming overhead. Could she stop them with sticks or stones?

As if in answer, their pitch increased, and her situation went from bad to worse.

The drone lifted skyward and her feet left the ground. Before she could reorient, Jo found herself dangling like a hooked fish.

Desperate to stop her ascent, she lunged for the lamppost. It was the old fashioned kind, a fluted black steel cylinder that crooked to suspend its lamp from above. A functional ornament retained by a city that clung to its grandiose past.

The fingers of her right hand caught the fluting. Pulling carefully on that precious purchase, she swung closer to the pole, but the drone's ascent denied her left hand a grip. Without a second to spare, Jo brought her legs into play. Quick as a falling cat she twisted and arced and swung them around the pole, crossing her ankles as the drone drove her higher.

Her legs latched around the top of the crook. But not at the knees. She caught it down by her calves.

With her head above the rooftops and her legs clinging to the pole, Jo felt like a worm in the beak of a bird. Refusing to become breakfast, she put everything into her legs. She willed them to become bands of steel.

The upward force pulled the cold coil hard against her diaphragm, restricting her breath and raising her panic.

She pressed the panic back down while refusing to release her ankles. She might suffocate or be ripped in half, but she vowed to fight up to that point. She vowed not to give. She stared up at the mechanical beast with a defiant stare and drew energy from her rage.

That was when she first noticed it. A familiar rectangular barrel with a yellow tip, a muzzle turning in her direction. A taser.

Her heart sank.

Her tears started flowing.

There was nothing she could do.

She had no shield, no place to hide. Just locking her legs demanded all the might she could muster. She wanted to shout "That's not fair!" but couldn't spare the breath.

Staring back at the beast above, Jo swore she would not yield.

3

Inch by Inch

Versailles, France

Michael watched the scene unfolding on the other side of the windshield with a fearful fascination he hadn't experienced since the second plane hit the World Trade Center on 9/11. Jo was clinging to the top of a lamp post while Raven strained to snatch her skyward. It was human versus machine—and for the moment the woman was winning. Surely she couldn't keep it up?

Just to be certain, Michael decided to tip the scales. "Hit her with the taser."

"Already aiming," Pavel replied, his voice cool as arctic ice.

Michael had investigated Jo, both immediately after an unfortunate event a few years ago, and more recently in preparation for the Raven trial. The Frenchwoman had a colorful background to say the least. She came from a family of con artists. According to the file mysteriously procured by Ivan, Jo's parents had involved her in the family business from the day she was born. They gave her daily on-the-job training, and skewed her formal education to facilitate the life they led. Gymnastics lessons prepared her to become an exceptional cat burglar, while acting and debate classes prepped her for sophisticated confidence scams.

She'd been on track to be a female version of Ivan until her soft side blossomed and fate intervened. After inadvertently swiping the briefcase of an American diplomat, she returned it in flamboyant fashion. This so impressed the ambassador that he recommended her to the CIA for field ops.

The future had looked bright for Miss Monfort until she landed on the team pursuing Ivan—for her very first assignment. Although she and Kyle Achilles ultimately foiled Ivan's plan, Ivan and Michael had escaped. That failure earned her the personal animosity of CIA Director Wiley Rider, ending her government career. Now she did P.I. work and security consulting—apparently pretty well, given her Versailles address.

But that too was about to end.

Ivan wasn't one to forgive and forget. In fact, the only reason he wasn't there to enjoy this little bit of revenge in person was that he was overseas, settling an even bigger score.

"Firing," Pavel said.

Tasers shoot twin barbed electrodes attached to long thin wires. Once they penetrate a target, the electrodes deliver 50,000 volts, causing considerable pain and disrupting voluntary muscle control.

"Merde!" Pavel said. "One electrode hit The Claw."

"I thought you were aiming?"

"She's wriggling around like a worm in the beak of a bird— and The Claw is center mass. Plus the rotor wash is wreaking havoc on the aerodynamics."

"You've got a second taser, right?" Michael asked, attempting to repress his growing sense of panic. He had no idea how Ivan would react if they failed. The possibility had never crossed his mind. Michael never came up short. He'd just flown in from a flawlessly executed mission in Moscow. To follow that with a flop was unthinkable. A "C" average for the day just wouldn't do. Granted today's mission was just a test run. Part of the meticulous preparation Ivan always put in before a big job. But the expectations were clear. Ivan paid top dollar for top talent, and expected nothing but shining successes.

"We've got one more," Pavel said. "Aiming. Firing."

Michael watched Jo flinch as one electrode penetrated her upper arm and another hit her thigh, but she didn't start convulsing and she didn't release her grip. "What's going on? Why isn't she flailing like a landed flounder?"

"I don't know!" Pavel zoomed in on the taser's silver barbs. "It's the leg electrode. It hit the loose fabric at the side of her shorts, but didn't penetrate flesh."

"Dammit! What now?"

"We just keep pulling. We've got plenty of battery. We'll pry her off."

"I'm not worried about the battery. I'm worried about the neighbors."

"She doesn't have the breath to scream. Not with all her oxygen going to her legs. And not with The Claw wrapped around her ribs."

"This was supposed to be a quick in-and-out grab. An easy victory. Proof positive."

Nobody replied to Michael's reproach.

Raven kept straining skyward.

Jo did not yield.

"Unbelievable," Michael added.

"Never seen anything like it," Pavel said, his voice also a mutter. "Where does she get the strength?"

They continued staring in silence at the petite P.I., waiting for her legs to give. Waiting to get on with their mission.

But her legs didn't give. Her arms came into play instead. She grabbed hold of The Claw ... and began pulling.

"What's she doing?" Michael asked, his voice cool but cracking around the edges.

"She's going on the offensive," Pavel said. "My god, look. She's ... it's ... is Raven dipping?"

"We have a problem, guys," Boris said. "Raven's only spec'd to lift 250 pounds."

"She can't weigh more than 120. No way she can pull 250," Michael said.

"You're forgetting to factor in adrenaline," Boris said. "Introduce enough of that and mothers can lift cars off kids. She is fighting for her life, after all."

They watched with wide eyes as the petite brunette pulled Raven closer, handhold by sweaty handhold, inch by incredible inch.

"How are we on battery?" Michael asked.

"We've still got 67 minutes, even with the extra load," Pavel said.

"Options? Can we ram her with Raven? Try to knock her loose?"

"Don't do it," Boris said. "The drone's not designed for that."

"I thought you compared it to a tennis racquet, light but

tough and strong," Michael pressed.

"That may be, but its not engineered to be a battering ram. This might be bad, but it could get worse."

Michael suddenly felt very aware of that possibility. Reporting a failed capture was one thing. Reporting the loss of a drone would be quite another. "Pavel?"

"I agree with Boris. Wise men never fire unfamiliar weapons."

Michael couldn't believe the words that were about to escape his lips. He certainly didn't want to think about Ivan's reaction to them. He took a deep breath. *One battle at a time.*

"Release The Claw. Abort the mission."

4

No Words

Versailles, France

As the drone disappeared into the dawning sky, Jo slid down the post that had saved her life. Uncertain if she should believe it was actually over, but unable to act otherwise, she collapsed onto the cool cobblestones. Even as joy and relief overwhelmed her heart, she found herself sobbing uncontrollably. Every muscle in her lower body burned from a chemical fire. She feared her legs would fold if she attempted to stand.

"Are you okay?"

Jo looked up to see the paperboy. He was on a bicycle built for a bigger body. She found herself struggling to answer his simple question. Compared to how she'd been a few minutes earlier, she was fantastic. Compared to her usual self, she was a wreck.

By nature and training, Jo tended to keep things to herself. Especially complaints. But even if she wanted to share her story, what could she say that wouldn't make her sound like a candidate for an insane asylum? *I was lassoed by a mechanical snake as I came out of my home this morning. Then a drone attempted to abduct me.*

"You're bleeding from your arm and chest." The paperboy pointed. "Was it locusts? I heard locusts."

Jo looked down and saw coin-sized spots of blood. When Raven retreated, it ripped the barbs from her flesh. She hardly felt it at the time, with her pain receptors already on overload, but picturing the process now made her grit her teeth. She'd seen taser barbs up close. They resembled fishing hooks. She would probably twitch at the sight of yellow plastic for the rest of her life, and angling was out of the question. "It's nothing,

Pierre. I'm just recovering from a particularly tough workout. Thank you for asking."

"Shall I help you up?"

"I think I'm just going to lie here for a few minutes. Enjoy the morning sky while I catch my breath."

Pierre looked up, shrugged, and pedaled on. A few seconds later, newspapers started thunking the ground.

She attempted to analyze what had just happened, if for no better reason than to keep her mind off the pain pulsing through her body. There on the cobblestones, she couldn't come up with a better explanation than the one that had first struck her. Ivan. She'd run awry of many people in her lifetime, but only two had the resources to call in a customized drone for retribution. Ivan the Ghost and CIA Director Wiley Rider.

She discounted the Director as a candidate. If Rider were inclined to turn his attention to retribution, she would be way down his list. Certainly not in the first hundred anyway. Ivan, however, was a different story. She'd dealt a serious blow to his reputation and his career. In fact, he hadn't been attributed with a single crime since she and Achilles had crossed his path years back.

That sounded like sufficient motive to her.

But what next? Where did that leave her?

She could go after him—but the problem with that plan was obvious. It was right there in his name. Ivan was a ghost. The law enforcement community knew almost nothing about him. European residence was assumed, as was Russian nationality— thus *Ivan*—but both were speculation, and neither really mattered. National borders were meaningless to men who flew on private jets.

They did know what Ivan looked like. Achilles had seen him, face to face. And while he hadn't captured a digital image, he had worked with Agency sketch artists to create a rendering that was almost as useful. At least temporarily. Jo had no doubt that Ivan had changed his appearance while in hiding these past few years. He was a meticulous planner who could afford the best plastic surgeons and brightest make-up artists. She was certain that his appearance was now indistinguishable from millions of other fortyish Europeans.

Perhaps, Jo reasoned, she was going about this all wrong. Perhaps the operative question was *What would Ivan do next?* Would he attempt to complete what he'd started this morning? On that topic, what had he attempted? And why had he used a drone? And what was his larger plan?

There had to be a larger plan.

While Ivan might be susceptible to the sweet siren song of revenge, he was not impulsive. He was a planner. A ruthless, inventive, patient planner. A man who devised complex schemes to create situations his victims never saw coming.

But what could that scheme be? Who would become his next victim?

Energized by the provoking questions, Jo peeled herself off the ground. Her legs didn't scream, but they protested—loudly. No doubt the insides of her lower legs would be badly bruised for weeks. Fortunately she didn't have far to go. Ivan had attacked on her doorstep.

Inspiration struck as Jo twisted the knob. Although Ivan's plans and motives remained a mystery, she knew her best next move.

She shuffled over the worn stone sill and limped toward the kitchen phone. Ignoring the stools, she grabbed the receiver and slumped back to the floor. She dialed a number she knew by heart but hadn't called for many months. An American number. A cell phone. Jo called Kyle Achilles.

5

Important

Yosemite, California

Kyle Achilles was at the crux of The Nose when his phone rang. Tell most people that was where you were and they'd look at you with crossed eyes. But say that to a fellow rock climber and you'd receive a slow nod of respect. Add that you were free soloing, and that slow nod would transform into wide-eyed wonder.

Once thought to be unclimbable, The Nose on Yosemite's El Capitan was the most famous American ascent in the sport climbing world. Three thousand vertical feet of granite monolith rising above one of the most beautiful valleys on earth. Thirty-one "pitches" of a 100-foot rope. Except Achilles wasn't using rope. He was free soloing. Climbing without protective equipment. Just sticky shoes, a bag of chalk and a whole lot of hope.

He'd just dislodged a mouse, sending it up his arm and down his back before it disappeared into a crack, when he got his second surprise in as many seconds. His phone rang.

Most climbers wouldn't have their phone on during such a dangerous climb. It would be powered down and in reserve for emergencies. But Achilles received emergency calls on a regular basis, so duty kept him connected. Nonetheless, he was not in a great position for chitchat. The crux of The Nose route had overhanging rock, so Achilles' shoulders protruded behind his ankles. He dug in on three points of contact and carefully slipped in an earbud using nothing but touch to guide his moves. "Yes."

"Achilles?"

A familiar voice, but one Achilles couldn't quite place. "Yes."

"This is Director Rider."

The head of the CIA wasn't the last person Achilles expected, but he might have been the second-to-last. Their relationship had ended three years earlier, and that end had not been amicable. They hadn't spoken since, and Achilles hadn't expected that they ever would. "Yes?"

"We need to meet. I'm in San Francisco. Can you be at the Top of the Mark at 11:00 p.m. tonight?" he asked, referencing the InterContinental Hotel's landmark rooftop restaurant.

Achilles had no interest in meeting with Wiley Rider, and he was certain Rider had no personal interest in meeting with him. Therefore it had to be professional. The CIA must need something pretty badly for Rider to suck it up enough to ask in person. Achilles made the calculation. It would take him four or five hours to get back to his car and another four to reach San Francisco. "I can."

"Good. Thank you." Rider disconnected.

Achilles had left the CIA specifically because of Wiley Rider. The Director had levered his way into the corner office at Langley by blackmailing key members of congress. He had used Ivan the Ghost to do that dirty work, and then attempted to cover his tracks by sending Achilles to kill Ivan. Achilles eventually figured out what Rider was up to—but couldn't prove it. So when Ivan escaped, Achilles resigned rather than selling out and spending his career serving a dishonorable man.

At the time, Achilles had fully expected Ivan to eliminate Rider for double-crossing him. But years had passed, Ivan had vanished, and Rider had remained king of the castle. Achilles' best guess regarding tonight's agenda was that Ivan had finally threatened Rider, and Rider was going to try to cajole Achilles into going after him with "you'll be next."

But that was just a guess.

Achilles wasn't one for pretenses or formalities, and he was short on time, so his only prep for the meeting was a quick shower in the Yosemite parking lot, cold water sprayed from a hanging plastic bag. Fortunately the scruffy look was trendy, and casual clothing remained hip with the Silicon Valley crowd.

Achilles entered the restaurant's dedicated vestibule at 10:58 pm and immediately spotted the telltale bodyguard.

The spotting was mutual.

The bulky suit gave him a thorough pat-down topped off by a magnetometer scan. Once satisfied, he used a key to summon the elevator. When it arrived, the bodyguard stepped aside, gesturing without saying a word.

No witnesses, Achilles thought. That fit his hypothesis.

The elevator door pinged open on nineteen to reveal another suit. This one gestured toward a stairway leading to the rooftop bar. He stayed put as Achilles climbed.

Emerging into the open air and a skyline view of San Francisco, Achilles spotted Rider standing by the rail. He was ostensibly dressed like his guards but in a suit that no doubt cost thousands more.

The Director turned around at the sound of Achilles' footfalls. He was not wearing a glad-to-see-you grin. In fact he did not look the least bit pleased. Meeting Achilles' eye he said, "This better be important."

6

Upside Down

San Francisco, California

Achilles understood that an attack was imminent the moment Rider's words reached his ears, but that was a moment too late. Even as the implication registered and the conclusion calculated, he detected an approaching hum.

As a former field op, Achilles reacted on reflex, diving and rolling for cover while shouting for Rider to do the same. But Langley's chief bureaucrat was exactly that. He had not come up through operations with a gun in his hand and a mic in his ear. His duck-and-cover reflexes had been honed in press rooms, not back rooms. The only assaults he ever dodged were verbal.

From beneath a marble-topped table, Achilles turned his head toward the source of the sound and caught sight of a descending drone. One of those pesky model helicopter-like pseudo-toys that were all the rage with techies and teenage boys. It dropped down from the sky a few feet in front of the spot Achilles' head had just occupied.

For a split second, Achilles felt relieved. Drones carried cameras. They were the paparazzi's favorite new tool, and Rider was a celebrity of sorts. But it wasn't a telephoto lens that Achilles observed dangling beneath the quadcopter's belly. It was a handgun complete with suppressor.

Achilles sprang to his feet and grabbed the back of a chair with both hands. He swung it around like a big fat bat, putting his back into it and hurtling the chair toward the electronic intruder with careful aim and considerable speed. The handgun barked at the same instant he released the makeshift missile. Three things then happened at once. The recoil propelled the drone backward a few feet. The chair flew through the empty air where the drone had just been. And CIA Director Wiley Rider took a bullet to the heart.

Actually four things. Achilles let loose a few expletives.

Before the chair crashed to the ground, he began calculating moves. Offensive and defensive. Achilles fully expected the drone to adjust its aim and empty its magazine in his direction. He searched for other objects to throw, scanned for sources of cover, and identified potential exits.

But the drone didn't turn on him.

It did the last thing he expected—but the first thing he should have anticipated.

It dropped the gun. A suppressed Glock 19.

While Achilles watched the sinful steel clatter onto the tiled floor, the drone shot skyward and disappeared, its mechanical whirr melding into the city soundscape.

Achilles muttered a few more choice words and ran to Rider —just to be sure. Rider hadn't twitched or flailed, grunted or groaned. He'd acted exactly as any mammal would if it suddenly found itself without a functioning circulatory system. He'd dropped like a glass brushed off the edge of a table. Only instead of shattering, he'd just slumped.

Achilles pressed his fingers to Rider's neck, and laid his ear next to Rider's nose. He got nothing.

Rider was gone.

Achilles looked back toward the dropped Glock and then over toward the door beyond. He had no doubt that within seconds the bodyguards would burst through with weapons raised, responding to the noise. He did have doubt that they would stop and assess the situation before firing. Their duty was to protect the director. Nobody would question an "overreaction" to such a clear and credible threat. If they did stop and assess, the situation wouldn't be much prettier. He'd be arrested and isolated faster than you could burn the Bill of Rights.

The next moves of the judicial dance played out quickly and clearly in Achilles' mind. It wasn't pretty. He had the means. He had the motive. He had the opportunity. Meanwhile, the CIA had a situation that would cause it great embarrassment. The only way to blunt that public relations nightmare was to "serve justice." *Swiftly, soundly and severely.*

Standing dumbstruck beneath that moonlit San Francisco sky, the conclusion came calling like a freight train. If he was still there when the bodyguards burst onto the murder scene, he might never see sunshine again—uncaged.

Achilles chose option B. He vaulted over the rooftop railing and began the 19 floor descent, wondering all the while if this evasive action was precisely what the real killer had planned.

7

Battle Prep

Versailles, France

Jo experienced a surge of relief when Achilles answered his phone. She hadn't considered the time difference until after the first ring, but by then the damage was done.

"Yes."

"Achilles, it's Jo Monfort. Do you have a minute?"

He took a second to answer. "How urgent is it?"

How urgent? She wasn't sure. But since answering the question would take as long as presenting the situation, she dove right in. "I think Ivan just tried to kill me."

Another pregnant pause, followed by an answer that shouldn't have shocked her, but did. "Me too. Just now. He did kill Director Rider."

Achilles pressed on before she could process his startling comeback. "Another few minutes and you wouldn't have caught me. I'm about to destroy this phone."

To buy herself a second, she asked, "Are you okay? You're breathing heavy."

"I'm about a hundred feet up the side of the San Francisco InterContinental Hotel."

"And yet you took my call."

"I thought you were Ivan. And since my phone is about to be out of order, I took the opportunity to hear what he had to say."

"I'm glad you did. We need to talk. Team up. Where should we meet?"

"What were you driving when we first met?"

Worked up as she was, the non sequitur struck Jo's racing mind like a speed bump she didn't see coming. Then she understood. Identity verification. "A black Kawasaki Ninja with neon-green highlights."

"There's a Mexican restaurant in Manhattan on the corner of 3rd and 50th. Dos Caminos. You can sit outside. I'll look for you there at 19:00 hours."

Jo checked her watch and did some quick calculations. CDG direct to JFK, eight hours. A six-hour time change working in her favor. A few hours on either side. "I'll be there."

She considered his choice of rendezvous location. Achilles had picked a place that could be observed from a hundred different vantage points. A meeting point that facilitated disappearing into a crowd. She'd have done the same thing if he'd initiated the call. A good sign.

"Fallback is 24 hours later at The Grill," he added before ending the call.

Jo ruminated on that last point for a minute. She'd never been to a grill with Achilles. In fact they'd never been to a restaurant. Their time together had been brief, but intense, and their shared hours had played a pivotal role in both their lives.

The location of the backup rendezvous came to her a few seconds later. She hadn't trained with Achilles, but everyone who went through CIA training at Camp Peary, *aka* Spy U at The Farm, knew Berret's Taphouse Grill. Their motto was "Beer on tap, oyster in hand," and they played live music on the patio. It was the go-to place for frazzled new recruits let off their leashes for a few precious hours.

The memory made Jo aware of her stomach. She looked around the kitchen. Normally she picked up bread and croissants at the end of her run, but she'd be skipping her regular workout today. Her legs wouldn't take it and her heart rate had been sufficiently elevated. Her flatmates would be disappointed when they came down for breakfast.

Jo lived with three other thirtyish women. The four of them were all single but looking. Likewise, all were successful professionals grateful for the pleasant company and prestigious address. They joked that their life was like the French version of the American show *Sex in the City*—but without the sex.

She turned on the teapot, grabbed some day-old bread and a hunk of chèvre, then sat at the kitchen table with a notepad and pencil. She wanted to sketch out the drone and its snakelike snare while their images remained fresh. She was certain those memories would never fade per se, but she knew they'd morph with time, the evil features exaggerating with every mental retelling. The drone would become bigger, its hum louder, the snake somehow both more steely and serpentine.

For fifteen minutes she munched the bread and cheese while working her sketches, paying particular attention to scale and the component locations. The four propellers. The winch. The camera and taser mounts. If she ever battled that bot again, she would be prepared.

Satisfied with her renderings, Jo used the notepad to leave her flatmates a message, apologizing for the lack of breakfast and telling them she'd been called away indefinitely.

Packing didn't take but a minute. She knew that Achilles was a wardrobe minimalist, keen on keeping his life simple and his backpack light. She mirrored that move, changing into jeans and a gray top before slipping on versatile black boots and a matching leather jacket. Thirty minutes later, she walked out the door with a satchel on her shoulder and determination in her heart—uncertain if she would ever return. Going after Ivan the Ghost had never been a winning proposition.

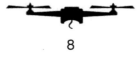

8

Spoiled

San Jose, California

Ivan's limo pulled to a stop beside the red carpet where the women were waiting. The *escorts*.

The American Express Centurion Card concierges had never let him down, but he was still amazed by the services they'd provide for a mere $2,500 annual fee. "Two escorts for 24 hours, waiting by the jet at midnight, please." Those twelve words were all it took—given that his preferences were on file and he had charged the jet to AmEx.

Ivan wasn't disappointed with the concierge's selection, and judging by the looks coming back at him, the escorts weren't either. Then again, they never were.

Ivan had hit the genetic lottery, and he knew it. He'd gotten the looks, the body, the brains and the means. Calling him one-in-a-billion was not hyperbole. Frankly, he doubted there were six people his equal on a planet of seven billion.

"Hello."

"Hi there. I'm Scarlett," replied the red head with a wink that made his heart rate rise.

"And I'm Daphne," said the blonde. "Where are we going?"

"You'll be back on this carpet tomorrow night. In between, you'll be enjoying this beautiful Gulfstream." What a thrill it was, offering lovely ladies a ride on a private jet.

"Where are we going?" Daphne repeated, her tone a bit tetchy.

Ivan wasn't used to back talk from anyone, much less the hired help. *What was it about Americans?* "It really doesn't matter, as you won't be getting off anywhere but here."

"I'm not leaving the country," she insisted.

"Me either," Scarlett said, taking Daphne's arm.

Ivan locked eyes with one, then the other. He could tell them that he was headed for the French Riviera, and that would probably change their tune. But he didn't like to be challenged, and their lack of logic vexed him. "It's a private jet, not a panel van, and this is Silicon Valley, not Tijuana."

Neither girl's expression yielded. That was the problem with the high-end escorts. They weren't hungry. "Suit yourselves."

Ivan headed up the airstair without a backward glance.

He didn't own the G650. Chartering jets was far more cost efficient than owning them, and infinitely more suited to the liquid-asset requirement of a man who might need to vanish at any minute. The downside was that he usually flew with an unknown crew, creating something he always preferred to avoid: unpredictability.

At the top of the stairs, he caught the eye of the flight attendant waiting in welcome, and reconsidered his aversion to unfamiliar faces. *What was it they said about variety being the spice of life?*

She gave a name with her greeting, but it went in one ear and out the other. What stuck was the emphasis with which she said, "It will be my pleasure to take care of you this evening."

He gave her a silky smile.

She gestured toward the luxurious cabin. "Do you expect the others shortly?"

"It's just me tonight."

Her eyes registered surprise—and perhaps something more.

Ivan grabbed a seat. As he settled in, the flight attendant brought him a chilled bottle of Icelandic Glacial Water and a frosty crystal glass. Setting the silver platter before him, she said, "Still sealed, as requested. First time I've seen this brand."

"A bit of purity in an otherwise tainted world."

"Is that the voice of experience I hear?" she asked while pouring.

He cocked his head and studied the flight attendant for a few seconds. Liking what he saw, he decided to engage. "You gave me a look, earlier."

"I might have spilled the water if I wasn't looking."

"Not that. You gave me a look when I told you I was the only passenger."

"Apologies if I offended. It wasn't intentional."

"I'm not offended. I'm curious. What were you thinking?"

She appraised him openly for a moment, after which Ivan expected her to ask if he wanted to hear the truth—as though anyone ever said they didn't. But she skipped the silly ritual. "I was thinking there had to be a story."

Ivan didn't buy it. "The look I saw was more judgmental than curious."

Another moment of appraisal ended with a shallow shrug. "This is a lot of plane for one person."

"You're pretty blunt for someone working in hospitality."

"I'm heading on vacation. Perhaps my mind is already there. Please forgive me." Her tone was more playful than placating.

"Where are you vacationing?"

"France. Thanks for the ride." She winked.

Playful. He liked playful. "Whereabouts?"

She shrugged. "Ne pas savoir est la moitié du plaisir."

Not knowing is half the fun, Ivan repeated to himself. *Talk about an opposite approach to life.* "You speak French like a native."

She inclined her head, acknowledging the compliment, but didn't spout the expected "Merci beaucoup." *Fascinating.*

Ivan found himself intrigued, but she'd touched a sore spot with her reaction to his flying alone. He raised the glass again in polite dismissal. "Thank you for the water."

Ivan didn't have regrets. He didn't think that way. Didn't look backward. But he had a sore spot, and this girl had found it in two seconds flat. She'd put a pin on the one thing he didn't have. Odd as it was for a man-of-mystery, Ivan dreamed of days filled with family and friends. He longed for a prestigious permanent address with personal photos on the wall. Club memberships and restaurants where they knew his assumed name.

Of course he also had much grander ambitions. He *always* had grander ambitions. He wouldn't stop until schoolbooks included his name. *Why was it that no matter what you had or what you'd achieved, you always wanted more?*

Ivan drank his water and pushed whimsy from his mind. Time to revel in the moment. He'd just completed a major coup.

One worth celebrating. He'd served revenge, clean and cold, to a man who had betrayed him. The Director of the CIA no less. And he'd framed his rival for it. He doubted there was another person on the planet who could have pulled that off. Not one of the seven billion.

He'd timed it perfectly as well. Crippling the CIA and forcing Achilles into hiding just when the world was about to need them most.

That called for a celebration.

He turned from the window toward the front of the plane. "Tell me, do you drink champagne?"

9

Reassignment

El Paso, Texas

Midnight phone calls rarely bring good news. Winning lottery numbers are picked early in the evening, and promotions are delivered in person. Unfortunately, SAIC Ripley Zonder of the FBI received those calls all too often. As Special Agent In Charge of the El Paso field office, he was point man on the border between Texas and Mexico.

His hand felt like lead as it reached for the phone. The remnant of a dream in full motion. "Zonder."

"Rip, it's Brix. Are you ready for a challenge?"

Rip was ready for his pillow and not much else. At that moment, he wouldn't get out of bed to attend the *Victoria's Secret Fashion Show*. A tip-driven bust on the border had kept him up for 36 hours. But Robert Brix was not a man you gave *No* as an answer. The Director of the FBI didn't just wield the biggest sticks in the world, he also controlled Rip's carrots. "Always!"

"Glad to hear it. I've got a new job for you. Starts in an hour."

"In an hour?"

"That's when your plane leaves. 03:00."

"Leaves for where?"

"San Francisco. I've just named you SAIC."

Well what do you know, a midnight promotion. The news perked him up as the questions flooded in. The first was *Why me?* He was a West Texas hound dog and San Francisco was more fit for poodles. But he chose a less challenging question. "Why the rush, sir?"

"Wiley Rider was just assassinated in the city. I want you running the investigation."

"The Director of the CIA is dead?"

"Shot in the heart during a meeting with a former agent. That agent is on the run, which is why I need a sheriff running the show. Someone who knows how to lead a posse. Tangney's good, but he's a numbers guy. Financial crimes."

"What's happening to Tangney?"

"Eric's getting your job."

"He's not going to be happy."

"Nobody's going to be happy until that assassin is a confirmed kill or behind bars."

"I'll grab my go-bag. Company plane?"

"Fueling up at Biggs as we speak. Kickoff conference is in four hours. And don't worry about Eric. Long term, his career will benefit from some time on the border."

Somehow Rip didn't think Tangney or his former team would see it that way. They would see one Texan favoring another—and they'd be right. But that didn't mean it wasn't a sound decision. Rip's role was to prove Brix right.

He slept and showered on the plane and arrived at his new office feeling about forty percent. The FBI's San Francisco field office was a typical nondescript high-rise office building, located amidst other high-rises just off Civic Center Plaza, a mile southwest of where Rider bit the bullet.

All eyes were on Rip as he walked to the empty chair at the head of the table. Few looked familiar. None were friendly. The big teleconference screen still showed the FBI seal—the stars, the stripes, the scales and the laurel leaves. Fidelity. Bravery. Integrity. Since Director Brix wasn't yet on the line, Tangney must have leaked.

It was time to form a first impression and Rip resolved to make it a strong one. He would not waste a minute waiting for Brix, despite the cover the Director might provide. He would not delve into personal politics, or delay progress with introductions. He would get straight to business. "Good morning. We've got a killer to catch and a trail that's seven hours cold. I've read the preliminary report from the crime scene, as I'm sure have all of you. We know *who*. We know *where*. We know *how*. With those three keys already in pocket, we're freed from the usual delays and distractions, so I'll accept no excuses.

Just one well-coordinated crunch to catch Kyle Achilles."

So far, so good. The eyes were still hostile, but the minds were engaging. "To do that, we need to understand him. His background, his motivations, his associates, his skills. Who here can give me the bacon without the sizzle?"

"I can," an unfamiliar agent said without hesitation.

"And you are?"

"Oscar Pincus, CIA. I was his last handler."

Oscar looked like he'd stepped off the bottle of Mr. Clean. One glance at the big bald prick and Rip pegged him as one of those slick Washington weasels who knew how to get dirty without letting anything stick. The kind of guy powerful politicians always kept in their corner. Their darkest corner. This one must have hopped on a plane even earlier than Rip had. That made sense. Upon losing their boss, the CIA would first scramble their own. Then they'd begin working to shift the blame. "You're in from Langley?"

Oscar nodded. "Achilles' last assignment was high profile, and he blew it. Director Rider fired him for it."

In other words, the assassin wasn't one of us. We dismissed him. A decent defense. "So Achilles was motivated by personal animosity?"

"And a misguided sense of justice."

"How long ago was he fired?"

"Three years."

"What's he been doing in the meantime?"

"Climbing rocks."

"Is that some CIA metaphor?"

"No. He's a professional rock climber."

Go figure. "That explains the dramatic escape. Is there money in rock climbing?"

"Can't be much."

Rip didn't think so either. "So he's broke and bitter and feeling cheated. He blames Rider and takes action."

"Or someone wants to make it look that way," Oscar added.

So the CIA was going to two-step this one, first add distance and then cast doubt. "You think it could be a setup?"

"It's possible. Invite men known to have a poor personal history, then use a long gun. Glocks are easily converted to carbines, and planting brass is child's play. Plus the killer left the weapon behind. That's not the mark of a seasoned operative, unless said operative is losing his mind."

Losing his mind. Make that a three-step. "Ballistics will clear that up."

Before Oscar could respond, the big screen flickered and the FBI logo yielded to Director Robert Brix's ruddy face. "Have you caught him yet?"

"Not yet, sir."

"Sorry I'm late, SAIC Zonder. Got another call. I trust you're getting full cooperation?" Brix made a point of meeting every eye so each agent would feel the weight. "I see Acting Director Riddle also sent his man."

"Good morning, Director." Oscar said.

Brix's gaze returned to Rip. "Afraid I have to run, but I wanted to check in. I've been rearranging my schedule so I can come out tomorrow."

"Tomorrow?"

"Today if you make the arrest."

"You'll be the first to know if we do."

Brix nodded and the screen reverted to the FBI logo.

"Was Achilles a good field operative?" Rip asked Oscar.

"His skills were solid. Some would say superior. Politics was his, um, heel."

"He have any friends left at the agency? Anybody he might turn to?"

"No. There's been a lot of turnover the past three years, and most of his work was in the field anyway. Solitary ops."

"Good to know. He have family?"

"A fiancée, Katya Kozara. She's Russian. And get this: she returned to Moscow two weeks ago."

That was a lucky break. The optics were right and it would give the CIA something to do. "I trust you're bringing her in."

Oscar focused intently on his fingernails. "We're working on it. Relations with Russia are a bit strained at the moment."

"Well, maybe this can make them better. Russians love locking people up."

"They didn't lock up Snowden."

Rip hated guys who made excuses before lifting a finger.

"Don't worry about bitin' off more than you can chew. Your mouth is probably a whole lot bigger than you think. Just focus on the prize. We get her, we get him. Game over."

10

Manipulation

French Riviera

Ivan's phone beeped as his plane descended below 10,000 feet, waking him. It was a single ping and not particularly loud, but it tickled the back of his brain. Few people had his number and none of them would leave casual messages. He checked the screen and groaned inwardly. The voice message was from the one man he couldn't ignore. He hit play.

Four words sprang from the speaker, stripped clean of salutation or sign-off. "Come see me immediately."

"Crap."

The noise roused the flight attendant, who rolled over to face him. They hadn't slept much, for all the right reasons, but she still looked alert. Perky even. "Who was that?" she cooed.

Good question. Vladislav "Vlad" Vazov, or *Little V* as everyone called him behind his back, was the son of Victor Vazov, one of Russia's oil oligarchs. The single best word to describe Vlad was *playboy*. But of course, that hardly described their relationship, or the reason for Little V's call. Speaking softly, Ivan said, "My boss."

"Your boss," she repeated, rising up on one elbow and uncovering a single beautiful breast. "I find it hard to believe that you report to anyone." She used her free arm to gesture around the jet, exposing the twin in the process.

So do I, Ivan thought.

As *The Ghost*, he had operated at the apex of the dirty-deeds business. He'd been a living legend. That was fine and good while it lasted, but it came with a downside he hadn't anticipated during the heyday of his acclaim. When one operated as a ghost, he had no verifiable income. No references. No collateral. None of the prerequisites for building anything big enough to be of interest to a giant like him. Yes, he'd done well financially. Very well. But he'd lived accordingly. So when the idea for his crowning achievement came to him, Ivan found himself far short of the financial foundation required to get it going.

He turned toward her. "I had to borrow money to build my business. The caller was my creditor."

"What business is that?"

An abundance of caution kept him from saying the name of his business. "A high-tech company."

"Sounds sexy." She traced a nail across his bare shoulder. "If you'd like, I'd be happy to come by your place to help work off any tension that might arise from your meeting."

I bet you would.

Ivan let her eat silence for few seconds before saying, "I owe him $600 million."

"$600 million," she repeated, her eyes growing wide.

Ivan nodded.

She dropped back onto the mattress but left her charms exposed. "Why call a creditor your boss? I've heard it said that *you* have a problem when you can't repay a million dollar loan, but it's *the bank* that has the problem if you can't pay back a billion."

"That's an acute observation."

"For a flight attendant, you mean?"

"For anyone. "

"I have my moments. Is it true? If so, then the banker's not really your boss, and we can play some more." She ran a fingernail across his shoulder.

This girl really was a sharp one, but she still had to go. He was nearing the endgame of his grandest operation and could afford no distractions, regardless of how smart, sweet, or stress-relieving. "Who says I borrowed from a banker?"

Her look shifted from puzzled to perturbed as realization dawned. "The mob? You've got the mob after you?"

Ivan shrugged.

She blinked a few times, then rolled into a seated position and began putting on her clothes. "We're about to land. You should

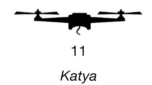

11

Katya

San Francisco, California

Achilles would have preferred a day at the dentist to the call he was about to make, but the entire 49ers defensive line couldn't have stopped him from making it.

Since he no longer had a phone and it was after midnight, his options were limited. He decided to hit the Four Seasons Hotel in Silicon Valley, which was near the storage facility where he kept his go-bag—his stash of weapons, documents, disguises and emergency cash. It was a big stash, all of it long-forgotten, off-the-books remnants from CIA missions. All of it untouchable except in emergency situations—kind of like a 401k.

Rather than asking at the desk, Achilles approached the valet, an Indian with a thick gold bracelet and lively eyes. Achilles held up a $100 bill. "I need to make an international call, immediately." He whipped out a second hundred. "For cash."

"Of course, sir. How long a call?"

"Less than five minutes."

Rather than picking up the phone on his stand, the valet said, "Please follow me."

He didn't take Achilles to the lounge or business center. He took him to the luggage storage room. Pulling out his own cell he called up an app. Skype. "Take your time." He handed the phone over, closed the door, and left Achilles in his own private phone booth.

Achilles sat on a hard-case bag while dialing, but got up again immediately. He was too nervous to sit. He began pacing while the call connected.

"Hello."

"Katya, I'm so glad you answered. Are you okay?"

"I'm fine. Just preparing for class. You sound stressed."

Relief swept over Achilles—but plenty of nervous tension remained. He had a big ask of Katya, and he wasn't sure she'd go along. Katya was fiercely loyal, but she wasn't a woman to stand blindly behind her man. She had fought her way up the academic ladder in Russia, and then made the leap from its top rung to America's, landing a plum professorship. Like Jo, she thought for herself, and acted for herself, and Achilles admired her greatly for it. But tonight, he needed her to follow his instructions. Tonight, he needed her to do as he asked—even though it would pain her greatly.

"I've just been framed for killing CIA Director Rider. Looks like it was Ivan the Ghost. By morning, half of U.S. law enforcement will be hunting me."

"Oh, goodness."

"It gets worse. They're going to come after you to get to me."

"In Moscow?"

"You're going to have to leave the university and go into hiding today. Immediately."

Katya only paused a single second. Her mind was the fastest he knew. "You've thought this through? Weighed the alternatives? Considered the consequences—to me and my career—and concluded that my leaving is the only way?"

"I have. There's no room for negotiation—*with the authorities*, I mean. They'll pounce like an angry lion. No chance to reason. No opportunity to fight. Absolutely no way to keep teaching. If you don't go, you'll be locked away and used as leverage against me."

Katya knew how serious Achilles' world was. She had firsthand experience with it. So she didn't push back with complaints about *career* or *commitments* or *students depending on her*. She didn't say, *I just got here*, or *That's not fair*. Instead, she said, "I can visit my aunt in Saint Petersburg. She'll be happy to see me."

Again, Achilles had to be cruel to be kind. "I'm sorry, but you can't visit anyone you know. The CIA will make capturing me a top priority. They'll use everything they have and will likely draft the FSB. You have to get off the grid. No cell phone. No computer. No friends. I'm *so sorry*."

Katya paused, and Achilles felt his heart stick in his throat. It only stayed there for a second.

"Where should I go?" she asked, her tone replete with resolve.

"You told me that when you were finishing up your dissertation, you went into isolation. You traveled to a small village beside a remote lake. Just you and your books. Do you remember the place? Don't say the name."

Achilles hadn't been there. He hadn't known Katya at that time. But one afternoon in Napa, she'd told him the story over a flight of five Cabernet wines. Following in the footsteps of a friend who had recently completed his dissertation, Katya had taken a train 250 miles east and glued herself to her books until her dissertation was done. Achilles remembered the name of the lake because they'd laughed about it. *Gryadetskoe* sounded a little like *graduation*. Her goal.

"I remember."

"You've got a few papers to publish, don't you? Part of your tenure track requirements? Can you do what you did then? Grab your books and research notes and go crank them out in solitude?"

"I guess so. If that's what I have to do."

"It absolutely is. Your attitude is amazing. I appreciate it more than I can say."

"How long will I need to stay there?"

"I don't know. Weeks. Maybe a couple of months. I'm so sorry."

After a pause, she said, "How will we communicate if I'm off the grid?"

Leave it to a math professor to probe the practicalities. "We won't. Too dangerous. I'm sorry."

"Stop saying you're sorry."

"I'll come get you when it's safe. In the meantime, I'm sure there will be some news coverage of my situation, even in Russia. If anything should happen to me, you'll hear about it. But I don't want you worrying about me. I'll be fine. Focus on making this an opportunity to get those publications cranked out."

"I will."

What a woman. She wasn't moaning about the career impact of walking away from a prestigious visiting professorship without notice. She wasn't complaining about leaving civilization behind. She was just doing what had to be done—for him. "I love you."

"I love you too."

12

Promotion

French Riviera

Like its creator, Silicon Hill was not what it seemed. On the outside, Ivan's business complex looked like a posh oceanfront community—secluded, exclusive and secure. On the inside, it appeared to be a high-tech research facility, complete with laboratories, dormitories, offices, eateries and recreational facilities. In actual fact, it was all those things—but it was also much more.

Michael was about to pull back the curtain for one of the engineers. *Welcome to Oz.*

Mickey Leonov was top talent on their primary legitimate venture, a shoebox-sized drone that monitored pipelines for oil and gas companies. And being of Russian descent, he had an intuitive understanding of both the privilege of insiders and the perils of crossing the powers that be.

Mickey's promotion wasn't planned, but the failure in Versailles required immediate corrective action. More action than could be completed by the current crew before Ivan's return. Michael wanted to retrofit Raven with improved offensive capabilities so that he could present the solution at the same time he revealed their shortcoming. Problem encountered, problem dispatched.

Ivan didn't know about the debacle in Versailles yet. Having taken a page from the playbook of Russia's previous president, he refused to discuss operations on the phone, even in code. He'd find out in person when he returned from California.

Michael, Boris and Pavel spent the drive back to the Côte d'Azur brainstorming fixes for Raven's flaws. They arrived home with workable solutions and implementation was now underway.

Michael phoned down to the laboratory. "Mickey, it's Michael. Please join me upstairs."

After a moment of stunned silence, Mickey replied with excitement in his voice, "On the second floor?"

The second floor was strictly off limits to non-executives. A call like this was tantamount to a promotion, and every engineer knew it. "That's right."

"I'll be right up."

In a stroke of genius typical of Ivan, he had named his company Silicon Hill. The obvious comparison worked as anticipated, and Silicon Hill quickly became the talk of Silicon Valley. Ivan's technology incubator boasted everything that Google, Facebook and YouTube offered its best and brightest —plus a beachfront location.

And not just any beach.

The most prestigious beach in the world.

The Côte d'Azur. The French Riviera. Home of Monte Carlo, Cannes and Saint Tropez. Topless beaches, tropical weather and mega yachts. Exotic cars, celebrity chefs and classy casinos.

Converted from a seaside estate, Silicon Hill's corporate compound centered around the previous owner's clifftop mansion. The ground floor of the two-story structure housed its large lobby, administrative offices, meeting rooms and an enormous kitchen. The second floor contained the executive offices, and the owner's residence which went unused. Vazov preferred his home on the grounds of the Monte Carlo Polo Club. All the legitimate creative work was conducted underground in a 20,000-square-foot finished basement that had once housed the most valuable exotic car collection in France.

Michael met Mickey at the top of the grand staircase that linked the lobby with the executive suite. "Right this way," Michael said, motioning toward the east wing, which appeared eerily quiet. "You expected to see more people," Michael added, reading Mickey's expression.

"I did."

"They're not here. They don't usually work *here*."

Mickey cocked his head. "They don't?"

"I know. You see them going up the stairs every morning and down them every evening, but they're not actually coming here. They're just passing through."

"Passing through?" Mickey's face displayed a gratifying disorientation. He really had no idea.

"You know the work we do here is highly confidential, right? Everything has to be kept secret until patents are issued or products are launched."

"Right. That's one reason Mr. Vazov has us living on his compound. It minimizes interaction with the outside world. We've figured that out."

Michael nodded while smiling inside. The hired help all thought Vlad Vazov was the brains behind Silicon Hill, when in reality he was just the bucks. This was intentional. An unwritten yet explicit clause in the loan deal. Vazov used the illusion to pacify his father—and Ivan was happy to be a ghost. "Well, Mr. Vazov has taken that approach one step further with his pet project."

"Pet project?"

"The team I'd like you to join." Michael stopped walking and turned to face the engineer. "But only if you're willing to keep it quiet—no matter what."

"No matter what?"

Michael reached beneath his jacket and pulled a handgun from the holster behind his back. He rarely carried. Ivan considered guns to be beneath them and preferred to get creative in situations where weapons were usually required. But in this instance, flashing a bit of cold steel was a smart tactical move, so Ivan would approve. "The pay is triple, but there are dire consequences for betrayal."

Mickey stared at the Sig with wide eyes for a few seconds.

Michael studied his face, looking for the decision.

"Everybody who comes up here—"

"Is part of that pet project."

"Triple the pay?"

Michael nodded.

Safety in numbers. The A Team. Mickey's calculations were obvious. "Well, all right then. Count me in."

Michael holstered the Sig and resumed walking. They passed

Vazov's office, Michael's, Boris's and Ivan's, then turned left into a short hallway made to appear longer by a mirror at the end. Michael passed Pavel's office and the bathroom without slowing, causing Mickey to fall back. At the last instant the glass slid aside, swiftly and silently, and he stepped onto an elevator. "Are you going to join me?"

Mickey followed him aboard, silently but with an expression that spoke volumes.

The elevator had no buttons or switches, and it didn't ask for a command, but as soon as Mickey cleared the threshold it sealed them in and started to descend.

"You know the previous owner had a huge car collection, right? All housed in the enormous underground garage where the laboratory is now located."

"I do."

"Well, he had another collection, a secret collection, as the world's wealthy often do."

Michael would have paid for a picture of Mickey's expression. "What kind of collection?"

"Artwork, armaments and apparatuses of a sexual nature. Much of it stolen, scandalous, or outright illegal. He kept it all on the next level down."

"Next level down? I had no idea—"

"This elevator is the only way to get there. Well, other than the cargo lift concealed in the laboratory floor."

Mickey was still processing the grand revelation when the elevator door opened and they found themselves looking at Silicon Hill's secret lab. Identical in size to the one above, it was similarly replete with storage racks and work benches and scores of high-tech tools. All the so-called executives were busy working on one of four big black machines, each roughly the size of a mattress.

"Those drones are enormous," Mickey muttered with wonder in his eyes.

"So are our plans," Michael replied. "Welcome aboard."

13

Little V

French Riviera

Exiting his limo at the Monte Carlo Polo Club, Ivan rolled his shoulders like a boxer about to enter a ring. Meetings with Vazov were always a battle of one sort or another. Vlad had an ego that outweighed his abilities tenfold, and the attitude of a man who thought the world owed him more than it had already given.

Ivan walked through a lobby festooned with trinkets and trophies and stepped out to the massive expanse of manicured grass. Polo fields were roughly nine times the size of football fields, with goal posts set wide enough apart that you could drive trucks between them—two at a time.

Ivan made his way to the owner's tent and availed himself of one of the chairs facing the throne. Vazov habitually sat with his back to the action in Japanese style, so as to be viewed against the best background. In his absence, this gave Ivan the opportunity to watch the match while waiting. Fortunately a flag indicated that this was the sixth and final chukka. He was eager to clear this hurdle, get home, and hear about Raven's test run.

A waiter appeared wearing the black and gold colors of Vazov's Team Excelsior, along with the requisite smile. Ivan ordered an Erdinger wheat beer and returned his gaze to the game.

People speculated that Vazov gravitated to polo because being on horseback literally kept the little guy out of his father's enormous shadow. Ivan saw the appeal, but developed his own theory. He suspected that Vazov simply liked to walk around with a polo mallet—given that swords were out of style. In preparation for a game of buzkashi, the Afghan analog to polo played with an animal carcass, he'd seen the playboy take the head off a tethered goat with a euphoric look in his eyes. Ivan shuddered to think how much practice it had taken to learn to strike a blow with that much force and precision—and how heartless one had to be to deliver it.

Sitting there waiting for Vazov to come galloping along, Ivan felt like a tethered goat. He didn't like the feeling.

The waiter returned with two frosty mugs as the bugle sounded: hefeweizen for Ivan and Panaché for Vazov, a fifty-fifty mixture of pale ale and fresh-squeezed lemonade. Ivan enjoyed a gratifying first sip as the black-and-gold team captain thundered to a stop before him. He had to concede that the scene made for an impressive sight.

Whereas Big V was a bear of a brute, with a thick neck, bald head and knuckles resembling walnuts, Little V was lean and athletic, with bronzed skin, thick hair and manicured nails. Obviously, the genetic roulette ball had favored his mother, a Latvian beauty queen. As far as Ivan could tell, the only things father and son shared were money, a name and a ruthless temperament.

"Walk with me," Vazov said, still in the saddle.

Ivan and Vazov shared the same height and build. In other words, equal footing. Apparently that didn't suit Little V at the moment. Ivan rose without responding.

"Bring the drinks," Vazov added, extending his left hand.

Ivan grabbed both frosty mugs and they began walking toward the stables.

The word "pony" conjures up the image of a diminutive horse breed, although in fact it references agility. Polo ponies average 15 hands in height, and weigh in at 1,000 pounds. Many are thoroughbreds and all are magnificent steeds.

Ivan remained abreast of the chestnut pony's shoulder, keeping his head too close for a mallet strike. He didn't think Vazov meant him any harm, but risk aversion was in his nature.

Vlad led them toward center field. Out of earshot, Ivan assumed. But it turned out to be more than that. Vazov came to a stop beside a neat line of polo balls. "We're just a month out."

Don't I know it, Ivan thought.

He had borrowed $300 million to found and operate Silicon

Hill. Yes, the legitimate drone business was finally making good money and several other product lines were coming into their own. However, like most startups, Silicon Hill had operated at a net loss for the first few years. With that in mind, Ivan and Vazov had structured the three-year loan to permit a single balloon payment at the end. To get those terms, Ivan had agreed to a twenty-five percent interest rate, and a few special provisions. Vazov would own Silicon Hill. One hundred percent. The company, all its assets, and the title of CEO. He controlled everything and kept all the glory. This was important to Vazov, as it made him look good to his father. It was favorable to Ivan as well, as it allowed him to remain in the shadows. A win-win.

Ivan did all the work, of course. Vazov was no more involved in drone manufacturing than Queen Elizabeth was in military maneuvers. He had absolutely no interest in anything going on at Silicon Hill if it wasn't public-relations related. And since everything that happened there was "confidential" and in "stealth-mode" he could easily dodge any technical question that ever came his way.

Aside from the above, the contract Ivan signed with Vazov was relatively standard save one very special clause. A few powerful sentences. Section 7 gave Ivan the right to purchase Silicon Hill from Vazov for a single dollar. Just one. But only after satisfying the loan. In full and on time. The initial $300 million plus $300 million more in interest.

Ivan's buy-out option would be expiring soon, and he had yet to make a single payment. If he came up short, he'd lose the option to purchase Silicon Hill—and still owe Vazov the $600 million.

If Ivan had hired lawyers, they'd have pressured him not to accept the draconian terms. Not to bet everything on an unpredictable timeline. But he'd worked without legal input, and was happy with the final agreement. In fact, the controversial term grew from Ivan's own subtle suggestion, although he had no doubt that Vazov would consider it his own stroke of genius.

Ivan looked up at his creditor. "A month from today, you'll get your $600 million. Not a bad birthday present. The big 4-0 right? I hear the party is going to be legendary."

They'd inked the contract on Vazov's thirty-seventh birthday. Vlad had been eager to make his mark on the world back then, and signing a $600 million deal fit the self-image he enjoyed. But Vazov didn't appear to be feeling sentimental today. He ignored the segue into the personal spectrum. Holding his drink rock-steady in his left hand, he whipped the mallet around with his right, cracking the nearest ball loud enough to send birds flying from distant trees and launching the white sphere a hundred yards down field. "Where have you been?"

"I had business in the States."

"You made me nervous, disappearing like that. Makes me wonder if you're preparing to vanish for good."

"Why would I do that?" Ivan asked, knowing full well. "Silicon Hill is worth far more than I owe."

Vazov smiled with his mouth, but not his eyes. "Much to my delight. But that's immaterial to our loan arrangement."

"What are you saying?"

"I'm saying that I'm inclined to keep you here until my party. I believe economists like to refer to the tactic as 'avoiding capital flight.' " Another swing of the mallet. Another mighty crack.

"I can't close $600 million worth of contracts from an armchair. I've got them lined up like dominoes, $10 and $20 million orders, but toppling them will still take finesse and personal assurances. I need freedom to travel."

"You have a team for that. Michael is quite capable. Meanwhile, I can provide you with everything you need to conduct your affairs, whatever they may be, remotely."

Vazov had no knowledge of Raven or The Claw or Ivan's plans. He had the intellectual curiosity of a turnip. He'd bet on Ivan because Ivan had been legendary as The Ghost, much the same way conventional venture capitalists would flock to blindly invest in anything run by Elon Musk.

"Is there another way I could put your mind at ease, Vlad? A show of good faith?"

Vazov finished off his Panaché and used his forearm to wipe his mouth. "The only show I'm interested in is the money."

How predictable. "How much money?"

"You've got thirty days to pay. Thirty days, $600 million, that's $20 million a day if I'm not mistaken. You can have those contract payments sent straight to my account. Easy as tipping dominoes, right?"

"You want me to repay you $20 million a day?"

"Beginning tomorrow."

Ivan camouflaged an irrepressible smile by downing the rest of his beer and standing to leave. "Beginning tomorrow," he repeated. "Straight to your account."

14

Four Questions

New York, New York

Wearing a black suit and tie, Achilles waited patiently for Jo to arrive from Paris at JFK International Airport. Air France had a flight from Charles de Gaulle landing at 4:05 pm, and he was virtually certain she would be on it. By setting a tight operating window, he'd limited her options.

The midtown Manhattan Mexican restaurant rendezvous was a ruse. A bit of misdirection. All part of Achilles' plan to beat Ivan at his own game. If Ivan had orchestrated or uncovered their meeting, he'd be disappointed.

Meanwhile, international arrivals was the perfect place for an interception. It provided an ideal observation point while funneling everybody through a single door into a room full of people watching and waiting. Dressed like a limo driver, complete with black sunglasses, a concealing cap, and a sign that read "J. le Carré," Achilles was invisible in plain sight.

He had acquired the uniform from a similarly-sized driver he'd hired for the day. Part of a package deal. While Achilles did the grunt work, the driver was waiting in his car, wearing Achilles' clothes and watching Netflix on his phone.

Speaking of phones, Achilles checked his own. Air France Flight 006 was right on time.

Josephine Monfort was a slim five-foot-seven with sharp features and eyes that looked like coal on fire, but it was her stride that caught his attention as she exited customs amidst the other "carry-on only" passengers. She normally walked like a swimmer exiting a pool, with blood pumping and muscles primed and brisk moves designed to fight the chill. But today she was limping with both legs, as though she'd ridden a horse from Paris rather than a plane. The lack of a roller bag also differentiated Jo. She just carried a satchel over her shoulder, traveling light, like a good soldier.

Achilles fell in beside another exiting passenger as if meeting him and followed Jo out onto the street, confirming along the way that he was the only person covertly in tow. Like half the travelers, she headed straight for the long snaking line to the taxi stand.

The world is full of scams and deals, tricks and shortcuts run by wily entrepreneurs. Among the ones perfected if not invented in New York City is the opportunity to skip the taxi line and go straight to a limo. Achilles blended right in as he closed on Jo. "No need to stand in line."

Jo whipped her head around with a smile already in her eyes. "It's good to see you."

"Likewise. Follow me."

~ ~ ~

Jo let out a long exhale as she slid into the restaurant booth across from Achilles, relieved that it was safe to stop moving and start talking.

After surprising her at the JFK taxi stand, Achilles had his driver drop them at the Warwick Hotel—in Philadelphia. They'd gone in its front door, out its back, and walked a few blocks south to a bustling boutique hotel off Rittenhouse Square. Alone at last in a quiet corner booth, both were eager to get busy.

Achilles dove right in. "Tell me about the drone."

Jo brushed the menus aside, pulled a sketchpad from her satchel and slid it to the center of the table. She had augmented it in the hours since first putting pencil to pad in her kitchen, and was now quite proud of the result. It showed both bottom-up and profile views.

Achilles leaned forward and studied her work with interest. "You sure about the size? Six feet square for the body?"

"It came at me from over my rooftop. It had been perched there, engines off, waiting for me like a hawk over a rabbit hole. I was able to use the roof tiles as ruler marks to take its measure. After the fact, of course."

Achilles read her labels. "Six cameras, four propellers, two tasers, a digital display and one winch."

"I think there's probably a seventh camera, watching the sky above, but I couldn't see it. In fact, I only saw two of the side cameras, but I extrapolated."

"Makes sense. A fixed one on each of the six sides, giving the landscape, and an omnidirectional one with zoom on the bottom. The virtual windshield. Pretty sophisticated. But then I guess it would have to be."

Jo nodded.

"What was displayed on the screen?"

"Nothing. It was black."

"How does the snare work? I assume that's what the rope is?"

"It's not a rope. It's metallic."

"A cable?"

"More like a mechanical snake. It struck and wrapped around my waist before I knew what was happening." She flipped the page to expose another drawing. "I think it's sections of aluminum tube strung together with wires and gears. And I'm not using the term *snake* lightly. The thing moves like it's alive."

"Some precision machining," Achilles speculated. "Like a series of handcuff ratchets connected and controlled by cables."

"That's my impression."

"How did you get away?"

Jo told him the whole story, beginning with her pre-jog stretch, ending with the paperboy, and including both taser shots with all the terror in between. The look in Achilles' eyes made her heart swell with pride.

"I think it's safe to say that virtually anybody but you would have been captured. I don't know if I could have held on through all that." As she watched, his eyes turned more serious. "If it is Ivan, and at this point I have no doubt, then it's also safe to say that he's busy fixing the drone's shortcomings."

"How could he do that?"

"I bet he'll swap the taser for a tranquilizer gun. I expect that he's also rewriting the rules of engagement to attack only when there's nothing nearby to grab as an anchor."

"You're talking as though the attack on me was a prototype test."

"Obviously he didn't choose you at random, so there was more to it than that. But yes, I think that's one reason. All sophisticated new weapon systems have to be tested on someone. Ivan knows you're tough and resourceful. A valid test. And he has a score to settle." Achilles flashed his eyebrows. "Two birds, one drone."

The comic relief didn't halt the sinking feeling spreading through her stomach. "So you think there will be more attacks."

"I have no doubt."

"But who? Where? Why?"

Achilles spent a moment tracing his finger over her drawing, as if it were a relic with a tale to tell. "I'm more interested in *How*."

Jo didn't follow. "The drone is the *how*."

"Not his *how*, our *how*. How are we going to find Ivan? Nobody ever has."

15

Drone Defense

Philadelphia, Pennsylvania

The daunting nature of the task before them put a momentary damper on their conversation, so Achilles and Jo ordered dinner. He indulged in the house special cheesesteak, and ended up struggling to keep his chin free of cheese. She maintained discipline with a Cobb salad, picking at the ingredients one by one, rather than mixing them all together.

Once both had blunted their appetites, Jo brought the conversation back to business. "How did Ivan kill Rider? The news only reported that he was shot at a rooftop restaurant in San Francisco."

Achilles gave the salt shaker a spin. "You're going to love this."

"What?"

He met her eye. "Ivan used a drone."

"No!" Jo slapped the table.

"Not a big one, like the monster that attacked you. A smaller version, like the ones kids use with cameras. Except Ivan's was armed with a Glock 19 rather than an iPhone."

"So while the drone was shooting Rider, you escaped over the railing? I'm surprised the drone didn't follow you down."

"When you called and I told you that Ivan had tried to kill me too, I was speaking shorthand. Actually I think he wanted me to get away. The drone dropped the gun to frame me." Achilles raised his eyebrows and waited for Jo to connect the dots.

"So you would be the focus of the FBI investigation," she said with an appreciative nod. "Ivan shielded himself and neutralized you with one blow."

"Exactly. He had the drone shoot from shoulder height at the spot where I'd been standing."

"So when Rider's bodyguards arrived, they found nobody but Rider. And who but you could go over the edge of a tall building and live to tell about it. They'll say you're the only person who could have done it. And they'll be right. And wrong. Because it wasn't a person at all."

"Yeah, I'm pretty screwed on that one. I ran a Google search to see if there was precedent for a 'drone did it' defense, but didn't find anything. That idea is not going to leap into anybody's mind."

Jo didn't offer a contradictory statement, but rather asked, "How did Ivan get you both there?"

Achilles gave her a you-don't-want-to-know look. "I got a call from Rider asking me to meet him there. And I presume Rider got a call from me asking him to meet me there."

"I don't follow."

"At the meeting, Rider only said four words to me before he was shot. He said, 'This better be important.' "

Jo chewed on that while she worked a piece of grilled chicken. "When you say you got a call from Rider, do you mean he called personally?"

"It sure sounded like him."

"And you think Rider got a similar call from you? Person to person? A call you didn't make?"

"I do."

Another bite of chicken followed by a chunk of blue cheese. She wagged her clean fork. "You've concluded that Ivan has a voice-replicating device. A device clever enough to fool you and the Director of the CIA?"

Achilles nodded. "That and more. I've been thinking about it. Knowing Ivan's crafty and meticulous nature, I bet he also has the ability to feed fake caller ID numbers into the system."

She swallowed some avocado. "By providing a familiar and fitting number, he'd slip right past people's usual defenses."

"Exactly."

Jo set down her silverware as her expression turned grim. "The possibilities for mischief and damage are endless—if he really can convincingly impersonate anyone on the telephone. And I'd say fooling the Director of the CIA is pretty much a ...

what do you say ... an acid test."

"You're right."

"Sweet mother. We're not going to be able to believe anything we hear on the phone until we've caught him."

Achilles nodded.

"That's why you asked me about the Kawasaki when we spoke. I thought you were worried someone had a gun to my head."

"Right again."

"What do you think he's going to use the call-spoofing device for?"

Achilles gave the salt shaker another spin. "There's no way to guess. But it's going to involve drones, and we can be certain it will be groundbreaking, devious and designed to make him more money than Croesus."

16

Ripping

San Francisco, California

Rip Zonder resisted the urge to work through the night, knowing he'd be a complete wreck in the morning if he did. As a result, he had an eight-hour recharge under his belt when Director Brix entered his new office. Unfortunately, he had little else.

"What do you have for me?"

Rip pulled a single sheet of paper from an uncomfortably thin file. "The ballistics are conclusive. The Glock found on the roof was the gun that killed Director Rider."

"Was there ever really a question about that?"

"The CIA guy, Oscar Pincus, suggested that Achilles might have been framed using a long gun fired from a surrounding building."

"Did he offer any evidence to support that theory?"

"He pointed out that a seasoned operative like Achilles would never leave his weapon behind."

"And yet he did. Any theories?"

"Either Achilles dropped it by mistake, or he didn't want to carry it while climbing, or he thought that by wiping his prints off it he'd create reasonable doubt. Hell, maybe he just wanted to mess with the investigation. A clever and effective plan, obviously."

Brix pressed on, covering the remaining bases. "You're certain that no one else could have been on the roof? No one could have hidden in the kitchen or disappeared down the stairwell into a hotel room?"

"Spunt would have seen him," Rip replied, referencing Ronald Spunt, the bodyguard who had ridden up the elevator with Achilles. "Other than over the rail, there was no exit off the roof that wouldn't have led the perpetrator right past their guy. That was why they allowed the private meeting to take place where it did. It was easy to secure and isolate."

Brix leaned back in his chair. "Have you figured out why they were meeting? Why the Director of the CIA would agree to a private, late-night rendezvous with a former agent he despised?"

"Spunt says it was arranged that afternoon. Achilles called with a meeting request and Rider agreed."

"Why did Rider agree to the meeting?"

"Nobody knows," Rip said.

"I can think of one reason, and one reason only. Blackmail. Blackmail could compel Rider to meet on that rooftop. If it was legitimate CIA business, it would get done in the office. Or more likely Achilles would go to someone else, someone with whom he has a better working relationship."

"I agree."

"Let's keep that speculation between us. As for the media, we have what we need. It's time to go public. How close are you to catching him?"

Rip considered his response. In fact, he was nowhere. But that could change at any minute. "We're just one tip away."

Brix snorted. He knew the score. He'd been there. "I'll have the press here in an hour. We'll announce that we're seeking Kyle Achilles for questioning, but we won't go any deeper than that. Let the reporters speculate. The news desks will love it. They'll get two or three cycles out of it, given the personal interest side of things, his being an Olympian and all. Might even lead to that tip you mentioned."

"And if exonerating evidence comes to light, we won't be on the record calling him a suspect."

Brix met his eye with a steady gaze. "That's not going to happen."

"I'm not suggesting it will. I'm just covering the bases."

Brix put both fists on the desk and leaned in. "Let me be clear. Our reputation is on the line. Decisive action is required. Swift justice must be served. We have everything we need to do that. Speculation and second-guessing will only serve to keep the story alive."

Rip didn't retreat. "I understand. No media leaks. No divided efforts. We catch him quick and put the screws on."

"You intend to put the screws on?"

"I intend to actively encourage a confession."

Brix leaned even closer. "There's no need for a confession. We have him, dead to rights. Take the advice of a man who's made the mistake of being soft and has suffered the consequences. You get a glimpse of this slippery fish, you pull the trigger."

17

Stunned

French Riviera

Ivan could tell that something was wrong from the moment he saw Michael. It wasn't that the former boxing champ wore a worried expression. He always looked as solid and unflappable as a Greek statue. It was the very fact that he was standing outside when Ivan arrived home, waiting.

The obvious conclusion leapt to mind. Michael had failed. He slammed the car door to punctuate his speech. "You let her beat you?"

Michael nodded.

"How did she do it?" Ivan asked, walking past Michael into the lobby. Despite the double dose of bad news, it was good to be home.

Visitors to Silicon Hill encountered three immediate attractions vying for their attention. First and foremost was the through-and-through clifftop view to the blue sky and azure ocean beyond. Majestic.

Second were the receptionists, Giselle and Girard. Blue-eyed, blonde-haired twins in their twenties, both more charismatic than magazine covers. Beautiful.

The third was a large-as-life portrait of Little V on his polo pony, a modern parallel to the famous portrait of Napoleon about to cross the Alps. Regal.

Ivan ignored the view, the receptionists and the portrait. He headed straight for the sweeping staircase while struggling to mask his concern and control his rage. Ivan prided himself on his ability to account for everything, but he had not predicted the possibility of Jo's survival. Given the resounding success of Raven's previous tests, her death had been a foregone conclusion.

Michael interrupted his thoughts. "Jo exposed both tactical and functional weaknesses. We've corrected for both."

"Show me," Ivan said, topping the stairs and turning left toward the hidden door.

Michael summarized the Versailles debacle while they rode down. Ivan had to admire the shrewdness of squeezing one's shortcomings into an elevator ride.

When the door slid open, it revealed a laboratory abuzz with activity and provided a natural change of topic. Michael gave Ivan a moment to let it soak in, then led him to the drone where Boris was working. The engineering genius was absorbed in alterations and oblivious to their approach. No doubt the headphones helped to isolate his marvelous mind. Boris was constantly plugged in to something with a strong beat.

Michael tapped the engineer on his shoulder.

Boris completed his adjustment before turning, then did a double-take when he saw Ivan. He pulled the headphones down to his neck, making the incessant electronic rhythms audible to all before a finger tap silenced them. He met Michael's eye but didn't speak.

"We'd like to see the improvements you've made."

Boris had the drone mounted on an articulating robotic arm that permitted positioning it at any angle. He manipulated the joystick to make the weapon system easy to view. "First thing I did was replace the traditional tasers with a military-grade prototype system."

"Military grade?" Ivan asked.

"It's more accurate, and it uses nanosecond pulse technology to deliver a different kind of shock. It renders the victim unconscious for about three minutes. No chance of fighting back."

Ivan cocked his head. "Why haven't I heard of that technology?"

"It's not commercially available. Pavel acquired it from the Austrian firm that's developing it in secret."

"Why in secret?"

"I don't know. Not my field. Probably has something to do with the fact that it can cause cardiac arrest."

"We don't want to be killing anyone either," Ivan said.

"Odds are just 0.2 percent."

No government would sanction a weapon that accidentally killed 1 in 500, but Ivan was okay with those odds. "Does the nanosecond pulse technology work the same as a standard taser?"

"Same barbs and wires. Different power supply."

Ivan nodded. "What else have you done?"

Boris gave the joystick another twist and the winch came into view. He pressed a button and fed out the end of The Claw. Two of the black aluminum segments had been replaced with copper ones.

"What's with the copper?" Ivan asked.

"I installed a traditional stun gun."

"And you couldn't make it work in black? I thought aluminum was conductive?"

"Aluminum is, but aluminum oxide isn't. And Pavel thought the visual aid might prove useful during deployment."

"I don't like the loss of camouflage."

"The shiny segments will be hidden when the winch is fully wound. After the Versailles experience, we thought it sensible to sacrifice a bit of defense for better offense."

"Anything else?"

"I'm implementing a design change that will speed up the snaring process, but it isn't ready yet."

"When will it be ready?"

"Soon. A day or two."

"Make it one."

Boris nodded.

Ivan turned to Michael. "Upstairs, you also referenced tactical corrections."

"Going forward, Pavel will avoid attempting captures in close proximity to anchoring handholds, like lampposts or trees."

Ivan grunted. "Give me the bottom line. What's your conclusion regarding our current operational status?"

"We're good to go."

"You're confident that Raven's ready for prime time?"

Michael met his eye. "I am."

"Good, because there's been a change of plans. We're going

live tonight."

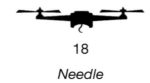

18

Needle

Philadelphia, Pennsylvania

Jo scanned the horizon as she exited the Philadelphia Museum of Art. No drones in sight. *Thank goodness for the little things.*

She was feeling refreshed but frustrated. While browsing the exhibits proved to be a delightful distraction, it brought her no closer to her goal. No closer to freedom from the fear that Ivan might inflict a final surprise at any moment. She'd be studying the sky every time she walked outdoors until one of them was dead.

How on earth were they going to find Ivan? Interpol had tried and failed. So had America's CIA and FBI, Britain's MI-5 and MI-6, and France's DGSI and DCPJ. Nobody knew where he lived or with whom he associated. What could she and Achilles do that the police hadn't already tried?

After a morning without discernible progress, they decided to stimulate their minds with fresh air and open horizons. The jogging route they selected wasn't quite as serene or picturesque as her usual tromp around the palace grounds, but the broad diagonal boulevard cutting through the City of Brotherly Love from the Academy of Natural Sciences to Fairmont Park's riverfront trails had proven to be both beautiful and invigorating. They put in six miles, after which she spent an hour wandering the museum in search of inspiration, while Achilles ran up and down the steps made famous by Rocky Balboa.

Jo walked across the broad courtyard toward the top of the steps, searching for Achilles. She stopped in the center where the statue of Rocky had once resided. Like millions had undoubtedly done before her, Jo put her feet on the brass footprints and looked out over downtown Philadelphia. As her eyes came to rest on the statue of William Penn atop City Hall, she resolved to return to this spot once Ivan was buried and raise her arms in triumph as Rocky had done. Jo liked circling back to visit vanquished problems once victory had been won. Little moments of positive reinforcement built up courage for battles to come.

She scanned the stairs, but Achilles was nowhere to be seen. Again she looked skyward, although that was silly. If he'd been snatched, there would be commotion all around.

She broadened her search and spotted him off to the side, doing sit-ups on the grass. The kind where you twisted at the top to touch elbows to opposite knees. She walked over. "Where do you get all the energy?"

"Nervous energy?" he replied with a wink.

"Forget I asked."

He rose and they resumed the run back toward Rittenhouse Square. For a few minutes, she forgot her problems.

"What are you up to these days?" Achilles asked. "What did Ivan interrupt?"

"Nothing related to drones or ringing of international intrigue. Just routine P.I. work. Looking for missing persons. Catching cheating spouses. Collecting business intelligence."

The third item on her list elicited a spirited response. "Corporate espionage?"

"Nothing glamorous or illegal. No hacks or bribes involved. Just a bit of clandestine observation and refuse collection. Competitors in certain niche industries like to keep tabs on each other, particularly when big contracts are accepting bids."

Achilles nodded. Not his thing, and probably not relevant.

A minute later he asked, "Is there anyone back in France who could be leveraged against you?"

"You thinking K&R? Kidnap and ransom?"

"To get you to surface. If Ivan wants to take another shot."

"Yeah, I get it. I have three flat-mates, but they're more casual friends of convenience than best friends for life. There's no man," she added. "What about you?"

"I'm engaged, but my fiancée is in Moscow for the summer. I let her know what's going on. She's laying low."

"Understanding woman."

"We've been through a lot together."

"So I'm not the only one?"

"Alas, no. I seem to bring troubles to all the women in my life, but for some reason this one sticks with me."

"Is she in the business?" Jo asked, referencing intelligence work.

"Hardly. Katya's a mathematics professor, at Stanford no less. But she was asked to guest lecture at Moscow State University this summer, her alma mater. It's a big honor—and I just torpedoed it."

"That's tough."

"Yes, it is."

"Why didn't you go with her? If you don't mind my asking."

"My history with Russia is—complicated. We agreed I'd be wise not to return and tempt fate."

Jo glanced over at her jogging partner. "Sounds like Katya's both smart and wise—yet somehow stupid enough to stick with you."

Achilles smiled. "Paradoxical, I know."

The friendly banter broke the tension. Jo felt blood flowing to areas that had been constricted. She'd done the right thing in calling Achilles.

He suddenly stopped running.

Jo stopped and looked back.

Before her eyes he grew a satisfied grin. "I know how we're going to find Ivan."

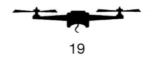

19

Invisible

French Riviera

Michael was nervous. Cautiously optimistic, but nervous. For better or worse, however, he had no time to dwell on emotion. The accelerated timeline had him hopping.

Michael's latest hop took him to Pavel's workbench. The pilot was busy practicing his maneuvers, and Michael spotted trouble. Big trouble. The display on the Drone Command Module was all out of whack.

Designed to be folded into a carry-on sized bag, the DCM consisted of a multifunction joystick and three laptop-size screens. The left screen displayed gauges, dials and flight controls. The right screen split camera feeds from fixed cameras facing all six directions. And the central screen displayed the main camera feed. Pavel referred to it as the "windshield."

At the moment, however, none of the displays were normal. The left and right screens were blank, and the windshield image was low resolution. "What's wrong?"

Pavel released the joystick. That move normally put Raven in hover mode as a fail-safe, but instead, it just froze the display. "Nothing's wrong. This is a simulation."

Michael felt relieved, but perplexed. "A simulation? Why bother with a simulation when you can practice with the real thing?"

"Mickey figured out how to run Google satellite images through a flight simulator. Now I can optimize our assaults in advance."

That made sense. Michael was pleased to see some independent innovation. Sometimes he felt like nothing happened if he didn't instigate it himself. "Will that help?"

Pavel put the joystick on the workbench. "I expect that we'll be making most of the grabs between dusk and dawn?"

"Whenever possible," Michael agreed.

"Low altitude navigation is challenging in the dark. By covering the terrain in advance, even using Google's daylight images, it will be easier for me to judge distances and identify landmarks. The simulation will also help with flight path planning. We'll want to pick the routes that are least likely to be observed."

"Good thinking."

"I'm pleased. Of course, before I can practice I need to know who we're going to hit. Have you decided?"

As part of the preparation for the rollout of Ivan's master plan, Michael had been analyzing dozens of potential targets. High-net-worth individuals within a day's drive of Silicon Hill. He was looking for opportunities to grab them. This proved to be easier than expected once he implemented the right tools.

GPS tracking got him ninety percent of the way there. Since everyone carried a GPS chip in their pocket, only two tricks were required: acquiring the targets' cellphone numbers, and hacking their telecom providers. Neither of those was particularly challenging when you had Ivan's connections and resources at your disposal. With that data in hand, the rest was routine analysis. Michael mapped out their movements over time, looking for patterns. Once his software identified the locations visited on a regular basis, Michael zeroed in on those that were prime for plucking people. Parking lots. Jogging trails. Backyards. Beaches.

"Looks like CJ LeClaire is our best bet for tonight. He's just come into a lot of cash, and he has a sundown yoga ritual with his husband that tees him up like a golf ball."

CJ was the CEO of LeClaire Designs, a fashion company that had recently signed a global distribution agreement with a major retailer. With that single signature, his net worth had jumped from low seven figures to middle eight. Nine figures was on the horizon if the LeClaire brand remained trendy. That possibility undoubtedly put the couple in an optimistic, forward-focused state of mind.

Michael called up a satellite photo of LeClaire's home on his laptop. "What do you think?"

"I like the isolation. And Saint Tropez is convenient," Pavel said.

"Convenient but a bit too close to home."

"Given the timeline though—"

"We'll take the risk," Michael confirmed.

Pavel reached for the joystick. "I'll start studying the terrain. Work out our approach and exit vectors."

Michael nodded and stood to leave, but Pavel cut him off by asking, "Why the rush? What happened?"

The question caught Michael by surprise. Pavel tended to be tight-lipped. No doubt this was a symptom of pre-battle excitement. Michael had known boxers who acted out of character before every big fight. He leaned in toward Pavel's ear. "Vazov is demanding daily payments on the loan."

"But it's not due for a month!"

"He's concerned that Ivan will skip town without paying."

Pavel contemplated that for a second. "Kind of like bail."

"Exactly."

"That's crazy. Ivan would lose everything if he ran."

And so would we, both men thought but didn't say.

The three executive members of Team Raven all knew about the loan because it affected their compensation. Ivan had granted each of them an equity stake in Silicon Hill, but like most bonuses, it was contingent on success. In this case, success was defined as Ivan taking ownership. The possibility that Ivan might not succeed had never concerned Michael. His boss was a legend. He always knew what would happen next, and how to leverage it.

Michael put an arm on Pavel's shoulder. "Vazov's just paranoid. Don't worry. Ivan can manage him. You focus on flying the drone and we'll be rich before we know it."

Pavel raised the joystick in salute.

Michael headed for the Tesla.

Boris had Raven folded for transport and now busy loading it aboard. The Model X's seagull wings were perfect for this, and with the second row of seats removed, there was just enough room.

"Everything good?" Michael asked.

Boris pushed the button that brought the wings down and sealed Raven in. Even though he'd seen the procedure a hundred times, it still struck Michael as something from *Star Wars*.

"It's good, but inefficient."

"What do you mean?"

"Folding and unfolding Raven takes time. So does loading. For fast deployments and getaways, we'd be much better off using a truck. We could just cut off the roof and fly Raven in. Plus we'd save weight without the hinging mechanisms."

Michael nodded. "It's common sense."

"Right!" Boris replied, obviously surprised that Michael was agreeing with him rather than defending Ivan's decision.

"I'm sure any experienced engineer would agree with you," Michael added.

"No doubt." Boris canted his head. "Do you think Ivan might change his mind? Perhaps after the first operation or two?"

"No chance."

Boris's expression dimmed. "Why not?"

"You might be an engineering genius, but Ivan is a tactical one."

"I don't follow."

"Precisely," Michael replied. He backed up a few steps and beckoned for Boris to follow.

Boris played along.

"What do you see?" Michael asked.

Boris shrugged. "A Tesla Model X."

"More generally..."

"A black car."

"Anything else?"

Boris studied the scene for a few silent seconds. "No."

Michael put his arm around Boris's shoulder. "That, my friend, is Ivan's genius. Even when they're looking for us, they'll never see us coming."

20

Chatter

Philadelphia, Pennsylvania

Jo studied Achilles' face in the afternoon sun as the Swann Fountain shot a geyser 50 feet into the air behind him. She saw genuine excitement sparkling in his eyes. Perhaps he really had figured out how to find Ivan. She didn't want to dim that glow, but there were practical issues to consider prior to pursuing Ivan, and she'd been meaning to ask one of them for a while now. "How will you get out of the country with the FBI and CIA hunting you, and your name on every customs agents' watch list?"

Achilles gave her a surprised look. "You never bought a passport before?"

"Never had the need. Do fake passports really work?"

"They're real passports. They work just fine."

"Where do I get a real fake passport with my biometric data in it?"

"You know those payday-loan and check-cashing shops you always see in poor neighborhoods?"

"Sure."

"We'll start there, since passport suppliers use them to get real passports."

"I don't follow."

"Most people who frequent those businesses don't have a passport and never expect to travel out of their home state, much less the country. But they are in desperate need of money. The passport suppliers offer them say $1,000 to get a new passport and turn it over."

"And then you buy it for what, $10,000?"

"Something like that. It's a very high margin business, given that the only expenses beyond an inventory of $1,000 passports is the equipment that does the biometric programming and the software to run it. I don't know what those cost, but they're one-time expenses."

"And that equipment is available?"

"It's not locked up the way you might think. The U.S. government outsources everything. The passports themselves are made overseas with components from all over the world. The biometric chips and software are outsourced to Germany, the Netherlands, Thailand and China."

"What about replacing the passport pictures?"

"Replacing them is tough, so they don't. The passport scammer in the payday-loan shop takes the photos himself using lighting tricks to minimize facial detail. Then he matches his customer with somebody who's close enough."

"And 'close enough' works in your experience?"

"Hasn't failed me yet. Since the passport control officer has biometric data, they tend to rely on that. In practice, they often don't check anything at all when the line is long. The Internet is full of stories of husbands and wives who get their passports mixed up and travel around the world without ever being questioned."

"Unbelievable."

"Combine human nature with a minimal wage, and you can't expect much else."

On that note, they left Logan Circle behind and began walking south on 19th. Once they'd passed the Academy of Sciences, Jo hit him with the big question. "So how are we going to find Ivan?"

He gave a one word answer. "Drones."

"Drones," she repeated. "As in surveillance? Turn his tool against him? I don't see how."

"Have you ever heard of a drone that could pick up a person?"

Jo thought about it. "No, come to think of it I haven't."

"I've seen videos of hobbyists who cobbled together one-seaters for short joy rides. And I've read about startups working on ultralight helicopters. But I've never seen anything nearly as robust or sophisticated as the drone you sketched. Have you?"

"No."

Achilles smiled and resumed jogging.

She raced to catch up. "How does not hearing about drones help us find Ivan?"

"Think about what he's doing from a historical perspective. His work may not rival the Wright brothers at Kitty Hawk, but transporting people by drone is revolutionary."

"That's an interesting perspective," Jo said, aware that her tone wasn't entirely sincere. "What's your point?"

"My point is that he's spearheading a very hot technology."

"Ivan has always been the leader in his field, but no one has ever tracked him down without insider knowledge."

Achilles' eyes twinkled, causing Jo's excitement to build. "Ivan's earlier work was different. Building a product isn't like constructing a caper. You can't work in a vacuum. For something as sophisticated as a drone capable of carrying a person in a combat situation, Ivan had to amalgamate multiple cutting-edge technologies. His power supply would have to be second to none. Each component would have to be extremely lightweight, strong and resilient."

"So?"

"In sum, the physical design of the drone that attacked you surely incorporates scores of insights gleaned from dozens of the industry's best minds. There's just no way he managed all that without assembling a team that's second to none."

Jo could feel the insight coming, but she hadn't quite grasped it yet. "So he had to recruit people."

"Right—"

"The best people."

"Right again."

Jo's mind was on a roll. "To do that, he'd have to compile a compelling offer."

"Such as?"

"This really isn't an area where I have any expertise. You're the man from Silicon Valley."

"Give it a shot."

"People like that would want more than money. They'd want 'the whole package,' whatever that means to engineers. Stock, I assume. Bonuses."

"Keep going."

Jo drew a blank and gave Achilles a give-it-to-me look.

"You can't steal Boeing's best aeronautical engineer without offering something more solid than a monthly paycheck and an unsubstantiated promise. The risk/reward ratio wouldn't work. Not for the guy everyone acknowledges to be the best."

"You're talking about reputation," Jo blurted. "Prestige."

Achilles didn't contradict her.

She considered her conclusion for a second. "Ivan has a reputation, a huge reputation. He's the world's most notorious criminal mastermind. He's *Ivan the Ghost*. But nobody knows who he is, so I don't see how that would help."

"You're right about reputation. That's the key. And you're right that most engineers wouldn't be attracted by the prospect of working for a criminal mastermind." Achilles nodded encouragement. "Keep going. Bring it home. Use a specific example, I find that helps."

Jo thought out loud. "How do you steal Tesla's best battery engineer? You show her something even better. Equally fascinating work, better perks, fantastic facilities, more prestige." She felt the light ignite. She got it now. "You couldn't keep an operation like that quiet. You wouldn't want to. You'd publicize it. At least within certain circles."

"Exactly."

"Ivan's got to be hiding in plain sight—like you did at JFK."

Achilles held out his fist for a bump. "And 'plain sight' is one place where the police wouldn't think to look for a ghost."

21

MiMiC

French Riviera

Ivan had a secret to share.

He loved moments like this. Moments when he got to give others a glimpse of his genius.

Exactly one hour before their departure on the first kidnap and ransom mission, he called the Team Raven executives to his office. It was a modest room in comparison to Vazov's spectacular suite two doors down, but his view was just as breathtaking and his round table seated four people comfortably enough.

They arrived as a group. Boris, the savant who was proving to be the best electromechanical engineer this side of Thomas Edison. Pavel, the ex-Air Force pilot who incessantly honed his skills on video games. And Michael, the team leader, the man who'd been by his side since high school.

Ivan got right to business. "Everything in order? Punch lists punched? Check lists checked?"

Each man nodded as Ivan met his eye.

"Any concerns? Now's the time to voice them."

Silence.

"Very good then."

With his team primed for the dangers and disappointments in the offing, it was time to send them out of the locker room and onto the field. But first, a bit of motivation. A brilliant new play. A secret weapon for their arsenal.

He picked up his mobile phone. It was an ordinary phone with an extraordinary app. He waved it beside his head. "You're all familiar with the software we're developing in the legitimate lab to help computers sound more like humans. But have any of

you heard of the side project Paul and Walter are working on?"
Paul Sturgess and Walter Moony were principal engineers
recruited for the project from Google and Apple.

Boris and Pavel shook their heads. Speaking slowly in speech
that just might have been tinged with resentment, Michael said,
"No, I haven't."

"Good. I'd hate for the world to lose their talent."

Ivan tossed the phone to Michael. "I call it MiMiC—short for
Mobile Impersonation Microphone. MiMiC has two very special
functions. The first allows you to customize the caller ID sent
to the recipient's phone. It's a relatively simple spoof, but an
important one. The second, however, is real magic. It enables
the caller to sound like anyone he wants. Tonight, for example,
when Michael calls Lawrence O'Keeffe, he will sound like
Melissa Theuriau."

Ivan paused, inviting questions. Two came at once.

"The anchor from M6 News?" Pavel asked.

"How does it work?" Boris asked.

Michael just smiled.

"I'll answer both questions at once, and will simplify for
clarity—although frankly I couldn't explain it any other way.
The nitty gritty of what Paul and Walter do is beyond me."

Ivan spread his hands professorially. "Picture a digital
recording. You've all seen those waveforms, right? Patterns of
vertical lines emanating from a central axis, kind of like a
heartbeat monitor but angrier."

Two of the three nods were halfhearted, but all eyes were
transfixed. Ivan continued, "If I read the first page of *War and
Peace*, I'll generate a different graphic than if Pavel reads it.
Similar, but different. What MiMiC does is digitally convert one
pattern to another. In real time.

"This may seem simple on the surface, like a basic addition
and subtraction operation, getting the sound peaks and valleys
to align. But that's because the waveforms we're used to seeing
portray sound in two dimensions. Human speech, however,
goes way beyond peaks and valleys. It has multiple dimensions
and is exceptionally complex. It's not just the pitch, tone, accent
and inflection of myriad letter combinations, but the speed at
which they're linked and delivered.

"Paul and Walter are the two best brains in the speech recognition and replication business. They came here with everything Apple and Google know on the subject. Even with all that knowledge and coding as a starting point, it still took them 18 months of 80-hour weeks to crack. But crack it they did. Now we've got MiMiC and they're set for the rest of their lives."

Ivan paused, giving the team time to ponder. He wasn't worried about their following the technical aspects. All three had engineering minds. But the volume of operational opportunities MiMiC opened was enough to color the ocean.

"Of course, MiMiC has to be taught how it's supposed to sound. That's accomplished by feeding it samples of speech, which is where Melissa Theuriau came in."

"Why Melissa Theuriau?" Pavel asked.

"How large a sample?" Boris asked.

"Sample size requirements vary. MiMiC needs thousands of letter combinations, each expressed in normal speech, exclamations and questions. With celebrities like Melissa Theuriau, it's no problem. Plenty of recordings are available. But with civilians, you need a good twenty minutes of varied discussion to capture the necessary range. Sometimes more.

"Paul and Walter set up the collection processor to display progress with red, yellow and green lights so you can measure progress in real time. Once MiMiC has enough data to function adequately during a typical business call, or a discussion between strangers, or a short conversation among casual acquaintances, red becomes yellow. Once you're good to go with anyone on anything, it turns green."

Michael raised a finger. "You'd still have to choose appropriate words. Suitable phrasing. Proper expressions."

Ivan turned to his right-hand man. "Exactly. MiMiC won't make a high school dropout sound like a college professor, or turn a Texas rancher into a Wall Street banker, but it will make Bill Clinton sound like Hillary—and it did allow me to impersonate the Director of the CIA."

Michael nodded as light dawned. He hadn't known how Ivan had arranged the meeting between Rider and Achilles. "Where did you get recordings of Achilles?"

"Press conferences from the 2010 Olympics. He did a long interview with his hometown news station."

"Genius," Pavel said, his admiration evident.

"I'm impressed," Boris said. A rare compliment.

Ivan added icing to the cake. "The advantages of sounding like a celebrity will be threefold. First, our victims will likely recognize the voice. Second, that recognition will distract them by raising all kinds of questions. Third, and my personal favorite, it will make their claims of drone abduction sound all the more absurd, should they choose to alert the authorities."

Smiles erupted all around.

Ivan basked in the warm glow of satisfaction for a few seconds, then handed Michael the MiMiC phone.

"Go get 'em."

22

LeClaire

Saint Tropez, France

Lawrence O'Keeffe loved his life. He loved his house. He loved his job. He loved his husband. The fact that they'd just come into big money didn't hurt, either. There were plenty of places to spend it in Saint Tropez, and since the money had been a long time coming, Lawrence had a list. Fortunately, CJ agreed with most of it.

Lawrence was thinking about that list as he and CJ began the warm-up portion of their nightly routine, a yoga regimen that would help keep them healthy well into their golden years. Lawrence knew he should be focusing on the sound of his breath, quieting the noise in his mind. That was never easy. A good CFO had to live and breathe the corporate numbers—the trends, the impacts, the implications. The stock market was a fickle master known to lash back with ferocity if neglected.

A strange hum interrupted Lawrence's background calculations. He looked up from a downward-facing pose to see a drone pop up over the hill. A big black one. He knew what that meant: the paparazzi had found them. CJ was new enough to celebrity status that the couple still found the attention more flattering than irritating.

"Yet another sign you've made it," he said as the drone zoomed closer. "We might be secluded from nosey neighbors, but apparently we're not hidden from paparazzi drones. Should we go inside or just ignore it?" As he asked the question, Lawrence automatically inventoried their outfits. All of it was LeClaire. "Might be good publicity."

"That's a bloody big drone," CJ replied.

They watched in wonder as the drone lowered a black cord. A

microphone? Were they hoping for an impromptu interview? That was a step too far. While Lawrence studied the unfamiliar contraption, the cord flicked closer and lassoed CJ's waist. Before either of them could do anything but scream, the drone yanked CJ into the sky. It rose straight up and then stopped, leaving CJ hanging like a yo-yo on a string.

Lawrence had no idea what to do. Should he call the police? Wait for instructions? Try to find something to cushion CJ's fall? The drone was just hovering there, about thirty meters up.

"Call for help!" CJ shouted over the hum. He was clinging to the cord with both hands despite the fact that it remained wrapped around his waist. Lawrence would be holding on too. He'd never survive the fall if it let go.

Obeying his husband's command, Lawrence ran back toward the house. They left their phones inside to avoid unwelcome distraction while working out. As he slid open the patio door, CJ's ringtone struck his ears. Lawrence snatched the screaming cell off the end table and read the caller ID. It didn't list a number or say, "Caller Blocked." It read, "Answer Me."

"Hello."

"It will cost you $10 million to bring him down slowly. Or you can select the fast option for free." The voice belonged to a middle-aged woman. It was clear, commanding—and familiar.

"What?"

"Our ransom demand is $10 million."

"Are you serious?" Lawrence ran back out into the yard. The drone was hovering, CJ was dangling, and nobody was laughing. "Of course you're serious. I'm sorry. I wasn't thinking."

"Go back inside. Make the transfer." The call ended.

Lawrence stared at the screen. The phone pinged and a text message popped up listing banking information. He ran for his computer.

As a Chief Financial Officer, Lawrence was conditioned to be wary of fraud and scams. Those alarms were ringing now, even though the veracity of the threat was beyond question. They didn't have the cash equivalent of $10 million in their personal account, but the corporation did. Was ransom for a CEO a legitimate corporate expense? Of course it was. How could he be thinking about accounting at a time like this? CJ's life was on the line. It was automatic. He couldn't help it. Finance was his comfort zone. His retreat. He loved the black and white certainty of numbers when the walls closed in. Oh, goodness. Focus!

Lawrence typed in all the transfer details, fumbling a few times in his nervous haste and wasting precious seconds. He double-checked all the numbers and hit "Transfer."

The computer thought. And thought. And thought. He glanced back and forth between it and the open door. The drone's rotor wash was blowing leaves across the hardwood floor.

Lawrence began banging the table. "Come on!"

"Transfer Complete."

He ran back outside with a prayer on his lips and hope in his heart.

23

Skolkovo

Philadelphia, Pennsylvania

Achilles enjoyed an insider's perspective on the startup world. His father and brother had both been senior executives at high-profile Silicon Valley ventures, and his home was but a mile from Stanford, the epicenter of modern invention. That said, he knew little about the state of drone technology.

He quickly discovered that drone manufacturers were popping up like coffee shops. The U.S. alone housed over 300. And they weren't all concentrated in Silicon Valley. Knowledge centers were developing all over the industrialized world. There were now dozens of drone-manufacturing communities that could hide The Ghost in plain sight.

So where to start looking?

Normally, Achilles could make a few calls and have knowledgeable friends point him in the right direction; however, his situation was anything but normal. In a stroke that was nothing short of masterful, Ivan had arranged to have half the federal government looking for him—wasting their time and isolating Achilles.

Achilles wasn't particularly concerned about getting caught. He knew how to beat the system, how to avoid tripping triggers, raising flags, or rising above the crowd. But the isolation complicated and constipated his investigation. And the government could always get lucky.

Achilles wheeled his chair back from the computer hutch and looked over at his partner. She was actively clicking away.

The Internet hub at their boutique hotel was smaller than the business centers commonly found at chains catering to corporate clients, but it did provide a couple of PCs with

Internet connections. "Any luck?" he asked.

"Yeah, you were right. This was much easier than I'd ever have expected."

Excitement and surprise washed over Achilles, tinged with a touch of skepticism. "What did you find?"

"Well, I'm not sure about the specific company yet, but it's got to be somewhere at Skolkovo."

Achilles felt like a fool. *Skolkovo! Of course.* Coming from Silicon Valley, he'd subconsciously been America-centric in his search. Jo, by contrast, had applied logic to a blank slate. Since they were trying to track down *Ivan* the Ghost, she'd looked at Russia first.

Russia doesn't typically come to mind when you think of technical innovation. Historically, they'd made their share of scientific breakthroughs. Certainly, the Soviet Union had been a leader in certain military, medical and aerospace niches. But if there was a single globally successful consumer product or service coming out of modern Russia, Achilles couldn't name it. Russia relied on its vast reserves of natural resources to power its economic engine.

Achilles recalled that former President Medvedev had tried to alter Russia's technological trajectory. At least on paper. In 2010, he founded and funded a whole city designed to develop breakthroughs. A Moscow suburb. The Skolkovo Innovation Center.

Achilles remembered wondering if the new technology park would go anywhere. Most of the Russian government's grand plans were really schemes to siphon rubles from public coffers into personal pockets.

Now that he thought about it, however, Achilles recalled a newsflash about a high-tech world conference being held there. The Technology Olympic Games or something like that. The news had shown a clip of Moscow's mayor bragging that the Skolkovo Hypercube now represented innovation much the way the Eiffel Tower symbolized culture. Achilles had let the political hyperbole go in one ear and out the other. But perhaps it wasn't a complete boondoggle.

"Show me what you've found so far."

Jo pointed to her screen. "Skolkovo is organized into five

technology clusters: Biomedical Technologies, Energy-Efficient Technologies, Information Technology, Industrial Technology, and Space & Telecommunications Technology. I'm not sure if drones count as Space Technology or Industrial Technology."

"We could figure that out by looking at the companies in each."

"You'd think, but it's not so easy. Skolkovo's latest annual report boasts 191 companies in the Industrial Technologies cluster and 170 in Space & Telecommunications, but it doesn't catalog them, and I haven't been able to find a list online. I expect the numbers have also grown since that publication, given all the infrastructure development that appears to be going on."

Achilles and Jo spent another half hour searching independently. Finding nothing drone-specific, Achilles again rolled his chair back from the hutch. This time Jo looked over at him. Her expression told him she hadn't found the detail they were looking for either. "One thing's clear," he said.

"What's that?"

"We're going to Moscow."

Jo blinked a few times. The fire in her eyes seemed to dim a bit more with each closure of her eyelids. "When we were talking about Katya, you told me your history with Russia was complicated. That you'd be wise not to return and tempt fate."

"It's a risk."

"Isn't it also exactly what Ivan will be expecting?"

"If he's there, I'm sure it is."

"And isn't Ivan always two steps ahead?"

"More like six."

"So we'll be playing right into his hand."

"I can't think of another way to play it. Can you?"

Rather than answering his question, Jo asked one of her own. "Doesn't that make it the very definition of a trap?"

"It does indeed," Achilles said, rising from his chair. "Should keep things exciting."

24

Tipping

San Francisco, California

Rip cradled the phone, hung his head, and cursed. With the Directors of both the CIA and the FBI looking over his shoulders like a pair of parrots, and the war room chaotic as a sports bar on Super Bowl Sunday, Rip had made exactly zero progress in his hunt for Kyle Achilles.

The assassin had simply vanished.

Rip shouldn't have been surprised. Achilles wasn't just CIA. He'd been the guy they sent to find people who couldn't be found. Still, between the press coverage making the public vigilant and the intelligence agencies all programming their electronic eyes, he'd hoped for a break. Naively, he knew.

Reality was, when individuals jazzed up with patriotism decided to help out by remaining vigilant, more often than not they spotted someone they thought might be the suspect in disguise. "I saw the man who killed the CIA chief, that Olympian. He shaved his head and grew a mustache, but I'm sure it's him."

What a quagmire.

A swamp to slog through.

There was a reason the faces on the FBI Ten Most Wanted Fugitives list didn't change much from year to year. Smart people motivated to stay hidden were hard to find when they had the whole world to hide in. Announcing Achilles' name had created the illusion of progress, but by tying up resources investigating false leads, the publicity had done more to hinder the investigation than to help it.

The electronic searches weren't proving to be any more helpful.

Hollywood had conditioned people to believe that eyes in the sky could scan faces the way AFIT, the new AFIS, did fingerprints. The perception was accurate, to a very limited extent. Facial recognition programs worked well in office buildings, where employees came and went through one or two carefully monitored doors and everybody allowed to enter was catalogued. But once you went beyond controlled buildings, the situation became hopeless.

There was no nationwide surveillance network to access. Larger cities had individual systems for monitoring activity hubs, busy roadways and bus terminals. But their cameras were neither designed nor positioned for facial recognition. Airports weren't much better. For the TSA to catch Achilles, he'd have to use his own name, or linger in front of a camera without a disguise. Rip had a better chance of winning the lottery than he did of getting that call.

There were special electronic surveillance setups at key locations around the globe, but they couldn't be activated en masse. The false-positive numbers on those systems were very high, so the manpower requirement would be insane. They could only be used when you knew where your target was headed. Rip had no idea where Achilles would be going, if anywhere at all. He might already be sitting back on a remote beach with a cold beer in his hand and warm waves on his toes, all set to lie low for years.

Rip had held high hopes for reeling Achilles in by capturing his fiancée, but Katya Kozara had vanished. She had phoned her sponsor at Moscow State University with a heartfelt apology for having to manage a family emergency, and hadn't been seen or heard from since. The FBI's Moscow office was not optimistic.

Katya's apartment had yielded no actionable clues to her whereabouts, but it had provided insight into Achilles' psychology. They'd found CIA-grade tracking devices in the purse and shoes she'd left behind. How insecure does a man have to be to track his woman's every move?

As Rip rose to return to his corner office, an office not likely to be his for much longer, his cell phone buzzed. He checked the screen. A Moscow number.

Rip looked skyward, said "Please," and answered. "Ripley Zonder."

"Agent Zonder, this is the call you've been waiting for."

The voice wasn't Russian. Rip was no linguist, but he recognized a French accent when a female was talking. Something about the *ooh la la* always tickled his ears. "Glad to hear it. Who is this?"

"Your investigation is going nowhere, but not for the reason you think. It's going nowhere because you're looking in the wrong direction."

"Good to know. What's the right direction?"

"Thank you for asking. The answer is *up*."

"Why should I be looking up?" Rip asked, thinking *I just did.* "As much as I like the sound of your voice, I'm going to be hanging up if you don't get more specific, fast."

"There was no video of the shooting on the Top of the Mark. No video. No witnesses."

"Who told you that?"

"Wrong question, but I'll answer it anyway. Your boss told me and everyone else during the press conference. He said you're looking for Kyle Achilles."

Rip caught a reflexive follow-up on the tip of his tongue. In situations like this, where an informant wanted to tell you something, it was best to let them stick to their script. "What's the right question?"

"Ask yourself why you should be looking up."

"I'd rather ask you."

"Good idea. Here's your reward. If you look up, you might see the real shooter."

"I don't follow."

"Find video showing the skyline around the hotel at the time of the incident."

"Why don't you save me the trouble and tell me what I'll see if I do?"

"It's not a matter of trouble. It's a matter of believing, as per that old axiom. Gotta go now. Good luck, Agent Zonder." She hung up.

Rip sat back down. He wanted to avoid the inevitable hijacking that would occur as he walked from the conference room back to his office. Requests for signatures or a moment of his time. He wanted to process the unusual conversation without interruption while it was fresh.

The call was unusual in both origin and content. It came from Russia, but the caller was French, and she'd somehow obtained the number for his cell phone. Then she spoke as an equal with a style that was both vague and direct. Had the investigation been going well, or had she said anything inaccurate, he would have hung up or transferred her to the tip line. Well, maybe not. He liked the sound of her voice and the stimulation of her wit. But she'd been spot on, and more. She'd pushed his buttons with the facility of someone who'd worn his shoes.

Rip wondered why she'd held back. She obviously wanted him to believe that Achilles had not killed Rider. She obviously wanted him to think she knew who had. Why not tell him? The answer, Rip decided, related to motivation. She wanted to make him curious.

By arousing his curiosity, the witty woman with the *ooh la la* voice had ensured that he'd do exactly what she wanted: look for video—not of the hotel and surrounding streets, he'd already done that—but of the skyline.

Walking back to his office, Rip found himself believing that this just might be his lucky break. And that wasn't all. He found himself hoping to hear from her again, and maybe even to meet her. *Ooh la la.*

25

Spark

French Riviera

The summer of his eleventh year, Ivan made a fantastic discovery, one that forever changed his life. He was goofing around at the Metro stop on his way to football practice when his ball smacked into the turnstile. Hard. Forcefully enough to dislodge a side panel and send it clattering across the stone floor while creating an echo that turned heads.

Ivan wanted to run, but he couldn't follow that instinct. The noise had attracted the gaze of a policeman, and he needed to retrieve his ball.

With slumped shoulders and downcast eyes, he picked up the fallen panel and attempted to press it back in place. The edges slid into their assigned slots, holding the panel snugly, but the screw that secured the union was missing. When he didn't find it on the floor, he removed the panel to search inside. He didn't find the screw, but he did find a surprise.

The metal box that caught the Metro riders' money was missing its lid. With the side panel removed, he could steal heaping handfuls of five-kopek coins—if no one was watching.

A backward glance revealed that the policeman had returned his attention to the attractive lady selling newspapers. A sideward glance, however, showed the tollbooth attendant to be staring in his direction. Her expression surprised him. It wasn't disapproving or disciplinary. It was fraught with fear.

He replaced the cover without the screw, retrieved his ball, and turned toward the booth rather than the down escalator. Keeping his eyes locked on the attendant, he approached the window.

She was a large woman, with ratty hair, a red face and thick wrists. She looked capable of picking him up with one hand, but she leaned back as he approached. Just a little, but enough.

"Give me a ruble and I won't tell."

Her lips puckered and her face contorted and her gaze shifted over his shoulder.

Ivan looked back toward the up escalator. The policeman was still there. Checkmate.

She slid him a ruble.

The note was worn and crumpled, but the rush from receiving it was the greatest of his life. He said, "I'll be back tomorrow," and Ivan the Ghost was born.

Twenty years later, Ivan made a similar discovery. A gift that would keep on giving. He felt that same euphoric rush looking at LeClaire's $10 million as he had that one ruble note. He hadn't just earned it. He'd earned it by spotting an opportunity and acting—boldly.

Like the realization of what was really happening at that Moscow Metro turnstile, the idea for Raven originated with a simple spark of insight. Ivan relived the memory as Michael pointed the Tesla east from Saint Tropez and began the drive back to Silicon Hill.

The spark struck his primed mind while Ivan lounged on the beach in Cannes, watching the beautiful people, listening to the sound of the sea, and soaking in the sun. At the next umbrella over, a slim, freckled boy with too much red hair was flying a remote-control helicopter while his voluptuous mother plowed through Samantha Christy's latest romance novel. Although she caught Ivan's eye initially, her son soon captured it.

The boy was stuffing toy soldiers into his helicopter, then taking it about twenty feet up and shaking it around until the soldiers fell out. Once Freckles tired of simulating paratrooping, he started lining up the soldiers on the sand and attempting to scoop them up on the fly by sticking a skid between their plastic legs. Watching the boy attempt what would prove to be an impossible maneuver, Ivan was struck by a simple but profound insight that would steer his life for years to come. If a person was abducted by an unmanned aircraft, nothing could save the hostage while he was airborne.

Disable the aircraft—the hostage dies.

Spook the pilot—the hostage dies.

Stall for time—the hostage dies.

There was literally nothing anyone could do to salvage the situation once the hostage reached breakneck altitude. It was as close to a black and white situation as Ivan had ever encountered in the dirty-deeds business.

And the beauty didn't stop there.

When you robbed a bank or stole a painting or boosted the family jewels, you put yourself at risk. You could be shot or caught or captured on film. Prison and death were clear and present dangers. That was not the case when using drones.

Given the capacity of remote controls, a drone pilot could work from anywhere in the world. If Ivan was cautious, he couldn't be caught in the act. Period. And if picked up for questioning, he'd always have an alibi.

The trick, he quickly realized, was getting paid. For his perfect plan to work, the ransom had to be paid while the hostage was still aloft. Cash was out of the question. Nobody had millions lying around, and even if they did, collecting it would cost him the remote advantage. That left online banking.

Could electronic transfers be completed fast enough? Ivan had doubts. And doubts upon doubts—because even if they could, those payments had to be irreversible and untraceable.

Still, the prospect was too alluring to dismiss.

He kicked at the sand as the glow of his spark dimmed. Rather than letting that precious ember extinguish, however, he kept on kicking. He kicked until ideas cascaded through his mind and revelations rekindled his fire. Standing on that sunny beach surrounded by Europe's rich and pretty, Ivan concluded that with the right drone there was no limit to the cash he could make, the glory he could earn, or the future he could hold—if he just figured out how to get paid.

26

Party Time

Moscow, Russia

Jo's head was spinning as Achilles pulled their rented BMW up to Skolkovo's guard gate and lowered the window. Spinning not from inertial force or jet lag, but from the rapid evolution of recent events. Once Achilles fixed on a target, he launched after it with all the speed, power and determination of a guided missile. She admired his brazen go-get-'em style while simultaneously worrying that they might drive full throttle into a wall. She was happy enough to take her chances with Achilles, however. Better to drive into a wall than be kidnapped by a drone.

Jo had never been to Russia, but she had crossed paths with a few Russian "businessmen" back in France. They were merciless brutes, but they also had brains. A dangerous combination.

"Vladimir and Patricia Makatsaria," Achilles said. "We're here for the investor reception."

Jo was relieved to see the guard wearing the same generic Russian rent-a-cop uniform they'd seen in photographs. Gray with red security insignia and a black beret. She was less comforted by the size of the guy and steadfastness of his expression. It revealed nothing. After a cursory glance at the empty rear seat, the guard pulled up a tablet and poised his finger for action. "Spell it."

"M - A - K - A -"

The guard cut Achilles off with, "Got it. Vladimir and Patricia. The reception is in the Hypercube. Just drive straight and you can't miss it. Parking lot is to the right."

As they pulled away, Jo asked, "Who are the Maka-whatevers?"

"The Makatsaria's are old friends. Tonight is their twentieth wedding anniversary. I'm supposed to be celebrating it with them and a hundred other guests at the art museum in St. Petersburg. Knowing Patty, it will be a first class affair, with a string quartet, sumptuous banquet and fireworks, but obviously I'm not going to make it. And just as obviously they have an ironclad alibi, should they need one."

"They just happened to be on the list?"

"No. But it was a simple hack to put them there. I just spoofed an email from Skolkovo's president to the lady listed as the media contact."

"Clever."

"I actually have friends from a former mission who are perfectly positioned to get us legitimate invitations. They work for the Bill and Melinda Gates Foundation in Moscow. But the CIA knows of our relationship, so that wasn't an option."

"Maybe you can introduce me to Bill and Melinda once this is a former mission."

Achilles chuckled and changed the subject. "Should be an interesting party, if you're into that kind of thing."

I could be into this kind of thing, Jo thought with a smile. While France was famous for its lavish parties and sumptuous champagne-soaked feasts, she had never been to one. Not, at least, as a legitimate guest. Her bank balance had always been at least three figures short. No doubt the shallowness of the relationships and pettiness of the one-upmanship at these high-society affairs would quickly have her eyes rolling. But still, she'd be willing to endure a life of pampered privilege for a month or six—with the right guy beside her.

They turned into the designated parking lot, cut the lights, and studied the scene. Resting on a rise beside a man-made lake, the glass block of a building looked as if it had been dropped from above by aliens, or a really big baby. The first floor of the Hypercube was entirely lit, whereas those above only displayed an occasional light.

"Looks like a Google building," Achilles said. "I'm sure that's no coincidence."

Peering through the glass walls at the glamorous dress of the champagne-sipping guests, Jo felt the familiar flutter of adrenaline hitting her blood. Phase one of tonight's incursion was all on her. Her operation to win or lose. Achilles was just there as window dressing.

Speaking of dressing, the alterations on hers were only hours old. Having grown up in the capital of fashion, Jo had not expected to find haute couture in the former capital of communism. She had been pleasantly surprised—both by the selection of dresses and the skills of her seamstress. The shops surrounding Lenin's tomb were anathema to his ideology, but they could hold their own against those on Boulevard Saint Germain.

Jo had no trouble discovering a design that met her tactical needs: long sleeves, short skirt and space to add concealed pockets. Its charcoal color wouldn't attract wandering eyes, and any attention it did draw would be diverted to boosted cleavage and exposed legs.

A chestnut wig with straight bangs and long locks rounded out her look for the evening. The total package she presented was chic enough to fit in among the spoiled millionaires' mistresses and wives, but not stunning enough to stand out. She'd be just another pretty face in the privileged crowd.

As Jo reached for the door handle, Achilles asked, "How long do you think you'll need?"

"Five or six."

"Six hours? I was counting on closer to one."

"Six minutes, silly."

"Six minutes? How could you possibly—" Achilles didn't finish his sentence. "I forgot whom I'm talking to."

Jo winked and got out of the car. Her mission was a simple swipe. She had a pocket to pick. Not just any pocket, of course. The pocket of one of the security guards. Phase two of tonight's mission required one of their all-access passes.

One potential target opened the door as she approached, ushering her from the dark to the light. Given the optics of glass buildings at night, Achilles would remain in the car where he could watch without being seen, and listen through a mic concealed in her ear. She spoke to him as she walked inside, her words punctuated by the tapping of stiletto heels. "I'll keep you updated with quick comments."

"Much appreciated. I'll keep quiet to avoid distracting you. I know what it's like at the tip of the spear."

Jo's first objective was blending in, becoming part of the crowd. She used a celebrity trick. When A-listers want to avoid attracting attention, they stick with common clothes, but go one step beyond the stereotypical baseball-cap-and-sunglasses camouflage. They carry a Starbucks cup. With nothing else on display, it's the first thing to ping people's radar, and it screams "I'm a local!"

Jo grabbed a glass of bubbly from a tuxedoed waiter toting a silver tray, and plunged into the crowd. She crossed casually through their midst, careful not to be the fastest mover, peppering her twists and turns with smiles and nods while her eyes wandered. Everyone else was working the scene—creating connections and making pitches. Forcing laughs and animating expressions. The only person availing himself of the famous neon-green beanbag chairs was an older, bow-tied gentleman. He was watching the silent slideshow projected on the wall while sipping a martini. Undoubtedly a foreigner.

Jo spotted her mark within twenty seconds of entering. He was bigger than she would have preferred—what did they feed the men in this country?—but the rest of his profile was right. Mid-thirties with a handsome face and eyes that weren't too bright. Enough experience under his belt to be bored by his routine, enough testosterone in his blood to be distracted by his dick.

She stopped before him and took a nervous sip of champagne, leaving lipstick. Once she had his eye, she pointed at the ceiling and smiled. "I left my purse upstairs during Pavel's pitch, and now the door is locked. Would you mind escorting me to get it?"

His eyes went from her lips to her glass and back again, with a slight detour a few inches down. When he spoke, his tone was apologetic. "My English not so good."

"Better than my Russian." She set down the champagne, used her thumbs and forefingers to frame a box on her bare thigh, and repeated the word Achilles had taught her, "Sumka." Again she pointed upstairs.

"Vasha sumka naverkhoo. Ponyal."

"Sumka naverkhoo," she repeated. Then she grabbed his arm and led him to the elevator before dereliction of duty could cross his mind.

27

Improvements

Loire Valley, France

They say that with sex, the second time is the best because the exploratory passions remain piqued, but the nervous tensions have eased. Michael found himself experiencing a similar excitement with Raven.

The maiden voyage with LeClaire could not have gone smoother. Raven had flown in and out without being seen. The ransom had been paid without dickering or delay. And Ivan was the happiest Michael had ever seen him. He resembled a prospector who'd struck gold after years of digging. Relieved, gratified and on the brink of serious wealth.

Now that they knew Ivan's grand idea worked, the Raven operations would be practically stress-free. What was left to worry about? There was no fear of capture. How could they possibly get caught? Even if law enforcement stumbled upon them in the Tesla with the Drone Command Module in operation and Raven flying, they were bulletproof. Pavel would just hit the SELF-DESTRUCT button and all evidence would vanish. Raven would explode into confetti-sized pieces, and the DCM would link up with one of Silicon Hill's legitimate little drones. Poof. Instant absolution.

Michael's only major concern was paying off Vazov before the deadline. Thirty ops in as many days would be a challenge, for sure. The real trick, however, would be keeping those victims quiet. Abducting people by drone would become much more difficult once victims became wary, neighbors began watching and law enforcement started scanning the sky.

But Ivan was oddly unworried about word getting out, so Michael suppressed his concern. At least verbally.

Ivan had joined the team for tonight's op rather than watching it remotely on his laptop screen. Claiming that he wanted to experience a capture live "just this once" and "see the improved Claw in action," he had relegated Boris to the Tesla's third row and hopped into the passenger seat beside Michael.

To connoisseurs of mechanical might, the captures were now as beautiful as any ballet performed by a prima ballerina. Michael was no artist or engineer, but after working closely with Boris and other brilliant scientists for years, he could appreciate The Claw's performance both as an engineering marvel and as an intricate amalgam of precision parts.

Thirty feet in length and an inch in diameter, The Claw resembled a finger with a hundred knuckles. If one had X-ray vision, he'd see that the two-inch segments of aluminum pipe were connected by cables and universal couplings, while the last four feet were also jointed with ratchets that allowed them to lock along a parallel plane like a long finger closing tight. Once those joints closed, their handcuff-like mechanisms could not be forced open. Once The Claw wrapped around your waist, there was no escape.

"What's better about the new capture system?" Ivan called over his shoulder.

Boris said, "It has a ninety-degree joint just above where the ratchets start. That allows us to swing the last four feet forward like a lance. With the press of a button, Pavel can place The Claw in perfect position for a wraparound. Then a second button closes The Claw. It takes no time at all."

"Walk me through it."

Pavel did. "I aim to fly Raven in from behind, fast and low, until The Claw is hanging down just behind the target's right side. Then I engage the lance function, jutting the last four feet up like the base of an 'L.' I activate the ratchets the instant the lance is beside his waist, looping it around his middle like a long metal finger closing tight. Takes less than two seconds in total."

"The concert of closing ratchets sounds like a rattlesnake," Michael added. "Increasing the fear factor."

"I practiced the maneuver for hours on end," Pavel

continued. "First on mannequins, then on animals, then on human volunteers. I practiced with them standing and fighting and fleeing. I practiced coming at them head on and from behind. I practiced swooping in at high speed and dropping down from high above. Meanwhile Boris optimized the engineering to make the motion fast as a finger snap."

"Show me," Ivan said.

28

Illusion

Moscow, Russia

Illusionists are specialists at manipulating perception. They leverage misleading expectations and utilize flashy distractions to conjure up false conclusions. As a con artist, Jo had mastered many of their tactics and would be using one tonight.

The secret to cons, like optical illusions, is taking advantage of anticipation. Feeding customers the appearance of something they've been waiting for while distracting them from what's really happening.

Illusionists can make a caged canary disappear, for example, by acting in the slim sliver of real estate that exists between the laws of physics and the boundaries of the human mind. While there is no physical constraint that prevents turning a tweeting tuft of yellow fluff into a wafer-thin pancake, everyone is born with a mental constraint. Fortunately, tonight Jo would be performing the more pleasant part of that trick. The reincarnation. She didn't have a twin canary tucked up her sleeve, but she did have a purse. Or rather a spring-loaded purse-shaped object made from the same material as her dress.

"Kakaya komnata?" the security guard asked.

Jo assumed he was asking *Which room?* She pointed to the right.

She'd picked the fourth floor because it had the fewest lights, and now turned right because that was the darkest direction. She led him around the corner of a bisecting corridor and stopped beside a conference room. She knew it was a conference room because a door plaque stated as much in both Russian and English. "Mendeleev Conference Room." No doubt an homage to the Russian chemist, given where they were standing.

"Mendeleev?" the guard asked.

"Yes. Da," Jo said with a smile.

The guard reached for his belt and produced the prize. It was white—good. It was plain—also good. It was slotted—still good. It was clipped to his belt by a retractable string—bad.

In preparation for tonight's incursion, she and Achilles had studied countless photographs and hours of YouTube video. Skolkovo was a prestigious place eager for publicity, so there was no shortage of selfie-video available to anyone who wanted to view the interior. She'd found footage showing a Hypercube keycard in action as an incidental part of an intern's unofficial tour. He had produced the keycard from his wallet, however, rather than the end of a string.

The guard held the card to the lock and Jo heard a click. Her plan had been to get ahead of him, using her body to block his view while she supposedly found her bag. But that had presupposed a simple pocket pick. Not a card clipped to a string.

Thinking on her feet, Jo allowed the gentleman to get the door.

The guard obliged.

Mendeleev's setup was modern standard, with roller chairs around a long laminate table and a large flat-screen on the wall. At this point, the natural move would be for her to return to where she'd presumably been sitting and produce her purse. She gestured instead. *Be a gentleman. I'm wearing ridiculously high heels.*

He walked around to the table, pulled aside the indicated chair and studied the floor.

She followed him, frowned, then smiled, pointed and tripped.

When you watch magicians perform card tricks, half the amazement comes from the apparent ease with which they do it. Cards fly around their fingers, darting in and out, up and down, as if piloted by microprocessors and pulled by strings. For the average person whose exposure is limited to card games at family reunions, the ease with which magicians manipulate those thin sheets of plasticized cardboard is miraculous. Most people couldn't do it in a thousand years. Except actually they could—if they put in a thousand hours.

The same principle applies to pickpocketing. It's all about practice, practice, practice. Instead of cards, pickpockets master buttons, snaps, zippers, bags, and of course, pockets. Endless repetition on mannequins rigged with buzzers and bells at first, then practice subjects. As a little girl, Jo had practiced by placing paper *into* people's pockets, little fairy fortunes for them to find. The one time a big hairy hand had wrapped around her thin little wrist only to find it grasping a message of good wishes, the man had actually teared up and handed her a few coins. No doubt her practiced expression of innocence had helped.

Although Jo had stopped grifting many years back, she'd kept her fingers nimble. It was a hard-earned talent she was loathe to let go.

As she fell forward that evening in the Skolkovo Hypercube, the mechanics of her moves came naturally as gravity. A cascade of activity designed to distract attention away from the hand that slips and flicks and tugs, freeing the precious piece of plastic into the palm. Then the quick switch inside the secret pocket, while she allowed herself to be helped up.

"So sorry," she said, eyes flicking up in acknowledgment before darting down in embarrassment. Then the discovery. "There it is!"

She walked past the guard to a seat further down. With her back to him and a chair blocking his view, she bent over. As her derrière undoubtedly drew his eye, Jo slipped the pencil-sized object from her sleeve. A quick flick of the thumb released the catch that bound the spring and *presto!* the purse appeared in her hand. Well, technically, the *clutch*. It didn't have a strap. "Got it," she said for Achilles' sake.

Jo rose and twirled and brought the prize up by her shoulder. Flashing a smile, she held it high just long enough to make the material match obvious then dropped it back to her side.

He wore an appropriately puzzled look. She had produced the purse from thin air.

Time to change the subject.

She pointed to the ground behind his right heel. "Is that yours?"

He followed her finger, then stooped to pick up a white card —the replacement she'd planted. "Thank you. I can't lose that."

29

Martin

Loire Valley, France

They parked the Tesla on a hill overlooking the Loire valley. They landed Raven a half-mile west amidst the grape vines. Their target, Christophe Martin, was due to come cycling their way at any minute as part of his weekly exercise routine.

Michael kept his binoculars trained on the road, but turned his head to look over at Ivan. "Is LeClaire keeping quiet?"

Ivan had been monitoring media outlets and police reports for any mention of their first attack. "Nothing."

"I must admit, I'm a bit surprised that the threat worked."

Ivan dropped his binoculars and looked Michael's way. "Really? After all these years of witnessing how quickly people yield to fear?"

Once CJ was safe on the ground, they'd placed another call to the LeClaire residence, warning Lawrence that they'd be back if the police were ever notified. "How are they going to explain the missing $10 million without a police report?" Michael asked.

"What good is a police report? It doesn't get their money back and it won't give them peace of mind. Quite the contrary."

"What do you mean?"

Ivan smirked. "Our threat aside, imagine the conversation. I'll help you get started. 'Officer, I was just kidnapped by a drone.' "

Michael played it forward. "A savvy police detective would play the odds and conclude that LeClaire concocted the story to steal the $10 million. Then he'd put LeClaire under investigation."

"Prolonging his nightmare. Plus there's our threat."

"I didn't game it out far enough ahead," Michael admitted,

kicking himself for allowing fear to override reason. He knew better than to second-guess Ivan's instincts when it came to anticipating reactions.

"Apparently LeClaire did."

While Michael reddened, Ivan pointed toward an approaching cyclist and asked, "Is that Martin?"

Michael turned back to his binoculars. "That's him. And we're in luck—he's wearing earbuds. Probably has music playing."

Christophe Martin was an attorney who had just received a $33 million fee as lead counsel on a mass tort settlement. He was based out of New York, but his wife preferred to live at their Loire Valley vineyard. Christophe joined her for most of the summer and the occasional long weekend. Ivan had bumped him to the top of the list on principle.

"You say the word," Pavel called from the back.

Michael started counting down. "Ten, nine, eight—"

Raven was exceptionally quiet for a drone of its size. The electric motors merely whispered, the rotor housings baffled their noise, and the propeller blades had been engineered for silent operation. But the hum of air displacement was impossible to avoid. Raven sounded like a swarm of locusts or a thousand flies. It also kicked up rocks and dirt when flying near the ground.

Michael and Ivan both had their binoculars locked on Martin. When the count reached one, a cloud of dust erupted amidst the vines about twenty yards from his position, but he sped by before they brought Raven high enough to be seen. Either he didn't notice the commotion or he didn't care.

Pavel began to follow the bicycle from a few feet behind. "He's clocking in at around 40 km/h. Pretty good for a suit."

They'd chosen to snatch Martin on his way out, rather than his way home, in part due to the location of the sun. With it blazing before his face, Martin would not be warned by Raven's shadow. He wouldn't see or sense it coming. There'd be no last second twist or jerk. One moment he would be cycling along, listening to his iTunes and watching his rpm's. The next he'd be airborne, fearing for his life. Michael zoomed the binoculars in on Martin's face and waited for the grab.

30

Vertical Vision

Moscow, Russia

While waiting in the BMW for Jo to exit the Hypercube, Achilles experienced emotions he usually avoided. Worry and regret. Not for Jo, she was in her element, but for Katya.

Achilles worried how Katya was coping. He had no doubt that she was making good use of her time and was comfortable enough. But nobody liked a state of limbo. She'd been sentenced to solitary confinement without knowing how long she'd be there or what was happening to him.

Achilles regretted coming so close and yet remaining unable to relieve her suffering. But like a parent exposing his baby to an immunization shot, by keeping away he was protecting his fiancée from a potentially fatal infection.

Ivan had begun this by manipulating him and Rider using one new technology, and then killing Rider with another. Who knew what other novelties he had up his sleeve. Perhaps he had somehow marked Achilles on that rooftop, and now knew his every move. That was highly unlikely, but then so was a drone assassination. Achilles simply couldn't risk contacting Katya until he'd removed Ivan as a threat.

As Achilles pounded the steering wheel, Jo emerged from the Hypercube without an angry guard in hot pursuit. She slid into the BMW and proffered the prized white card.

"You made that look easy," Achilles said, accepting the gift.

"Once you've put in the hours required to develop fast fingers, there's not much to it beyond basic psychology."

Achilles was keen to change mental gears, and learning a pro's insights seemed just the ticket. "Basic psychology?"

"I offer up a familiar framework and allow my marks to fill in the rest. In this case, I went with damsel-in-distress. With men of a certain age, it trumps dereliction-of-duty every time."

Achilles was eager to learn more from Jo about her special talent, but ignored it for now. They were exposed, the clock was ticking, and the important work still lay ahead.

Extensive online research and a few confirming phone calls indicated that the only active drone program on Skolkovo's grounds was housed at Vertical Vision, a startup owned by oil oligarch Victor Vazov.

Achilles drove to the Industrial Technologies section and parked behind a building Vazov leased. The 10,000-square-foot facility housed both Vertical Vision and Blowback Systems, a windmill manufacturer. A windmill manufacturer, Achilles mused. At least one oil oligarch was thinking ahead.

Achilles selected a spot with low lighting and reached around to the back seat where duffel bags held security uniforms. The outfits matched Skolkovo's right down to the red SECURITY patches, everything but the cute little Sk logo stitched in neon green. Acquiring them had been disturbingly easy. Jo took a printout from an Internet photo into an industrial supply store. She asked the clerk to match it, much the way one would ask a beautician for a celebrity haircut. "Our best seller," had been the response.

As Achilles put the duffel on her lap, Jo stayed his arm. "Let's not bother. You were right about Russia. Nobody's going to believe I'm security, regardless of my attitude and uniform. The chauvinism is neck deep around here."

Achilles met her eye. "The idea is to avoid standing out while walking around. Nobody gives a second glance to two guards on patrol."

"But our only walk is going to be between the car and the front door. After that, any encounter will be up close and personal. Better to set the stage for that."

Achilles recognized a good idea when he heard one. "So our story is that we slipped away from the investor reception to stage our own private party?"

"Yes. Only instead of etchings, you'll be showing me your drones."

"How very inventive of me, and obliging of you."

"Think we can sell it?"

"No problem. You're looking hot enough to make a good dog break his leash." True as it was, Achilles regretted the compliment the moment it left his mouth. He had no intention of straying. Hopefully Jo understood that. Not to assume that she'd even be interested.

They put on a bit of a show while walking to Vertical Vision's door. The enthusiastic alpha dog leading his lass by the hand.

Then the moment of truth arrived.

The white card.

Achilles had bet that security guards carried master keys, not just for a single building, but for the entire complex. Although Skolkovo was inherently sophisticated, and best practice was a zoned defense, Achilles was reasonably confident they had gone with universal master keys. Why? Working with master keys was simple and easy, and in all his years, he'd never lost when betting on lazy.

The lock clicked.

They stepped inside.

People tend to assume that sexy startups have glamorous offices. At least that was Achilles' impression. It had been his own until he visited a few Silicon Valley darlings and found them to be more like warehouses than palaces. Most of their layouts look the same. Farms of generic, second-hand cubicles crammed into sprawling open spaces. The decor is driven by economics. Prior to a "liquidity event," a blue-chip buyout or an initial public offering, startups treat cash like the last bottle of water.

Vertical Vision appeared to be no exception.

The lobby was furnished with a couple of chairs, an end table and a trophy case. No waterfall or oil paintings. No marble floor or mahogany desk.

"That's not good," Jo said.

"It's pretty typical."

"Not the decorum. The drone in the trophy case. It's the size of a shoebox."

Vertical Vision made drones for inspecting gas and oil pipelines. Thousands of miles of pipelines. Pipelines running through all kinds of inclement, uninhabited terrain, bringing energy from distant corners to ports and population centers. Those pipelines needed constant inspection for cracks, leaks and corrosion—not to mention criminal endeavors to siphon off profits. By using drones to do that inspection, pipeline owners got the golden trilogy, the almost mythical combination of better, faster and cheaper.

The drone had looked much larger when pictured online. "Maybe it's just a model. A miniaturized reproduction of the real VV1." Achilles stepped closer and pulled up the flashlight on his phone, supplementing the streetlight streaming through the windows.

"The case isn't locked," Jo said, swinging the glass panel open.

She extracted the object of their attention with the swift precision of a professional jewel thief and presented Vertical Vision's flagship product to Achilles. The weight was an immediate giveaway. Batteries were included. But he flipped it over to inspect the underside just in case. "This is no mockup. It's the real deal. A genuine VV1."

"It looked so much bigger in the website videos," Jo said, disappointment dripping from her voice.

Achilles handed her back the drone. "I'm sure that was the intention, given the price."

"I was thinking Ivan just used a different shell and made a few minor tweaks, you know? As camouflage. But it would take a hundred of these to get me off the ground."

"At least."

Jo replaced the drone and closed the glass with a clink. "All that work, and we ended up in the wrong place."

31

Headset

Saint Tropez, France

Michael watched with unfettered fascination as Pavel initiated the attack. First thing he saw was a dust devil come to life among the vines. Then a black beast rose from the burgeoning cloud, steady and powerful. Pavel took it up to an altitude of forty feet, spent a second orienting, then shot off after the cyclist like a guided missile.

He swooped Raven in from behind, bringing its altitude down to twenty feet while matching Christophe's speed. From where Michael watched, the scene looked like a cyclist pulling a big black kite on an invisible string. Then the string became visible as Pavel lowered The Claw. "Here we go."

Pavel accelerated, quickly closing the gap between pedaling man and mechanical bird. When The Claw drew even with the rear wheel, he said, "Initiating capture." He raised the lance with a button push, then nudged Raven forward and to the left, bringing The Claw up against the cyclist's side. The instant it made contact, Pavel hit a second button, wrapping The Claw around the man's waist like a prehensile tail. Before Martin had a clue what was happening, he was airborne—and so was his bike.

"Crap! His shoes are still clipped to the pedals," Ivan said. "Take him up fast. I don't want him getting any ideas about using the bike as a weapon. I want him too scared to move."

"Roger that."

Raven soared skyward with effortless grace. "Christophe's at 120 feet, the height of a ten-story building."

Ivan said, "Lower the headset."

"Lowering."

The final tactical hurdle of the kidnap and ransom scheme was figuring out how to communicate with the victim. This hadn't been an issue with LeClaire since his husband was present. Lawrence hadn't needed convincing to make the payment. But in more instances than not, the person transferring funds would not have visual contact with the victim.

Three-way calling provided the perfect solution. Even if a wife didn't care for her husband, she could hardly waffle or question payment with the husband shouting "Pay it!" in her ear.

Unfortunately, with the victim hanging directly below Raven's rotors it was difficult for him to hear. Boris had struggled to find an eloquent solution, but in the end the best he could do was tie a helicopter headset to a cable.

Michael watched Martin while a winch lowered the tool. He was clinging to The Claw with both hands.

"Doesn't look like we'll need to try out the new taser on him," Ivan said through a rueful grin. "Time to get the wife on the phone."

Ivan had a watcher on Martin's house. An outside contractor Michael hadn't met who knew nothing about their operation. Ivan had instructed him to remain out of sight unless she tried to leave, or didn't answer her phone, at which point he'd intervene. If her power went out or her Internet connection failed, he'd supply a laptop computer. Ivan left nothing to chance.

It didn't matter which member of Team Raven spoke to her on the phone. Thanks to MiMiC, the speaker would sound like Gerard Legrand, Chief Detective of Centre-Loire Valley. That extra touch was typical Ivan. A meticulous move. If the Martins went to the police and weren't laughed out of the office at first mention of a drone abduction, they would eventually speak with Chief Detective Legrand. Michael could picture their faces now as they recognized the voice from the phone.

Ivan said, "Remember to sprinkle 'you see' into the conversation." Legrand had a habit of ending his sentences that way.

"Roger that. I've got the wife on the phone," Michael replied.

"The idiot hasn't put the headset on yet," Pavel said.

"Why the hell not?" Ivan asked.

"I'm thinking he closed his eyes, so he doesn't see it," Pavel said.

"Can you whack him in the head with it?"

"It only has vertical movement," Boris said. "I'll add a ball joint before the next mission."

"I can get his attention," Pavel said, jiggling the stick.

"She hung up," Michael said.

Ivan rolled his eyes as the headset clunked Martin in the head.

When Michael saw Martin grab the dangling earphones, he said, "Redialing."

"Hello."

"Listen carefully, Mrs. Martin. Your husband will be dead in ten minutes if you don't do exactly as you're told."

"What? Who is this? What do you mean? What's wrong with Christophe?"

"What's wrong is that he's about to fall to his death."

"Fall? Fall from where? What are you talking about?"

"We'll let him explain." Michael flipped the switch that activated the headset mic.

"Maureen, oh my God. This thing just pulled me up into the air—" Michael flipped the switch back to the off position. Enough said. They were burning clock. Or rather, battery.

"Christophe? Christophe!"

"We silenced his microphone. He's still talking, but he should be listening. As should you, you see."

"Put him back on! I want to talk to my husband!"

"You need to listen to us now. If you want to save him. Do you want to save him?"

"Of course I want to save him."

"I can drop him right now if you want? You could collect the life insurance, you see. Find another man."

"What do you want?"

"Good question. Good question, Mrs. Martin. That's the question that will save your husband. Here's the situation. Would you like to hear the situation?"

"Yes."

"Good. Your husband is hanging from a helicopter a mile in

the sky. That helicopter is battery operated, you see. If the battery dies, the helicopter falls, and well..."

"What do I have to do?"

"Just a bit of typing."

"Typing?"

"Typing. You can type, right?"

"Of course."

Michael said nothing.

"What do I type?"

"A password, an account number and an eight-figure payment."

"What?"

"Christophe, why don't you explain it to your wife." Michael said, flipping the switch.

"It's a ransom payment, honey. Go to my computer. Quickly, please."

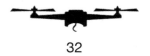

32

Barriers

Moscow, Russia

As Jo turned to leave, Achilles held up a hand. "I'm not ready to dismiss Vertical Vision just yet."

"They make toys, Achilles. The thing that grabbed me was a monster."

Achilles didn't move. "But the drone that shot Rider was about the size of this one. Granted, it was black and the VV1 is white, but a can of spray paint would take care of that."

Jo stepped back toward the display case. "Would this be a match if it was black?"

"I can't say. My focus was on the gun. But the size and shape are right."

"Hundreds of companies make drones of this size and shape. It's standard. You're grasping at straws because we don't have any other leads."

"No. I'm trying to think like Ivan."

"What do you mean by that?"

"Your reaction is exactly what Ivan would be aiming for. Absolute incredulity. No need to look twice."

"By that logic, every yogurt factory and turnip farm could be cloaking his secret lab."

"Yogurt factories and turnip farms can't hire cutting-edge aeronautical engineers and material scientists. They can't explain any of the myriad interactions required for high-tech research and development. The Internet searches, the conference attendances, the tool purchases."

Jo pointed at the drone. "They also can't justify interest in anything bigger than a breadbox. Let's get out of here. We'll think it through someplace that's not patrolled by men the size of major appliances."

Achilles still didn't yield. "We're dealing with Ivan."

"Do you think I've forgotten that? Even Ivan can't hide a mammoth behind a mouse. Come on, let's go."

"Modern windmills are mammoths."

"Windmills?"

"Victor Vazov's other business. Under this same roof."

Jo sucked on that for a second. "Motors and rotors of considerable size."

"And batteries," Achilles added.

Jo whipped the keycard from her secret pocket and stepped to the rear of the lobby. "What are you waiting for?"

The click of the keycard revealed an enormous room dimly lit by scattered LEDs. Status lights for plugged-in pieces of electronic equipment.

The space itself was a cavernous open plan arrangement. The kind that was all the rage in high-tech. A spruced-up warehouse with a ceiling high enough to fly small drones or work with giant windmill blades. Twenty feet by her estimation.

Although unoccupied, the room was abuzz with the sound of electronic activity, dulled but distinct. Jo looked over to see Achilles smiling.

He leaned toward her ear and whispered over the ruckus. "Is that how the drone sounds?"

She dashed his hopes. "No. That's the wrong pitch and it's much too varied."

Achilles found a bank of switches just inside the door. He flicked the furthest and augmented the glowing LEDs with dim emergency lights, creating the atmosphere of an overnight airplane flight. "Shall we explore?"

Clusters of low partition cubicles filled the foreground, one flavor workstations good for every rank. Some dedicated to drones, some to windmills, others to administration. Beyond them were long white workbenches, steel shelved supply stations, and organized tool racks. The only enclosed quarters were off to the sides, common areas or whole departments, judging by the spacing of the doors. All the way at the back, banked by packaging and storage stations, a modest production area beckoned.

"Looks pretty lean," Jo said, surprised.

"That's the name of the game these days, along with flexibility and collaboration."

They wandered about until they found the source of the mechanical noise that Achilles had hoped was drones. A bank of six large machines lined up beside tool racks. Each with rapidly moving parts, vibrating, twisting, or turning behind clear polycarbonate walls. "Stress testers," he said. "Putting parts through millions of cycles to check for fatigue. The engineers probably just run them at night, due to the noise."

They spent ten more minutes wandering from table to table, workbench to workbench, talking little, taking everything in. Nothing reminded Jo of the drone she'd seen in Versailles.

When they reached the back of the room, she turned to Achilles. "Conclusions?"

"I saw no sign of the big drone here."

"Me either."

"Surprisingly, they're not making the little drones here either."

"Sure they are." She pointed to stacks of VV1 boxes off to her right.

Achilles shook his head. "This is a quality-control testing and packaging operation. Likely just enough for the made-in-Russia stamp, but no more."

"So what's our next move?"

Achilles gestured toward the perimeter.

"The conference rooms?"

"Not just conference rooms. One function you never leave out in the open is finance. These identical cubicles give everyone the appearance of equality, but you can be certain that illusion stops short of their paychecks."

Accounting proved easy to find. One of the back corners was dedicated to it. Achilles translated the sign on the door, which of course was locked. Jo's stolen white card generated a red-light response. She rapped her knuckles on the door, confirming its metallic nature. "There's nothing to pick, and it won't be easy to break down."

Achilles backed up a couple paces to study the scene. He smiled after a few seconds then held up a finger. "Hold on a minute."

He trotted back to a workbench they'd passed. She expected him to grab an electronic gadget, something he could use to overcome the lock with sheer computing power. A CIA hack. But Achilles went the opposite direction on the evolutionary spectrum. He came back holding a utility knife. A box cutter.

Jo was no handyman, but she knew her way around locks and doors. She didn't see this working. "You're going to get us in with that?"

"I am."

She pondered that proposition for a second. "Are you going to short the lock?"

Achilles slid out of his suit coat and dropped it on the floor. "No."

"Do you know some trick to retract the latch."

"Nothing like that."

"What then?"

"Use your lateral thinking."

He had a habit of doing that, she noted. Guiding her toward his conclusions rather than presenting them. She rapped on the metal again. "My lateral thinking tells me even an axe wouldn't cut it."

"An axe was my first choice, but I didn't see one lying around."

She stepped aside. "Have at it."

Achilles stepped aside too, in the other direction. He lunged forward and stabbed the knife into the wall at hip height, burying the entire inch of exposed blade. He left it protruding perpendicularly and turned to face her. With a stiff arm, he grabbed the handle and dropped his weight onto it. The drywall yielded. The blade cut a straight line from hip height down to the base board.

While she shook her head at her own shortsightedness, Achilles repeated the procedure half a pace to the left, creating a parallel slice. Then a hearty stab and heavy two-handed tug across the top completed the third side. At that point he set aside the knife, rolled onto his back, and used his feet to punch out a door. Well, half a door. He had to repeat the procedure for the drywall on the other side of the studs, cutting a slit down the middle and kicking from there. Before she knew it,

33

Bingo!

San Francisco, California

The very best thing about being an FBI agent wasn't the pay, or the brotherhood, or the work itself, although all of those were wonderful. The big prize was the badge. Whipping one out was like presenting a golden ticket. Everyone respected it. Everyone feared it. And guilty or innocent, everyone gave you their full attention when they saw that shiny shield.

Flashing your credentials wasn't nearly as effective over the phone.

Character limitations on the length of caller ID ruled out displaying *Federal Bureau of Investigation*, and *FBI* just wasn't as intimidating when delivered in the same plain electronic print that displayed toll-free numbers. People who would never slam the door on a badge might not hesitate to hang up. But Rip decided to give it a try before involving the New Jersey field office.

"EarthCam. How may I help you?"

"Good afternoon, this is Special Agent Ripley Zonder with the FBI." He spoke the three familiar letters with crisp enunciation. "I need to speak with your head of technical operations."

EarthCam made money selling ads on webcam streams from places like Times Square and the Eiffel Tower. Included in their lineup was a 360-degree camera showing the skyline in San Francisco. By the grace of God, that camera clearly captured the InterContinental Hotel as seen at rooftop level. But the devil also got his due. The view was from the south, so the restaurant where Rider was killed was not in view. Still, Miss Ooh La La had said to check the skyline, and the skyline was in view. Crisp and clear.

But it was the current skyline. EarthCam displayed live coverage. Rip needed historical footage.

Did EarthCam record? If so, for how long? Video sucked up a lot of memory, so surely any recordings would be regularly overwritten. Daily? Weekly? Monthly? He was about to find out.

The Jersey girl manning the phone at EarthCam snapped to with due deference. Minutes later, CTO Ron Stotyn gave him the good news. Each of his cameras had a dedicated eight-terabyte drive. Enough to store four weeks of recordings when utilizing the same sophisticated software that streamed television. Best of all, Ron could grant the FBI remote access to the drive, with EarthCam's compliments.

To Rip's further delight, the recording offered the same user interface as the live camera, permitting him to change angles and zoom. Rip adjusted both, rewound to the time ten minutes before Rider drew his last breath, and hit play.

Having watched many a surveillance tape over the years, Rip had come to his desk prepared. Pastrami on rye with Swiss and a big fat pickle. The first thing he noticed beyond the superb quality of his sandwich was the big difference in midnight lighting between El Paso and San Francisco. The sky over El Paso was nearly black at night, whereas San Fran was a medium gray. The second thing he noticed was serenity. Despite the active luminescence, very little was happening.

The scene stayed still as a painting right up to the minute of the murder. Then an object fell from above. It just dropped down onto the hotel, landing beyond his view but presumably on The Top of the Mark. Rip nearly choked on a fat piece of pastrami as he rocketed forward in his chair. He hit rewind and then slow motion.

There it was again. Not an illusion. Not a camera glitch. Neither a fly buzzing past nor a drop of water on the lens. Rip paused with the object near the top of the building and zoomed in. It was the size of a basketball and shaped like a T. Its color was black. Rip rewound a few frames and then played the recording forward at normal speed. The object wasn't dropping —it was flying. He was looking at a drone. "Bingo!"

It got better.

And then it got worse. Much worse. Bad enough that Rip immediately summoned his entire team.

The four agents who were in the office gathered around Rip's computer. "This recording is from the night of Director Rider's murder." He hit play.

"Whoa! What's that?" Oscar said.

"Keep watching."

They did. A mere seven seconds later the same object shot skyward again.

"It's a drone," Clancy said.

"Where did you get this?" Oscar asked.

"From a commercial webcam. A company that streams live cityscapes to put eyeballs on advertisements."

"I saw that but dismissed it along with all the others. It doesn't show the restaurant or the wall leading up to it. No camera has the right angle. What made you think to study the skyline?" Adams asked.

"A tip, actually. A French woman calling my cell phone from Russia."

The room went quiet while everyone took in the new twist.

Rip plowed forward. "I want to try tracking the drone. It's a long shot, but long shots are all we have right now and maybe we'll get lucky. Start with the FAA. They keep a catalogue of companies in the business. There are about 500 manufacturers worldwide and probably twice as many models of drones. Go through them all and see if you can identify the one in the picture. I know it's grainy, but have the geeks in the basement do their best to enhance the images. Look for distinguishing features and find the best match."

"Sir, aren't we missing the big picture?" Clancy asked.

"What big picture?" Oscar asked.

"No, we're not missing it," Rip said with somber voice. "My next call will be to Director Brix. I'm sure within the hour, he'll brief the National Security Council."

"What big picture?" Oscar repeated.

In answer, Rip pulled up two video stills. "This one's from the descent. This one's from the ascent. Notice the difference?"

"It's not the same drone," Oscar said.

"Yes it is," Clancy contradicted. "It just left something

behind."

"And that would be?" Rip prompted.

"A Glock 19," Clancy said.

"Precisely."

"Achilles had a drone bring him a gun. That's how he got it past security," Oscar said.

Rip ignored the CIA guy and turned to face the brighter members of his team. "I fear Director Rider's death marked the birth of a new terrorist threat. I can't fathom how we'll defend against it."

"Terrorist threat?" Oscar scoffed.

All eyes locked on Rip's lips as he slid aside the curtain. "Assassination by drone."

34

Victor

Moscow, Russia

Fourteen minutes after crawling through the cutout door in strappy heels and a short dress, Jo found what they'd come for. She held the paper aloft like a winning lottery ticket. "You were right!"

Most modern financial records exist only in electronic form. Gone are the days when "the books" are actual paper ledgers. Storing and sorting electrons is far more efficient. But when products ship, paper goes with it in the form of a packing slip. It's the kind of documentation that accountants love. No marketing glitz, no legal flimflam, just the facts. Shipped from. Shipped to. Product. Quantity. Date.

Achilles abandoned his filing cabinet and walked toward Jo. "What did you find?"

"Packing slips for 'VV1 Kits'. Shipped six at a time—from France."

"Ivan likes France."

"Don't I know it."

"Who's listed as the shipper?"

"There's no business name, just an address—on the Côte d'Azur no less."

"That has to be it. Pocket one of the papers and put the rest away. No sense making it obvious what we were looking for."

"We're leaving?"

"What *bold* begins, *moderation* must finish."

"Huh?"

"It was a Granger saying. We have enough, let's not push it."

Jo had heard Achilles' mentor speak during her CIA training, so she understood the deference. Of the powerful men she'd met in her life, only a few had struck her as truly wise. Granger was one of them, and he also had a charitable side. A rare gem indeed.

She folded the packing slip and slid it into the secret pocket that had hidden the passkeys. Then she squared everything else away.

While Achilles got the lights, she crawled back out the doggy door—right into the muzzle of a gun.

Jo had been shot once, at close range. She never saw the weapon and had no memory of the incident, but she'd spent weeks in recovery and her sternum still ached when she stretched. Nonetheless, the doctors told her she'd been incredibly lucky. She wondered now if she had any luck left.

Her eyes flew to the end of the muzzle and she found it impossible to look away. Would it all end here on this gypsum covered floor, a thousand miles from home? Would she vanish without a trace? She stared into that dark abyss until Achilles appeared at her side. Then her rational mind overrode her lizard brain with a simple deduction: if her assailant was going to fire, he would have done so already.

Actually, there were two assailants. A matching set. One for her, one for Achilles. Both wore suits rather than uniforms. Both carried semi-automatics designed for concealed carry. Bodyguards, not security.

The pair was guarding a man who didn't appear to need it. A big bear of a brute, with a thick neck, bald head and knuckles resembling walnuts. Late-fifties by wrinkle count, but mid-thirties by physique, with an arrogant stance, clever countenance and commanding presence. A beautiful woman clung to his side. Not a tart or prostitute. A wife, judging by her jewelry, wardrobe and 50 year-old hands.

Another couple, also dressed for the party, waited wide-eyed a few paces back. Investors apparently, and unaccustomed to the sight of guns.

Jo had worked her way out of many a fix with quick wits and a clever tongue. In the background, her mind was already working. But misdirects and deceptions couldn't save her today. She didn't speak Russian.

Achilles did.

He spoke two words.

Jo understood both of them. "Victor Vazov."

The oligarch himself, Jo realized. He hadn't plastered his face all around the web like some CEOs. No mystery to that corporate strategy. Not if the goal was attracting investors, rather than frightening them.

Victor studied her for a long, thick second. Then Achilles. His gaze was like that of a housewife in a butcher shop— skeptical and appraising. When he spoke, he spoke to her, genteelly and in English. "Good evening. May I help you?"

She turned toward Achilles, anxious to read his expression.

"Don't look at him," Victor admonished. "That's not polite. I've just asked you a question."

No doubt Victor considered her the weak link. A woman rattled. Jo could work with that. She shrugged and donned a meek expression. "We saw an opportunity to score, and we took it. Surely you can appreciate that?"

"What opportunity?"

"A distracting party. An unguarded safe."

"There's no safe here."

Jo shrugged. "We were misinformed."

Victor raised his eyebrows. "Indeed you were. Not only did you set yourself up for a lengthy prison stay, but you missed a nice party. Since no real harm was done, I'll thank you for identifying a weak spot in my security and wish you the best with the judge." He gave a quick farewell bow of his head, spun on his heels and headed for the exit with his lovely wife at his side and the other couple two steps ahead.

The bodyguards remained, waiting for the police to arrive. Supposedly.

35

Double Take

Lyon, France

Arno Chauveau pulled his putter from his bag for the thirteenth time that evening and sized up the short grass between sumptuous puffs on his hand-rolled Dominican. The hole was par five, but he'd killed the drive and hit the green in two. A perfect putt would bag him an eagle.

He played the course almost every Friday night, and always as the last one through. His workweeks were stuffed solid with stress, and this was his favorite way to unwind. His ritual. With no one behind him, he could take it easy. Enjoy a cigar and half a flask of brandy. With no one accompanying him, he had no pressure to perform. So, of course, these games were always his best.

He practiced the putt, lubricating his shoulder joints while slipping into rhythm. It was getting dark. He'd have to switch to a glow-in-the-dark ball for the next hole. His night vision wasn't what it used to be, but he refused to let his age change his behavior. That was Arno's secret to staying young. Refuse to yield.

Once his practice swing felt right, he took a half-step forward, addressed the ball, and—*What the hell was that?* Arno turned toward the woods behind him and the source of an unfamiliar disturbance. It looked and sounded like a tiny tornado had just touched down on a beehive. The wind grew more intense as he studied the foliage. Loose ash flew from his cigar, sending sparks onto his sweater, while a black shadow moved overhead. Not a shadow, rather some kind of hovercraft. Fascinating!

Something tapped his foot. He looked down to see his ball,

rolling from the wind. As he bent to retrieve it, something encircled his waist. Something hard. It wrapped all the way around. He abandoned his putter and cigar, and grabbed the offending object with both hands. Thick as a broomstick and metallic black in color, it was hard, cold and completely unyielding. As panic engulfed him, his feet left the ground.

The hovercraft sucked him skyward until he was just above the trees, but not within their reach. Once it stopped ascending, it started flying backward. Away from the clubhouse and out over the woods.

Was he hallucinating? Had someone spiked his cigar or tampered with his brandy? Surely this couldn't really be happening, yet somehow it was. Glancing up at the big black all-too-real machine, Arno found pride in the fact that he hadn't soiled his pants or begun frothing at the mouth. He sought to build on that emotion.

He had worked his way up the real estate development business from the bottom, starting with high-rise construction work in his youth. The experience of working on girders had tamed his fear of heights and trained him to think clearly under duress. He owed much of his success to the lessons he'd learned and the discipline he'd developed at altitude. He drew on that experience now.

Instinct told Arno that the smart move was to seize control, to leap for the treetops when an inviting branch appeared below. But the coil encircling his waist would not yield. He had little choice but to hang there and take it. For the moment, at least.

To keep himself calm, Arno occupied his mind by attempting to guess what would happen next. Analytically. Remotely. As if watching himself in a movie.

He didn't get far.

The hovercraft halted before he got to his first good guess. It halted high above Carter Creek, a shallow stream running erratically through the thick woods. The stream looked cold, its rocks hard and jagged. Very uninviting. Arno chose to look upward instead—and got the answer. A negotiation would be next.

A headset was dropping down. Dangling on a thin cable, it stopped right before his eyes.

He slipped it on.

"Mr. Chauveau, we're calling with a request."

I bet you are, you wily bastard. "I'm listening."

"We're about to get your CFO on the phone. We're going to give him a bank account number, and you're going to tell him to wire $10 million to it. Immediately."

As a seasoned negotiator, Arno's impulse was to ask what would happen if he didn't place the order. Get them to reveal their hand. But in this case, that answer was obvious. Dickering over the price seemed neither wise nor dignified. He had no leverage, nothing with which to bargain. They had him over the proverbial barrel. Way over. He'd have to be satisfied escaping with life, limb and pride intact. With living to fight another day. That wasn't so bad. "And if I comply?"

"You get to putt for an eagle."

Arno looked up again. The hovercraft had four rotors arranged equidistant from a central winch, a winch that controlled the mechanical cable from which he hung. Next to the winch was a digital display. Two numbers, glowing green, counting down.

"It's minutes of remaining battery power," the voice replied in answer to his unasked question. "Of course, we'll lighten the load well before we run out of juice so we can bring our baby home safely."

Bring our baby home, Arno repeated to himself. He'd heard that phrase before. Come to think of it, he'd heard that *voice* before. Who was it? He'd remember. By God, he'd remember. Then payback would come tenfold. He would have the last laugh. "Get Elizabeth Piper on the line," he said, referencing his CFO.

"She's already on hold," the familiar voice said.

"Arno?"

"Hey, Lizzie. We need to make a transfer. $10 million. Immediately."

"What's going on? Can you turn off the hair dryer—it's kinda hard to hear."

"It's not a hair dryer, and you wouldn't believe what's going on if I told you. Did they give you an account number."

"Yeah. You sure this is what you want? $10 million to Highlife Insurance in Antigua?"

"I'm absolutely certain."

"Okay. Should I consult with Uncle Saar first? Or send him to the golf course?"

Saar Shmueli was head of corporate security. A former Israeli Defense Forces major, Saar was as smart and serious as soldiers came. "No. I need you to make the transfer immediately." He looked up at the green clock: 41 minutes. Not a lot of time to deal with computer glitches or pesky procedures. "Time is of the essence."

"Hitting send now," Piper said.

"Waiting for confirmation," the familiar voice said.

Fabre! The voice was Emile Fabre. He'd fired the bastard years back for theft. As vice president of sales, Fabre's job was closing the big deals. "Bringing babies home" he'd called it. Many of those deals were contracts requiring kickbacks. Arno had caught Fabre doubling the ask and pocketing half. He'd dismissed him on the spot. Fabre had gone on to become CEO of a rival corporation, something Arno was constantly reminded of since Fabre built his personal brand by jumping in front of every camera that came along.

So now that he was fat and happy, Fabre wanted revenge. Payback. Well, two could play at that game. He'd serve it up himself, old school. Baseball bats and brass knuckles rather than high-tech toys.

"Funds received," Fabre said.

Arno exhaled. He knew Piper would pay, but felt a warm wash of relief nonetheless. "So set me down already!"

"Sure. Just one more thing first," Fabre said, his voice taunting.

"What's that?"

"Another $10 million."

36

Three Heads

Quantico, Virginia

Rip didn't immediately inform Director Brix of the drone discovery as he'd told his team he would. He set up a meeting instead. As any corporate climber would testify, it was best to present progress in person—especially when your record showed more misses than hits.

Before heading to the airport, he had told the team where he was going and directed strict silence regarding the drone. The look in Oscar's eyes told him that his order had come too late. No doubt the CIA's representative had rushed to inform Langley the moment their meeting ended.

That suited Rip just fine.

His phone rang as the plane was landing at Reagan National. Caller ID indicated Agent Clancy. "Yes."

"I've got a tentative ID on the drone. It's a modified VV1, manufactured by Vertical Vision and used for surveying oil and gas pipelines."

"Tentative?"

"The photo resolution is too rough to be certain. And VV1s are white, whereas the drone in question is black. But paint is cheap and the VV1 is the only drone I've found with matching ears."

"Ears?"

"They're antennae, but—"

"I get it. Anything else?"

"No, sir."

"Thanks, Clancy. Good work."

An hour later, Rip walked into the corner office in Quantico. His boss wasn't alone. CIA Director Kevin Riddle was also seated at the table. Two directors, twice the credit. *Thank you, Oscar Pincus.*

"Have a seat, Rip," Director Brix said. "Director Riddle was just telling me that you have evidence of drone involvement in his predecessor's killing?"

Despite the cordial tone, Brix was undoubtedly pissed that Riddle received first word. But Rip was confident his transgression would soon be forgiven. He'd emerge from this meeting with two gold stars. "That's right. Given the severe ramifications, I thought we should discuss it in person."

Rip whipped open his laptop and showed them the video from EarthCam. Then he pulled up stills of the drone coming and going.

"What have you concluded from this?" Brix asked.

"I see two possible scenarios. One, Achilles used the drone to slip a gun past Rider's bodyguards. Two, a third party used the drone to kill Director Rider and frame Achilles for it."

"Which do you consider more likely?" Brix asked.

"Using a drone to deliver a weapon is a lot more complicated than hiding one."

"But potentially more reliable," Brix countered, playing devil's advocate. "A gun might be discovered."

Rip nodded diplomatically. "I take your point."

Riddle said, "Achilles could have hidden a ceramic knife without fear of discovery. In his hands, it would be just as deadly. For that matter, Achilles wouldn't require a weapon. Not against a politician."

Rip didn't contradict him.

Brix cracked the knuckles of his left hand, one after the other, his eyes on the ceiling. "If the drone pulled the trigger, then we're looking at something very different from a disgruntled former employee taking revenge. Potentially something much bigger."

"What are you thinking?" Riddle asked.

"Either someone wanted Rider dead and figured that framing Achilles was the best way to get away with it. Or killing Rider served a different purpose entirely."

"Such as?"

"Suppose, for example, you want to convince prospective

clients that you can kill anybody. Anybody at all. A sheik. A sultan. A president. Killing the Director of the CIA would be one hell of an audition. You do that, and you could name your price. Nine figures wouldn't be out of the question."

Riddle nodded somberly before turning to Rip. "What are you thinking, Agent Zonder?"

"I have to admit, the audition angle didn't occur to me. My thoughts went straight to the broader security picture and got hung up there."

"Broader security picture?"

"Our country is packed with guns and it's filling up with drones. Once people realize they can combine the two to kill with anonymity, we're going to find ourselves living in a different world."

Rip watched the two powerful men absorb his words like heavy weights laid on raw shoulders. Nobody said anything for a few beats.

Brix was first to break the silence. "We need to keep this development quiet."

Riddle immediately concurred. "Agreed."

"My team knows to keep quiet," Rip said.

"We should personally reinforce that message," Brix said to Riddle before turning back to Rip. "Looks like finding Achilles is more important than we thought. It's not just optics anymore."

"I agree," Riddle said. "Achilles knows what happened on that roof. If he was framed, he'll likely know who did it. The urgency of finding him just increased tenfold."

Brix said, "So as far as everyone not on the team is concerned, Achilles will remain our prime suspect. There will be no public mention of the drone. Rip, your team should investigate the drone angle with strict discretion."

Rip was tempted to ask Brix if this negated his previous order to shoot Achilles on sight, but bit his tongue. "Understood. We've tentatively identified the model as a VV1, manufactured by Vertical Vision in Moscow."

"The bloody Russians," Riddle said. "That makes sense."

"Vertical Vision is owned by Victor Vazov, the oil oligarch," Rip added.

Riddle raised his eyebrows. "I'll see if he's crossed paths with Rider."

"There's another Russia connection," Rip said. "The call that got me searching the sky for drones was made from Moscow, although I'm pretty sure the caller was a French woman."

"A French woman? With what intent?" Brix asked.

"She appears to want to get Achilles off the hook."

"You think he was with her when she called?"

"At the very least, she'd spoken to him after the event."

"How old did the woman sound?" Riddle asked, his voice suddenly more energetic.

"Young enough to have me thinking *ooh la la*, but old enough for me to take her seriously. Early thirties, I'd guess."

"Did you mention that to your team? Does Oscar know about the French woman?"

Rip had kept her tip to himself until the video yielded fruit. "We didn't discuss her."

Riddle slammed the flat of his hand against the table, causing the others to jerk their heads. "Achilles' last partner was a French woman. A rookie. They only worked one operation together. It was a high profile assignment and they blew it. Cost both of them their jobs. That operation was an attempt to capture Ivan the Ghost."

37

Separation

Moscow, Russia

Achilles knew what was coming before it happened. After a dozen paces, Victor Vazov raised his left index finger and stopped walking. The oligarch's good-cop routine wasn't so much for Jo as for his wife and the foreign investors. He said something sotto voce to the missus, then returned to the nearest bodyguard and spoke, while she escorted the guests toward the door.

After listening to Victor, the bodyguard motioned for his partner to accompany the boss. He did so without taking his aim from Jo's center mass.

As Victor walked off, Jo whispered, "What did he say?"

"Apparently the garbage truck comes in the morning. We're supposed to be in it."

"No talking!" their minder growled. He kept his Glock 19 on Jo's chest, but locked eyes with Achilles. A sound tactical move. "Get back inside." He gestured toward the hole with his chin.

Achilles put his arm around Jo to guide her.

The bodyguard cut him off. "Just you. She stays here."

Achilles had faced scores of tough choices over the years, but he couldn't recall another one this gut wrenching. He couldn't leave Jo alone with Vazov's brute. The way she looked in that dress, with her lithe legs, boosted bust and sparkling eyes, no magic was required to read his mind. But Achilles also couldn't cover the ten feet between them faster than the twitch of a trigger finger. Sure, the brute would hesitate. Even pros would think twice before shooting a beautiful, young, non-threatening woman. But the order had been given. They were going out with the trash and this guy's orders were to put them in the can.

Doubt would only buy half a second.

"Move!"

Achilles moved. Not out of fear, but out of faith. Faith that Jo could take better care of herself than he could.

No sooner had he squirmed back through the hole then something slid across it, blocking any attempt at retreat. A file drawer from the look of it. Not a serious physical barrier, but an audiovisual one that doubled as an early-warning system. It put a lightning attack out of the question.

Achilles spent a few seconds trying to overhear what they were saying, but it was hopeless. The stress testers created too much cover noise. So what next? He couldn't just wait around. That was contrary to his nature under routine conditions. In this case, the friction from flying neurons would light his hair on fire if he didn't move.

He looked around the room. The finance department was twice as deep as a normal office, and three offices wide. It was also twice as tall. To separate it from the rest of the bay, the architect had taken the walls all the way up rather than suspending a ceiling. It was more aesthetically appealing, and probably cheaper.

The roof was supported by scaffolding that zigzagged in the standard perfected by big box stores. An elevated highway for anyone who cared to climb, but leading nowhere. The HVAC vents, while sizable and sturdy, weren't large enough for shoulders like his. He knew that from experience. If the building was burning and he needed to escape, he could rip a vent from its moorings and climb through the gap into the next room. But that avenue wouldn't help him now. His escape had to go undetected, and the camouflaging sound of the stress testers wasn't sufficiently loud.

The ceiling was a nonstarter.

He fought the urge to obsess over Jo and forced himself to focus on rescuing her. The clock was ticking. Each minute he failed to act was another she had to suffer.

He walked around collecting weapons, while contemplating his options. A few letter openers, a spherical glass paperweight and a hefty pair of scissors made it into his pockets.

What about a fire? An alarm would initiate a rapid response

—followed by two swift shots from a Glock. A call to the police would get the same result. Nobody else could get there in time, not that he could call anyway as a wanted man. He was on his own.

The phone was out. The ceiling was out. The walls were out. That left the door.

Door locks are much more malleable from the inside than the out. Or rather their latches are. While on the outside, the latch is shielded from access and view by the frame, on the inside it's exposed. It has to be to allow the door to swing.

Latches differ from bolts on two key characteristics. First, they have a cutaway radius. Second, they can be moved even when the door is locked. Without both of those features, the door wouldn't swing closed on its own. Someone would have to turn the handle. The downside to these convenient features is security. Any motion mimicking the press of a door frame will cause the latch to retract. This is why you can open loose-fitting, low-quality doors—like those on cheap hotel rooms—by sliding a credit card between the latch and frame.

Achilles was on the inside, however, so to take advantage of that engineering loophole, he would have to pull on the latch's radius, rather than pushing it. He slipped a paperclip from his back pocket, and set to work.

Given the innocuous nature of paperclips, combined with their multiple uses in emergencies, Achilles always tried to keep a few paperclips handy. It was a thing with him. Had been for years. This time, however, the mighty paperclip let him down. The spring on the latch was stronger than the paperclips he could fit in the gap. He would have to use wire. Hopefully, he could yank one from inside some piece of electronic equipment and floss the latch open. Fast.

A scream interrupted his search. An anguished, primordial shout, lasting only a second. Was it masculine? Or was that wishful thinking?

He lunged toward the hole but immediately stopped himself, the front of his mind overriding the lizard brain in back. *Don't play into his hand.* He forced himself to maintain tactical discipline and fought the urge to scream Jo's name.

He readied his weapons and perked his ears. The paperweight

held high above his head, the scissors clenched for stabbing. For several long seconds, he heard nothing over that damn robotic whirring. Then the file cabinet slid aside.

His striking arm strained higher.

His stabbing arm pulled further back.

Shadows signaled the moment of truth. Then a bloody hand came into view, holding a Glock.

38

Instant Gratification

Moscow, Russia

Ivan ended up seeking professional assistance to solve the problem of getting paid while the victims were still in the air. He didn't like involving outside consultants, in part because of security concerns, in part because he liked to figure things out for himself. But after spending a few frustrating days fumbling around the Internet, he decided that banking was too complicated and mission-critical for guesswork.

He used connections to find the best darknet banker in the business, then shelled out a hundred grand to get tutored in the tricks of his trade. They met for the weekend at a mountain retreat on the island of Corsica—home of the French Foreign Legion's parachute regiment, and source of the banker's beefy bodyguards.

Speaking through an endless stream of blue cigarette smoke, Markos set him straight. "The banking world isn't what it was even a few months ago. There's so much competition for hiding ill-gotten assets that banks are tripping over themselves to attract the illicit trillions circulating around the globe. Long gone are the days when Switzerland was the only game in town. Nowadays, every island state and third world dictatorship is looking to skim a commission off that golden river."

Ivan was thrilled by the news, but feared his circumstance might be an exception. He wasn't talking about a low profile op. By the time he rode off into the sunset, his heists would be making the nightly news on a daily basis. "What if the FBI or Interpol get involved?"

Markos scoffed. "Independent bankers are making way too much money to give a damn what Western governments want.

Think about it. Even if their commission is only 0.1 percent, they still make $1,000 for every million transferred. That's $1,000 for a few minutes of work. It adds up fast, and leaves plenty to pay for pricey lawyers and pretty receptionists."

Made sense to Ivan, but he wasn't there yet. "I'm not going to be able to wait days or even hours for funds to clear. I need instant transfers that can't be revoked or traced."

Markos gave a knowing nod. "Instant used to be a problem, but not anymore. Countless new transfer systems have cropped up—the PayPals of the world. As for irrevocable, that depends on the recipient bank, for which I refer you to my previous point about commissions."

"I'm not sure I follow."

"If a banker is making thousands of dollars a day for moving zeroes around the Internet, and some suit shows up flashing a foreign badge and asking him to bite the hand that feeds him, is the banker going to say *Yes, sir* or *Piss off?*"

Ivan pictured the scenario and it made him smile. He wasn't a big fan of the police. "And untraceable? Can the police get the records?"

"Snowden showed us that the U.S. government doesn't ask for permission. If they want to trace your transfers, they've got the tools and talent to do it. But it takes time. Took them years to track down the guy behind Silk Road, the online narcotics supplier."

"So I might be safe in the short term, but eventually they'll catch up?"

Again Markos scoffed. "Not at all. The question isn't if they'll be able to trace your transfers, but what they'll trace them to. If you use a fake ID or shell corporation to open an account—" He tilted his head back and blew smoke into the air.

Ivan smiled as the smoke vanished.

He had his answers.

He was tempted to hire Markos to arrange and manage the Raven extortions for him. To set up scores of accounts at dozens of banks, so he'd never have to use the same one twice. But since they had met, that was out of the question. There were plenty of talented bankers who had never seen his face. He asked Markos one final question. "Suppose I want the FBI to trace the money?"

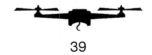

39

The Path

Moscow, Russia

Achilles felt his heart leap with relief as Jo followed the Glock through the hole. She was bloodied, but didn't appear to be bleeding. She set the gun down with a clunk and slid it aside. Then she jumped into his arms like a scared child. She hugged him hard as her silent sobs turned to stuttered wails. Forcefully enough to relieve some of his worry.

He wanted to verify that she'd completely extinguished the threat, but kept his impulse in check. Jo needed him to hold her.

A minute was all it took.

Her sobbing stopped and her grip slackened off. Her breathing became regular.

Achilles mirrored her actions.

She shook her head and started to speak, but choked up. "Sorry about that. It—. It was pretty rough there for a minute."

"The blood, is it all his?"

"Yes."

"He didn't hurt you?"

"No."

"He didn't—?"

"No. He never touched me."

Relief washed over Achilles. Taking life was traumatic, but infinitely better than losing it. "Oh, thank goodness."

Jo backed up a step to signify that she could stand on her own, making them both acutely aware of the fact that she was naked.

Achilles pulled a black sweater off the back of a nearby chair and handed it to her. "Shall we get out of here?"

"Please."

Achilles led the way back into the main room. The scene before him told the tale. A trail of clothes led to a body. Dress. Bra. Panties. All spaced a few paces apart. All leading to the source of the bleeding.

The bodyguard's face and throat looked like they'd suffered small-caliber exit wounds, but Achilles knew a bullet wasn't the source of the damage. The lethal weapons were lying beside the corpse. Jo had used her shoes, her stiletto heels.

"You conned him. You promised to give him the time of his life if he'd let you go. You told him you'd fly back to France and nobody would ever know. Then you started dancing."

Jo said nothing.

Achilles understood that she didn't want to relive the scene, but he sensed that there was more to her silence. "He wouldn't have let you go. He'd have had the time of his life, and then he'd have shot you in the back of the head."

Jo said nothing.

"It was him or you, him or us. You didn't just save your own life, you also saved mine."

Jo said nothing.

"Let's get out of here."

"I'd like that."

He picked up her clothes and handed them over. "Take a minute to wash up in the bathroom."

"Good idea."

Once the bathroom door closed behind her, Achilles grabbed the stilettos and ran to the men's room. He gave them a thorough washing followed by a thorough drying using a combination of paper towels and the electric dryer.

When Jo exited the ladies' room, she looked up at him and then down at the shoes in his hand. She stared at them with quivering lip, digesting what had happened.

Achilles realized that she was standing at a mental crossroads with a choice to make. Relive the perils of the past, or focus on the promise of the future. Walk toward the dark, or into the light.

It was his turn to say nothing. He could show Jo the road to rapid recovery, but she had to choose to take it.

She made her decision. She reached for the shoes. "Better than barefoot."

"You're going to be fine," Achilles said, and he meant it.

40

Not Enough

French Riviera

Michael had seen Ivan pull off dozens of incredible capers, but he still hadn't lost his sense of awe at seeing the master in action. It wasn't the massive amounts of money Ivan extracted so much as his unconventional methods. Ivan had a way of finding pressure points that didn't involve physical force. No ball-peen hammers or blow torches for The Ghost. He was graceful. His tactics weren't just more pleasant to employ, they were also more effective.

Michael was sad that their collaboration would soon be coming to an end.

His oldest and essentially only friend was about to hit the beach with hundreds of millions of dollars in the bank.

They had never specifically discussed what would happen to Michael at that point. It was an awkward topic. While Michael had begun in an authority position as a mentor hired by Ivan's father, their roles had reversed over time and Michael was now completely dependent on Ivan. For nearly thirty years, Ivan had paid all Michael's bills without question, and put a fancy roof over his head. He'd given him a gold credit card rather than a paycheck.

Michael had next to nothing in the bank, but he had stock. He was set to receive a two-percent stake in Silicon Hill, once Ivan took ownership. Two percent of a $600 million business. Twelve million. Enough to retire on quite comfortably.

But he wasn't looking forward to retiring. He would miss the adventure. The thrill of the hunt. The pressure of the heist. The adrenaline rush of outsmarting everyone and walking away with millions. Those were priceless experiences.

And he would miss Ivan.

Michael couldn't help but worry about his friend. What if something went wrong and Ivan couldn't pay Vazov back in time? He'd learned to never question Ivan's plans for the simple reason that only one of their minds worked six moves ahead. But still, he was worried. He didn't see how they'd be able to pull off enough kidnap and ransoms, K&Rs, to raise $600 million before the deadline.

Since *his pension* was also on the line, Michael screwed up the courage to ask. He caught Ivan alone in his office and delivered a prepared line. "Not bad, collecting $40 million in three days."

"I'm pleased."

"That double dip with Chauveau was a particularly brilliant move."

"All according to plan."

"Glad you brought that up. I have a question regarding the plan."

Ivan raised an eyebrow. "Go ahead."

"Are you really planning to pay Vazov back? The full $600 million?"

"Every last dollar."

Michael shrugged. "I always figured you'd play him the way you play everyone else. Press on a pain point and get him to walk away. Especially with the way he treats you."

Ivan smiled. "I can't have the Russian mafia after me."

"It's not going to be easy, meeting that payment schedule. We're already $20 million behind."

Ivan raised his eyebrows, but said nothing. He didn't seem to share Michael's concern.

"I have a few additional targets lined up, but to pull this off, we have to identify dozens more. Then we have to identify an opportunity to abduct them in a predictable, private setting. These first three have been the low-hanging fruit. Going forward, we're going to have to climb higher. By the end, we'll be way out on slim limbs."

"Your point?"

"We can't afford a single miss. Not a day. Not a target. Not if we're going to raise $560 million more before the deadline. And we have to continue bringing in $20 million a job, with a couple of $30 million days thrown in. That's one hell of an assumption, even for you. If I may say so."

"You just did."

Michael moved his hands to the small of his back and clenched his fists in frustration while keeping his face calm. "You know Vazov wants the company. You know he'll hop on any opportunity to keep it. If you come up a few million short, he's not going to say 'close enough.' "

"I'm well aware."

"How can you possibly be so calm about this? Either I'm missing something, or you are. I know the former is much more likely, but I feel I deserve to know."

Ivan stood and walked to the window, hiding his face. "I have a confession to make. I've gone behind your back."

Michael felt his stomach drop. "Why would you do that? Have I let you down?"

"I didn't want to distract you."

When had Ivan ever worried about distracting him? For twenty years Ivan had treated him like he had Atlas's shoulders, capable of bearing the weight of the world. "So what have you done?"

"I contracted out a bit of research—to some friends—in America. Had them do some ground work as well."

"Ground work? America?"

Ivan whirled back around. "We're moving the operation to the U.S. Raven is being crated and a new Tesla will be waiting when we land. We're leaving at 2:00 a.m. to take advantage of the night shift at both airports."

Michael knew what "the night shift" meant. Ivan had explained it years ago prior to another assignment. Jobs at private aviation facilities were very cushy in comparison to those at standard commercial facilities. Everyone fortunate enough to capture a coveted position clamped onto it with both hands and a broad grin.

The broad grin was a requirement. People who pay for private planes often expect to walk around with lips glued to their tanned asses. Some make a sport of sacking the servants who don't demonstrate due deference. So privileges are extended and eyes averted and gratuities paid. Especially after hours.

"Where in America?" Michael asked.

"You can't guess?"

Michael probably could. He knew Ivan, and he knew Raven.

"Has to have a high concentration of wealth."

"Of course."

"But not a big city. Raven needs room to operate. We want people living in houses."

Ivan said nothing.

"Palm Beach?"

"Palm Beach is flat. Too easy to spot Raven coming and going."

Of course. All of Florida was flat. *Where else?* Certain suburbs around New York City might work. Suffolk, Westchester or Fairfield counties. But somehow those didn't feel right. They weren't Ivan's style. So what was? Lightning struck and Michael grabbed it.

"Silicon Valley."

41

Genetic Dice

Airborne

Moscow, Russia to Nice, France

They paid for Wi-Fi on the flight to France. As usual, it was overpriced and underperforming. Achilles didn't mind, as long as it kept Jo's mind moving. He didn't want her dwelling on the stiletto scene. Bad experiences had a way of digging in and setting up camp if you gave them time to fester.

Fortunately, they appeared to have struck gold at Vertical Vision. The address on the packing slip Jo had uncovered was exciting.

She looked over from her laptop. "Google says it's a business called Silicon Hill. Have you heard of it?"

"Rings a bell, but not a loud one."

"You're going to like this. Their CEO is Vladislav Vazov."

"Vladislav, not Victor?"

"That's right."

"Must be his son. Is there a picture?"

"I'll find one."

Jo had no immediate success, but she kept on looking. She spent the entire four-hour flight from Moscow to Nice researching Vlad Vazov and his company. She shared bits and pieces as she uncovered them. She saved a number of links and files. But she presented no pictures of the man himself.

"Silicon Hill was founded three years ago. It's a privately held corporation."

"What's its principal business?"

"It's classified as a technology incubator. A home for startup technologies."

"No mention of drones?"

"No mention of anything specific. They're all in 'stealth mode.' In the articles, Vazov positions his company as France's answer to Silicon Valley. He claims to have attracted some of the world's best talent. He says they have all the resources of the California counterpart, but with a much better view."

"Did you find a list of major shareholders?"

"There's only one. Vazov owns it all."

"Well, then he must be exaggerating about the quality of his talent. You can't get the best without stock options."

"Apparently, that's where he's been most inventive. Silicon Hill isn't just a company—it's a compound. The engineers and technicians all live within the walls. Vazov equates working for him to life at an all-inclusive resort."

"Sounds like a page from the Soviet playbook. A technology city."

"Look at this," Jo said, pointing to a picture. "I suspect it's a bit more glamorous than anything the Soviets ever built. Vazov converted the estate of a deceased billionaire. Check out the main building."

Achilles did. It was an aerial shot staged to show off both the front of the main building and its clifftop view of the beach.

Jo scrolled down to a secondary picture, taken from higher altitude. "Silicon Hill occupies a hundred acres of prime real estate. Four hundred meters of oceanfront stretching a whole kilometer inland."

"Did you find anything from a major media source? *Newsweek* or *The Wall Street Journal?*"

"The primary hits have all been puff pieces in technology journals."

"Places you can pay to brag," Achilles said, as much to himself as to Jo.

"Why do you ask?"

"Just starting to work the problem."

"The problem?"

"Getting in." Achilles changed the subject, not wanting Jo to dwell on their last incursion. "What does it tell us about Vazov?"

"Not much. He's 39 and single. One piece noted that he

belongs at the top of Europe's most eligible bachelor list."

"Any personal details? His nationality?"

"It confirms that his father is a Russian oligarch and his mother's a Latvian beauty queen, but there's very little else. As one article put it, Vazov loves to talk about his business, but he clams up when the conversation turns personal. There is a hint, however. The same article that mentions his bachelor status says he and his father are known as Little V and Big V. That might reference more than their ages."

"But there's no picture?"

"Surprisingly not. He's awfully camera shy for a CEO. The only photos I've found show him from behind, surveying his empire"

"Not even a group shot or distant photograph?"

Jo shook her head. "No. I suspect that either the woman we saw with Victor isn't Vlad's mother, or the genetic dice favored his father, or—" Jo suddenly stopped talking. She grew a faraway look that slowly turned into a smile.

Achilles had no idea what she was thinking, but he was thrilled to see the immersive therapy session working. "What is it?"

"I just got a crazy idea. Maybe it's the trauma speaking, or maybe it's just wishful thinking, but I swear I think it fits."

"Fits what?"

"Our quest."

Achilles began to worry again. "I don't follow."

"I think Little V is Ivan the Ghost."

42

Identity Crisis

Airborne

Moscow, Russia to Nice, France

Achilles had serious doubts that a man as crude and brutish as Victor Vazov could have sired a handsome charmer like Ivan the Ghost, but he bit back the urge to immediately refute Jo. Perhaps her intuition was better than his. In any case, the discussion would be therapeutic.

He glanced around. They were at the back of the plane, with an empty middle seat between them. There was no bathroom line, and the flight attendants were providing white noise from the galley with an animated discussion of Facebook posts. "Tell me your thinking."

Jo leaned closer. "For starters, at around forty, Vazov's age fits. His nationality and region of residence are also right."

She paused for comment, so Achilles gave it to her straight albeit with a sympathetic tone. "You can't visit a five-star hotel in Europe without running into a rich, forty-something Russian."

Jo continued, undeterred. "As the son of an oligarch, he'd have the financial resources and criminal connections required to get started in the style favored by Ivan."

"I refer you to my last point."

"Having Victor Vazov for a father would also explain Ivan's brains and missing moral compass."

Achilles' worries began to fade. She was thinking clearly, although not necessarily correctly. "It's a common mold. And speaking of molds, Ivan looks nothing like Vazov. Not his height. Not his build. Not his face."

"So Little V draws his physical appearance from his mother."

"Possible, but not probable."

"If Ivan's identity fell within probable parameters, he would have been caught years ago."

Achilles had to give her that. "Agreed. Why don't you tell me what triggered your conclusion?"

"The drone connection was a biggie. How many rich Russian Europeans have connections to drone manufacturing?"

"I don't know, but I bet if we look hard enough we'll find hundreds."

"Perhaps. But there's also the secrecy. There are no photos of Little V on the web. I could understand being camera shy if you look like Big V, or if you're trying to be a ghost, but if your looks come from a Latvian beauty queen, there has to be a compelling reason."

Achilles pointed to his computer screen, which displayed an article written in Russian. He'd been doing some research of his own. "There is. Vlad Vazov was kidnapped. Twice. The first time when he was sixteen years old, the second when he was twenty. The article ties it to a long-standing blood feud between the Vazov and Gulin families, but it doesn't disclose additional detail other than to say that after the second kidnapping he dropped out of university and moved to the South of France."

"Huh. That's interesting, and it's good to know Vazov has a blood rival, but it doesn't change anything."

"It explains why he doesn't want people to know what he looks like. And it explains why the Vazov's are so big on security."

"But it doesn't contradict my theory."

Achilles decided that going along would be wiser than attempting to change Jo's mind. There was no downside to it— they were following the drones to Vlad Vazov regardless—and perhaps she was right. "So what's your suggestion?"

"We find him. If he looks like his father, we know he's not Ivan. If he's more like his mother, then we'll move on to stage two."

"Stage two?"

"We arrange a situation that lets you look him in the eye, listen to his voice, and study his body language. Since you've confronted Ivan before, you'll know if Vazov is The Ghost—regardless of any surgery he may have had."

Achilles couldn't fault her logic, even if he questioned her premise. "If Vlad is Ivan, he'll see through my disguise the moment we're face to face. We'll need to orchestrate that encounter to occur away from crowds and bodyguards in a setting that allows me to take immediate action."

Jo reached over and set her hand on his arm. "Thank you. I'm glad we've got a goal. Now, let's get working on a plan."

43

The Golden State

Silicon Valley, California

Michael held the binoculars with his left hand while drumming the dashboard with his right. He was nervous. Nervous for himself, and nervous for Ivan.

California was not going as planned.

Ivan's "friends"—he had yet to identify them—had done a good job selecting targets, even with no knowledge of Raven. They had identified key executives in companies flush with cash, and then had uncovered times in their routines that were "good for a grab." That was the guidance Ivan had given. It translated to times when the targets were alone in isolated locations. Early morning meditations. Late night love affairs. Walks in the woods or along lonely beaches. Thus far their intel had been spot-on.

But the numbers were insufficient.

California was only yielding $10 million per op, plus they had missed two days due to the relocation from France and another when their target took ill. As a result, they were $90 million behind schedule on Vazov's repayment plan.

Ivan had hinted at a kicker to come, but so far, Michael hadn't seen it. He began to worry about his retirement fund. It was an odd sensation, and a first, fretting about Ivan not coming through.

Michael and Ivan were on a hillside above their latest target's sprawling Los Gatos estate, whereas Boris and Pavel were parked on a fire road deep in the woods. The split was designed to help avoid detection. Normally Michael would be by himself, but Ivan had elected to join him. As to why, Michael wasn't sure.

Ivan leaned forward and muted the hands-free call to Pavel and Boris. "Would you mind stopping that?"

"What?"

"Your fingers are drumming the dashboard."

"Sorry."

"Something bothering you?"

I've got a growing list, but this really isn't the time for it. Michael needed to focus on the job. If they screwed this up, they'd be another day behind. Another $20 million in the hole. He ignored the question.

He wondered if Gordon Sangster would look the same in person as on the cover of *Wired* magazine, with slightly wild red hair, eyebrows in need of trimming and a perpetual half-smile that marked him as the smartest guy in the room—at least in his own mind.

Their target was set to show any second. He had a daily ritual. The celebrity CEO loved to walk around his hillside garden in the evening. He'd hold a martini glass in one hand and a pair of shears in the other. He'd prune his babies to the sound of Bach and the sight of the setting sun. Michael found it ironic that the prime purveyor of artificial exercise environments relaxed by connecting with Mother Nature.

"Best to get it off your chest," Ivan pressed.

It's now or never, Michael realized. Without taking his eyes off the target yard, he said, "The miss with Miller has put us behind, and odds are he won't be the last target to become sick or have a change of plans. I'm worried about you."

"You're worried about me? Why on earth would you do that? Have I ever failed to deliver? Even once in all our years together?"

"Well, no, but—"

"Have I ever come up short? Ceased to amaze? Underperformed?"

With his eyes buried in binoculars, Michael couldn't see Ivan's face. He couldn't tell if the offense was genuine or just Ivan pulling his chain. Perhaps he was testing Michael's discipline to keep his eyes on target. Undeterred, Michael decided to stick with his program. "We're nearly a $100 million behind schedule, and further hiccups are bound to happen. I'm sure Vazov is salivating as we speak."

"You expect hiccups?"

"It's only going to get harder. One of these times someone will go to the police."

"You're right."

Michael was shocked. Shocked and horrified. He didn't want to be right. So far, every CEO had kept his abduction secret— exactly as Ivan had predicted. Ivan insisted that the last thing any CEO wanted was talk of his demise, given the resultant blow to his image and hit to his stock price. "I'm right?"

"Soon our little secret won't be a secret anymore."

"So what then? How will you pay off Vazov in time?"

"If I tell you now, I'll ruin the surprise."

Before Michael could concoct his response, Ivan added, "There he is. Sangster's in the garden."

Michael realized he'd been looking without paying attention. He unmuted the call to Pavel and Boris. "We're a go."

"We're a go," Pavel repeated.

44

Tele-phony

Quantico, Virginia

Caller ID on Rip's vibrating phone indicated a CIA number. Probably Pincus with an update. He was comparing the recording of the French woman's voice to that of Jo Monfort, and he was looking into Vertical Vision. "Zonder here."

"Rip, it's Kevin Riddle."

The Director of the CIA. Calling him directly. And using his first name. Something was up. Probably something his boss wouldn't like. "How can I help you, Director?"

"I'm looking for the latest news—unfiltered."

In other words, he wanted to circumvent his FBI counterpart. Brix hadn't actually berated him for allowing Riddle to receive first word about the drone, but they both knew he'd crossed a line and damaged their relationship. Now Riddle wanted another taste. Rip wasn't about to make that mistake.

"I know this call is unusual," Riddle continued. "Perhaps a minor protocol deviation. But I thought it might be mutually beneficial if we opened up a channel of direct communication. This is a joint investigation, and it was my predecessor who died."

Rip remained silent while his processor whirred. Riddle had used the magic words: *mutually beneficial.* He was offering to become an ally.

"Surely there's no harm in your occasionally accepting my calls and giving me latest news directly. So here's the deal. I'll never speak of our arrangement. Never hint at it. Never acknowledge it, even if we're alone together. But I will remember it. I will remember you. And I will be there if you should need me."

Could anyone fault Rip for assisting the Director of the CIA? It wasn't like he'd called Riddle. He was simply responding to a direct request from a ranking team member. No, he decided, nobody could fault him—if he called Brix immediately afterwards to report the call.

And there was the rub.

If Rip reported it, he would lose with both directors. If he kept it secret, the arrangement would be win-win for him and Riddle. The proposal felt exactly like that of a beautiful woman asking him to cheat on his wife. And it was coming at a moment when he was worried about divorce.

He decided to stick a toe in the water. See how it felt before plunging in. "Was it Jo Monfort who called me?"

It was Riddle's turn to remain silent.

Rip waited.

"We believe it was."

The water felt warm and refreshing. Rip put his other foot in. "Were you able to link Victor Vazov with Director Rider?"

Another substantial pause. "No, we didn't find any connection. What's your latest thinking on Vazov?"

The temptress had unbuttoned her blouse. Time for Rip to choose: *walk away* or *unzip*. He looked toward heaven and rolled his eyes. Did men ever walk away? "Our analysts remain confident that the assassin employed one of Vazov's drones in San Francisco."

"But what about Vazov's personal involvement?" Riddle pressed.

"After 9/11, we didn't suspect the airline CEOs. I think the same reasoning applies here."

"You might have been more suspicious if it had been Aeroflot rather than American and United. Vazov's drones are relatively obscure, or rather, specialized. The VV1 was an odd choice."

"I agree. The drone selection does point to Russian involvement. Between that and the call from Monfort, I'm favoring the theory that Rider was killed by Ivan the Ghost."

Riddle replied with a tinge of excitement in his voice. "I can't fault your reasoning. Do you think Ivan was working with Achilles, or against him?"

"Could be either. We have to assume they've teamed up until the facts indicate otherwise."

"I agree. Do you have any clue as to Ivan's whereabouts?"

"None. He remains as ghostly as ever."

"And Achilles? How close would you say you are to catching him?"

"He's no less ghostly at the moment."

"Thank you for your candor, Agent Zonder. Keep on it."

As Rip hung up, he found himself feeling better than he had before the call. He felt he'd acquitted himself well. He had gained a powerful ally without giving Riddle any information Brix didn't already possess. That made the call inconsequential —and thus not worth reporting.

Just ten miles away in the heart of Silicon Valley, Ivan also hung up a phone. Then he kissed it.

45

Sightseeing

French Riviera

Jo pulled a rented Peugeot up to Vazov's security booth and lowered the driver's side window. The actions earned her a blast of hot air and an inquisitive glance. A bald guard with small ears and a sweaty lip asked, "May I help you?"

"We're with the *San Jose Mercury News*. We have an appointment with your public relations manager." She handed over a business card. *Bridgette Simpson, Editor-at-Large.*

"Yes, Miss Simpson. Chantal is expecting you. How many are in your party?"

"Just me and my photographer."

Achilles was disguised with a thin mustache, round black wire-rimmed spectacles, and the kind of golf cap often worn backward by men with thinning hair. He inclined his head toward the guard.

The guard politely returned Jo's card. To her relief, he did not ask her to pop the trunk. "Chantal will be waiting for you in front of the main building. The road will fork a few times, but just keep climbing. If you end up in the ocean, you've gone too far."

Achilles had conjured up the idea of posing as reporters from Silicon Valley's premiere newspaper. Jo had taken it from there. *An insider's perspective on life at Silicon Hill* was how she had pitched it. *Tagged onto the end of her vacation,* she'd confided. "You get exposure. I get expenses." Vazov's public relations manager had seized the last-minute "win-win opportunity" with both hands.

It took a good five minutes to drive up the hill at sightseeing speed. They spent every second studying the compound. The construction was all of a similar style, with off-white stucco walls and red tiled roofs. The grounds were sun-drenched and artfully arranged to leverage the natural landscape. Lots of rock and wild grass interspersed with lush trees and flowering bushes. Despite the heat, Jo kept the window down to enjoy the fragrant air. "Did you know the perfume industry began not far from here?"

"Yes, in Grasse. Can you believe this place? I'm ready to move here and I haven't even seen the ocean yet."

"I don't see how an engineer could resist, especially if she's young and single."

"I trust that's one of the questions on your list?" Achilles asked.

"Actually, I've got a dozen regarding recruitment tactics and retention statistics."

Although they were posing as a team, reporter with photographer, the mission tactic was to divide and conquer. Jo would be exercising her interpersonal skills in the role of reporter, while Achilles broke away to take photographs. He was "a creative genius" who "requires solitude and isolation."

When they finally reached the hilltop, Chantal was waiting for them as promised. She wore a patterned summer dress reminiscent of the wildflowers they'd driven past. Purple and orange on a beige background. She extended a hand as they stepped from the car. "I'm Chantal. We spoke on the phone."

"I'm Bridgette. Nice to meet you, Chantal. This is Kevin, my photographer. He doesn't speak French, but then he doesn't need to. Thank you for agreeing to the interview."

Chantal ushered them through enormous glass doors into a lobby expertly designed to showcase its oceanfront location.

Jo stopped cold and spread her arms before bringing them to her heart. "What a spectacular view!"

"It never fails to take my breath away," Chantal concurred.

It truly was a more spectacular view than most people would ever see. After soaking it in for an appropriate period, Jo turned to the left and found two blue-eyed receptionists smiling at her, perfect as fresh flowers. She nodded acknowledgment before glancing to her right. The wall opposite reception was dominated by a life-sized oil painting of a man playing polo. She made a point of studying it.

"Our CEO, Mr. Vazov," Chantal said with a touch of pride.

"I wondered. You know I couldn't find a photo."

"Mr. Vazov likes to have his cake and eat it too."

"Pardon?"

"Fame and fortune with anonymity."

Jo heard Achilles' camera clicking while they spoke but didn't look in his direction. She wanted to keep the spotlight off him.

"Smart man. After all, who doesn't detest the paparazzi?"

Chantal nodded approval. "Who indeed?"

They walked past a sweeping central staircase and stopped before the big windows with the boastful view. "We're in through here," Chantal said, gesturing left toward a suite of glass walled conference rooms. "Ours is the corner one, the Azure Room. I think you'll like it."

Achilles cleared his throat loud enough to draw attention.

Jo looked back to see him wave a circle with his index finger. She leaned in and touched Chantal's shoulder. "Best if we let Kevin do his thing while we chat. He's a genius with a lens, but —well, I'm sure you know artists."

Chantal smiled understanding. "Absolutely." She turned to Achilles and spoke in English. "Enjoy your quest for the perfect shot. I'm sure you'll find it. There's so much to choose from. Ask Giselle if you require assistance." Chantal gestured toward reception.

Achilles met the blonde receptionist's eye, then inclined his head toward Chantal and touched his cap.

The game was on.

46

Checkpoint Charlie

French Riviera

Silicon Hill's lack of security surprised Achilles. Aside from the front gate, there appeared to be no guards. No cameras either, at least within the main building. And to his knowledge he hadn't passed through a metal detector. While that environment was normal enough for office parks, it was atypical for criminal enterprises.

Of course, the lack of conventional defensive devices didn't mean that security was slack at Silicon Hill. Defense came in many forms. Which was more secure: a jewel locked in a stainless steel vault, or one hidden where thieves would never look?

Achilles reminded himself that he was dealing with Ivan. Or not. Which of course was the point. The master of camouflage would blend into the background. Were you looking at a lizard, or just a pile of leaves?

The person portrayed in the lobby painting might well be the same man Achilles had once met on the back of a mega yacht, giving credence to Jo's theory. The basics seemed to fit: age, race, size and build, as did the facial features. Then there was the location and the flamboyance, both of which synched with their previous encounter.

But he was still far from sold.

Achilles found the first element of a sophisticated security system almost immediately. The staircase labeled as leading down to the East and West Wing Labs was located behind and beneath the central sweeping stairway. To reach it, a person had to pass through one of several sets of swinging glass doors. Each set was split barroom style, and rose floor to ceiling.

Functionally, the arrangement was reminiscent of a subway entrance, with multiple side-by-side channels, but the floor-to-ceiling glass construction was foolproof and far more elegant. Watching from behind his camera lens as employees came and went, Achilles observed that the system was smart enough to always open the door away from the user. Whether he or she was coming or going, the doors swung away swiftly, then closed just as quickly. No way you could surreptitiously tailgate someone.

Achilles decided to try the direct approach. Walking as though guided by his camera lens, he approached one of the doors.

Nothing happened.

No alarm. No flashing red light. Just the absence of motion. It was like he didn't exist. He figured RFID chips triggered the doors, rather than motion. Employees probably had them embedded in their identification cards. Very elegant. Very unobtrusive. Very effective.

An employee exited as Achilles was failing to enter. A younger guy, with bright eyes and a California look. Achilles said, "Excuse me. When does Mr. Vazov usually arrive?"

"Vazov. He usually doesn't. But then I'd be playing polo too, if I had the option." The Californian gestured toward the painting as proof positive and kept going.

Interesting.

Achilles walked back to Giselle. "Would you kindly buzz me into the labs."

"Afraid I can't do that. They are restricted to authorized employees only."

"I just need to snap a few quick photos. For the paper. We're going to make everyone back in Silicon Valley very jealous."

"I'm sure you are, but I really can't help you. I've never been down there myself."

"Seriously?"

"Stealth mode. Laboratory access is strictly for team members only."

"Which lab team is bigger, East Wing or West Wing?"

"I couldn't tell you. From up here I can't see which way people turn."

"Do you know where the senior engineers work?"

"Everyone here is pretty senior."

Achilles felt like he was playing ping pong. It was his serve, but he had yet to score. "Where's Mr. Vazov's office?"

"It's upstairs with the other executives, but he's not here today."

"Tomorrow?"

Giselle appeared ready to answer but stopped herself. "I thought you were flying back to the States tonight?"

So Chantal had passed along the context of their visit. She was thorough. "In the morning. Late enough that we might manage a shoot if he's an early riser?"

"I'm afraid not. And anyway, he's not big on being photographed."

"Just painted," Achilles said with a wink.

Giselle smiled.

"I won't take up any more of your time."

"Do let me know if you need anything."

Gaining access to the labs would require stealing an ID card. Jo could do that in her sleep, but Achilles wasn't willing to risk it. He suspected that the RFID chips triggered more than just the laboratory doors. A smart security system would have them connected into everything. The housing, the athletic facilities, the restaurants. What better way to keep track of your people— or ensure that the loss of a card was quickly detected?

That left Achilles the second floor for now. The executive offices. The trick would be reaching them. The   sweeping stairway was in full view of reception. Part of the decorative architecture and yet the functional equivalent of Checkpoint Charlie. To reach the second floor undetected, he was going to have to get creative.

47

Insufficient Funds

Silicon Valley, California

The selection of a specific target from the thousands of options available was largely dependent on three factors. First, the individual or his company needed instant access to at least $10 million in cash or credit. That wasn't too much of a stretch in Silicon Valley. Second, target executives had to have a habit that left them alone and isolated at a predictable time. Michael had expected that to be challenging, but it turned out that most people maintained a habit that made them vulnerable. The challenge was proving to be the third requirement: the ability to get Raven in and out without detection.

Pavel and Boris had practiced unloading and reloading Raven in and out of the Tesla to the point where they worked with the efficiency of a NASCAR pit crew. About ninety seconds at either end. But those ninety seconds had to happen in a concealed location accessible by the Model X. And on nights like tonight when that location didn't have line of sight on the target, Michael had to operate elsewhere. He didn't like splitting up the team or operating alone. And he didn't like Ivan looking over his shoulder.

"I'll make the ransom call," Ivan said, plucking the MiMiC phone from Michael's hand.

What was going on? Michael tried to take the change of plans at face value. Ivan was here, so of course he wanted to get behind the wheel and have some fun. But things were rarely that simple with Ivan.

Michael pushed his worries from his mind, and resolved to enjoy the show.

With The *new* Claw, the grabs practically ran on rails. Of

course, with the boss by his side, fate might want to make tonight an exception.

He and Ivan watched from their hillside with rapt fascination as Raven swooped in like a shadow. Pavel dropped The Claw just one second before the strike. As Sangster turned to investigate the buzzing sound, Pavel closed The Claw and scooped the screaming CEO from the ground.

Michael had questioned the wisdom of abducting anyone holding pruning shears, fearing what a motivated man might do to The Claw, but Sangster dropped his tool to the dirt beside his martini, precisely as Pavel predicted.

"A thing of beauty," Ivan said as Raven ascended. "Like watching an eagle catch salmon."

"Pavel's really got it down," Michael concurred as the headphones descended.

Ivan went to work with the phone. He put Sangster on hold —talk about a double entendre—while connecting with Sangster's CFO, George Milton.

During the half-dozen calls he'd made, Michael had honed his extortion technique to minimize their exposure time. The clock was the key. The display of remaining battery life. By artificially reducing that number to nine minutes, he eliminated all hesitation and dickering. Everyone knew what it meant to run out of power. Everyone had also encountered online delays due to slow connections or technical snafus. Combine those with the threat of impending death and nobody's focus wavered.

Ivan created a three-way call and began talking. "Listen up! Both of you. This is a ransom call. Mr. Sangster, the number you see blinking above in bright green is the remaining minutes of battery power. Mr. Milton, repeat after me. If I see any sign of the police, or we don't receive a $20 million transfer in the next nine minutes, your CEO will be dead."

"If you see any sign of the police, or you don't receive a $20 million transfer in the next nine minutes, my CEO will be dead."

"Very good. I've just texted the account number to your phone. Now, get typing."

"Pay it, Jim. Pay it now!" Sangster screamed. "I'll explain later, but for God's sake don't waste time asking questions."

"How—What—" Milton cut himself off, catching himself doing exactly what his boss had just forbidden.

Michael leaned toward Ivan and whispered in his ear. "They don't have $20 million."

Ivan didn't react.

"Just pay the money," Sangster repeated, his voice cracking. "If you don't, I'll be dead in eight minutes and thirty-seven seconds."

Milton's tempo remained calm and controlled, but his timbre edged up. "We don't have immediate access to $20 million. We have $3 million in cash and $15 million in overdraft instant credit. We could borrow the remaining $2 million, no problem. But not in the next eight minutes."

"Is that enough?" Sangster shouted, his voice imploring. "Is $18 million enough?"

Ivan said nothing.

"Hello? Are you there!"

Ivan said nothing.

"Maybe the call dropped," Milton said.

"Is $18 million enough?" Sangster repeated.

Ivan said nothing.

Sangster said, "Pay it."

"We don't have $20 million to pay."

"Don't screw around. If $18 million is everything we've got, pay him $18 million and include a note in case he isn't listening. I'm down to seven minutes."

"Initiating the transfer."

Michael looked over at his boss, impressed. Ivan had gotten them to give him everything they had.

"Transfer complete," Milton said. "Do you hear that? We've given you everything we have available. Let him go now. Please!"

Ivan said nothing.

Michael had his laptop open and refreshing. The account they'd given Milton was in Barbuda, and after tonight, it would never be used again. It was programmed to immediately forward any funds received to another account, which had a similar imbedded instruction funneling the money to Vazov. All arranged at considerable expense, Michael assumed, by Ivan's darknet banker.

The $18 million appeared. He gave the thumbs up to Ivan.

Ivan broke the silence. "Not good enough."

"We can pay the remaining $2 million tomorrow."

"Now or never," Ivan said.

A cacophony of pleas and promises erupted. It morphed into an explosion of threats and curses when Ivan failed to reply.

Michael looked over at Ivan, but Ivan remained focused on the windshield. He muted all the microphones and set down the MiMiC phone. Then he spoke into the car's hands-free phone. "Can you hear me, Pavel?"

"Loud and clear."

"Wait until the timer hits zero, then drop him."

48

Child's Play

French Riviera

Achilles studied the comings and goings of Silicon Hill employees while photographing the sweeping stairway that led up to the executive suite. Oddly enough, nobody appeared to be using it.

Whereas there was a steady trickle of scientists going down to the labs, Achilles hadn't seen a single person going up to the big offices. He extended his observation period by pretending to fuss with various camera settings.

Still no action. Not one *executive* in sight.

Interesting.

Achilles walked to the far end of the lobby, to the glass doors in the glass wall that separated the climate-controlled environment from the spectacular view. He exited onto a travertine terrace and looked around. It was enormous, about 6,000 square feet by his estimation, and furnished to resemble the quintessential five-star French alfresco restaurant, with round-topped tables, wrought iron chairs and colorful umbrellas. No doubt this was where employees enjoyed their meals and Vazov wooed investors. As for Achilles, if he had to pick a place to come and die, this would be it. And die one could. He estimated they were 400 feet above the surf.

He walked to the semicircular stone wall surrounding the perimeter and looked down at the beach far below. Beautiful white sand, a long pier capped by an inviting pergola, and an envy-inducing motor yacht.

Looking at the cliff beneath his feet with climbing in mind, he spotted what looked like an elevator shaft. Of course, down wasn't his area of interest. Achilles wanted to go up.

Turning back around to study the stone facade, he immediately characterized the climb to the second floor as child's play. Quite literally, the type of thing that might be attempted by a foolishly naive and naively fearless kid. For Achilles, the trick would be climbing without being seen.

The central second floor balcony was about twenty feet overhead, and empty. Even with camera equipment dangling about his neck, reaching it would only take a climber with his skills about six seconds. He just had to avoid the eyes of everyone inside.

Achilles wandered back toward the building and out of view of anyone inside. He stopped with his back to the stone and planned his next moves, while playing with the lens. If he came face to face with a person or six after vaulting over the railing above, he'd raise the camera to his eye and say, "Much better." Then he'd snap a few shots and ask the employees if they'd mind posing for a few photos behind their desks or a conference table. "I really want to put our readers into the executive suite at Silicon Hill." Flattery mixed with misdirection rarely failed.

He went for it.

The stonework felt hot as a pizza oven, but he moved fast enough that it didn't matter. Swinging onto the balcony, Achilles quickly surmised that it belonged to an office, and that office was mercifully empty. At least of animate objects. Slipping inside, he found it full of information. The room was so grand that it could only belong to the big cheese himself.

Hand-scraped hardwood floors were partly covered with Persian carpets. Soft leather furniture formed various configurations around the edge of the room, while a grand desk stood in the center. It was glass-topped and kidney-shaped, with spindly legs carved from olive wood. More form than function in Achilles' opinion—but very nice form.

Oddly absent was the matching credenza or anything resembling a vanity wall. He found no diplomas, no trophies, no awards, no display of celebrity photographs. There were no business materials. No business cards, no envelopes, no letterhead, or stack of messages. It contained nothing that revealed a name or displayed a face.

But Achilles knew it belonged to Vazov.

That meant it belonged to Ivan, if Jo was right and they were one and the same.

Achilles knew it from the oil paintings. One big, bright, brash scene hung from each plaster wall. Original LeRoy Neiman's perhaps, although Achilles wasn't one to know. But the subject matter was indisputable. The sport of kings. Polo.

49

The Drop

Silicon Valley, California

Michael was used to Ivan throwing tactical curveballs, but he still couldn't believe his ears. "You're going to kill Sangster? After he paid us everything he had?"

"Come again," Pavel said.

Ivan locked his eyes on Michael's as he spoke into the phone. "Wait until the timer hits zero, then drop him."

Pavel didn't reply immediately. Michael wasn't certain the pilot would cross the line, but Ivan's eyes beamed with confidence. They waited. One second. Two seconds. Three seconds.

The team had known all along that killing might be in the cards. Every soldier knows that when he enlists, although not everyone in uniform is capable of murder. For most, it's back of mind, not front. An abstraction filed away with other potential unpleasantries like auto accidents and cancer.

Ivan had primed them for the possibility from the beginning. Their first assignment had been the assassination of Jo Monfort in Versailles. But that had been different. A targeted hit. A settled score. A non-innocent. Gordon Sangster was no one to them, and he'd just forked over $18 million. True, he was considered to be a tyrannical boss, one known for publicly berating employees who displeased him and for going through secretaries faster than coffee cans. But he was contributing to society. By moving millions of fat asses from couches onto VR exercise machines, he was succeeding where generations of doctors had failed. He didn't deserve to die.

Pavel's reply crackled over the phone. "Roger that."

Michael was about to ask Ivan what killing Sangster would accomplish, but paused to ask himself instead. Ivan was undoubtedly several steps ahead. He thought aloud, with Ivan's eyes still locked on his. "The police will get involved. Given Sangster's profile, there will be media coverage. Given the amount of money involved and the extraordinary nature of the kidnapping, it will go viral."

"Yes, it will. Then what will happen?"

"Law enforcement at all levels will get involved—city, county, state, federal."

"Because one man died?"

Michael recognized a leading question when he heard it, but it took him a moment to figure out where Ivan was going. "The others will come forward. The other victims. Once the Sangster story hits the news."

"Why would they speak up now, if they wouldn't earlier?"

Michael could tell that Ivan was just testing him now.

"Now they can do it anonymously through a call to the press. People will believe them, but their stock price won't be affected."

Ivan's eyes flashed approval.

Michael pictured the ramifications. "It will become a media frenzy. The talking heads will start speculating 24/7. The news channels will rush to parade experts. Drone experts. K&R experts. Self-defense experts. National defense experts. Experts on aliens. Religious scholars. Conspiracy buffs. Within a week, there won't be a person on the planet who isn't aware of drone abductions."

"Keep going."

Michael's head was reeling. Why hadn't he thought of this earlier? It was thinking like this that made Ivan *The Ghost*. He continued billowing forth his stream of consciousness. "Everyone in Silicon Valley will be watching the sky. Gun sales will skyrocket. CEOs will stay indoors. They'll begin checking their cash on hand, setting up $20 million lines of credit... So that's it? You're using the scare to double our average score?"

"No."

"It's awfully risky. Catching people will become much more difficult. And when we do catch them, they'll— Did you say *no*?"

"I did."

"You're not killing Sangster to up the ransom demands to $20 million?"

"I'm not."

"Why, then? Why attract so much attention? Why let our targets know we're coming. Why make the whole world aware?"

"So they'll be prepared."

"You want them prepared?"

"I do."

"For what?"

Ivan smiled. One of those long, thin, distant-stare smiles. "Phase two."

Before Michael could ask what the hell Ivan had planned for phase two, Pavel broke in over the speaker phone. "We're down to thirty seconds. Sangster is freaking out."

"What's he saying?" Michael asked.

"I can't hear him. You've muted his mic. But I can see him banging the headset and yelling into it. His eyes are locked on the clock, and he looks like he's about to stroke out. He might be dead before he hits the ground."

Ivan unmuted Sangster's mic.

"...for God's sake. I swear you'll have it tomorrow. Just set me down. We'd pay you now if we could. Don't you see? Be reasonable." He released The Claw to spread his arms wide, appealing to heaven. "For God's sake, don't drop me."

Pavel began counting down. "Ten, nine, eight ..."

Ivan muted Sangster's mic again. He was a strategist, not a sadist.

"...four, three, two, bomb's away."

50

Apparitions

French Riviera

Achilles searched Vazov's office top to bottom but found nothing of interest. In fact, he found almost nothing at all. Beyond the telltale oil paintings, the most interesting thing he uncovered was dust.

There was too much of it.

It wasn't that the carpets hadn't been vacuumed or the hard surfaces wiped. They had. But the combination of stillness and cleanliness left an artificial feeling in the air. The undisturbed feeling that could best be described as prolonged absence.

Achilles got the distinct feeling that people rarely visited this room. The complete absence of wear and tear told him they never had. He crouched and canted his head to study the floorboards from the right angle in the right light. He found no discernible traffic pattern. Conclusion: for all its splendor, Vazov had never inhabited this office.

While Achilles mulled on that little twist, he decided to explore the rest of the second floor. Peeking out into the hallway it seemed not a soul was around. Such a sharp contrast from the bustle below.

He started searching the offices along the south wall, assuming they belonged to Vazov's lieutenants. While each boasted the same splendid view and fine furnishings, none were nearly as large or grand as the one where he'd started. No oil paintings or Persian rugs. But the interesting difference was that they didn't feel abandoned. They showed signs of activity. Reading materials—none of it helpful—along with the tiny dents, scratches and smudges that inevitably accompany regular use.

Achilles moved quickly, acutely aware of having limited time. While Jo was slick enough to keep the interview going indefinitely, his absence would start to look suspicious. Chantal might also have another commitment, real or invented, leading to a polite eviction at any second.

He was standing behind one executive's desk when someone walked past the door. Achilles had left it the way he'd found it, cracked open. He crept silently toward the gap between door and frame and peeked out. The man was walking toward the stairs.

The moment the man descended from view, Achilles stepped into the hallway. He had a puzzle to solve.

The man had come from the end of a hallway Achilles had already cleared. The dogleg corridor from which he'd emerged contained three offices: one facing south, one facing west, and a corner enjoying both views. The inside of the dogleg housed only a bathroom, large and unisex. Although Achilles had searched all three offices, he had ignored the plumbing.

He glanced into all three offices again before turning his attention to the bathroom. The fittings were reminiscent of a five-star spa facility. All polished granite and stone tile. In addition to a urinal and two stalls, it included a shower, complete with its own changing room. Taking a shower explains why someone would be there for the time it took Achilles to search the three other rooms, but the floor wasn't wet and the wicker hamper was devoid of dirty towels. The air was neither spoiled nor humid.

Mystery unsolved. But time to move on.

Since Jo had not texted him a warning, Achilles decided to press his luck and explore the opposite end of the corridor, the rooms east of Vazov's office. It would be a bit trickier. To get there, he'd have to cross the top of the stairway, exposing himself to anyone looking up from the lobby.

The way the bathroom door opened, the first thing you saw was the floor-to-ceiling mirror that capped the hall. In it, Achilles spotted yet another person disappearing around the corner. That seemed virtually inexplicable. The office across the hall had been empty when Achilles entered the bathroom.

He crept to the end of the corridor, just to confirm that the man would follow his predecessor down the stairs. Once he did, Achilles backtracked. The dogleg gave access to only two rooms, the bathroom at the left end and the office at the right.

He glanced in the office for a third time. It appeared identical to his earlier visit. Unchanged and undisturbed. No way two men had been hanging out.

Achilles decided to play a hunch.

He returned to the corner office. Stepping behind the door, he placed it in the three-quarters closed position, making it possible to observe the short corridor through the crack without being seen. Then he waited.

He would have loved to text Jo to ask how it was going, but didn't want to disrupt her discussion. Her mission was to keep things rolling until he signaled that he either had what they'd come for or had reached some other conclusion. That other conclusion came about four minutes later, when a third man suddenly appeared.

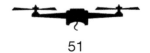

51

Plan O

French Riviera

The conference room to which Chantal led Jo was the third of three situated side by side: Coral, Turquoise and Azure. Each had floor-to-ceiling glass walls on all four sides, with opaque film cut into intricate floral patterns providing partial privacy. Each looked out across a blue sea and down on white sand far below. At their centers, hopelessly vying with the view for attention, were exquisite tables carved from solid limestone surrounded by luxurious natural-leather chairs. Smiling faces occupied two of those chairs.

"Allow me to introduce Tanya Stewart and Steve Derr. Tanya is a software engineer from Mountain View, and Steve is an electrical engineer from Sunnyvale."

After shaking hands and exchanging pleasantries, Jo took the two California converts and the PR manager through a list of questions designed to delight and disarm them. She buttered them up by asking about the perks, which were indeed incredible. Free housing was huge for anyone accustomed to paying California rents. The food was fantastic and also included. "It's like getting a twenty-percent pay raise and thirty percent more quality time, what with not having to shop or cook or commute." When Jo asked Tanya if she could quote her on that, Steve chipped in with his prepared line. "It's a little like joining a five-star army, except that nobody's shooting at you. We work hard then play hard and bond like brothers."

"Another great quote." Jo looked up from her list of questions. "Let's move on to the fruits of your labor. Can you give me any demos? Show me what you're working on? Put some meat on these bones I'm sketching?"

"That's one place we can't go," Chantal said. "I'm sure you're used to hearing about *stealth-mode* back in California. We have to keep everything confidential prior to product launch."

"Of course. But Silicon Hill has been operating for three years now. Surely you have some products out in the field?"

The Californians looked at each other, while again Chantal chimed in. "We do, of course. But nothing is marketed under our name, so nondisclosure agreements apply."

"You can't show me anything?"

"We can give you a tour of the recreational facilities. The housing, the restaurants, the athletic facilities, the beach. When's the last time you visited a corporate beach?"

Jo considered pressing it, but decided to save the tough reporter act for later. If she needed it. Her primary goal was giving Achilles time to operate. "This will be my first."

"Well, all right then. Isn't that the very definition of newsworthy?"

"I suppose it is."

"And of course, there's the corporate yacht." Chantal tossed this out like a forgotten garnish, parsley on a steak au poivre.

"Corporate yacht?"

"A 66-foot Marquis Sport Yacht. The *Bright Horizon*." Chantal moved her arms in a flourish as she spoke the name. "Why don't you call Kevin and we'll head down."

Jo looked at her feet. "Kevin's best left alone once he's in his groove. And I'm afraid I'm not wearing the best shoes for a hike."

"No hike involved. There's an elevator at the other end of the lobby. A glass elevator actually, running down the face of the cliff."

"An elevator to the beach," Jo said. "I think I've got my title." She wrote the phrase in caps atop her notepad, then pulled a cell phone from her bag. "I'll text Kevin in case he needs to find me."

She typed.

He typed right back. A single letter. "O." As in, Plan O. Obviously he was on to something. He was going to hide out overnight.

52

Laws of Physics

San Francisco, California

Rip kept a clean desk. Not just free from clutter, but devoid of the distracting doodads people tended to place there—the pen and pencil set, the business cards, the family photos. He wasn't one for family photos, and he used drawers for the rest. Even the phone. His workspace was for two things: doing and thinking.

When he was doing, he pulled out whatever he needed, be it his laptop or the relevant paperwork. When he was thinking, he fiddled with a Newton's Cradle.

Five steel spheres dangled in the cradle. Spheres number one and five swung in sequence, while remarkably numbers two, three and four remained still. Unmoved but transmitting. Action and distant reaction. Always equivalent. Click click, click click. Rip found it meditative. Relaxing. His job would be much easier if people were so predictable. Their actions rational, proportional and measured. Alas, logic did not rule the jungle.

Rip was factoring Ivan the Ghost into his calculations when he looked up from the cascading spheres to see Oscar in the doorway. The CIA's liaison wasn't wearing his usual smug expression. "Yes?"

"Josephine Monfort went off the grid. She flew from Paris to New York and vanished—the day after Rider died."

Of course she did, Rip thought. Anything else would have constituted a break, and breaks had been scarcer than grass 'round a hog trough. "You reckon she's with Achilles?"

"That's one scenario we're considering. It fits if Achilles was framed using a drone. Frankly, I find that a stretch. They only worked together for a few hours, and that was years ago."

"But during those hours, they were chasing Ivan the Ghost, right?"

"Unsuccessfully."

"What's the other scenario you're considering?"

"That Achilles and Ivan have teamed up. Monfort somehow got wind of it and is trying to stop them without sticking her neck out."

Rip used a forefinger to stop the swinging spheres and motioned for Oscar to take a seat. "You worked with Monfort?"

"Not really. I assigned her to Achilles, but we never met. I know that sounds strange, but it was a crunch. The operation moved unexpectedly from London to Monaco, and she was the only agent immediately available."

"So you don't know if she's worth her weight in walnuts?"

"I know she failed on her first and only CIA op. Along the way, she got herself shot. She's lucky to be alive."

"But you never met her?"

"No."

"You didn't visit her in the hospital?"

"She was in France. I was in D.C. She resigned shortly after her discharge."

"By which time Achilles was also out?"

"Correct."

"So chasing Ivan was his last mission as well?"

Clancy burst into the room before Oscar could answer. "Excuse me, but I thought you'd want to hear this right away. There's been a killing in Los Gatos. A kidnapping gone awry."

"Los Gatos is your jurisdiction," Oscar added, in case Rip didn't know.

"Somebody famous?" Rip asked.

Clancy nodded. "Gordon Sangster."

"The virtual reality guy?"

"That's right."

"Let me finish up here and I'll come find you."

"That's not it. The urgent part, I mean." Clancy drew a deep breath. "He was killed with a drone."

"They shot him with a drone?"

"Not shot. Dropped. A drone picked him up and the

kidnapper demanded $20 million in ransom. When his CFO only paid $18 million, everything they had on hand, they dropped him."

"Wait a minute. How big was the drone?"

"We're not sure. Nobody saw it."

That didn't make any sense to Rip. "Sit down and walk me through it."

Clancy did—the conference call with Sangster's CFO, the shortage of funds, the pleas, the transfer, the drop, the body.

"And nobody saw anything?"

"Sangster's home is up in the hills on a three-acre lot. Isolated and wooded. LGPD is interviewing neighbors as we speak, but so far they've got nothing."

"Any chance the CFO invented the drone story to conceal a theft? Either premeditated or opportunistic?"

"Opportunistic?" Oscar asked.

"The CFO might have seen Sangster fall from a tree and decided on the spot to leverage it into an $18 million payday," Rip replied.

"That's the working hypothesis until the coroner confirms cause of death. The lead detective says Sangster wasn't found beneath a tree. If he was dragged out in the open, or if he had been climbing for that matter, the coroner will find signs."

Rip looked across the desk at his subordinates. "On the one hand, the drone we saw in the video was much too small to pick up a person. So if Sangster was killed by a drone, it wasn't the same one. On the other hand, if Rider and Sangster were both killed by drone, they're the first two ever recorded in the civilian sector. And they've taken place within a few days and a few miles of each other. It's hard to believe that's a coincidence."

Both men nodded agreement. They didn't like coincidences either.

"So the cases are likely related. Rider and Sangster were probably killed by the same perp."

Clancy said, "Bear in mind that Sangster wasn't a straightforward assassination, according to the CFO. It was a K&R gone bad."

"Bad for Sangster. Not so bad for the perp. $18 million." Rip leaned back in his chair and clasped his hands behind his head.

"Let's think about that for a minute. Kidnapping by drone with an immediate ransom demand. Tactically, it's brilliant."

"Brilliant fits our Ivan the Ghost hypothesis," Clancy said. "But it puts our careers in the crapper. Nobody's ever been able to find Ivan the Ghost."

"You're right," Oscar said.

"It gets worse," Rip said.

"How could it?" Clancy asked.

Rip lifted three spheres and set the cradle in motion. "Whoever is masterminding this, he just made $18 million for an hour's work with a drone. No way he's going to stop with one victim."

53

Mirror, Mirror

French Riviera

When is a mirror not a mirror? When it's a door. Achilles had just confirmed his hypothesis with his own eyes.

Conclusions flowed freely from there. His first order of business was to share one with Jo. He would be spending the night.

Although the mirror had not appeared in his crystal ball while planning the incursion, Achilles had anticipated the overnight potential. In fact, he'd projected it as the second most-likely scenario and as such they had scheduled their visit near the end of the workday. His most-likely scenario had been getting nowhere, due to stonewalling or surveillance he couldn't circumvent.

He sent the O for overnight text.

Jo would now wrap up her meeting. She'd inform Chantal that her photographer had developed a migraine—not unusual, roll eyes—and had retreated to the car for a nap. Also not unusual. But no worries, he had the perfect photo for the story.

At the front door, if not before, she would say her goodbyes. She'd drive off fast enough to avoid onlooking eyes, leaving the guard booth at the bottom of the hill as the only hurdle.

Good security operations were run with surgical precision. They kept track of how many people went in, so they could match the number against how many came out. The best security systems matched the faces of people exiting to photos of people entering, so they'd know who remained inside. Easier to look for missing people when you had a picture.

To earn two check marks, Jo would stop halfway down the hill as if to talk on the phone. She'd then fold down the back seat and pull a mannequin from the trunk. A mannequin with a thin mustache; round, black, wire-rimmed spectacles; and a black golf cap—worn brim forward and pulled over closed eyes. While Achilles waited for Jo's "All clear," the mirrored wall continued coughing up men. It slid without any noise and did so very quickly. The third time it opened, Achilles caught a glimpse inside. To his surprise, the mirror didn't conceal a secret laboratory. At least not directly. It opened onto an elevator.

The minute he saw it, Achilles felt foolish for his lack of foresight. Of course the drone laboratory was underground. That offered all kinds of tactical advantages, and Ivan always sought those. Achilles had been thrown by having the entrance to the underground lair on the top floor. Again, knowing Ivan, this was something he should have anticipated.

His phone vibrated. A text from Jo. "Made it out."

"No issues?"

"My tongue is tired, but I'll survive. Tell me!!!"

"Found elevator to underground lab. RFID required to open."

Jo spent a few seconds digesting that one, then typed, "What's your plan?"

"I'll sleep on a couch and go down with the first guy who shows up in the morning."

Achilles did exactly that.

Every corporation that has a career ladder also has an employee who shows up first. The early bird. The overachiever. It wasn't so much a rule as a law of the corporate jungle.

Achilles waited for his early bird just inside the adjacent office's door. Out of sight, but unimpeded. He pounced the instant the mirror started to slide. He pushed the man into the elevator with his left hand, while his right rendered a reeling uppercut blow.

There's a science to knocking someone out. It's kind of like playing pool because you're aiming to initiate a specific sequence of physical reactions, reactions that literally rattle the recipient's brain. You have to hit him hard enough to send his big ball of gray matter bouncing off two walls. When done with enough speed and force, this causes electrical signals to overlap and overload, shutting the brain down. It does this for its own protection, like a circuit breaker in a lightning storm.

Achilles got his haymaker in before the early bird knew what hit him, but they both ended up splattered with hot coffee. He drank what remained in the cup on the way down. His hadn't been a particularly restful night.

He pulled the ID card from the pocket of his unconscious victim and read it aloud while they descended. "Mickey Leonov. Sorry about that, Mickey. Nothing personal."

The best thing about his early-bird approach was that Achilles didn't have to worry who would be there when the door opened at the bottom. Of course, that was about all he knew.

The unknown he was most interested in was how long he had before the next employee arrived. Since he had no way to know and Mickey couldn't tell him, Achilles had to assume *not much*.

Not much turned out to be sufficient.

The elevator door opened and there it was. The big black drone. Clamped in the grasp of a robotic arm that presumably allowed the engineers to position it at any angle.

He dragged Mickey off to a nearby corner and left him sitting there with his back to the wall and the empty coffee cup in his hands. He'd appear to be napping when the next employee came along, if they noticed him at all. The ruse might add time to his getaway clock.

Within two minutes of the knockout punch, Achilles had everything he required. Absolute, 100 percent indisputable confirmation. Silicon Hill was the source of the drones.

He made a quick video of the drone, its control module and the surrounding lab. Then he snapped off a dozen different pictures.

The elevator had not waited while he worked. No doubt it automatically returned to the second floor, thereby minimizing the odds of someone walking into the mirror. He pressed the button—and the elevator came back empty. Had it not, Achilles would have tried slipping aboard after it emptied without attracting attention. Instead, he blocked the elevator door with a three-ring binder and dragged Mickey back aboard. He'd leave him on the floor with his ID in his pocket and his coffee cup in his lap.

Mickey would have no recollection of how he ended up in

the elevator. That was the reason for the lightning attack: it afforded the brain no opportunity to make a mental recording. When he awoke, Mickey would be confused and embarrassed. He'd assume his headache was the result of falling and whacking his head. Maybe he'd see a doctor, maybe he'd try to forget it. It didn't matter either way to Achilles, since he'd be long gone.

While riding back to the second floor, Achilles selected the drone photos on his phone, typed in Jo's number, and hit SEND.

54

Deflation

San Francisco, California

Rip was glued to the television monitor when Oscar bounded into his office. The CIA agent started to speak, but stopped when he saw that Rip was already watching the news.

Rip motioned to a seat and turned up the volume on the pretty blonde reporter. "Since the murder of Gordon Sangster, three other CEOs have come forward under the condition of anonymity. All reported that they too were abducted by drones and held for ransom. In their cases, however, each was gently returned to earth after the ransom was paid. Why was Sangster treated differently? Why was—"

"It's just as you predicted," Oscar said.

Rip hit the mute. "Lot of good it did us. We're still way behind the ball."

"What do we do now?"

Oscar had asked the right question for a change. Rip stood. "Grab your coat. We're going to Channel 4." He would have preferred to use Clancy or Reynolds as the second badge, but Oscar would suffice for intimidation purposes. He didn't have to speak. Just glower. He was good at that.

"I'll call to confirm that the station manager is there," Oscar said.

Rip turned to face the CIA guy. "You don't get out from behind a desk much, do you?"

Oscar reddened. "Pardon me?"

"We never call ahead. Forewarned is forearmed."

"But—"

"No buts. Just shock and awe."

Rip was half tempted to run the two miles to Channel 4's

Front Street office. He'd like to watch Pincus turn even redder. Plus Rip needed the exercise. He hadn't yet developed a running routine in San Francisco. But it wouldn't do to arrive flushed and sweaty. That would turn shock and awe into bemused curiosity. So he had Oscar drive.

They rode a few blocks in silence, but as he turned onto Broadway, Oscar asked, "Why would Ivan kill a man who paid $18 million when he let the others live after paying only ten?"

Rip had asked himself the same question. "It's a message. A lesson."

"*Do as I say, or die.* I get that. But the CFO said they couldn't pay. Not on the spot. Not $20 million. You don't kick a dog because it can't sing. There's no lesson in that. Just cruelty."

Rip was beginning to think the CIA was better off without Rider, at least if Oscar's lateral thinking skills were representative of the former Director's inner circle. "The message wasn't for Sangster. The message was for his next victims."

"You think he wants them to know he's not bluffing?"

"I think he wants them prepared. You can bet that as we speak, every CEO in Silicon Valley is tasking his CFO with arranging an instant line of credit."

Oscar gave a jaywalker a honk and finger wag before responding. "That's good for us, right? No more murders, but plenty of opportunities to catch Ivan red-handed."

"That's your conclusion?"

Oscar paused again. Once bitten, twice shy. "Yes."

"Because it's logical? Straightforward even?"

"Exactly."

"Well, then we can be certain that's the one thing that won't happen—if we really are dealing with Ivan the Ghost."

Oscar closed his eyes and bowed his head. A suitable response, but tactically ill-advised while driving, even at San Francisco city center speeds. He rebounded two chilling seconds later. "So what will happen?"

Inevitable as it was, the question still deflated Rip's puff. Not what he needed going into a shock and awe performance. "I have no idea."

55

Divide and Conquer

French Riviera

After leaving Mickey on the elevator and sneaking out of Silicon Hill, Achilles found Jo in the hotel dining room. She was enjoying a croissant and coffee over the morning paper. He signaled the waitress to bring more of the same and joined her.

Jo looked up from the paper, mixed messages on her face.

"What is it?"

"Ivan struck in California."

"Struck how?"

"With a drone. He's been ransoming CEOs. Holds them in the air until they pay up, and drops them if his demands aren't met. The story broke overnight. He killed Gordon Sangster, the virtual reality exercise guy. Ivan demanded more cash than Sangster had in the bank."

"That doesn't sound like Ivan. Does it say it's him?"

"No, no. The police don't have a clue. But it has to be Ivan. Here, read this."

Achilles devoured the full front-page story while Jo watched the video of the secret laboratory on his phone. He set down the paper as his breakfast arrived. "You're right, it has to be Ivan. But Ivan doesn't make tactical mistakes, and demanding more than a man can pay appears to be one."

"What are you saying?"

Achilles ripped into his croissant. "Ivan's plan must go beyond simple K&R."

"There's nothing simple about kidnapping someone with a drone. It's a brilliant, bulletproof plan. Obvious once you think of it—but only Ivan did."

"And now we know why he went after you."

"He needed a guinea pig. I have never felt so small."

"You'll be a giant again before this is over."

Jo raised her coffee. "Here's hoping. Did you have any trouble getting out this morning?"

"None at all. Silicon Hill's ground security is movie-theater style. Unidirectional. And the wall, well, you know."

"They still haven't made one that can stop you. So what now? Do we call Zonder and have the FBI storm the compound?"

"No. We keep our find quiet."

"What! With everything that's going on in California, you'll be a hero. They'll have to believe you regarding Rider and the drone."

"The CIA doesn't have to believe anything but its own conclusions, and it takes its own sweet time making those. Plus my goal isn't to become a hero. My goal is to catch Ivan. Once the FBI shows up at Silicon Hill, Ivan vanishes."

"So we do nothing?"

"We *say* nothing."

"But we go to California, to catch Ivan?"

"No, we stay here. For now."

Jo set her cup down and grabbed Achilles' hands across the table. "Talk to me, Achilles."

Her intimate move surprised him, for a second time. He ignored it. It was probably subconscious. "Why did you call Ivan's drone kidnapping plan *bulletproof?*"

"Because there's neither recourse nor wriggle room. Not for the victim, not for law enforcement. Once he's got his guy in the sky, there's nothing anyone can do. You can't delay or fail to pay. You can't shoot it down or pressure the pilot, not when he's —" Jo trailed off. When she spoke again her voice was softer. "Ivan could be anywhere."

Achilles nodded. "The drone pilots fighting the Taliban aren't in Afghanistan. They're in Florida or Nevada or Colorado. Half a world away and safe as a king in his castle. I think it's safe to say Ivan is no less savvy. It's also safe to say the FBI has California covered. I don't know what we could do there that they aren't already doing."

"You have another angle?"

"There's one I'd like to try. It assumes you're right about

Vazov being Ivan."

"You've warmed to that idea?"

"I'm still skeptical. But I don't have a better tactic for tracking Ivan down."

Jo withdrew her hands and assumed a thinking pose. "Tell me."

"When I hunted people for the CIA, I occasionally did it through their purchasing habits. Artwork. Automobiles. Wine. Watches. People with power tend to get obsessed with their image. They want to be *that guy*, and they want everyone to know it. And it's not always expensive stuff. Sometimes it's silly things. Russia's Prime Minister got nailed in a colossal corruption scandal due to his obsession with tennis shoes and untucked shirts."

Jo's expression said she didn't quite follow. "Did you find a peculiar purchase in Vazov's closet?"

"Not exactly. And not his closet. His office. It's very nice and very new. Too new. Virtually unused."

"Maybe he had it remodeled while he was in California."

"No. It didn't have that brand new smell. Quite the opposite. It felt abandoned. Same goes for his residence. Half the second floor is Vazov's personal suite. I broke in overnight. It's beautifully staged but has never been used."

"I still don't follow."

"Hang with me for a second. Do you recall the huge portrait in his lobby?"

"Vazov on horseback doing a Napoleon impression."

Achilles nodded. "There were similar paintings in his office. Not of Vazov, but of polo players."

"You think polo is his hobby?"

"More like an obsession. Silicon Hill is a unique entrepreneurial endeavor and an impressive accomplishment. But the vanity shot isn't one capturing an inventive moment or even the great man surveying his empire. It's him swinging a mallet."

"Maybe we're just missing the symbolism."

"Remind me to call Robert Langdon."

Jo flashed a lopsided grin. "Seriously, that's pretty thin."

"I'd agree with you, if it weren't for an unguarded comment.

I asked a passerby when Vazov usually gets in. He said, 'He usually doesn't. But then I'd be playing polo too, if I had the option.' "

"So you want to start snooping around local polo clubs?"

"How many can there be?"

56

Goal Posts

Los Angeles, California

Given the size of the media swarm that engulfed Silicon Valley, you'd have thought it was hosting the Olympics. News trucks outnumbered taxi cabs and hotel rooms became hard to find. Dozens of Bay Area police forces were burning through overtime budgets responding to drone-related reports, and most local mayors had enacted bans prohibiting the operation of drones.

All were going to be disappointed.

Team Raven had left town.

Michael was thrilled to leave the circus behind, but he was nervous about setting up the tent in L.A. For their purposes, Silicon Valley was an exemplary location, offering a high concentration of extreme wealth paired with perfect geography. The endless expanse of rolling hills and wild lands surrounding the valley floor provided an abundance of isolated environments ideal for eight-figure estates and unobserved abductions.

Los Angeles, by contrast, was a concrete jungle. Ten million homes packed into a coastal basin and connected by a clogged highway system. While there were plenty of ultra-wealthy neighborhoods in the greater metropolitan area—Manhattan Beach, Beverly Hills, Hidden Hills, Rolling Hills, Bel Air—there was limited isolation. Especially for activities taking place at an elevation of eighty-five feet.

The fact that falls from altitudes of eighty-five feet and above were one hundred percent fatal was one of many that had made the news. As Ivan had predicted, the talking heads jabbered on about little else. The surviving CEOs had all come forward under the condition of anonymity to share their experiences in scintillating detail. The strange sound preceding the strike, like locusts or a rattlesnake. The cold constriction around their waists, a steel shackle that would not yield. The incomparable terror of being torn from the earth and tethered to a UFO. The accounts went on and on in dramatic fashion, feeding voracious appetites for vicarious experiences of the most famous abductions since the Lindberghs lost their baby.

Ivan maintained a mischievous look in his eye throughout. That "all according to plan, my plan" look. Michael knew it to be a sure sign that the great man was happy. It occurred to Michael that Ivan was only happy at times like these, when the dominoes he'd so ingeniously arranged were toppling according to plan—racing toward an inevitable and yet unforeseeable conclusion.

Michael couldn't believe that Ivan would really give it all up. The Ghost was fooling himself, pretending that it was all about the money. His bank balance was just a scorecard. It was icing on the cake. The real gratification, the true impetus for his action, was proving that he could outwit the rest of the world combined.

Ivan had an unparalleled ability to invent and implement schemes that showered money. Schemes so cunning and complex that nobody could second-guess his next move. That unique ability to outwit was his bliss. His passion. His calling. It gave him a sense of satisfaction no bank balance could replicate.

"You're looking at me funny," Ivan said, setting down his silverware.

They were in a booth at the Tune-In Diner, one of those restaurants with televisions on the wall and speakers at each table. *Take your table, choose your channel and tune in.* Perfect for couples tired of talking, or those with children they needed to keep occupied. Ivan liked it because all the background noise kept conversations private, and half the on-screen action these days revolved around Raven.

Michael set his fork beside his plate. "Are you really going to do it? Walk away, I mean. Leave The Ghost behind and become ordinary."

"There's nothing ordinary about being a billionaire."

Michael shrugged. "It's passive. *Being* isn't *doing*."

Ivan resumed the attack on his steak. "This game I play is no different from other contact sports. It's physically dangerous, mentally demanding and ultimately exhausting. It favors the young. If I keep going, I'll fade. Bit by bit. Imperceptibly perhaps. But eventually, I'll get sacked, or benched, or knocked-out—choose your metaphor. Best to retire while wearing the heavyweight belt, the Super Bowl ring."

"You've been wearing those for years."

Ivan speared another rare chunk of red meat. "I intend to take my title to the grave—many years from now."

"So you're not going to retire?"

"Oh, I'm going to retire all right."

"I don't follow."

Ivan waved his knife. "We're about to take bold to a whole new level. Before we're done with Raven, we'll have moved the goal posts so far down field that our record will never be beaten."

57

Three-Day Plan

French Riviera

They found the club. It wasn't hard. There were only a few polo clubs in the south of France, and the Russians all belonged to the same one. The newest one. The Monte Carlo Polo Club. Once they knew where to focus their efforts, Achilles and Jo dug deeper and discovered that the MCPC was owned by none other than Vlad Vazov. Little V himself.

Shortly after that discovery, Achilles enjoyed another breakthrough. He got one of those ideas where your mind lights up like Christmas and a grin connects your ears. He was brainstorming ways to confirm that Vazov was Ivan without being recognized. The idea appeared as insights usually do, with a warm flash of excitement. He could spy on Vazov using a drone.

Achilles found poetry in turning The Ghost's own weapon against him. He also found merit in learning to fly one of the machines. Know thine enemy, be prepared, and all that. The icing on the cake was that he didn't need to be particularly concerned with camouflage. What more natural place to fly a camera drone than over a sporting match?

His bright idea literally took a nosedive hours later. No sooner had he breached the aerial border at the Monte Carlo Polo Club than his shiny new toy dropped like a swatted fly. It didn't act like it was supposed to when there was a simple signal disruption. It didn't hover or return to base. It simply plummeted.

"Did you hit the wrong button?" Jo asked, glancing over from her 25x70 SkyMaster binoculars.

They were "picnicking" atop the hill nearest the MCPC,

which was a half-mile away. While too distant for definitive facial recognition even with a telescope, the hill was close enough to watch the game through high-powered binoculars. It even gave them a partial view of a house hidden from the road at the far end of the field. A sprawling compound built in the same Mediterranean style as the clubhouse, but with security enhancements sufficient for storing nuclear weapons. Vazov's real house, no doubt.

Achilles pointed to the display on the drone control unit, where "Connection Lost" was flashing in red. "Talk about an understatement."

"What happened?"

"Vazov obviously has defensive measures in place."

"A jammer?"

"Something more serious. I'm thinking either an EMP cannon fried its circuits or a counter-drone weapon switched off its power."

"You sure it wasn't just a fluke?"

Achilles wasn't completely certain, so they sent in a second drone. A different model from a different manufacturer. It met with a similar end. "They must scrape drones off the field like bugs off a windshield."

"So what's next?" Jo asked. "How do we give you a good look at Vazov without giving him a good look at you?"

Achilles whipped out the idea he'd been working when the drone tactic came to him. "It's become clear to me that the club is our best and perhaps only way to approach Vazov in an unsuspicious manner. The polo field is the one place where he isn't cordoned off by bodyguards. It's also a place where attention isn't on faces—it's on horses and mallets and, of course, the ball."

"So?"

"So I need to get myself onto the polo field while Vazov is playing."

"You mean as a referee or something?"

"I'm thinking as a player on an opposing team."

"You ever played polo before?"

"No. I've never even held a mallet. But I rode a lot as a kid. Horses are big in Colorado. I figure I can become reasonably competent in a couple of days with intense private lessons."

"Private lessons?"

"I'll pay the club pro whatever he asks. That will give me an ally and get me out on the field. It will also provide plenty of time in the club. Who knows, maybe I'll receive a social invitation to something Vazov is also attending. Or maybe I'll find the means to swipe his phone or steal his wallet. Once I'm inside, opportunities will present themselves."

"What if Vazov gets a good look at you—while you're seeking opportunity? If he is Ivan and he recognizes you, it's all over. You'll be surrounded by his men."

"I won't give him the opportunity."

They both knew that was easier said than done, but Jo let it slide. "You really think you can get onto an opposing team? Sounds like the very definition of something that's easier said than done."

"It probably is. I'll know by the end of the first day."

"How so?"

"Either the club pro will call me a natural, or he won't. If he doesn't, then we'll try to find some other situation that brings me face to face with Vazov without making him suspicious."

"And if the pro does call you a natural?"

"Then I work my butt off to impress him enough that he recommends me as a substitute if somebody doesn't show up for a match against Vazov's team."

"What are the odds of a player not showing up?"

"Under normal circumstances, not very good, given that there are only four people on a team. But that's where you come into play."

"Me? How so?"

"When the time comes, you're going to ensure that the right guy fails to show—without warning."

"Really? And how do I do that?"

"I have no idea. But I'm completely confident you'll figure it out."

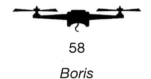

58

Boris

Los Angeles, California

Boris often heard that he had an unusual mind, although he wasn't sure what constituted *usual*. Everyone seemed unique to him. Of course, they were referencing his aptitude for engineering—which was entirely natural if not usual.

Since his single-digit years, Boris had devoured and absorbed engineering texts like so many lollypops. Laws, rules, theorems and hypotheses, all of it stuck. Now, if he studied an object in operation, be it a predatory bird or a nuclear submarine, he could deconstruct the design in his mind. Kind of like X-ray vision.

And that was only half his talent.

The lesser half.

His mind also worked the other way. If he knew what he needed, he could create a design. Plausible, if not practical.

While this struck most people as a remarkable ability, for Boris it was just there. An intuitive application of basic mechanical principles—and some advanced ones. The challenge he faced was finding projects that cranked his intellectual motor.

Most employers were looking for incremental improvements. Sleeker models. Iterations. Designs that would increase their share of proven markets. That wasn't Boris's thing. He wanted to break barren ground. Open new markets. Be an engineering entrepreneur. But the money just wasn't there. Not in Russia anyway. Not until Ivan came along.

Ivan brought him the idea of Raven and the money to make it happen. Boris took it from there.

It had been a great ride, but this one was nearing its end. Ivan had brought him along for maintenance and troubleshooting as a one-man pit crew. There wasn't much of that required, so his role had morphed into mundane things like driving.

Until today.

Today's assignment began with boosting the truck they would use during their "Los Angeles premiere." A generic white model the size of a UPS truck, with a roll-up door and a pullout ramp. Having him steal a car, even when it required disabling the GPS, was like having Rembrandt paint your house.

But Boris didn't mind.

He was happy to be busy with his hands.

And the next steps would be far more exciting.

Once he had the truck, his next move was removing the roof. A clean cut that wouldn't be noticed from the ground. One that would allow Raven to fly in and out without getting snagged.

Then the real fun started.

For Raven to fly in and out of a truck, Boris had to make two of the rotors retractable during flight. Otherwise it wouldn't fit.

There was no weight problem, as Raven carried no cargo during those parts of the mission, but it still presented a tasty engineering challenge.

Normally Raven folded away for transport like a transformer from the movies. The rotor blades rotated to stack and the rotor housings folded in half. The rotor arms telescoped and The Claw winch flipped aside. But that all happened with the drone on the ground. Boris had just made it possible to retract two rotors with Raven in the air. It was a temporary fix, and not particularly pretty, but Ivan said it only had to work for one mission.

With Raven ready, all that remained was camouflaging the truck. Boris painted *Elite Exterminators* in blue on both sides, and slapped *Toxic Hazard* warnings all around. The resulting drone transportation vehicle was exactly what law enforcement was looking for, except that they were looking 400 miles north in Silicon Valley.

When the truck was ready, Ivan revealed another pleasant surprise. He put Boris back to work on the drone. "I want you to remove the components required for folding. Everything but your new additions. Should knock off about ten pounds."

"It's really not necessary," Boris replied, reaching for his socket wrench. "It won't impact performance in the least. Not that I'm complaining. I'm happy to do it."

"Do you really think I don't know what I'm doing?" Ivan asked, surprising Boris with a tone that was anything but inquisitive.

"No, it's just—"

"Then don't tell me there's no need."

The abandoned warehouse where they were working went quiet.

"We're all just a bit mystified," Michael said, wading into the cooling water. "You indicated that tomorrow's mission is going to be special, and you've had us prepare a new truck, but otherwise you've been tight-lipped about it."

Ivan said nothing.

Reading Boris's mind, Michael motioned toward the discarded roof and socket wrench. "You're also adopting tactics that you once dismissed for being shortsighted and ordinary. Then there's the Sangster drop."

"What about the Sangster drop?"

"It cost us our invisibility. We're exposed now, and as a result, a bit nervous."

"So, what are you: nervous or mystified?"

Michael blanched, but stood his ground. "The two are related. We just want to know what's going on."

"What's going on is business as usual. I devise a plan. You execute it. Everybody wins."

"The plan appears to be changing. Usually, you have everything scripted—our moves, their moves, from bitter beginning to elusive end—with uncanny foresight and precision. Suddenly, however, we're altering a fundamental part of the operation. Plus, we're way behind with Vazov's payments."

Ivan looked down and shook his head.

Boris couldn't tell if the move signaled contrition or exasperation.

You could have heard a spider sneeze while everyone waited for an outburst. But when Ivan spoke, his tone was measured. "Guys, I'm conducting a symphony here. You're focused on the beat, but there's a lot more to this tune than percussion. I haven't deviated one note from my original plan. The music isn't changing. It's just becoming more complex as the rest of the orchestra chimes in. Get used to it."

"It might help if we knew the whole score," Michael pressed.

"To the contrary, it would distract you. For this to work, you need to be focused on flawless execution. Keep the faith, and be ready to roll with the new van and revised Raven in the morning." Ivan turned to leave but then paused mid-stride. With a softer tone, he added, "We're going to Venice Beach."

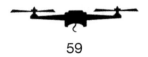

59

Lessons

French Riviera

Jo looked up as her date arrived, and smiled. It was a genuine smile, with sparkling eyes and flashing teeth.

Crafting cons was the part of her old life that she missed most, and she was glad to be back at it. Cons gave her the intellectual satisfaction enjoyed by generals and corporate captains, coupled with the thrill of being part of the action on the ground.

It didn't hurt that this particular ground was in the Casino de Monte-Carlo. As the center of the nightlife scene in the small principality of Monaco, the casino's architecture befitted the most exclusive real estate on earth. It looked to Jo like a gilded version of Notre Dame Cathedral, except that the stained glass windows were on the ceilings rather than the walls, and the floors were covered with colorful carpets.

Her date was Fernando Aguilar. Fernando was a thirtyish Argentinian with dark, soulful eyes and windswept hair. At five-foot-six, he was the shortest man Jo had ever dated, but he carried himself like he was six-foot-six, and the boots didn't hurt.

Fernando stood as the maitre d' escorted her to his table on the terrace. "I'm so glad you came."

"I thank you for the invitation. If your goal was to impress, you've already succeeded."

Once she was seated, their waiter pulled a bottle of rosé from a waiting ice bucket. He poured two glasses with the aid of a white napkin before vanishing.

Jo had spent her afternoon at the Monte Carlo Polo Club watching Fernando's Team Eagle play Vazov's Team Excelsior.

She had smiled and cheered through six chukkas, meeting Fernando's eye at every opportunity, and then encouraging and accepting a date once the game concluded. She had tried to study Vazov as well, but he never approached the visitor bleachers.

Once they'd clinked glasses and tasted their wine, Fernando said, "So are you going to tell me?"

"Why I was watching the game?"

"I'd love to know."

"Surely you have a guess by now?"

"I've tossed around a few ideas."

"Your first guess?"

"You're a talent scout looking to poach players for a new club."

She ran her finger around the side of her glass, playfully clearing a path of condensation. "Not even close. Guess again."

"You're a private investigator, looking for stolen horses."

"Stephanie Blanc, P.I. has a nice ring to it, but no. I'll give you one more shot on goal. You get it right, I give you dessert after dinner. You get it wrong, you buy me one of those flourless chocolate soufflés I saw on the way in."

Fernando inhaled long and hard. "I'm known for performing under pressure, but I don't know. Not a recruiter or an investigator—that only leaves about a hundred options. I'm going to have to play the odds and say tourist. You're a tourist who had an extra afternoon and thought it would be fun."

Jo wet her lips. "I can already taste the chocolate."

"D'oh! That's two losses today. But you've got to tell me now. What brought you to my game?"

The waiter appeared before Jo could answer. She ordered the John Dory Supreme, while Fernando went for a medium-rare sirloin with Béarnaise sauce.

"I'm not going to let you eat your fish until you tell me."

"I was doing research."

"Research? What kind of research?"

"I'm a novelist. I write romance novels."

Fernando threw up his hands. "That's not fair! No way I was going to guess that. But then I suppose that's why you made the offer. You knew your virtue would be safe."

Jo had indeed, but she had a few reasons prepared just in case. "It was plenty fair. Think about it." She leaned in and lowered her voice. "Romance novels always involve a dark, handsome foreigner."

Fernando swallowed dry. "Lots of horses too, I suppose."

They both laughed. He had a nice laugh, warm and soothing. More like a purr than a cackle.

The rest of the conversation went so well that Jo nearly forgot she was on a job. She'd been expecting an arrogant playboy, given that he was a handsome polo player and this was Monaco, but he was charming. Anything but self-absorbed. She wished she'd found another way to do what needed to be done. She wished she'd picked another victim. But Ivan had to go, and there was no turning back now.

Jo palmed her dessert spoon while their entree dishes were being cleared and excused herself to the ladies' room. She locked herself in a stall and pulled a baggie from her clutch.

Her goal was to put Fernando out of play, quite literally. To keep him from showing up for his next game, she'd considered tranquilizers, but decided that would arouse suspicion. She'd considered arranging an accident to break his foot, but that seemed extreme. She'd considered giving him the time of his life, but the game wasn't until after lunch and every appetite had its limits. In the end, Jo decided to go with food poisoning.

Food poisoning wouldn't cast suspicion or leave a scar, but it would make the idea of hopping on a horse unbearably nauseating. Which kind of food poisoning? She wanted to use Staphylococcus due to its rapid onset and short duration, but couldn't come up with a way to procure it. She eventually settled for the less elegant choice of Salmonella.

She bought a family-size pack of chicken drumsticks from a bargain grocery store and went to work. The final result was a powder derived from dehydrated slime, a powder packed full of the pesky bacteria.

While the toilet one stall over flushed, she gave the back of her dessert spoon a good lick then plunged it into the baggie. It came out with a coating of crystals on the underside. *Bon appétit*.

Dessert was waiting when she returned to the table. A chocolate soufflé fit to photograph. "You waited. I don't know if I'd have been so strong."

"It's all yours."

"No way. I'm not dining alone." Jo pulled an invisible switcheroo with the silverware on the table while pouring the tiny pitcher of crème fraîche onto the molten chocolate. With a broad smile and a mischievous wink, she plunged her special spoon into his side of the soufflé. "Now open wide."

Fernando shook his head while smiling with surrender, but instead of leaning forward with open mouth he put his hand around hers and cleaned the spoon without breaking eye contact. The sweet sensation of *mission accomplished* soured a second later when he dipped the spoon back into the soufflé and brought it to her lips. "Your turn."

Staring at the sickly spoon, Jo kicked herself for failing to foresee this possibility. When she was little and learning the family business, her father had forced her to live with the consequences of her mistakes rather than coming to her aid. Once, she ended up spending the night beneath a bed in a brothel. Another time, she spent the weekend locked in a cigar shop without food or water. She had cursed her father for hours on end, but she'd also learned to master the situational analysis required of a master criminal.

Apparently her skills had rusted and her senses had dulled during her years of making a legitimate living. She was certain she'd never forget this lesson. She could practically see the Salmonella swimming around the spoon. Talk about the very definition of taking one for the team. She opened wide.

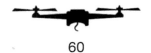

60

Muscle Beach

Los Angeles, California

Venice Beach is one of many legendary locations in Los Angeles. Famous for a pedestrian promenade stocked with artists, psychics and street performers, it is also the epicenter of modern bodybuilding. Every day, rain or shine, fitness fanatics and action flick fans flock to watch bronzed brutes pump iron in an open air pen on the sand.

Tonight, however, anyone attempting to reach the pen would encounter police barricades. Whereas tourists might conclude that it was a crime scene, the locals would correctly identify a movie shoot. In this case, that movie was *Big Ambition*, an action film starring A-list muscle man, Preston Jenks.

Boris drove the white exterminator truck while the others rode in the Tesla. He was wearing coveralls, complete with booties, gloves and a hooded mask. The idea was to hide his features while leaving no DNA behind. And the getup appeared perfectly normal for someone spraying insecticide.

He'd managed to make the modifications in time, but they were crude and temporary. They clashed with his sense of propriety. He'd itch until he had the opportunity to redesign the whole frame with appropriate elegance. But that would have to wait until they were back in France. Meanwhile, Raven would perform as required.

The ability to fly Raven in and out of the truck was a big relief. Especially since the Sangster incident had turned up the heat. No doubt Pavel could even pull it off while the truck was driving. He was every bit as intuitive with aeronautics as Boris was with engineering.

What wasn't intuitive was why Ivan had waited to adopt this

tactic. Boris had suggested it way back at the beginning. Something told him he'd be slapping his forehead before it was over, marveling at Ivan's insight. The man had mastered operational tactics like no other.

Boris turned the truck off Electric Avenue onto Westminster. Almost there and so far, so good. He'd garnered a few funny glances due to the protective garb, but nobody had honked. A few turns later, the driving app told him his destination was a hundred yards ahead. When he closed to forty, he saw the signs.

The same "friends" who scouted the scene had reserved parking spots using folding signs stolen from the Sheriff's Department. For the truck, this was the driveway of an empty house two blocks north of the movie shoot. For the Tesla, they'd reserved a spot two blocks south of the shoot in a beachfront public parking lot with line of sight on the action.

After parking and locking the truck, Boris stepped across the street into a grove of bushes and stripped off the coveralls. He stuffed them into a backpack and ran south four blocks to rejoin the team. "We're good to go," he said, a bit out of breath. "It was an excellent choice of location. Minimal foot traffic in the immediate vicinity and no reason for anyone to give the truck a second glance."

Ivan nodded.

"Are you going to tell us why we're here now?" Michael asked.

"We're here because this place has exactly what we need."

"And what's that?" Michael said, playing along.

"Rolling cameras, a clear flight path and an accessible movie star."

"Accessible movie star! You can't be serious?"

Ivan remained silent, but raised his eyebrows.

Boris felt his stomach drop as Michael replied. "You are serious. We're actually going to kidnap Preston Jenks?"

"We are, and we're going to do it on camera with the whole world watching."

"But why?"

Ivan flipped open his laptop. "All part of the plan."

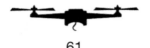

61

Game Over

French Riviera

They came for him ten minutes before the 2:00 match. Three players from Team Eagle. Number 3 spoke while 2 and 4 held back atop their chestnut mounts. "Feel like a real match? We're down a man today."

Achilles tried not to appear too eager. "I saw you talking to Nic. Did he say I'm ready?" Nic was the club pro, a champion from the 1980s. He was also Achilles' trainer, or rather Sergey's, as that was the name Achilles was using.

"He said you're green as a spring leaf, but a natural athlete. He said you've got a lion's heart and a cat's reflexes."

Lions were cats, although Achilles wasn't going to quibble with the compliment—bought though it might have been at the price of 500 euros an hour, mount and tack included. He had run up an astronomical tab over the past three days, but the opportunity to join Team Eagle for a game against Vazov's Team Excelsior was worth it—especially given that the funds came from an operational account long-forgotten by the CIA. Jo was the one with the lion's heart, the one actually paying a price. He shuddered to think what she had done.

Achilles met the player's eye. "I'll do my best to prove Nic right."

"I'm Andrey," the team captain said, tossing Achilles Team Eagle's number 1 jersey. He gestured to the two other players. "And this is Pablo and Paulo."

"Just focus on defending against their 4. Andrey and I will handle offense," number 2 said.

The numbers in polo designate position rather than rank, with 1 being the foremost and 4 the rearmost on the field.

Number 3 was typically the team captain, the tactical leader, while 2 tended to go to the best player, as its back and forth nature made it the most difficult to play. That left positions 1 and 4 as the most suitable for novice players, and Achilles' size inclined him toward 1. He was a big guy requiring a big pony, meaning more speed and less agility. Better for offense than defense. That suited Achilles just fine, as it would maximize his mingling with the opposing players.

Achilles popped three pain pills while following his teammates to the starting line. He'd found that learning effective mallet work came easily, given his strength and hand-eye coordination. Riding hadn't been problematic either. Muscle memory returned as readily as it did when riding a bike. The rub came from clinging to a horse for eight hours a day. Saddle sores were no laughing matter.

Achilles and the other three Eagles rode straight for the starting line. He studied the opposing team the whole way. The closer he got, the clearer it became that identifying Ivan during play would not be so easy. Vazov's features were partially hidden beneath a helmet and behind protective goggles. There wouldn't be much conversation on the field either, so identifying Ivan vocally would also have to wait until a break or the traditional after-game drink.

The umpire rolled the ball without fanfare once everyone was at the line, and the game was on. For the first chukka, Achilles found himself fully focused on just surviving, both literally and figuratively. Polo was a fast-moving, hard-charging, dangerous sport. He hadn't come this far to take a mallet to the head or get kicked from the team.

Seven-and-a-half minutes of play later when they headed for the sidelines, Achilles was no closer to identifying Ivan than he had been days earlier. The break between chukkas didn't change things, as Excelsior returned to their sideline across the field. Between swapping ponies and swallowing water, the three-minute break was hardly restful. The other Eagles remained quiet as each gathered his thoughts, but Achilles did get a back slap from number 2 as they returned to the field.

And so it went until the last twenty seconds of the third chukka, when Achilles gave his team a 5-4 advantage and ended the first half. Tactically it was a blunder, because it brought attention to him, but his competitive nature had kicked in and he'd gotten lucky.

Rather than heading in the usual direction when the bugle sounded, his fellow Eagles turned their ponies toward Excelsior's side and rode for the owner's tent. Achilles felt a drop of adrenaline kick in. This was the opportunity he needed. If he positively identified his nemesis, he planned to put the tapered end of his mallet through Ivan's eye socket right then and there. With a proper swing, he could bury it a good four inches. On the other hand, if he looked Vazov in the eye and determined that he wasn't Ivan, Achilles would attempt to ingratiate himself. Maybe garner a drink or dinner invitation from the man who supplied Ivan his drones. Maybe get a fresh lead on The Ghost.

"They do things a bit differently at Club Monte Carlo," Andrey said, removing his helmet as they rode. "The home team hosts halftime refreshments while staff members stomp the divots."

Helmets off was a double-edged sword for Achilles. It would make his job easier, both the identification and the assassination, but it would also expose him. His disguise was thinner than he would have liked. It had to be. The number of hours and amount of sweat involved ruled out makeup and prosthetics.

He wore a blonde wig with hair considerably longer than his norm, and contacts that turned his dove gray eyes a pale blue. The combination gave him an entirely different demeanor, much softer and less serious. He believed it would hold up to anything short of facial recognition software, or trained and suspicious eyes. But you never knew.

Vazov's four bodyguards greeted the eight players with mugs of a drink that looked like light beer but was probably Panaché, a mixture of ale and lemonade that seemed to be the club drink.

Everyone dismounted, grabbed a beverage, and crowded around Vazov, who addressed the group with lifted mug. His movements did not feel familiar, but this circumstance was very different from the first time Achilles met Ivan.

"Well played everyone."

Achilles had expected to feel a chill the minute Vazov opened his mouth, but the voice, like the stance, did not resonate with any in Achilles' memory. Feeling anxious and emboldened, he met Vazov's eye. Something was brewing there, but it wasn't surprise from an unexpected recognition. Achilles felt a savage stab of disappointment. Vazov wasn't Ivan. Vazov wasn't Ivan!

While Achilles processed that kick in the crotch, the toastmaster approached him, and looked at him—but spoke to Team Eagle's Captain. "Andrey, I see that you have a new player to thank for your lead. Where's Fernando?"

"Out with food poisoning."

"Well, that's no fun. And where did you find your substitute?"

"Nic recommended Sergey. He's his new star pupil."

Achilles tried not to let his disappointment show as he again met Vazov's eye.

"Sergey, you say? Are you certain?"

"I have no reason to doubt it," Andrey replied, his voice suddenly wary.

"And why would you? But I have men working for me whose job it is to doubt. One of them, Gleb here, just told me a different story." Vazov gestured toward one of his bodyguards.

The man whipped a piece of paper from his breast pocket. A printout with a picture on it. Achilles' official photo from the 2010 Olympics. Still speaking to Andrey, Vazov said, "Gleb told me your man's name isn't really Sergey. He told me he isn't even Russian. He's American. And not just any American. An American assassin. Don't let the wig fool you. Your new number 1 is Kyle Achilles, the disgruntled former agent who killed CIA Director Wiley Rider."

All eyes began boring into Achilles.

Powerful grips grabbed Achilles' arms from behind, sending his mug to the turf and his operation to the toilet. They secured his wrists, locked his elbows, and forced his face to the ground. "The game's over," Vazov announced. "Everybody go home."

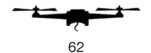

62

Big Ambition

Venice Beach, California

Pavel joined the Air Force because he wanted to feel the excitement, power, thrill and rush of flying a fighter plane at twice the speed of sound. He wanted his nickname painted on a cockpit and wings pinned to his uniformed chest. He wanted the ability to obliterate Russia's enemies, and attract her hottest babes.

He achieved all of it.

There was no stopping him.

He entered the academy with an intuitive feel for aerodynamics and blew through his training with a white-hot passion. The Russian Air Force teed it all up and he knocked it all down—fixed wing and rotary wing, transport planes and fighter jets. There was just one thing standing between him and a stellar career. When he wasn't training, Pavel hated life in the military.

The pay was pathetic, the food basic, and the accommodation spartan. He was willing to look past all that to pursue his muse, but then plunging oil prices took the Russian economy to its knees, forcing the military to cut more than corners. Once oil dipped below $50 a barrel, he was lucky to get more than an hour a month behind the stick.

For most of his fellow flyboys, the smart move was obvious. Go commercial. But Pavel wouldn't consider it. While commercial airline pilots made good money in positions of authority and prestige, flying passenger planes didn't feed the passion that brought him to aviation. Adrenaline didn't flow during routine trips from point A to point B.

Fortunately for Pavel, Ivan came calling.

When Ivan offered the opportunity to work on aviation's cutting edge, he got Pavel's full attention. When Ivan coupled that opportunity with a healthy paycheck and big bonus potential, Pavel was sold. When Ivan threw in life on the Côte d'Azur, Pavel couldn't agree fast enough.

He put his heart and soul and every available hour into learning to play Raven like Beethoven's piano. By the time he found himself looking across sun-drenched sand at a movie crew a quarter-mile down the beach, he wasn't just ready, but eager to perform. The crowd didn't matter. The police didn't matter. The pressure didn't matter. He was an athlete set to explode. Bring it on!

"Ready when you are," Pavel said.

"Our scene's up next," Ivan replied. He was reading from the shooting script. *Big Ambition* had a total of four scenes taking place on Muscle Beach, and the third appeared to be the best for the grab. It had Jenks doing a SEAL-style workout in the sand at the surf's edge.

"Are you going to tell us why?" Michael asked, looking over at Ivan from the driver's seat.

"Why tell when I can show?"

Pavel was certain Michael was rolling his eyes, figuratively if not literally, but he couldn't confirm it while seated behind the Drone Command Module.

"Tell me again, how much are we behind with Vazov?" Ivan teased.

"$152 million."

Ivan didn't comment further, and a moment later there was a lot of movement on the set. "Looks like it's a wrap on scene two. Let's get out and watch them prep scene three with the stand-in. Pavel, this should give you everything you need to time the grab."

"Roger that."

The cameras were already in place about twenty feet from the surf, allowing for both wide-angle framing shots and the obligatory zooms onto firm flesh glistening with sweat and sea spray. Twenty minutes later, the man of the hour reemerged from his trailer, wearing nothing but body-hugging black shorts and an aw-shucks smile.

"He's a monster," Pavel said. "You can't always be sure, given what they can do with camera tricks, but this guy really is huge."

"Let me guess," Boris said. "Jenks weighs in at two hundred sixty pounds."

Michael's fingers flew across his phone. "Exactly two hundred sixty, at least according to Google. How'd you know?"

"Ivan had me remove the mechanisms that allow us to collapse Raven. By cutting those ten pounds, he took the cargo limit up to two hundred sixty."

"That was part of it," Ivan said. "But only a small part. I'm sure Pavel would have managed to get Jenks off the sand even with the hinges on."

"So why, then?" Michael asked.

"Ask me again in an hour, if you still haven't figured it out."

Pavel interrupted the heated discussion with a hotter announcement. "They're going straight to the surf shot. No down time, no fussing around. Time to rock."

63

Amusements

French Riviera

Vazov's men kept Achilles' face planted in the grass until all the players had left the premises and the club doors had been locked. Then they secured his wrists and ankles with thick zip ties, and rolled him over like a rug.

Achilles looked up to see Little V looking down. The playboy wore a contemptuous smile and held a polo ball.

Made of high-impact white plastic, polo balls weigh four ounces and have a diameter of three-and-a-quarter inches, making them slightly bigger than baseballs. Vazov pressed the plastic against Achilles' lips and waited for him to pucker. "If you drop it, I'll hit it where it lands."

All things considered, Achilles decided to remain still and silent. It wasn't easy, keeping his breathing regular and body from quivering with all the adrenaline coursing through his veins. And, irony of ironies, he'd still be with the CIA if he was good at puckering.

A few seconds after Vazov disappeared from his view, Achilles heard the scrunch of leather followed by pounding hooves. Feeling that vibration, he couldn't help but do the calculation. Polo ponies weigh a thousand pounds and charge at 30 mph. It would take six pro football players to generate that much momentum. Hardly a fair match against his nose and lips. He tried telling himself that it could be worse. Given the way his cinched hands were clasped beneath his hips, his genitals were also protruding. Nonetheless, Achilles decided he'd prefer a spoonful of Salmonella. It heartened him to know that as bad as Jo had it, she was doing better than he.

While the hammering of hoofbeats shifted from receding to

approaching, Achilles sent off a quick prayer that Vazov was talented enough to compensate for the ball's raised position. Then he pushed all thoughts of peril aside, closed his eyes, and thought about Katya. The way her face seemed to soften right before she kissed him. The way she stood naked on the scale every morning, making his day before it got started. The way she smiled when—

Crack!

His lips tingled and the tip of his nose ignited, but his head remained on his shoulders and his heart remained in his chest.

He opened his eyes.

Vazov reversed course and trotted back. "Would you prefer to talk, or shall we continue working to improve my swatting skills? It's entirely up to you."

"A chat sounds nice, but I'm going to need a fresh mug of Panaché. I fear I spilled the first one you gave me."

His quip generated a creepy half-smile that soon vanished. "Consider that last comment your final free pass. Anything short of serious conversation won't hold my interest. Understood?"

Achilles gave a single nod.

"Why are you here?"

Forewarned, Achilles bit back his reflexive reply. "Polo seemed the best way to meet you."

Vazov summoned another half-smile. "Go on."

"Upon becoming persona non grata in the U.S., I asked myself where I'd most like to live. I got the French Riviera in answer. Since I need to work but don't speak French, I decided to find an English or Russian-speaking employer. Since I need to avoid law enforcement, I figure it's best if that employer is similarly predisposed."

"You want to work for me?" Vazov asked, his voice surprisingly devoid of inclination or emotion.

"I do."

The Russian transplant chewed on that for six beats of Achilles' heart. "Why me in particular?"

"You're the right age, and you've got panache. Given those, I thought you might be someone I could bond with. Especially if I also played polo."

"What makes you think I'm looking to hire anybody?"

"In a word: need. My undercover work revealed that you've got a big one."

"What exactly do I need?"

"A new head of security." Achilles felt the bodyguards tense. He suspected he'd see bulging necks and bared teeth if he glanced back at them, but he kept his gaze cool and locked on target.

Vazov engaged, but he came out firing. "Gleb was good enough to catch you."

"Only because of a fluke. If the Eagle's attacker hadn't eaten a bad shrimp, I'd still be within striking distance and beneath your radar."

"My men might not be perfect, but what makes you better?"

"Beyond having worked for the world's most revered intelligence agency?"

"Beyond that. The CIA did fire you, after all."

"And I did take out their director. But beyond balls and brains and connections galore, I'm also a guy who can outfight your best fighter and outshoot your best shooter."

This time the bodyguards let their exhalations be heard.

Achilles ignored them.

"My men are good. Very good. *All* of them."

"They might be good, but they're not good enough. I'm better, and I can prove it—against all of them."

Achilles finally earned Vazov's full smile. "Now that, I must admit, sounds amusing."

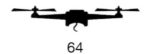

64

Altitude and Attitude

Venice Beach, California

The Drone Command Module was Pavel's own design, and he loved it. It was light and modular and slipped into a standard padded backpack for transport. The three laptop-size screens folded like a vanity mirror and ran for hours off the built-in battery, when not plugged into the Tesla's power supply.

The joystick was an X52 Pro system manufactured by Saitek. It snapped into a custom-fit lap desk that strapped securely to his thighs.

The makeshift cockpit he created at the back of the Tesla resembled the flight simulators in which he'd practiced for years. He had installed blackout window tinting all around, and an articulating arm that suspended the monitors from the ceiling.

The one thing Pavel had not practiced was flying Raven in and out of the truck. Boris had been modifying it up to the last minute. That was a violation of Ivan's meticulous mandate, but for some reason, that shortcoming hadn't bothered the boss. For his part, Pavel was more excited than nervous. Flying in and out of the truck would be fun, if not challenging. And snatching a mammoth movie star mid-shoot would be outright exhilarating.

Michael counted down. "Three, two, one—"

Pavel started the two extended rotors at their slowest speed, knowing that operating them within the truck's confines would create turbulent conditions. They'd padded the floor and walls with packing foam, but why take chances? He slowly raised Raven up until it just cleared the truck, then extended the two collapsed rotors. Once they were locked into position, he slammed on the thrust and popped the drone into the sky like a champagne cork. "Liftoff!"

He took it straight up. Way up. High enough to put the shoot in the middle of his screen, even though it was a quarter mile to the southwest. There were three advantages to this tactic. First, it moved Raven out of ordinary sight lines. People don't walk around city streets staring at the clouds. Second, it made navigation a breeze. A straight line. A runway approach. Finally, it gave him speed.

Under its own propulsion, Raven maxed out at 60 mph in still air. And Pavel didn't have still air. He had a mild headwind coming off the ocean. By adding downward momentum, however, he could approach 70 mph even battling the breeze.

That breeze was a blessing in disguise. By muffling the sound, it would help him strike without warning. Seconds were crucial when success depended on surprise.

Pavel took the throttle to full and dove at Jenks like an eagle that had spotted a mouse. Graceful, fast and focused. The secret to successful strikes was keeping an unwavering eye on the target. In this case, that target was Preston Jenks' waist. The point where his black shorts met chiseled abs.

Pavel ignored the crowds and the trucks. They were background noise. He ignored the cameras and the grips. They wouldn't interfere. His battle was with the big man himself. The up-and-coming action hero. The muscle man movie star. All Pavel had to do was get The Claw wrapped around Jenks' waist. The rest was up to Ivan.

65

Attitude

Venice Beach, California

Preston Jenks was on the brink of superstardom, and he knew it. He also knew many an actor who had reached this point and blown it with a bad script or flat performance. *Big Ambition* could make him or break him, so he was giving it one hundred percent.

They had started with the day's dialogue and melodrama scenes, shooting the sensitive shots while he was freshest. Finally, they'd come to his favorite. Not just for the day, but for the whole film. It wasn't the climactic sequence, where he solved the crime, killed the crooks and saved his costar. It was the training montage.

Jenks had grown to six-foot-six and two hundred sixty pounds while working out to similar scenes. Sylvester Stallone had set the standard in the Rocky films, and still held the title. Jenks was determined to become the Rocky of his generation. He had watched Rocky preparing to battle Apollo Creed, Clubber Lang and Ivan Drago a thousand times. When he worked out, he played those soundtracks. *Gonna Fly Now. No Easy Way Out. Eye of the Tiger.*

The producers had pulled together a killer soundtrack for *Big Ambition*, a collaboration between Pitt Bull, Ryan Tedder and Adam Levine. But it didn't evoke inspiring images. Not yet. He hadn't shot them. So he had *Hearts on Fire* playing in his mind when he hit the sand, determined to surpass Stallone—or die trying.

Working out on the ocean's edge had been his idea. It seemed natural for a hero who had once been a Navy SEAL. He began with push-ups, one-handed of course, up and down, in and out of the breaking waves. Once his biceps were burning, his pecs were pounding, and the veins were bulging from his neck, he switched to Burpees, adding double-leg kickbacks and arm-raising jumps to the pushup routine.

It struck him on the fourth jump, a whip that lassoed his waist and clamped down like a cold collar of steel. His first thought was heart attack. His second was a change to the script. Before his third thought registered, before he snapped out of his training trance and into the external environment, his feet left the ground.

The wind and noise and screams registered all at once, crashing in harder and colder and faster than the waves below. He looked up and saw the source of everything. Some big black flying machine. A drone. Had Hollywood decided to cash in on the Silicon Valley story? Was the director springing it on him as a surprise in order to capture an authentic reaction?

He looked down at the crew. The cameras were still on him. The cast was staring. The director was on the phone.

It took him higher. Way too high for comfort. High enough to see Marina Del Rey, the Santa Monica Pier and the Financial District.

He clutched the constraining cable with both hands. It was an impulsive move, and one he immediately regretted. He was a tough guy, being caught on film. He couldn't appear scared. Image was everything.

Determined to salvage the situation, he readjusted his grip, putting one hand well above the other. Then he started to climb.

Jenks had no idea what he would do when he reached the mechanical beast. Disabling it would literally be suicide. But he thought about the cameras and the nightly news, and continued putting one hand over the other.

It hit him like a mule kick to the solar plexus. Blinding pain. Loss of breath. Complete muscular disfunction. His hands released of their own accord and he dropped back to a dangling position. No doubt the crowd below had gasped, but he couldn't hear it over the rotor wash.

What he did hear was the drone commander's message. Loud and clear.

He looked up to see a green display come alive. A clock in

countdown mode. Twenty-nine minutes. He'd heard the testimony of prior victims on the news. He knew what it meant. As he studied the numbers—shocked and transfixed, contemplative and terrorized—a set of padded headphones dropped down on a wire.

Jenks placed them over his ears and adjusted the mic, but didn't speak. No doubt they were watching and would speak when ready. Instead, he put on a smile and waved down at his fans.

"Now that's the attitude." The voice was distorted, almost robotic. "When a situation is out of your control, best to enjoy it. You do understand that it's completely out of your control. Physically at least. Don't you, Preston?"

"If you say so." They wanted money. He knew they wanted money. But he was going to make them ask for it. The cameras were rolling, and his attitude would be reflected in his body language. Best to method act this one.

"We're going to let you relax for this one. First, however, we need the number for your agent. The one that's sure to get him on the phone, quickly."

He rattled off Johnny Fainsilbler's cell. It was easy to remember.

"And your accountant?"

"I don't have his number memorized."

"Who is it?"

"Benny Cohen. The firm's in his name."

"Very good. I like you, Preston. You're the real deal. Tough under fire. No stupid questions or silly threats. This is going to cost you a little money, but you keep your cool and you'll more than make it up in publicity. This may look like a holdup, but it's really a gift—so long as you maintain the right attitude."

Publicity. Publicity. He'd been focused on image, on minimizing damage, on not crapping the bed. The idea of upside hadn't entered his head. But the crook was correct. *This* performance could be his breakthrough. "You mind if I put on a bit of a show? A few crunches, some pull-ups, leg lifts, stuff like that?" He began fantasizing the answers he'd give from talk show chairs, bromides about attitude and determination.

"That's the spirit. Just don't attempt anything looking like an assault. If you go offensive or climb past the halfway point, we'll put you down. Hard."

"Roger that."

66

Lucky

Venice Beach, California

For only the second time since the damn drone investigation began, Rip got lucky. He'd learned nothing of practical value from the surviving CEOs, and he'd heard nothing more from Miss Ooh La La. But a regional meeting happened to have him in the Los Angeles office when the Preston Jenks story broke.

Now the clock was literally ticking.

The big green display gave Jenks 23 minutes to live.

He set the timer on his watch to match it, while talking to his L.A. counterpart. "How far is Muscle Beach?"

SAIC Christopher Ott rose and grabbed his suit coat. "About eight miles. We'll take the 405 to Venice Boulevard. It's a straight shot."

"How long?"

"Ten minutes if we're code three."

As an investigator, Rip rarely rode with his lights flashing and sirens wailing. When he did, it was to plow through traffic in pursuit of a hot crime. It gave him a rush better than any amusement park ride. The power to part cars and run reds was intoxicating. So was the knowledge that he might be only minutes from catching the bastard who had become the bane of his existence.

Los Angeles had over ten thousand officers to police its four million residents. No doubt a good chunk of them were converging on Venice at that very moment. Ivan had made his first mistake, and by God, Rip was going to exploit it. "Make sure LAPD has a chopper on the scene."

"Already there," Ott replied, pointing through the windshield. "As are the news crews."

Rip refocused and counted three helicopters a few miles ahead, circling the smoggy sky .

"It's a bloody brilliant plan, using drones," Ott said. "I mean, what are we supposed to do?"

"Tell me about it."

"Any offensive action, and they drop the vic. And defense?" He snorted. "Forget about it. We bring in an air cushion and all they have to do is move a few yards to the left or right."

"Welcome to my world."

"I assume their banking is similarly impervious?"

"Clarice is working it personally," Rip said, referencing the star of the FBI's Financial Crimes Division. "But she told me it will take weeks to follow the trail, and warned that it would likely lead to a dead end."

"Well, at the very least, we're about to capture their drone. No way it can outfly our birds."

Rip hoped Ott was right. The conclusion seemed inescapable, but he had his doubts. Even the great Houdini had nothing on Ivan. The Ghost's plans were original and his executions were flawless. A brilliant gambit seemed more probable than a big blunder.

Jenks emerged into view as they passed an obtrusive building. He was about a hundred feet above the beach, dangling by what looked to be a black rope. And he was acting oddly. "Is he doing crunches?"

"Sure looks that way."

"I know working out is a good way to combat stress, but that seems extreme."

"He's not working out," Ott said with a knowing nod. "He's working the cameras. Playing to the crowd."

"You Angelenos are a special breed."

"People act differently when cameras are rolling. You ever watch one of those funniest home video shows? Everybody hams it up, goes a bit crazy."

"If you say so."

The traffic gridlocked as they neared the shore. Between the infamous drone and the famous victim, the sexy story had the looky-loos out in droves. People were abandoning their cars to watch the action. It made sense. If police cars couldn't get through, neither could tow trucks.

Rip checked his wrist. Fourteen minutes remaining. "Let's leave the car and run."

"Roger that."

The LAPD had reinforced the studio's barricade, using SWAT vehicles and officers in riot gear. The scene reminded Rip of the Fourth of July, with mobs of people all pointed in the same direction and staring at the sky.

Rip and Ott badged through the barricade and spotted a Mobile Command Post, a beefy vehicle that looked like a blue and white armored car extended to the length of a bus. Rip sensed a change in his partner's mood as they ran toward it.

Twelve minutes.

As they neared the door, Ott said, "I should warn you, the MCP means Captain Garwood is likely running the show. He's not a big fan of the FBI in general or me in particular."

Rip reached for the handle without hesitation. "Well, that's not likely to improve when he finds out he's no longer in charge."

67

The Fifth Man

French Riviera

Vazov's four bodyguards cleared the club's private dining room of a long oak table and eighteen matching chairs, creating an arena. A gladiatorial arena. Despite the genteel surroundings, Achilles knew the Marquess of Queensberry's rules would not apply. This was going to be a cage match.

Little V had not allowed vanity to guide his bodyguard selection. He hadn't surrounded himself with petite protection. In fact, he'd gone the opposite direction. He'd recruited men massive enough to make almost everyone appear inferior. At six-foot-two, Achilles usually stood above ninety-five percent of any crowd. But standing amidst Vazov's men he found himself to be below average. Three of his opponents were of similar size. The fourth was a colossus.

Achilles had studied them over the past few days. Glimpses and snippets of their behavior led him to believe that they were top of the line—for hired muscle. Despite their size, they remained unobtrusive yet attentive. But Achilles had also seen the glorified bouncers demonstrate a lack of leadership and dearth of tactical thinking. Professional bodyguards would never busy both hands serving beers, or let an unknown within arm's reach of their principal. Achilles likened his opponents to fraternity brothers more than soldiers.

Despite their apparent lack of coordination, however, he still preferred to take them on one-by-one. Divide and conquer. Establish artificial order and then inject chaos. "Who's first?" he asked.

The bodyguards looked at one another. It wasn't an easy question. There weren't just tactical considerations—pride was on the line.

Achilles beckoned toward the beefiest bodyguard, a six-foot-eight wrecking crew with hands the size of hams and shoulders that would support a bridge. Start with the biggest guy was Achilles' rule. Take him on while you're fresh and demoralize the others with his defeat. "Come on, big guy. Let's get this party started."

Ham-hands stepped forward.

Vazov intervened. "No. Gleb goes first."

Ham-hands receded, his expression unchanged. Achilles was tempted to say "Good boy!" but bit his tongue as all eyes turned toward a bald guy with a wrestler's cauliflower ears.

Gleb stepped forward, rolling his shoulders.

One of the things that made Achilles an accomplished climber was his "ape index." The proportion of his wingspan to his height. Ideally, the two were identical, as illustrated by Da Vinci's *Vitruvian Man.* By that standard, Achilles' reach was five percent longer than it should have been. He took advantage of that aberration and the momentary disruption to jab baldy square in the nose. Hard and fast. Hard as a hammer. Fast as a falcon. Kabam!

Cartilage cracked, blood erupted, lips split and eyes rolled. Gleb was gone before the fight began.

Achilles didn't follow the jab with an uppercut or knee to the groin. Both would have been overkill and wasted precious time. He attacked bodyguards two and three instead.

He loosed a lightning left cross on the nearest jaw, following it all the way through. The blow caught number two totally unprepared. A split-second earlier, he'd been a spectator surrounded by burly friends waiting for a show. Then, before he realized what was happening, his head was twisting up and around like a stubborn lid letting loose. This caused his brain to smack against the left side of his skull hard enough to send it rebounding back against the right. Ding, ding.

While number two's lights extinguished, Achilles pivoted back around. Winding into a half-crouch, he filled his leading arm full of monstrous momentum and funneled all the power through to his right elbow. He plowed it squarely into number three's solar plexus, dead center, no tilt, no roll. The blow was as perfectly placed as any Achilles had ever dealt. It compressed nerves and expelled air and robbed the stunned bodyguard of the ability to breathe.

While three doubled over, Achilles unwound, reversing his momentum and rising up toward full height. Along the way, he put his right knee into play, whacking it against number three's exposed temple like a bowling ball on a ten pin. The bodyguard spun and sprawled and curled up on the floor. Gasping for air while grabbing his head, he looked ready for a blankie.

Five seconds from first blow to third man down, with no lasting damage done. An entirely acceptable outcome, in Achilles' opinion. Of course, the first three-fourths of most marathons were easy, and the big hill still lay ahead.

Achilles took a long step back and a deep breath in before again beckoning toward the beefiest bodyguard. "Come on, big guy. Time for the grand finale."

Ham-hands had to step over his fallen comrades to reach Achilles. A disheartening act, to be sure. The tactical equivalent of a gut punch. But the big guy looked unmoved. Perhaps he held his smaller colleagues in contempt. Perhaps his heart was just as hard as his pecs.

Achilles searched for early signs of his opponent's fighting style. Would he assume a full-frontal crouched stance, like a Greco-Roman wrestler? Or would he present a profile with fists up and on guard, like a boxer or martial artist? Would he put his weight onto one leg, leaving the other free to kick, or spread it out, ready to dance and deflect? Whatever the style, Achilles would counter with something different, avoiding conditioned reflexes and practiced combinations. Aikido would be his first choice, the Japanese technique of using an opponents size and strength against him. But the choice wasn't Achilles' to make.

As so often happens, Achilles' battle plan changed with his opponent's first move. Ham-hands adopted a style best described as "tank." A straightforward assault intended to crush Achilles beneath a rolling wave of brute size and savage strength.

Achilles held his ground and waited for the inevitable haymaker to come. Ham-hands launched the right cross with his second step, a powerful blow swung from the shoulder—a blow designed to break Achilles' jaw and put him on the ground. Achilles didn't step back or dodge. He didn't attempt to block or deflect. He simply presented a different target.

Using his neck like a third arm, Achilles snapped his forehead at the fist. He timed it to make contact at the apex, thereby maximizing momentum. The meeting proved no contest. None at all. An intricate amalgam of hard and soft tissues striking a thick arch of solid bone was the equivalent of a car colliding with a concrete wall. The colossal fist crumbled. It buckled and crunched and splintered, becoming worse than useless. In the blink of an eye, it transformed from a powerful weapon into a source of enormous pain.

Achilles didn't stop there, not with Vazov's big gun. As the giant began to bellow, Achilles put his own right arm into play. He swung it up along his opponent's centerline until the heel of his palm plowed into the broad chin like it was punting a football. The giant jaw slammed shut amidst a spray of blood and his head wobbled like a punching bag. Without a word, Vazov's last bodyguard slumped to the floor.

"Impressive, Mr. Achilles." Delivered in a cool, crisp tone, the intent of Vazov's words was ambiguous. His actions were not. He spoke with his SIG Sauer trained on Achilles' center of mass. "Now, grab the ground before I blow out your knees."

68

Garwood

Venice Beach, California

The LAPD's Mobile Command Post contained two working rooms. Nearest the door was the communications hub, housing computers, phones, clocks and racks of radios with backup batteries. Rip and Ott walked right through it and into the command room.

Eleven minutes remaining.

Monitors lined the walls. High definition displays of the MCP's rooftop cameras. One showed a wide-angle view of the crowds, the barricades, the beach and the drone. Another focused on the drone and its hostage. The third zoomed in on Jenks, who was now doing one-armed pull-ups using the cable that suspended him.

Rip walked straight to the man with captain stripes, who was in heated conversation with two lieutenants. An interesting discussion Rip didn't want to interrupt.

"You're saying we have reports of two ransom demands?"

"That's correct. One to Jenks' agent, the other to his accountant."

"For $20 million each?"

"Correct."

"And both are paying? The perp's going to clear $40 million?"

The lieutenant nodded.

"I get the accountant, but why the agent? Those guys are sharks, but they don't have that kind of cash."

"Beats me."

Ott said, "Agents liaise with production companies that take out insurance policies on actors critical to the completion of films."

Garwood turned toward Ott, briefly and without warmth. Then he shifted his gaze to Rip.

"Captain Garwood, I'm Ripley Zonder. I run this investigation for the FBI."

"I'll be with you momentarily. Give me fifteen minutes."

So much for diplomacy. "Since this will be over in ten, you'll be with me now."

Garwood puffed up. He was a large man. Looked a bit like Terry Bradshaw, a retired football player with thinning hair and a few too many doughnuts behind his belt. "Excuse me?"

"Have you thought of a single scenario that could save the hostage?"

"We're working it."

"You are?"

"We are."

"Well, then that's the problem. You can't save the hostage. Only the ransom can do that. What we can do is prepare to catch the perps."

Garfield rolled his eyes and gestured with his arms. "This isn't a tea party."

"We need to follow the drone to the people who control it."

"I've got a bird in the sky and two dozen cruisers on the ground."

"That's another problem."

Garfield stepped into Rip's space. "I'm pretty sure I know what I'm doing."

Rip didn't budge. Texas would never yield to California. "At some point, the drone is going to make a break for it. He's likely got something unexpected planned. An unconventional maneuver. We want to let him think he's succeeded in evading surveillance."

"Do we now?"

"We do."

"And just how do you propose we make that happen, without actually losing him?"

"Order the news cameras out of the area. Bring in a second helicopter at maximum altitude and sufficient distance to stay off the drone's surveillance cameras. Once it's in place, put the visible helicopter down on the beach—when he asks you to."

"When he asks me to?"

"He's got to ask, right? The only other move is surrender."

Garwood pondered for a slow second, then grew a rueful grin. "Are you officially assuming command? Is the FBI taking operational control?"

"Just for the next fifteen minutes."

Garwood turned to his lieutenant. "Make note of the time. Agent Ripley Zonder of the FBI now has operational control." Without pause, Garwood then called into the next room. "Branson, order the news choppers out of the area. No civilian aircraft within two miles of Muscle Beach."

"On it," Branson called back.

"Anything else?" Garwood asked.

"Yes. Drones can fly places helicopters can't. Inside parking garages or sewer systems or subways, for example. Let's use that fancy map of yours to identify locations like that and position patrol cars accordingly."

Garwood nodded, but said nothing.

"Instead of planning to follow him, we'll get ahead of him instead."

The countdown clock clicked down to seven minutes.

"The drone's descending," Ott said. "The ransom payments must have posted."

All eyes turned to the central monitor.

"Impossible," Garwood said, his tone mocking. "They haven't asked us to ground our bird."

He was right, which meant Rip was wrong. He had no idea what Ivan would do next, but he sensed a disaster.

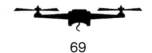

69

The Bottom

French Riviera

Looking up at Vazov's gun and the stern face behind it, Achilles got the feeling that his gambit was about to backfire. He'd put the four bodyguards down without serious damage to promote the illusion that he wanted to lead them, but now that he was under the gun, their first impulse would be revenge.

"Shall we move on to the marksmanship contest?" Achilles asked.

Vazov harrumphed. "After that last display, do you really expect me to give you a gun?"

"I expect you to want an upgrade."

"You obviously know how to knock heads. And I'm willing to concede that you know how to shoot. But brawling and blasting aren't the primary requisites for my bodyguards."

Gleb and the third bodyguard rose slowly to their feet while Vazov spoke. Gleb looked like a vampire clown, with his swollen nose and blood-covered chin. Number three just looked dazed. Dazed and angry.

Achilles ignored them. "What is your primary concern?"

Vazov gestured toward Achilles with both index fingers. The bodyguards responded by grabbing Achilles' arms and employing a wrist lock favored by cops and bouncers. It put his torso under their control while leaving his legs free to respond to their guidance.

Achilles didn't resist. No point. Not with the Sig squared on his chest from a distance of ten feet.

Vazov grew a satisfied smile. "My primary concern is loyalty. There will always be somebody tougher out there, tougher even than you, Achilles. No sense fretting over that, not if what you've got is solid."

Achilles glanced down at the two on the ground. "What you've got doesn't look very solid to me."

"Ah, but it is. These men will do as I say, without question, without waiver. They are loyal." The two downed bodyguards began to stir while Vazov spoke, as if buoyed by his words.

"What makes you think I wouldn't be loyal?" Achilles said with what sounded like sincere concern.

"Experience has taught me that there are two kinds of people in this world. Those whose core driver is logic, and those whose core driver is emotion. The split has nothing to do with intelligence or education or demographic detail. The assignment is purely Darwinian. A genetic coin toss. Random chance. And neither is necessarily advantageous over the other. But only one type will remain loyal no matter what. You, Mr. Achilles, are not that type. If you were, you'd still be at the CIA. You'd have gone along, and gotten along. You'd have been loyal to your director."

That wasn't an explanation Achilles had been expecting nor one he was prepared to counter. At that moment, literally under the gun, he wasn't sure if Vazov's words were exceptionally insightful or complete crap. Analysis would have to wait. "That was a very different time, in a very different place. Circumstances have changed. I've changed."

"Not a risk I'm willing to take. But I do want to thank you for exposing several weak spots in my security. I won't forget your contribution."

Vazov turned his attention to Gleb. "You look terrible. I want you and Gary to go to the hospital. Get that nose taken care of. In fact, I want you both to get head scans. Make sure there's no hidden damage."

"Will do, boss."

"On the way, I want you to stop by the marina. You'll find padlocks and spare anchor chain in the aft storage compartment of the *VaVaVoom*."

Gleb and Gary looked confused.

Achilles wasn't.

He didn't jump in with bargains or pleas. Both would be pointless and neither was his style. Intuitively, he felt that his best move was to hurry things along, to get himself alone with the two dazed bodyguards before the others regained their feet.

"The chain is for our guest here," Vazov said, gesturing toward Achilles. "Take him out far enough that you can't see the shore—then show him the bottom."

70

Ka-BOOM

Venice Beach, California

Michael was battling mixed emotions as the drone descended, its mission complete. He was thrilled that they'd secured $40 million, pissed that Ivan hadn't informed him of the plan, and anxious that the walls were about to come crashing down around them.

He was, however, better off than Boris.

Boris was the designated driver for their new transport vehicle. He'd be behind the wheel when Pavel landed Raven in the back, presumably with police in hot pursuit. Or so Michael assumed. Ivan hadn't yet ordered him back to the extermination truck.

The other guys hadn't said anything either, but Michael knew they were no less nervous.

"We're fifteen seconds from release," Pavel said. "I trust I don't need to point out that the instant Jenks is on the ground, we become vulnerable to all types of attack. Overt and covert. We have three choppers to contend with, and I've seen dozens of cruisers on the ground. Meanwhile, our battery life is down to twenty minutes, and it will take Boris five of those just to get back to the truck and retract two rotors."

"I'm well aware of all of that," Ivan replied.

"So what's the plan?"

"Up and out."

"Up and out?"

"Up as high as you can take it, out over the ocean as far as it will fly. Ten miles or more would be optimal."

"Roger that," Pavel said as they all wondered *optimal for what?*

The four sat in silence until Pavel chimed in with the

countdown. "Three, two, one, releasing. Jenks is clear."

Uproarious applause broke out all around the Tesla and across Venice Beach as the movie star landed in the sand. While he trotted back toward the barricade, raising one arm and then the other to wave at fans, Pavel complied with Ivan's instructions.

The helicopters responded in kind, moving to match Raven's altitude while maintaining a defensive distance. No doubt they found the move baffling and were left wondering what to expect.

They weren't alone.

At least for a few seconds.

Then the clouds parted and Michael saw the light. "You're planning to self-destruct."

"Of course."

"Way out over the ocean. So the components will get a saltwater scrubbing and the pieces will be hard to find."

"The pieces," Boris repeated, his tone wrought with wonder. "That's why you had me remove the hinging mechanisms. You didn't want to leave any evidence that Raven could fold."

"And the truck," Pavel said. "It's nothing but a decoy. A misdirect. A red herring. It's bloody brilliant!"

"Did you expect anything less? Seriously. I do this every time. What's a guy got to do to get you gals to stop worrying?"

"I appreciate the misdirect, but I'd still rather we didn't have the police involvement," Michael said.

"Or the public awareness," Pavel added. "They make our job considerably more difficult."

"Really?" Ivan challenged.

"Undoubtedly."

"And what is our job?"

Pavel tilted his head quizzically. "Kidnap and ransom."

"No."

"No?"

Ivan shook his head. "You're operating on the wrong level."

"On the wrong level?" Pavel repeated, slowly.

"Think bigger."

"Think bigger?"

Ivan looked from person to person. Nobody offered a guess.

"Our job is making money. Transferring it from other people's bank accounts into our bank accounts. The Sangster sacrifice and the Jenks job just made that a whole lot easier."

"They did?" Pavel asked.

"How?" Boris asked.

"We'll come to that, but first things first." Ivan motioned toward the Drone Command Module. All eyes went to the first screen, the one with the controls, the one with the red button.

"Ka-BOOM!"

71

One Pop

French Riviera

First, they snugged zip ties around his wrists. Right there in the polo club's private dining room under the gaze of Vazov's gun. Then they added ankle ties. Not like before, not a tight truss. Gleb used multiple ties to create a chain just long enough for Achilles to hobble.

Vazov taunted him. "I must say, that looks pretty solid."

It was. Serious gymnastics would be required to overpower two captors with zip-tied hands and feet. Achilles was always up for those. Free-solo climbing was often the very definition of serious gymnastics. But elaborate acrobatics required room to move and time to act. He didn't expect either to be forthcoming, much less both at the same time.

They shoved him into the back of a black SUV and buckled him in the middle. Gleb took the wheel, while Gary kept a Sig trained on Achilles from the passenger seat. The setup reminded Achilles of a similar scene in Quentin Tarantino's *Pulp Fiction*. The story didn't turn out well for the man in back. Marvin lost his head to a bump in the road.

Achilles tried to think of some angle to gain advantage. Some distraction or offer or countervailing concern. He came up blank. He'd just beaten the crap out of these guys. They wouldn't be charitably inclined. And their boss was a sadistic billionaire. Hard to trump that.

Achilles was familiar with Port Hercule, the famous Monte Carlo Marina. It was right in the middle of some the world's most expensive real estate. Much too expensive for a large parking lot. It was also a beehive of tourist activity. A walk through that beehive was bound to offer opportunity to a bold man ready to grab it.

Unfortunately, Gleb didn't drive toward downtown Monte Carlo. He took an earlier exit toward Cap-d'Ail instead. Achilles watched with a sinking heart as they drove right into a smaller marina and parked within spitting distance of a glistening white 50-foot yacht with *VaVaVoom* painted on its hull.

The two bodyguards surveyed the scene before opening their doors. While there was plenty of activity out on the road, the marina itself appeared tranquil.

Gary kept a Sig poised to bark, while Gleb pulled Achilles out of the car. Then Gleb kept Achilles pressed against the hot black metal until Gary joined them. Without a word, the pair of wounded warriors grabbed an arm each and frog-marched Achilles up the gangplank onto the *VaVaVoom*.

They wasted no time in manhandling Achilles below deck. Once out of sight, the bodyguards lifted his arms as high as they could go while bound behind his back, then higher. They kept pressing upwards until Achilles was forced to bend over. When they had his torso parallel with the ground, each swept a foot out from under him.

Achilles went down hard, landing on his chest and chin. Gary kept Achilles' arms held perpendicular to the ground but also stepped on his neck. Then Gary used his free hand to point his Sig at Achilles' head. "This look solid to you?"

"Looks solid to me. Keep him like that while I grab the chain."

It was solid. Too solid. Were it not for the gun, Achilles would have tried kicking for Gleb's leg. But as it was, that would have been suicide.

They kept him in that ultimate submissive position while Gleb bound his ankles with anchor chain. The bodyguard wrapped it around eight times, before fastening the ends with a heavy padlock. The click was as ominous as anything Achilles had ever heard.

"That should do it," Gleb said. "Go free the moorings. I'll take the wheel."

They left him alone during cast-off. Achilles didn't know if Gary would come right back or if he'd stay topside while they sailed out of sight of the land. Regardless, Achilles had to work fast. He needed a knife to free his hands and a sliver of metal to pick the lock. Neither was readily apparent.

He was in the main room, a combination of kitchen and living room. It appeared to have two staterooms forward, and a third plus a toilet aft. By the time Achilles finished his survey, the engine was rumbling.

Under normal conditions, a person can't pull himself up onto his knees from a face down position with his arms tied behind his back. The leverage isn't there. But the sixty pounds of steel wrapping his ankles changed the equation. It all came down to hamstring strength, and Achilles had plenty. From that kneeling position, he squatted backward until his thighs had the angle to power him to his feet.

The yacht started moving.

While face down on the floor, Achilles had held hope that he could shed the chains by shucking his polo boots, but once he assumed a standing position, it immediately became apparent that they were wrapped much too tight. Without wasting time on laments or curses, he hopped to the kitchen and began rummaging.

The second drawer revealed a paring knife with a stained wooden handle and a blade that had endured a hundred sharpenings. He reverse palmed the knife and wriggled the blade beneath a zip tie, forcing it all the way to the hilt. Then he torqued. The tie resisted for a few strained seconds before popping all at once.

Achilles didn't pause to celebrate or rub his wrists. He didn't remove the tie circling his other wrist. He moved directly to the padlock. It was a brass contraption with a hardened steel shackle. Prying it apart would take tremendous leverage. That left sawing and picking. Neither posed a problem for Achilles' adept fingers, given the right tools.

He didn't have them.

There was no pocket for paperclips in the back of polo pants, and he hadn't wanted them worming around inside his boots, so he'd broken his habit and gone without. The drawers didn't offer up replacements. They didn't hold a hacksaw either.

By this point the powerboat was racing across the water, rocking the hull with the thump-thump of conquered waves. At that speed, Achilles wouldn't have long. Where to look next? He could search for bobby pins in the bathroom or try to find tools.

He went for the tools, having seen where Gleb had gone for the chain.

The supply closet lacked the fine finish of the rest of the yacht, but it served its purpose. Achilles' eyes went straight to a yellow plastic toolbox on the bottom shelf. It didn't have a hacksaw, but it held screwdrivers, pliers and a hefty hammer.

Achilles removed the smallest slotted screwdriver and wedged the tip into the keyhole. Then he started pounding. He pounded straight and true. Gently until the screwdriver was seated, then letting loose with all his might. Once he had a good half-inch of penetration, he went to work with the pliers, trying to force the cylinder into submission.

The chain tightened. He ignored it. The screwdriver flexed. He gripped harder. The cylinder snapped. He began to exhale, but stopped mid-puff. The shackle hadn't popped open—and there were footfalls on the stairs.

72

Cascade

Albuquerque, New Mexico

When you drink a really fine wine, the fulfillment is multifold. It begins with buying a four-figure bottle. The promise of prestige. The suggestion of sin. The twinkle in the sommelier's eye. It continues as the senses are invited in. The cork pops, piquing the ears. The wine swirls, caressing the eyes. The aroma wafts, arousing the nose. All before that first magnificent taste tickles the tongue.

Ivan enjoyed a similar symphony of satisfaction when implementing his plans. Each element contributed to a cascade of emotions that grew ever faster as it progressed toward the ultimate conclusion, an apex of enjoyment that only he could foresee.

He felt that magical tingle while reaching for the MiMiC phone. An anticipatory rush. As with a thousand-dollar bottle of wine, however, he wasn't entirely certain what to expect.

He programmed his caller ID to display the Hoover Building's switchboard. He could have used the Director's office number or even Brix's personal cell, but he figured the switchboard was the least likely to raise questions. With that virtual mask in place, he proceeded to dial Rip Zonder's mobile number.

Agent Zonder answered on the second ring. "Ripley Zonder."

Since Ivan wasn't certain how the FBI Director addressed his subordinates, or what kind of relationship Rip had with Brix, he skipped the greeting, confident that MiMiC would do its job and Zonder would recognize Brix's voice. "What the hell just happened?"

"The drone self-destructed."

"You certain it wasn't shot down?"

"One hundred percent."

"So we lost our only lead."

"That's one way to put it."

Ivan liked this guy. He had spunk. Too bad Ivan had to crash his career. "Do you have an alternative interpretation? One less likely to result in my standing before the Resolute Desk in the Oval Office with my pants around my ankles?"

Zonder remained cool and composed. "We could claim victory. Report that the drone is no longer a threat."

"That's one way to spin it. Might work too, if they don't have another."

"No reason to think they do."

"But every reason to assume it."

"If you want to play it conservative, report that we 'reduced the threat.' "

Ivan let Zonder stew for a moment. "That's worth considering. What will you get from the drone wreckage?"

"It's too early to say, but I'm not expecting much. Examination of the video revealed that the explosives were arranged to obliterate the device."

"Aren't all explosives arranged to obliterate?"

"Excuse me, I should have been more precise. Rather than using a single central repository that might have left the distal components intact, the engineer placed explosive charges on all four rotors plus the central housing. Each of the five appeared powerful enough to do the job alone. We're not expecting to find anything bigger than a nickel."

"You talk like you haven't found squat."

"The water in the area of the explosion is a quarter-mile deep."

"A quarter-mile?"

"He flew out past the shelf. No doubt that was intentional."

"No doubt. Give me the bottom line."

"We'll eventually be able to identify the country of origin for the components and explosive, but not much else."

"So after spending millions of hard-earned taxpayer dollars and holding my breath on camera for two months, I'll get to go to the press with 'Made in Taiwan.' "

Rip said nothing.

Ivan sighed. "Write it up and send it to me as a debriefing. A flash report. Word it as though this conversation never took place, and get it to me within the next two hours."

"Yes, sir."

"Now, just between us, and without any wishful thinking or ambiguous political drivel, do you have any concrete leads on the perp? Or his whereabouts? Or his next targets?"

Rip paused for half a beat, weighing the cost of candor against the price of peddling bullshit. "No, sir."

"Any reason to believe we'll catch him if we don't get a lucky tip?"

Another brief exhale. "No, sir."

"Any hope we can offer the people or the President?"

"Not at this time, sir."

"I appreciate your honesty if not your lapse of competence. Call me immediately if any of that changes." Ivan hung up without waiting for a reply.

Smiling at his phone, he scrolled to the bottom of the MiMiC app, slid an indicator to the left and hit the play button. The familiar voice of FBI Director Brix emanated from the speaker. "...do you have any concrete leads on the perp? Or his whereabouts? Or his next targets?"

"No, sir," SAIC Ripley Zonder replied.

"Any reason to believe we'll catch him without a lucky tip?"

"No, sir."

"Any hope we can offer the people or the President?"

"Not at this time, sir."

"I appreciate your honesty, if not your lapse of competence. Call me immediately if any of that changes."

Ivan stopped the recording and spoke a single word. "Gotcha!"

73

Two Thuds

French Riviera

Achilles turned to see both bodyguards barreling his way. They hadn't waited to reach their destination before coming for him. They hadn't stopped the motor. A savvy tactical move. Would he now pay the ultimate price for overlooking the autopilot option?

Payment began to look inevitable.

Events quickly cascaded in the wrong direction.

Gleb pressed the Sig's cold snout against the base of Achilles' skull, while Gary secured a fresh lock and rebound his wrists. The click and ziiiiip sounded like nails pounding into his coffin.

The pair paused to gloat while Achilles stood there helpless as a bowling pin. "How's it feel, knowing what's coming? Knowing you're about to die gasping for breath?" Apparently they didn't want an answer as Gleb punched him in the solar plexus the second Gary stopped talking.

They scooped him up when he doubled over and carried him up onto the deck. It should have been challenging with sixty pounds of steel wrapped around his ankles, but they did it without breaking stride. Gleb grabbed him by the waist of his pants, while Gary hoisted the chains. Achilles had to arch his back to keep his head from clunking on the stairs—easier said than done while gasping for air.

They dropped him at the top of the stairs without further word.

Gleb disappeared, while Gary stood watch. A moment later the engine died. As the yacht came to a stop, Achilles became acutely aware of the rise and fall of the ocean.

Gleb returned and spoke through a smirk. "We're going to

give you a choice. You can either hop or roll to the edge."

Achilles had always been an optimist. No way you could free-solo without a positive outlook. No way you could endure an Olympic training regimen or an undercover operation without the core belief that everything was going to work out. But there on the deck of the *VaVaVoom*, with bound arms and shackled ankles and beefy gunmen at his back, with hostile intent infusing the air and an ocean of isolation all around, Achilles struggled to find hope.

But not for long.

He gave up on hope and went with rage instead. Being beaten by Ivan the Ghost was one thing. He was a one of a kind genius, whose reputation was well deserved. But being bested by a Russian playboy was completely unacceptable. No way would Achilles go quietly at these amateur hands. No way would he disappear into the depths with a simple *bloop*.

He shifted his focus from saving himself to taking the smug bastards with him.

Rock climbers develop phenomenally strong fingers. The strength of their grip is second to none. Hand over hand, Achilles had climbed for hundreds of miles. By his fingertips, he'd hung for thousands of hours. If he could get a grip on a wrist or a shirt, he could drag the owner to the bottom. And if he could clamp onto the other with his teeth, he could drown them both.

As he pictured the scene, Achilles was struck by a plan. A far-out hail Mary kind of plan. A plan that offered hope where there had been none. The big one had the padlock key in his pocket.

While the objects of his animus watched with twisted grins, Achilles used his hamstring lift-and-squat trick to return to standing. Surveying the scene, he saw that Gleb had done as instructed. Whatever direction he looked, Achilles could see neither boat nor land.

"Hop to it," Gleb commanded, motioning with his gun.

Achilles hopped three times, then pretended to break down. Still a good ten feet from the water's edge, he bent over and began sobbing.

The reaction was one that he had feared, but not the one he

had expected. He heard two gunshots ring out in rapid succession. The world around him—didn't change. It didn't snap to black or fade to white. He didn't feel a sharp jolt or an overwhelming burning sensation.

He heard two thuds instead.

Then a familiar voice. "See what happens when you go in without me?"

Achilles looked up toward the sun. "Jo?"

"Who else?" She swung down from the roof where she'd apparently been impersonating a starfish. A seasick starfish with a Glock.

Achilles was having trouble adapting to this dramatic, magnificent, benevolent twist of fate. "How?"

"Bed was boring, so I grabbed the binoculars and a blanket, stuffed a thermos of hot tea and a pack of Pepcid into my satchel, hopped on the motorcycle and went to our picnic spot to watch you play." She looked simultaneously radiant and pale.

"Some picnic," Achilles said with a shake of his head.

"One to remember. Or forget."

"Amen to that. How'd you end up on the yacht?"

"Following you from the club was a breeze on two wheels. So was slipping aboard while they brought you downstairs. The tough part was timing my strike. I initially hid in a bow box half-stuffed with spare life preservers. It was the first suitable place I saw and I grabbed it not knowing how much time I'd have. But tactically, it was unsuitable for launching an assault. Too visible. Once both guys went back down for you, I made my way onto the hard top, where I waited for clean shots." She gave him a sideways glance. "Surely you knew I'd have your back?"

"I thought you were on your back. You've got food poisoning."

"What's that got to do with anything?"

Achilles smiled. "Apparently nothing. You mind grabbing the key from the hairy guy's pocket? I'm anxious to change my footwear."

Once freed, Achilles dragged his would-be assassins to the dive platform. He bound their ankles together with the familiar chain and snapped the lock back into place. "Better you than me," he said, and gave the pair a shove.

"How you feeling?" Jo asked as they watched the bodies vanish with a *bloop* and a few bubbles.

"Relieved, but not satisfied."

"How so?"

"Vazov is an evil crook, but he isn't Ivan."

Jo put an arm around his shoulders. "You're certain?"

"Absolutely."

"Merde. So what next?"

Achilles gestured toward the captain's chair. "You know how to operate one of these things? I've got a deck to swab."

She gave him a puzzled look.

"I'd hate to return Vazov's yacht in bad condition."

74

Canary

Albuquerque, New Mexico

The Standard Diner in downtown Albuquerque was anything but standard, at least if Michael compared it to the other places they'd stopped on the long drive from California. Cloth napkins, granite countertops and brick walls painted the first impressions. The rare ahi tuna salad on the menu completed the above-standard picture.

Team Raven began the migration from L.A. before the smoke from the explosion had cleared. Four guys in the Tesla taking turns at the wheel. A straight shot east on I-40, with an overnight in a nondescript Arizona motel.

Michael had spent a good chunk of the drive staring at the empty space in the middle of the car, and contemplating what the loss of Raven meant. Now that the shock had settled in and they'd gotten some rest, it was time to press Ivan for answers. He'd wait for the food to arrive.

The waitress appeared as if on cue, but Ivan beat Michael to the punch. "Have any of you figured it out yet? Our next move?"

They were seated at a square four-top table in the corner. Michael looked left to Boris, then right to Pavel before replying. "I think it's fair to say we're full of faith but curious, concerned and confused."

"That sounds like a rehearsed line. Is the sentiment shared?"

Pavel and Boris nodded.

"Good." Ivan took a big bite of his Reuben. The thick, marble rye sandwich was piled high with corned beef, sauerkraut and a special sauce that oozed around the edges, begging for a lick. Ivan chewed while they stewed.

Michael broke the silence. "Why is that good? Why would you want your team, your support staff confused?"

"Isn't it obvious?" Ivan met each man's eye. "Apparently not." He took another bite before continuing. "We're in uncharted territory, guys. Nobody's attempted anything like this before. I think I've got it all gamed out, but you know me, I like to be meticulous. That's pretty important when one's up against the combined forces of the CIA and FBI."

"How does keeping us confused contribute to meticulous?" Pavel asked. "I'd think it's just the opposite. I think four minds are better than one."

Ivan let the question hang.

Boris bit. "We're canaries."

Ivan brought finger to nose. "Exactly."

"I don't follow," Pavel said. "Call me stupid."

Michael didn't follow either, but he kept quiet.

"You guys know me. You guys know Raven. You guys know everything we've done, why we've done it, and how. If you still can't figure out what I'm going to do next, then I don't need to worry about the feds figuring it out, either." He chomped on a couple of fries. "Evidently, I'm carefree."

Michael set down his salad fork. "Now that you have your peace of mind, are you going to invite us behind the curtain?"

"No."

"No? Why not?"

"We're still mining coal, so to speak. But I'll give you a peek. We're going to strike another movie star, here in Albuquerque. An off-camera grab, but still good for $40 million. Then we'll do a public grab in New Orleans. After that, we'll have another sit down and you can tell me if you've figured out what's next."

"How are we going to strike anyone else after blowing up Raven?"

"Oh, I've had two other drones shipped over. They're both on location."

Excluding the initial prototypes, Team Raven had only produced four drones. Two were now available to complete their mission. Michael did the math. It wasn't difficult. "After Jenks, we still owe Vazov $482 million. That means we need to earn nearly a quarter billion per remaining drone. We got less than half that amount out of the first one."

"We were just warming up," Ivan said.

"My point exactly. That was before the world was watching and law enforcement was on high alert. When we hit Albuquerque, that will put the whole country on notice, not just California. We'll be lucky to get more than a few ops per drone after that."

"You're exactly right."

Michael thought about that for a second. "You've factored that in?"

"Of course."

How could I ever have doubted. "Care to clue us in on how we're going to make our number?"

"You've got clues."

"We do?"

"The same ones the FBI has, as befits your function."

"As befits our function," Michael repeated.

"Canaries in a coal mine," Boris said.

Michael was less than thrilled with his new title. "Care to point us in the right direction, since we're not professional investigators?"

Ivan spread his hands in gesture. "Do what they do. Look for a motive that goes beyond the immediate monetary return. Ask yourself why I killed Sangster, then kidnapped a movie star on prime time TV. Keep asking yourself as you see what we do next—and let me know immediately if you figure it out."

75

Broken Branches

French Riviera

Jo surprised herself by docking the *VaVaVoom* without scraping fiberglass or cracking wood. They tied it down in its assigned berth, and left the yacht looking as if it hadn't moved.

She paused as they were walking up the dock. "Why not steal Vazov's yacht? Or burn it? Get a jab in."

Achilles attempted a mischievous grin, but retained a rattled look. When he spoke, his tone lacked its usual exuberance. "I like your thinking, but as a rule I find it's better to confuse an opponent than to taunt him. Missing men will play to Vazov's paranoia. Are they dead? Arrested? Did they defect? Are they revealing secrets? He'll also worry about me. Am I still out there? Will I be returning? How did I get away?"

Jo saw Achilles' point, but liked the exploding-yacht idea. Let Vazov watch his baby burn on the evening news, then spend the night answering questions for the gendarmes.

But she trusted Achilles, and it wasn't her call.

He commandeered Vazov's SUV and she followed on her bike. They drove to the underground parking lot at the Monaco Heliport, and abandoned the SUV between a Porsche and a Rolls Royce.

From Monaco, they drove straight back to the hotel on her motorcycle. She was dying to sip peppermint tea and drink Pepto-Bismol, while he was looking forward to the first meal of the rest of his life. Her hand went to her stomach, however, when she heard his room service order. "Bouillabaisse?"

Achilles grew a guilty look. "Sorry. I suppose that's insensitive. I'll change my order. I felt like celebrating the fact that I can eat fish, rather than vice versa. Thanks to you," he added.

"No need to change it," she replied.

Their eyes met briefly before both looked away.

After a few seconds of strained silence, Jo said, "You're absolutely certain that Vazov isn't Ivan?"

"Positive. Our eyes met for the very first time there on the polo field."

"You were right."

"I wish I wasn't. Ivan played us, Jo. He played us like a deck of stacked cards."

"He plays everyone. That's what Ivan does, and he's the best in the world at it."

Achilles began pacing. "What bothers me most is that I didn't feel like I was being played. Before it all finally went south, I felt like I was getting the best of him. Unravelling Ivan's deepest secret and sneaking up on him from behind."

Jo wasn't sure where Achilles was headed. "You think there was more to it than simple misdirection? You think Ivan actually wanted you to investigate Vazov?"

"I do. I think he specifically set me up. Seems obvious in retrospect."

"Why would Ivan send you after Vazov?"

"I wish I knew."

"Earlier, when I suggested burning Vazov's boat to get his goat, you said the best practice was to confuse your opponent. But Vazov's not your opponent. Ivan is."

Achilles moved to the balcony window and spread the curtains wider, startling a seagull. "Clearly, they're connected. Vazov is making Ivan's drones. We know that for a fact. I've seen it with my own eyes. But just as clearly, we know that Vazov isn't in Ivan's innermost circle. If he were, he would have recognized me."

Jo followed Achilles to the window. "Do you think Ivan wanted to pit you against Vazov?"

"I do."

"But how could he predict which of you would win?"

"He couldn't. Obviously, it could have gone either way."

"So what was the point?"

"That's what we need to figure out. I'm going to go for a run.

Let you get some sleep while I generate a few endorphins."

"What about your bouillabaisse?"

"It can wait."

"Really? Cold fish soup—?"

"Figure of speech."

"I have a better idea. Let's call Agent Zonder."

Her suggestion put a bit of spark back in Achilles' eyes. "Any particular reason?"

"Gathering intelligence—and planting it. I suspect he'll be receptive to anything resembling an olive branch. While you were tied up, Ivan was wiping the floor with him." Jo recounted the debacle in Los Angeles that left the police looking helpless on live television.

Achilles shook his head. "Law enforcement has never outwitted Ivan during the commission of a crime."

"But *we* did once," Jo said. "And we will again."

Achilles pulled up a pet program on his laptop, a VOIP service that allowed him to spoof his calling location. He set it for Moscow's Sheremetyevo International Airport, since that was sure to catch Zonder's attention. Once he'd entered Zonder's cell number and hit *call*, he pivoted the laptop toward Jo. "I wonder if he's figured out who you are yet?"

Jo had little doubt.

Zonder picked up on the third ring. "Ripley Zonder."

"Remember me?"

"I'll never forget you, Agent Monfort."

Jo gave no reaction to the use of her real name. "Did you find my last tip useful?"

"Very much so. Thank you. Do you have another for me?"

"I might. But you have to earn it."

"And just how do I do that?"

"You skip the boilerplate about not commenting on an ongoing investigation and tell me what you've learned."

Silence.

Jo waited.

More silence.

She continued waiting. She knew it would come.

"We identified the drone as a VV1. Everything else is supposition."

"And what are you supposing?"

Zonder mumbled something to himself before replying. Jo couldn't hear the words, but the tone wasn't hostile. "Director Rider's assassination is related to the drone K&R operations taking place around the country."

"And?"

"And Ivan the Ghost is behind both."

"Right on both counts. What else?"

"It's your turn, Jo. Are you working with Achilles or against him?"

The question caught her by surprise. She hadn't considered the against-him interpretation. "With him, against Ivan."

"So Ivan framed Achilles."

"Yes."

"Why?"

"Four birds with one stone. One, for cover. Achilles is the only law enforcement officer known to have laid eyes on Ivan. Two, for concealment. To hide his own involvement. Three, for distraction. To focus law enforcement on hunting the wrong man. And four, for revenge. Achilles is the only person to have thwarted one of Ivan's plans."

"Well, at the very least you've short-circuited his distraction plan."

"Does that mean you're hunting Ivan?"

"We are."

"Do you have any leads?"

Silence.

Again, Jo waited.

"What's your involvement?"

"Ivan tried to kill me with a drone—the big drone—the same day he shot Rider with the little one."

"What happened? How did you escape?"

"Not relevant."

"Why did he want to kill you?"

"We think he was using me as a guinea pig."

" 'We' being you and Achilles?"

"Yes."

"Why don't you come in and work with us? Together, we'll be more efficient."

And there it was, the inevitable surrender request. "We know how politicians work. Your director will throw Achilles in jail and claim victory. Probably lock me up too, as an accessory."

"I could make arrangements to—"

"We've got a good thing going," Jo interjected. "Don't blow it with promises you know you can't keep."

Silence.

More silence.

Jo hung up.

76

The Big Easy

New Orleans, Louisiana

Albuquerque was a breeze. An evening grab in the isolated suburb of Corrales. $20 million from the star of Woody Allen's latest film, and $20 million more from the studio. It reminded Michael of the early grabs in Silicon Valley.

He wasn't expecting tonight's operation to be so simple.

Ivan informed them that New Orleans would be a public grab, but he had yet to supply the particulars. Michael found the exclusion increasingly frustrating. For decades, the two of them had been a team. Michael had felt like the father of a brilliant child, offering guidance and support in some areas, while watching with wonder in others. But now Ivan was acting like a kid going off to college and leaving his "clueless" parents behind. Michael wondered if that was it. If Ivan was simply moving on? But he worried there was something more. He worried that he'd somehow offended his best friend.

"Listen to this," Pavel said, waving his phone from the back seat of the Tesla. They were on their way to the French Quarter for a K&R Ivan had yet to define. *"The Times* is reporting that the effect of the Preston Jenks kidnapping is exactly the opposite of what common sense would dictate. Rather than becoming more reclusive, movie stars are out in droves. Sightings are way up. Even the A-listers have begun parading around public locations."

"Of course they are," Ivan said with a smile. "Predictable as dominoes. We gave Jenks the PR boost of a blockbuster movie with a cast of one."

Michael reflected on that eye-opening insight, while Pavel swiped over to a related story. "According to *Hollywood Insider,*

Jenks made more off his kidnapping than we did. Everyone knows his name now, not just the action flick fans."

"Is that it?" Michael asked. "Is that how we're going to pay off Vazov? Hold out the net and let the fish leap into it?"

"No," Ivan said, the hint of scorn in his voice digging deep as a dagger. "That's not it at all. But keep guessing."

Boris broke the tension by announcing, "There it is, on the right."

Michael saw the red neon sign half a block ahead. He turned the Tesla into the parking structure and took a ticket.

"Take it to the roof," Ivan said. "Park in the southeast corner. We'll be able to see Bourbon Street from there."

Minutes earlier, they had left Raven prepped and primed in an abandoned waterfront warehouse with a large broken window. Although the drive back across the Mississippi River had required a circuitous route, Raven was less than a mile from their current location as the drone flies.

Michael put the car in park.

Pavel checked his controls and confirmed, "Raven is ready to rock and roll."

Ivan said, "Very good. Our target is Emmy Delaney. She'll be parading down Bourbon Street atop a float in 23 minutes. Pavel, please familiarize yourself with the terrain."

"Roger that."

"Emmy Delaney," Michael repeated. "We're kidnapping America's sweetheart? She's only seventeen."

Ivan said nothing.

"Why take unnecessary risks? Why not stick with low profile victims? There are plenty of them with cash."

"Isn't it obvious?"

Michael momentarily closed his eyes. "No."

Pavel and Boris held their tongues while Ivan looked over from the passenger seat. "I don't want low profile."

"What's to be gained by high profile?"

"Isn't it obvious?"

Michael was tired of this game. "No."

"You began with a faulty assumption. The risk *is* necessary."

Necessary for what?

Ivan ended the conversation by opening his laptop. While he

went to work, Michael tried to puzzle out the long game. He didn't get anywhere before Boris brought everyone's attention back to the moment at hand. "The parade is coming. I've got eyes on Emmy."

Ivan glanced back at Pavel. "Go."

From their perch atop the parking garage, they saw slivers of Bourbon Street through breaks between buildings. They couldn't yet glimpse the parade, but they could hear it coming. Michael shifted his gaze to Ivan's laptop, where the live feed from Raven's main camera streamed like the aerial coverage of a football game.

As Raven began its swift descent, the crowd appeared oblivious to the approaching threat. All eyes were riveted on floats or on tiny screens held high above heads.

Then it happened.

Even though Michael knew it was coming, even though he'd seen it happen dozens of times, the swiftness of the snatch still surprised him. One second America's sweetheart was doing the princess wave, the next she was wrapped in a metallic ring. Pavel made it look so easy.

Thousands of spectators gasped and screamed as Raven lifted its latest victim high into the humid air—then flew away.

77

Messaging

New Orleans, Louisiana

Ivan experienced a profound surge of satisfaction as Raven swept America's sweetheart into the sky. Emmy Delaney was the woman that half of the world's teenagers wanted to be. Young, beautiful, talented, famous, rich, respected, healthy, happy—and now completely under his control. Her life was on an amazing trajectory, a rocket to the moon, but he could crash it with a snap of his fingers.

That was power.

The surge passed quickly. Ivan wasn't in this for influence. He wasn't after a rush. He wanted self-respect, satisfaction, and recognition—not just as a master criminal, but as a man who changed the course of human history, forever.

So far so good.

At that moment, perched atop a New Orleans parking garage, Ivan was taking on the whole world. Quite literally. And he was winning.

That left only three blank boxes on his big list. All would soon be checked. The first was money. Enough money to give him whatever he wanted, whenever he wanted it. Instant gratification, for the rest of his life. The second was freedom. The ability to enjoy everything the world had to offer without worry. Freedom from the fear that law enforcement might be closing in, or that a vigilante was on his trail. Freedom to make friends and start a family. The third was everlasting fame. Ivan would have that too. His final masterstroke would pen his name beside Nobel's and Oppenheimer's in the big book of human history. He was going to change the world.

With a shake of his head, Ivan returned his focus to the

game. Pavel now had Emmy dangling over Jackson Square, the historic park dedicated to the Battle of New Orleans hero who had gone on to become President. They'd whisked her three blocks east from her float on Bourbon Street, while the drunken crowd gave chase.

He turned to Pavel. "Put her directly over the statue. If she falls, I want her skewered."

"Roger that."

Ivan felt Michael flinch beside him. A subtle twitch, but telltale nonetheless. His friend was growing squeamish.

On the one hand, Ivan felt for his former mentor. He understood the difficulty of adapting to a state of relative ignorance after being on the inside for so long. On the other hand, Michael's lack of faith frustrated Ivan to no end. If Ivan had ever failed to deliver, even once, he might understand the skepticism. But his record was perfect. There was no basis for anything but full faith and allegiance—unless Michael somehow sensed what was coming.

Ivan seriously doubted that. Even the pros never saw Ivan the Ghost coming, and Michael was no pro. Not once in their twenty-plus years had his predictive powers proven remarkable.

As he glanced over, Michael made the jackpot gesture. "The twenty from the family is in the bank."

"And the producers?" Ivan asked.

"They're working on theirs."

Now that the show had gone airborne, they could observe the action directly. But Ivan watched the live news feed on his laptop as well. Raven was hovering a full 130 feet above the ground, level with the spire atop St. Lewis Cathedral. This was by design, for the cameras. As predicted, they were making the most of the artistic elements, using 19th century architecture and 21st century aeronautics to frame the timeless image of a damsel in distress.

Emmy Delaney was not attempting to mimic Preston Jenks' breakthrough tough-guy performance. And why should she? She wasn't seeking action-hero roles. She was a sweetheart hoping to make the move to leading lady.

While neither calm nor cool, to Ivan's eye Emmy appeared collected. No surprise there. One didn't become an international celebrity at seventeen without a Mensa membership and Spartan discipline. Watching with an analytical eye, Ivan understood that she was drawing her acting cues from images of Fay Wray in King Kong's palm. "Savvy move," he muttered. "She's co-opting a classic."

Michael didn't comment.

The police already had two spotlights in action, one from the ground, another from a hovering helicopter. A news chopper added a third. No doubt the crowd had swelled to the size of a U2 concert, but buildings blocked Ivan's view of the ground.

Time to give them a show.

He pulled up a special app on his laptop and began typing.

In addition to the broad framing shot, the news cameras were favoring two focal points. The first was the victim. A tight zoom on a terrorized face. The second was the clock. The bright green digital countdown displayed on Raven's belly. They tended to split the screen, displaying one above the other on the right side, with a broader context shot capturing the entire scene on the left, including their reporter.

Ivan was about to change all that. As the clock flipped from 11:48 to 11:47, he hit a button and the display went dark.

The crowd gasped loud enough for Team Raven to hear it six blocks away. The buzz of frantic conversation erupted a moment later.

After a suitable pause, Ivan hit another button and brought the display back to life. This time, however, it didn't display a clock. Instead, it began scrolling a message: GROUND THE HELICOPTERS. OR ELSE.

The background buzz grew louder.

Ivan had no doubt that within seconds his words would be creeping across Headline News crawlers on screens around the world. The only outstanding question was how the pilots would react.

But not really.

No way, no how, could any police or news organization defy his order. Not with the world watching. Not with the resultant consequences so apparent and dire.

"What's going on?" Pavel asked. Raven's digital display wasn't visible from their position.

"It's a minor coding modification," Boris replied. He pointed to the appropriate display on the Drone Command Module. "Ivan asked me to keep it confidential."

Pavel studied it for a second before asking, "What's the purpose? They might land now, but they'll still chase Raven the moment we release the hostage. It accomplishes nothing."

Ivan didn't answer.

"You can be sure it accomplishes something," Michael said. "We just don't see it yet. And neither do the police."

As those words resounded in the Tesla, the helicopters backed off and disappeared behind surrounding buildings.

Ivan tapped his keyboard and the countdown clock reappeared. 8:38, 8:37, 8:36—

"$20 million from the producers just cleared," Michael said with obvious relief.

Ivan smiled. "Well, all right then. Pavel, set Emmy down. Put her atop the horse so she can hug General Jackson. Throw our sweetheart a bone and give the photographers a money shot for tomorrow's front page."

78

Fair Warning

New Orleans, Louisiana

Applause erupted across the French Quarter when Pavel released America's sweetheart atop Jackson's statue. The ruckus crescendoed and cameras flashed like fireworks as Emmy wrapped her arms around the bronze embodiment of America's 7th President in a wholesome hug. Her next move was no less savvy. She turned her attention toward the sky as her captor climbed away—just like Fay Wray had with King Kong.

As predicted, the other helicopters rose like wraiths from behind surrounding buildings. They swung their spotlights on Raven and began edging closer.

Pavel didn't move. He waited for orders.

Ivan returned his attention to the laptop and began typing. The clock disappeared and the command reappeared. GROUND THE HELICOPTERS. OR ELSE.

"What are you doing?" Michael asked.

"Giving fair warning."

"But we have no leverage."

Indeed, the police helicopters did not budge.

Pavel kept quiet. As a former fighter pilot, he was accustomed to waiting for orders. He might be the master of his machine, but he wasn't the strategist in this situation—nor had he been in any other. He hadn't risen to the rank of general during his service, so being sidelined didn't bother him. The same could not be said for Michael.

Pavel respected Michael. He was disciplined, fair, and had been a boxing champ back in the day. That made him tough, smart and determined. But blind obedience was a trait he'd never learned, and at times like this, it was mission critical.

As if making Pavel's point, Michael stated the obvious. "If we make a threat, we have to deliver. Otherwise, we lose the power to inflict fear."

While Michael spoke, the side door of the police helicopter opened and a gunman appeared. The crowd on the ground reacted by backing away, even as a truck hauling barricades arrived.

Pavel seized the opportunity to switch the subject. "The police can't shoot because of the crowd. They're playing for the cameras."

Ivan wasn't moved. He turned to Michael and stared. He stared while the tension built and the helicopters hovered and the world watched. He stared while his message crawled across millions of television screens and Michael's mouth went dry. He stared until Michael coughed, then he said, "I deceived you guys earlier."

"You did?" Michael asked quietly, as all ears strained.

"I did."

"What about?"

"The money shot—it's not going to be Emmy atop the horse."

Pavel felt his own throat begin to go dry as Michael asked, "What then?"

Ivan turned his attention Pavel's way. "Head for Plaza Tower. Fly fast and evasive."

"Roger that," Pavel said, grabbing the stick.

When it opened its doors in 1969, the 45-story structure was the tallest in New Orleans. Alas, the glory didn't last. One Shell Square beat it by six stories just three years later. Twenty-nine years after that, however, Plaza Tower regained renown with a new tallest ranking. But this time the title came with an asterisk. An adjective to be more precise. Toxic mold and asbestos made Plaza Tower the tallest *unoccupied* building in the city, a distinction it's held ever since.

Pavel plotted a course that took them straight across the city, 1.05 miles south by southwest. Without fanfare or warning he pressed the stick, transitioning to forward flight as fast as a hovering hummingbird.

Although he appreciated the mechanical marvel at his

command, Pavel was not thrilled to be taking Raven into combat. Helicopters were faster, tougher and had a greater range. Raven's only advantages were a smaller size and greater maneuverability. Then there was firepower. He was pretty sure the police helicopter wasn't armed beyond the gunman inside, and damn sure the news bird wasn't, but he couldn't beat even a single machine gun when his only weapon was a taser. "We've got sixteen minutes before our batteries fail and Raven falls from the sky."

"Keep it low, no more than 100 feet," Ivan said.

"Yes sir," Pavel replied.

"Plaza tower rises for 45 stories, but I want you aiming for the tenth floor as if you're going to ram it."

"Roger that."

Pavel spotted the abandoned building dead ahead, with red rooftop lights flashing. A dark monolith blocking out a big swath of city lights, creating an atmosphere of desolation and foreboding.

Pavel raced toward his target at full throttle, rocking Raven back and forth as if avoiding TIE fighters with an X-wing. He had no idea what Ivan would have him do next, but he was excited to find out.

The police chopper followed about three seconds behind and fifteen feet above. A bit closer than standard pursuit formation. Pavel figured the pilot was compensating for the fact that Raven was a black bird flying at night. The news helicopter remained five seconds behind it and another fifty feet above. Pavel didn't know if they had a standard, but that felt about right.

What was Ivan up to? Had he hidden gunmen in the abandoned tower? Did he plan to fly inside? The whole planet was about to find out.

"At the last second, I want you to slip around the tower to the left, hugging it tight. Do it without slowing down."

"Roger that."

"Circle clockwise, keeping close to the tower so they lose sight of you."

"Will do."

"The moment you're hidden from the police chopper's view, stop all forward movement and take it straight up to an altitude just above their bird."

"Vertical evasion. Roger that."

"What about the news helicopter?" Michael interjected.

Ivan ignored the question and asked Pavel, "Can you pull it off?"

"I can temporarily lose them, no problem. But if they've got a veteran behind the stick he'll reacquire us in about four seconds."

"Then that's how long you have."

"To do what?"

"Drop The Claw into the enemy's rotor, and hit Raven's SELF-DESTRUCT button."

79

Missing Picture

French Riviera

Achilles burst onto the balcony his room shared with Jo's. Having just pounded out thirteen contemplative miles running along the beach, he was dripping with sweat and brimming with excitement. After days of getting nowhere attempting to anticipate Ivan's next moves, he finally had an idea he could work with.

He was eager to share it with Jo, but before he got the words out, she shared news of her own.

"While you were out running, Ivan wiped the floor with law enforcement. Again. This time in New Orleans." Jo recounted the debacle that downed a police helicopter and killed four officers on live television.

Achilles shook his head. "Ivan's never been one to issue hollow threats."

"Or tolerate disobedience," Jo said. "But the New Orleans police don't know it's Ivan."

He flopped onto a lounge chair, twisted the top off a cold bottle of water, and shared his own revelation. "I was wrong earlier."

"How so?" Jo asked.

He drained the bottle before responding. "I said Ivan couldn't predict whether I'd kill Vazov or vice versa. But of course he could. I've been so stupid."

"What are you talking about?"

Achilles tossed the empty bottle and went to work with a hand towel while he spoke. "No way he'd leave the outcome of my meeting with Vazov to chance. Ivan always lines up every domino before he topples the first."

"You and Vazov aren't inanimate blocks of wood. How could he expect to control your meeting?"

Actually, people are highly predictable. Marketers and propagandists proved that every day. But Achilles wasn't about to chase that rabbit. "He didn't need to manage our every action to manipulate the outcome. He just needed to control the flow of information."

"I don't follow."

"He's got an inside man, Jo. Or rather, he had an inside man."

That perked her up. "One of the bodyguards?"

Achilles nodded. "The bald guy from the boat. Just before his thugs jumped me, Vazov gloated that Gleb had uncovered my true identity."

"Inside guy or not, you still escaped."

"Only thanks to you."

Jo cocked her head. "But Ivan knew about me."

"Yes, he did. And he accounted for you in his plan. You were supposed to have died back in Versailles. He pushed that domino at the same time he sent me on the path to Vazov. Ivan's only shortcoming was failing to account for the miracle of your survival."

"But that was weeks ago. He's had time to adapt."

"Calendar time, but not free time. Ivan's in the midst of a wild and crazy operation in America. He's bound to be completely consumed with its execution. He's got no time to concentrate on anything else. Trust me, you can't rewrite the field manual while in the field. That's something you do during breaks between operations."

"But this is Ivan the Ghost we're talking about. He's the best there ever was. Surely he has the ability to adapt on the ground. Every field agent does that."

"Ivan doesn't work like everyone else. He doesn't improvise, he plans—with incredible detail. That's what makes him so special. He spends years designing operations as complex as Swiss chronographs—the big ones that factor in leap years and phases of the moon. Then he executes, trusting the machine he built to run with clocklike precision. He has faith in his ability to account for everything during the planning stage, and history has justified that faith."

"Until now."

"Until now. This time he didn't account for your miraculous escape screwing up his plan to have Vazov kill me."

"Which was supposed to happen when his man Gleb unmasked you at a vulnerable moment."

"Exactly."

Jo stood silently, intermittently twirling a lock of hair around her index finger and tugging on it.

Achilles waited quietly while she puzzled it out.

"If everything you say is true, about the dominoes and faith and the informant, then Ivan's plan for you started with framing you for Rider's murder, and ended with having you killed by Vazov's men."

"Correct."

"What was the point?"

"*That* is the billion-dollar question."

Jo gave him a knowing look. "If I know you, you have a hypothesis."

Achilles wished he could justify her confidence. "I haven't come up with anything that accounts for everything, not when you factor the drone kidnappings into the picture."

"So what do we do?"

Achilles tossed the towel through the balcony doorway and onto his bed. "I don't know, but I think we need to back up to figure it out."

Jo's eyes grew wide. "Back up? As in retreat?"

"Back up as in change our perspective. We thought we were looking at the big picture, but we haven't been. We couldn't have been. What we see doesn't make sense, and Ivan's plans always make sense—in hindsight. We need to picture his plan with foresight."

"But Ivan's genius is devising endgames that nobody can predict. That's why he never gets caught."

"I know."

"So how do we predict his plan this time?"

"We put our heads together, take what we know, and apply it to the broader picture."

Jo's face contorted into an expression one might describe as less than optimistic—which was exactly how Achilles felt.

80

High Net Worth

Northern Kentucky

Michael didn't understand the man racing through the back woods of Kentucky on a $140,000 motorcycle. Why would anyone with a net worth of nine figures risk his life against a random encounter with a stray deer or loose gravel? And Billy Burns wasn't just zipping around corners at breakneck speeds. He was doing it without the protection of full leathers or a brain bucket. Just boots and a black jacket—emblazoned with a rebel flag.

To Billy's credit, the roads were remote and the weather was dry. He'd found the equivalent of a private racing track, a six-mile loop full of twists and turns, with only a single stop sign.

Michael had his eye on that sign because Raven was waiting in the woods behind it.

The Confederate P51's top speed was a full 100 mph above Raven's, so the stop sign was important. Billy habitually ignored it—as did others if the bullet holes were a clue—but nonetheless the 90-degree turn took his speed down to the mid double-digits.

Michael, Pavel and Boris were parked atop a neighboring hill, waiting for Billy to come back around, while Ivan dealt with other business.

After New Orleans, they embarked on what the three now dubbed their America Tour. To help them better blend into the heartland, they traded in the Tesla for a Chevy Suburban. White with blackout-tint on the windows. Its 0 to 60 acceleration was three times slower than the Tesla's, and its handling wasn't nearly as tight, but they'd never been forced to test their car's capabilities. Hopefully that lucky streak would hold.

Team Raven switched their focus as well—from CEOs and celebrities to high-net-worth individuals. People whose only notable characteristic was a very big bank account.

Pavel made conversation while they waited for Billy to come 'round. "I gotta say, I like these nobodies a lot better. Why deal with lawyers and corporations and helicopter attacks if you don't have to?"

Michael knew he should keep his mouth shut, but he couldn't resist venting. "Because these guys don't have enough cash on hand. Their money is all tied up in real estate or family businesses or long-term investments."

"What are you talking about? Every one of them has shelled out $10 million."

"$10 million a pop is only half of what we need. As of today we're $150 million behind with Vazov, and the trend isn't in our favor. Plus we're down to our last drone."

"Man, you gotta have faith in Ivan. You told me yourself he's never let you down."

Boris shocked them both by wading in. He was usually the silent stoic, only speaking when the mission required. "I have to admit, I'm a bit baffled by the way things are evolving."

"How so?" Michael asked.

"The downside of involving the media and antagonizing the police is abundantly clear. The upside isn't. This change of tactic is contrary to the thing I appreciate most about Ivan. The quality that drew me to him."

"Namely?"

"His ability to operate as a ghost."

While they reflected on Boris's observation, the deep bass of the P51 began rumbling through the Suburban's open front windows, signaling Billy's impending arrival.

Pavel pulled the joystick's collective, raising Raven into the air and positioning it in a predetermined striking posture, with Claw dropped and lance raised. Once Billy passed a rock they'd positioned beside the road as a visual aid, Pavel would take Raven to full speed and set it on an intercept course. The idea was to rocket up at an angle while the target slowed for the turn.

Michael cocked an ear, but couldn't hear the drone over the raucous rumble of the mighty motorcycle. Billy, of course, wouldn't hear a thing. He wouldn't be studying his surroundings either, just the next few seconds of road.

The three stared down from their hilltop as the target approached, 200 pounds of rebel atop 500 pounds of steel. Or rather aluminum, Michael corrected himself. The P51 looked like a monster, a triangular wedge of mechanical might that Boris claimed was very high-tech. He raved about its carbon fiber wheels, quadruple front discs and 6061 aluminum construction. Impressive as that apparently was to those who understood such things, Michael suspected that Billy would soon be happy to swap the Confederate for four standard wheels and a driver's airbag.

Pavel pressed Raven into action as Billy roared past the rock.

Two heavy heartbeats later, Billy swung around the corner as if the stop sign wasn't there and began accelerating up the winding road that would take him higher into the hills.

Raven swooped down like a falcon attacking a flying duck—and missed.

Michael couldn't tell if Billy swerved to avoid something in the road or if he somehow sensed the predator behind. Whatever the reason, Pavel's first miss took everyone by surprise.

While the trio held their breaths, The Claw closed on thin air and Billy hit the brakes. As Raven flew by, Michael saw recognition dawn. The infamous drone. The serpentine snare. The ransom demand. Once the tumblers had clicked in their victim's mind, Michael saw something that shocked him to his core. Billy smiled.

He yelled something they couldn't hear and hit the gas with enthusiasm as Pavel brought Raven back around. The P51 exploded forward like a bullet from a gun—and the chase was on.

Except, of course, it wasn't.

Raven couldn't hope to keep up with the Confederate, even cutting corners by flying straight above the winding road.

Within seconds, the motorcycle vanished along with their payday.

"What do we do?" Michael asked.

"Drive!" Pavel commanded. "We'll intercept him on the other

side of the hill."

Boris hit the gas without further hesitation, putting all 355 horses of the 5.3 liter engine to work.

It felt pitifully slow.

Now that they finally needed the Tesla's ludicrous speed, they didn't have it.

"He'll be heading for home, taking the road he knows," Pavel continued. "He'll stick to the next five miles of his course before branching off toward Lexington. We'll go the other way around. Clockwise, that branch is just one mile from here."

"Won't he take a random route in the name of evasion?"

"You saw his face. He's excited. He's riding lightning, so he's thinking speed. That's his tactic and he'll maximize it using the road he knows."

"You can't snare him at 160 mph."

"No, I can't. That's why we have to intercept him in the Suburban."

"Roadblock?" Boris asked, driving like he was attempting to qualify for the Indy 500, and doing a fine job despite the limitations of his ride.

"Yeah. Preferably just after a curve."

"If we create a roadblock, he'll see us. And he'll see the car. He's bound to give the police our description."

"Three white guys in a Chevy? That might be a problem in Kyoto, but not here in Kentucky."

Boris shook his head. "I hope you're right, because about twenty seconds from now we're going to find out."

81

Bad Returns

French Riviera

Vlad Vazov liked to live on the edge. In fact, he insisted on it. And when you're the only son of one of Russia's richest men, you tend to get what you want.

Whether his aversion to *average* or *normal* or *ordinary* experiences was a genetic predisposition or the result of a spoiled youth, Vlad didn't know or care. He just knew that he craved extremes the way other people craved coffee—or chocolate or poker or porn. His brain didn't sit right in the absence of risk and stimulation. That was why he loved polo.

No other team sport offered both extreme danger and intense competition without also subjecting you to an unpleasant environment, be it inclement weather or common people. He had tried to get his fix from solo activities—skiing and sky diving and rock climbing—but they didn't satisfy his social nature or need to command other men. In that latter regard, and perhaps only that latter regard, Vlad resembled his famous father.

So polo it was. Polo and the appearance of enough ancillary activity to keep his father both distant and content. The figurehead position at Silicon Hill checked that box nicely—with prestige as a welcome bonus.

His father had given him the $300 million to get Silicon Hill started, not knowing the details of his arrangement with Ivan. When Ivan paid out, Vlad would tell his father he'd sold the business. Then he'd pocket the proceeds and "retire." He'd gain financial independence and his father would get bragging rights. The whole plan was nothing short of brilliant.

Not so brilliant was the performance of his bodyguards.

Achilles had chewed through them like a Rottweiler on a new pair of shoes. He would be upgrading, just not with ex-CIA agents.

Vlad checked his watch. Gleb and Gary had gone incommunicado. It was probably nothing, but he wasn't taking chances. He eventually sent Sergey and Alex after them, and locked himself in his house—a house that was essentially a 10,000-square-foot panic room. They'd been gone for three hours. It was getting late and he was anxious to finish the practice session their departure had cut short.

Motion on one of the security monitors caught his eye as he reached for the phone. Turning toward the bank of screens covering one of his study walls, Vlad saw an SUV driving through the guard gate. Sergey and Alex were back.

He met them at the door and immediately knew the news wouldn't be good. Their body language wasn't telegraphing happy.

"No sign of them, boss," Sergey said.

"The boat's at the marina, but the car's at the heliport," Alex added.

Vlad wasn't sure he'd heard correctly. "At the heliport?"

"We called Mercedes and had them track the GPS," Sergey said.

"No police involvement," Alex added.

The Monaco Heliport was almost exclusively used to shuttle people between Nice International Airport and the Principality of Monaco. The scenic seven-minute flight gave visitors their first taste of the glamour most were seeking when visiting one of the world's most exclusive pieces of property. But Vlad knew that flights could be arranged to anywhere in Southern France or Northern Italy, even Switzerland and Lichtenstein.

Questions pelted him like feces flung from angry monkeys. Had Achilles bought off Gleb and Gary? Did the CIA intervene? Were his henchmen being debriefed by his enemies at that very moment? Vlad grasped for affirming answers.

"How did the boat look?"

Sergey shrugged. "Like usual."

"No sign they took it out?"

"None."

Last he'd seen them, Achilles was bound hand and foot, and buckled into the back seat with a Sig's sights centered on his chest. Escape was impossible. So had Achilles been assisted, or had Vlad been betrayed? That was the killer question.

"What's your next move?"

The bodyguards glanced at one another before Sergey spoke. "We figured it best to get your direction on that."

So they had nothing. Vlad appraised his two remaining bodyguards. Sergey had retired from Moscow's Dynamo hockey team. He never wanted to see ice again, but was as cold and hard as a Russian winter. Alex had become a bouncer in his teens and moved to bodyguarding in his early twenties. At three hundred pounds, he weighed nearly twice what Vlad did, and at six-foot-eight he approached Vlad's horseback height. "Let's have that discussion out on the field. Follow me."

Vlad had not yet disciplined his men for being bested by Achilles. He resolved to rectify that while pondering his predicament—and verifying that Achilles hadn't robbed either bodyguard of his balls.

He motioned for the men to follow him and headed for the stables. Without a word, he hopped on his horse and trotted toward the nearest goal posts, forcing them to follow at a run. Once he neared the posts, he turned around and gestured with his arms like a runway traffic controller. "I want you to stand directly between the goal posts."

The men complied.

Vlad continued gesturing with his arms until his bodyguards were lined up equidistant between each other and the goal posts, effectively creating a set of human goal posts. "Perfect. Now don't move."

A dozen polo balls remained scattered about the near end of the field, remnants of his earlier practice session. Vlad trotted out and spun around to survey the scene from center field. His human goal posts were a yard shorter than the originals, and spaced only one-third as wide, but both were equally unmoving. So far.

With a quick kick and a staccato shout, Vlad took his mount to a full gallop, charging toward the furthest ball at a peak speed he knew was north of 50 mph. Standing in the stirrups he whipped the mallet through a full arc, connecting at the midpoint and creating the sweet crack all polo players crave. The ball flew straight and true, passing between his men at knee height.

Neither appeared to flinch, although their sunglasses blocked Vlad's view of their eyes. He took it down to a trot and circled back around.

The second ball nearly clipped Alex's elbow, but again neither man moved. He put the third and fourth through at head height. Both men were sweating visibly, but then the late afternoon sun was still hot and bright, and they'd been running.

As Vlad was about to hit the fifth ball, his watch alerted him to an incoming call. A rare call from Ivan. He'd been wondering when the inevitable extension request would come. Torn between taking the call and finishing his practice, Vlad decided to do both.

82

The Finger

Cleveland, Ohio

Whereas only hours earlier Ivan had been euphoric, an unexpected development back in France had his mood morphing from irritated to concerned. It began when his spy, Vazov's security chief, failed to confirm the execution of Kyle Achilles. Gleb had texted, "It will be done in an hour." Then six hours passed without word. Now Gleb wasn't answering his phone.

Ivan was holed up in a Cleveland hotel room with a laptop to his left and a cell to his right. The laptop displayed a live feed of the Kentucky operation that ought to be kicking into action at any moment. The phone displayed another French number—a number he was reluctant to call.

After a few seconds of hesitation, Ivan hit the green button.

"If you're calling to ask for an extension, you can forget it. I've waited long enough." Vazov had a habit of getting right to the point. Rich brats could afford to do away with pleasantries.

Knowing this, Ivan had his reply locked and loaded. "Well, then I'm glad I don't need one."

This clearly caught Vazov by surprise, but he recovered quickly. "My bank account begs to differ. You're $150 million behind on your payments, with just ten days to produce the remaining $350 million."

Ivan wanted to point out that he was actually $250 million ahead according to their written agreement. He wasn't contractually obliged to pay anything in advance. But he bit back that retort and leveraged the convenient opening. "You sound frustrated, Vlad. What's going on?"

"Frustrated? No, I'm beyond frustrated. Hold on a sec."

Ivan heard the thunder of hooves and the crack of a polo mallet. Some background commotion followed, then Vazov yelled, "Be glad it wasn't six inches lower."

"You still there?" Vazov asked.

"Yep. You feeling better?"

"Not really. Tell me, how do you find good men?"

Now we're talking. "Why, what happened?"

"I caught an American infiltrating my club. An allegedly-former CIA agent. I asked two of my guys to show him the ocean floor. They drove off with him bound hand and foot—and haven't come back. Their car turned up at the Monaco heliport."

Exactly what Ivan had feared. "Whoa!"

"Tell me about it."

"So the American is alive?"

"I can only assume."

Damn! "You think your guys took a bribe or made a deal?"

"An hour ago, I would have said 'never.' But there are only a few scenarios that explain the facts in evidence and those are two of them."

While Vazov was speaking, Ivan watched Pavel miss his mark in Kentucky. The motorcycle swerved and accelerated and disappeared from the screen. Vazov asked him something, but the words didn't register. "Vlad, I'm sorry. Something's come up requiring my immediate attention. Good luck with your runaways. We'll talk soon." He hung up without waiting for a reply.

Pavel had missed. Pavel had missed and Achilles was alive.

Achilles was alive!

He was alive, and now he knew that Vazov wasn't Ivan the Ghost.

He was alive, and still on the hunt.

Did he know anything? Did he know enough? Ivan couldn't calculate all the ramifications on the spot. In any case, Achilles would have to be eliminated. Quickly. That planning and execution would have to wait, however. He had to handle Kentucky first.

As he hit the speed dial that would connect him with Michael, Ivan felt something he hadn't experienced in living memory. A cold finger of fear ran up his stomach and around his heart.

83

A Terrible Truth

Northern Kentucky

Michael pressed the phone to his ear as Pavel shouted "Here. Stop here!" and Boris screeched to a stop with a twist of the wheel that left the Suburban blocking both lanes of the road. Billy Burns could still squeak by, but he'd be risking ditches on both sides. "Can I call you back in five minutes? We're pretty busy at the moment."

"I can see that," Ivan said. "Put me on speaker."

Michael did.

Ivan immediately took command. "Boris, back up so he can't pass behind you! Pavel, hover Raven behind the Suburban so he won't see it when he comes around the corner!"

"Roger that."

"How far is it to the corner? How much time will he have to react once he sees you?"

"About a hundred yards," Boris said. "That will give him less than two seconds at a speed north of 100 mph."

"Okay. Okay. When he sees you, he'll aim for the hole. That will be impulse. Motorcyclists are conditioned to automatically avoid hazards. Meanwhile, the back of his brain will be warning him to watch out for Raven. So the instant you spot him, pull Raven into view above the gap. At that point, he'll have no choice but to—"

"There he is!" Michael shouted.

Pavel swung into action.

Time seemed to slow as Michael watched Billy's emotional roller-coaster ride. The awareness of an unexpected obstacle.

The hope of an untended gap. The horror of an impending attack. As Raven rose to fill the void, Michael heard the frantic screech of clamping brakes and the frenetic squeal of burning rubber. He saw Billy's realization that he had to reverse course, his fear that he wouldn't have time, and his bracing for the inevitable collision.

The P51 slid sideways, eating concrete with the broad side of both tires, while Billy struggled to remain upright.

Pavel pounced on the opportunity. Determined to limit his losing streak to a single miss, he kept his eyes locked on the proverbial ball. But rather than chasing his quarry, he positioned the snake on an intercept course and let Billy come to him. "Gotcha!"

He spoke too soon.

Billy didn't release his bike.

The rebel kept his hands rapped around the handlebars, effectively anchoring himself with 500 pounds of metal. Moving metal. The P51 and its rebellious rider slid into the Suburban, dragging Raven behind like a big black balloon.

Suddenly, Billy was right there on the other side of the tinted glass, leering in at them with defiance in his eyes. Michael had never been up close and personal with one of their victims. When Billy raised a fist, Michael found himself feeling an affinity for the rich hillbilly.

It didn't last.

Billy remembered Raven and resumed his two-fisted grip on the handlebar.

"Zap him with the stun gun," Ivan shouted.

"I am," Pavel replied. "The leather jacket is shielding him. It's a thick son of a bitch, designed to prevent road rash."

"So shoot him with the taser!"

"Working on it. I gotta hit his legs, but the angle's not right."

Michael turned his attention to Raven, which was attempting to tug its prey away from the Suburban by lining up the force vector with the bike's wheels. Billy was foiling that effort by clamping on the brakes.

"He can outlast Raven's battery," Ivan said. "You've got to hit him over the head. Stun him into losing his grip."

Boris said, "I don't know what the new Taser will do if it hits his head. Remember, we switched to an experimental military-grade system, one that typically renders victims unconscious for three minutes."

"I'm not talking about the Taser. Michael, get your ass out of the car and punch him in the face. Or the kidneys. Or wherever it takes to make him let go of the damn handlebars."

Everybody looked at Michael.

Without a word, Michael opened the passenger door and walked toward the back, intent on approaching the raging rebel from behind. The P51 had no mirrors so Billy wouldn't see him coming. Michael would end this embarrassing incident with a single sucker punch.

He marched around the rear of the SUV, fists flexed and shoulders forward—and caught Billy's eye in the Suburban's rearview mirror. *Crap!*

Michael moved fast, closing the gap while rolling back his right shoulder, readying to release a mighty blow to the base of the biker's unprotected skull.

Billy moved faster. Or at least further. With a twist of the wrist, his motorcycle lunged forward like a cheetah at the start of a strike. He arced around until he was pointing parallel to the road and out of punching range. It was only a few yards, but it was enough to illuminate a terrible truth. Terrible for Michael and Ivan and Boris and Pavel. The P51 could drag Raven—and this was their last drone.

84

Emergency

Northern Kentucky

Ivan felt his own fists clenching as Billy Burns outmaneuvered them again. It was one thing after another today. "Get Michael back in the car and chase the bastard!"

"On it," Boris said.

"What are we looking at? How's Raven stack up against the bike?" Ivan knew his engineer would have checked the P51's specs. He was like that.

"Their torque and horsepower ratings are surprisingly similar, but Raven is in the air while the motorcycle is braced by the ground. Bottom line, we can slow him, but we can't stop him. Oh, and by the way, the bike's full name is the P51 Combat Fighter. How's that for ironic?"

Nobody chuckled.

Pavel said, "We're down to 36 minutes of battery life."

Ivan wasn't particularly worried about battery, yet. Billy used his cell phone for electronic banking, so they wouldn't burn clock getting a third party on the line or convincing him that the threat was real. Billy would personally make the transfer—as fast as humanly possible—once they had him hanging at altitude.

Ivan heard the car door slam and knew Michael was back. He couldn't see the Suburban, just the live feeds from Raven's cameras. Those cameras showed that Billy was getting the hang of driving with a tether. He couldn't open the throttle wide because that put too big a strain on his hands. They were at their limit anchoring him to the bike. And on top of that, he needed his hands to control the brakes, clutch and throttle. Ivan figured Billy's grip would give well before Raven's battery.

But he wasn't without worry.

Kentucky was full of trucks sporting shotgun racks and NRA stickers. The last thing the current clusterfuck needed was a showdown with a couple of good ol' boys eager for glory.

Ivan got an idea. "Stop fighting him. Put Raven in neutral and let him pull you without resistance."

"Roger that," Pavel replied.

Ivan loved military men. No backtalk. No fuss. Just rapid execution on tap.

Billy responded as predicted. As the tension eased off, he rolled his shoulders, subconsciously at first and then deliberately. After a few seconds, he gave the bike more gas.

Ivan waited for Michael's usual challenge, but it didn't come. Perhaps the failure had humbled him, temporarily of course. "Now fly with him. Don't give him any resistance."

Again, Pavel complied.

Again, Michael remained silent.

Again, Billy went faster. That was good. Faster was Ivan's goal.

"40–50–60–70 mph," Pavel announced.

Ivan smiled. It was almost too easy. "Next tight turn, I want you to go full throttle against it. He turns right, you pull left."

"Roger that."

Six seconds later, Pavel executed as ordered. While Billy took the bike into a half hairpin at 70 mph, Raven suddenly shot sideways, pulling hard against the turn and wreaking havoc on the centripetal forces that kept riders glued to the ground. Billy fought it, but momentum was against him—as was the edge of the road. He held on for about a second and a half before losing control of the curve. With the P51 destined to go over the edge, Billy had to choose between riding it into the wooded ravine or releasing. The former would be suicide, but Ivan knew better than to second-guess pride.

Billy released.

Ivan saw no explosion and heard no crash as the $140,000 toy disappeared into the wooded ravine, but celebratory whoops erupted from the Suburban. They'd won.

"Back to business as usual, boys," Ivan announced, although he wasn't so sure. He couldn't be sure of anything with Achilles on the loose.

When Ivan planned his operations, he used a sophisticated software program that allowed him to connect people, places, ideas and actions according to their relationships and interdependencies—all against the dimension of time. He reckoned the resultant map resembled a NASA playbook, although he suspected that it was even more sophisticated. People were less predictable than particles, and Ivan didn't get to operate in a vacuum.

He'd begin a full-blown impact analysis of the Achilles factor as soon as he hung up the phone. Even without examining that spaghetti bowl, however, Ivan knew that minimizing Achilles' ability to interfere would be the smart move. He'd done that from the beginning by setting the CIA and FBI after him. But this unpleasant new twist called for increased heat. Even with the distraction of an ongoing op, Ivan only needed seconds to figure out how to apply it.

As part of the prep for every K&R, Ivan fed MiMiC every available recording of the victim's voice. That way if the victim freaked out or blacked out in the midst of the operation, Ivan could continue the banking conversation in his place. To date, it had never been necessary but, Ivan being Ivan, he remained prepared. For contingencies. Like this one.

He tuned back in to the Billy Burns operation. Ivan expected to hear a barrage of cussing and bluster, but Billy sounded more like a businessman than a biker. Of course, he was a businessman. An oil businessman. He bought land and drilled holes. He'd made a fortune tapping Mother Earth, and now Ivan was going to make a fortune tapping him.

"Why don't we make it $7 million, and part as friends?"

By Ivan's accounting, Billy was the first with the balls to negotiate. He admired the machismo, foolhardy though it was. Shame that the southern gent was about to become the victim of bad timing.

He texted Michael while Michael was explaining the facts of life to Billy. A few seconds later, Michael texted back. "Billy doesn't have $20 million cash. Intel says fourteen."

"The ask is twenty."

"We'll get nothing."

"The ask is twenty."

Ivan set down his burner cell and collected his thoughts. He heard one additional text from Michael come through, then another, but he didn't bother glancing at the screen. There was nothing left to say and he had more pressing business.

His thoughts in order, Ivan picked up the MiMiC phone. He typed Billy's cell number into the CALL FROM box and selected *Billy Burns* on the VOICE menu. In the CALL TO box he typed 9-1-1.

85

The Show

Cleveland, Ohio

Kevin Thompson was not among the top five earners on Cleveland's basketball team, but he still took home over $10 million a year. In Michael's book, that was the ideal scenario. You get the pay and the play without the paparazzi problem.

Michael enjoyed a similar setup of sorts as Ivan the Ghost's invisible sidekick. Or at least he used to. Although he was still playing the game, Ivan no longer consulted him on strategic planning. Michael had no idea why, and it frustrated him to no end. He was also nervous about his big payout, his championship bonus. In that regard, he was no longer alone.

"Why on earth did Ivan call 9-1-1 posing as Billy Burns?" Boris asked. "What good does it do us for them to have his last words leading every newscast?"

"I want to know why he walked away from the toughest $10 million we ever earned." Pavel added. "It makes no sense. And now, going after celebrities again with all the attention they bring. Why do that when we don't have to? Seems crazy."

They were parked outside a boutique hotel in the old money part of Cleveland, out by the Cleveland Clinic and the Institute of Art, waiting for Thompson to emerge from his latest extramarital rendezvous. He kept a room there for discreet meetings with fans of a certain caliber, and made use of it more nights than not.

"It makes sense," Michael said with a ring of certainty. "We just don't see it. Consider that a good thing. If we can't see Ivan's play from our courtside seats, the FBI's got to be completely clueless up in nosebleed."

Boris wasn't buying it. "Frankly, I'm less concerned about

capture than I am about losing my bonus. How far behind are we?"

By bonus, Boris was referring to the one-percent share of Silicon Hill he'd receive when Ivan bought it back from Vazov. While Michael was contemplating an appropriate answer, the passenger door opened and Ivan slid in. They hadn't seen him for days, but he still skipped the pleasantries and got straight to business. "What's our status?"

"The girl's been there for nearly an hour. Thompson showed up twenty minutes ago."

Ivan turned to Pavel. "Where's Raven? I didn't spot it."

"There's a grand old cemetery, just north of here. Thompson's Maserati is parked in that direction at the edge of the lot, isolated from the danger of undisciplined doors. I can fly Raven to it faster than Thompson can walk."

"Good."

Ivan turned back to Michael but adjusted the rearview mirror so that he could glimpse the boys in the back seat as well. "I'm sure you have a few questions after Kentucky?"

Nobody commented, but the absolute stillness told Michael that Ivan had their undivided attention. Michael had to split his own, lending Ivan his ears while keeping his eyes on the hotel exits.

"Let me begin to answer by throwing a question back at you. What's the biggest industry in the United States?"

Boris was first to struggle past the non sequitur and offer a guess. "It's got to be healthcare, if the nightly news is any indication."

"Nope. Healthcare is number two."

"Retail trade," Pavel guessed.

"That's number four."

"Manufacturing?" Boris asked.

"Durables are number three. *Insurance* is number one. Insurance companies bank $1.2 trillion in policy premiums every year. $1,200,000,000,000. That's thirteen digits of bank. Four commas. A staggering sum."

Michael had no idea why Ivan was talking about the American economy, and given that nobody else was reacting aloud, he figured he wasn't alone. He was about to ask when the hotel's side door opened and a six-foot-seven shadow emerged. "Thompson's on the move!"

The announcement acted like a firing pin pressing Pavel into immediate action. He had his hands maneuvering controls before Michael closed his lips.

The other three locked their eyes on the celebrity basketball player. He was crossing the parking lot with what Michael considered an appropriate swagger. He had just completed nature's primary conquest and was walking toward the embodiment of another.

Raven appeared over his head like a blustery black cloud.

Thompson glanced back to investigate the atmospheric disturbance, but only halfheartedly. He didn't break his stride. Reaching the Maserati, he grabbed the driver's door handle— and nothing happened.

Like most popular automotive technologies, touch-activated door locks first appeared in luxury vehicles and then spread down the auto industry ecosystem, replacing button-activated systems in all but budget brands. From a user perspective, the touch-based systems are both more fun and more convenient than the button-activated ones. From an engineering perspective, they are essentially identical, save for the initiation mechanism. Both require wireless communication between the key fob and the car's computer control module. Both operate on the industry assigned frequency of 433 MHz.

If you want to prevent a key fob from locking or unlocking a door, all you have to do is blast the car's computer control module with enough noise at 433 MHz to prevent it from hearing the key fob. It is a process known as jamming, and Team Raven was using it to keep Kevin Thompson preoccupied and stationary for a few crucial seconds.

"Bingo!" Boris said as Pavel picked Thompson from the pavement while he fumbled with the fob. Boris spoke too soon. The basketball player grabbed the door handle and locked it in his iron grip.

Raven pulled hard enough to flip Thompson upside down, but the player held fast.

Pavel didn't hesitate. He shocked Thompson with the stun gun.

Thompson flinched as if it was the car and not Raven that had bitten him. The instant he released, Raven rocketed skyward.

Michael immediately initiated the ransom call with Thompson's agent.

Ivan said, "The art museum is a mile southeast of here. Pavel, I want you to dangle Thompson over the patio outside the East Wing. It's the big glass cube they use for special exhibitions."

"Roger that."

"You'll find it lit up bright for a fundraiser tonight. We're going to give the highbrow Cleveland crowd some unscheduled entertainment."

86

New Policy

Cleveland, Ohio

When Pavel joined the Voyenno-Vozdushnye Sily, the Russian Air Force, he did so knowing that he was volunteering to become a tool. An instrument of destruction. A weapon wielded by his motherland.

Except not really.

It wasn't Mother Russia that issued orders. That function was fulfilled by a squadron commander, or a group commander, or a wing commander. All flesh and blood mortals. All fallible. All subject to human foibles and fatigues. Everyone has a boss, of course, but only commanders send you into combat. Only commanders get you killed. Pavel had breathed easier after resigning from the military and leaving that vulnerability behind.

It wasn't until Kentucky that Pavel realized he was back in a combat role—and subject to a commander's whims. Prior to Team Raven's physical confrontation with Billy Burns, the remote nature of drone operations had kept his exposure on par with playing a video game.

Kentucky was also the first time that Pavel questioned the wisdom of his new commander. Walking away from an eight-figure payday? Killing an admirable, innocent man? Then impersonating their victim on a 9-1-1 call, a call that garnered round-the-clock media play and made them public enemy number one? Pavel didn't see the strategic genius in that. Then again, maybe it took one to know one.

And today. *What was all that talk about the relative rankings of American industry?* One had to wonder if the great Ghost was becoming unhinged. Was Ivan going to take them all down in a self-destructive psychosis, like the loony leader of a crazy cult?

Or was he crazy like a fox? The foxiest fox in the forest. Pavel was far from certain, but wary ... wary he was.

Now was not the time for timidity, however. Pavel called on the discipline he'd developed during countless hours of intense training to push those thoughts off the side burner and out of his mind. With a long, slow exhale, he returned his full focus to the battle at hand. The victim was airborne. The ransom payment was processing. The media, fans, onlookers and police were swarming the scene like ants and bees. *One of Cleveland's beloved sons was battling mortal danger!* The sensation was irresistible.

"The first $20 million is in," Michael reported.

"Family?" Ivan asked. Families were usually fastest because their stakes were the highest.

"Franchise. The team is riding high on a PR wave and the owners aren't about to jeopardize that. The family tells me they're facing technical challenges, but assures me they will work through them *pronto*. Their word."

"Sounds to me like it's time for act two," Ivan said.

Act two? What act two? Pavel wondered. He heard Ivan typing with dramatic flourish and saw that he was interfacing with the Drone Command Module, as he'd done when issuing the OR ELSE warnings back in New Orleans. Given the way the software worked, Pavel wouldn't see the message any sooner than the rest of the world. He was clueless as to what it would be, but figured it would answer his question about crazy.

He looked over to see Ivan paused with his right index finger raised over the keyboard. Ivan met his eye and asked, "What do you pay for auto insurance?"

The pilot didn't see that question coming, but he had the answer on the tip of his tongue. Pavel had the need for speed, so he drove a Porsche—and the insurance wasn't cheap. "About a thousand euros a month."

"So you've got a good policy? High coverage limits?"

"Yes."

"Ever have a major accident?"

"No."

"Ever expect to?"

"No."

"So why shell out every month?"

Pavel shrugged. "Because you never know."

"So you're paying for peace of mind."

Pavel thought about it. "I guess I am."

"So tell me this: if your bank account was flush, if you had more money than you'd ever really need, what would you pay for peace of mind?"

Again, Pavel thought about his answer. Again, it didn't take long. "Whatever it took."

"Without hesitation?"

"Sure, so long as I remain rich."

Ivan turned toward Boris and then Michael. "You guys feel the same?"

"Sure," both said, their tones telegraphing the same trepidation Pavel was feeling.

"Excellent! Because we're banking on that being the prevailing reaction." Ivan punctuated his exclamation by pressing the return button and changing Raven's display.

87

Percentages

Cleveland, Ohio

Pavel shifted his focus from Ivan to the section of the Drone Command Module that mirrored Raven's digital display. It took him a second to decipher the green text crawling across the screen, so unexpected was the content. The drone's countdown clock hadn't been replaced with a demand or a warning. The message was simply a web address. "What's at fallingstars.info?"

"It's a simple interface where people can check to see if they're on the list."

"What list?"

"The list of our intended victims. Our targets for kidnapping and ransom."

"We're publishing the whole list?" Michael asked with elevated tone.

"No. Not publishing as such. Nobody can see the list or even learn how long it is. They can only check to see if they're on it."

"Why *fallingstars?*" Boris asked.

"Psychology. The name is a double-pronged psychological attack, a subliminal one-two punch. First, it plays to their superstitious natures by reminding them of their fate, their stars." Ivan paused there, reading Boris's face. "You don't seem impressed."

"How many rich people are superstitious these days?"

Ivan smirked. "All of them."

"All of them?"

"To one degree or another. Even you are superstitious, my friend."

"I most certainly am not."

Ivan gave Boris a mischievous look before reaching into the

Suburban's armrest. He pulled out the pencil and sketchpad they used when planning ground operations, and handed them to Boris. Then he pulled a one-dollar bill from his wallet and began speaking slowly. "Write this: I Boris Aleksandrovich Vedernikov ... hereby sell ... to Ivan Ignatovich Sonin ... for the sum of one dollar ... my eternal soul."

Boris was not a religious man. He was an engineer, a pragmatic atheist, a what-you-see-is-what-you-get kind of guy. Nonetheless, his furiously scratching pencil suddenly stopped moving when Ivan said *eternal soul.* "Huh... Well I'll be."

Pavel was also impressed. Where did Ivan come up with this stuff? "What's the second psychological jab in *fallingstars?*"

"An ego play. The name implies that only stars get selected— and who doesn't want to think they're a star?"

"I'll buy that."

Boris chimed back in after a quick rebound. "That's why we grabbed Gordon Sangster and Preston Jenks and Emmy Delaney and Kevin Thompson. Because people will want to group themselves with stars they admire—business stars or movie stars or sports stars."

"That and the publicity," Ivan said.

"I take it the *fallingstars* list includes more names than are on our actual hit list?" Michael asked, his mind still stuck on practical matters.

Ivan turned his direction. "But of course. I included every American whose household investment portfolio exceeds $10 million."

"How big's that list?"

Ivan cracked a rare, full-faced smile. "625,000 people."

"625,000 people," Michael repeated, speaking slowly while his colleagues whistled.

"Why give them warning?" Pavel asked.

"To frighten them, of course."

"To what end?"

Boris leapt in with the answer. "It's the oldest tactic in the marketing playbook. First you scare them, then you sell them."

"Sell them what?" Michael asked.

"Insurance," Pavel said, recalling Ivan's earlier line of questioning. "Ivan's going to sell them insurance."

"What kind of insurance?"

"K&R of course," Ivan said with a nod to Pavel.

"And how is that going to play out?" Michael pressed.

"We'll give the world a day or two to work itself into a full-throated frenzy, then we'll add another page to fallingstars.info. The opportunity to buy an extraordinary insurance policy, one that's lifetime in length and crystal clear in coverage. For a mere $100,000 we'll permanently remove a name from our target list."

"Will they pay?" Michael asked. "Surely law enforcement will offer reassurances of swift justice, giving people pause."

"No doubt they will. We, however, will continue kidnapping people who don't pay. Furthermore, each day I'll also have a message delivered to a select person from the same community who did pay, congratulating him on dodging a bullet that otherwise would have been delivered."

"Social media will be all over that," Michael admitted.

"It gets better," Ivan continued. "Within an hour of the FBI press conference you're astutely predicting, I'll deliver this recording to the *New York Times*, Fox News and a couple of talk-radio shows—just to keep the big boys honest. It's a phone conversation between the Special Agent In Charge of the investigation and the Director of the FBI, with the latter being played by yours truly." Ivan swapped screens on his computer, pulled up the recording, and hit play. "Do you have any concrete leads on the perp? Or his whereabouts? Or his next targets?" "No, sir." "Any reason to believe we'll catch him if we don't get a lucky tip?" "No, sir." "Any hope we can offer the people or the President?" "Not at this time, sir." Ivan stopped the recording.

"That will do it," Michael said. "Although it's a shame to reveal the existence of MiMiC."

"I doubt the FBI will reveal it. They gain nothing by publicly exposing MiMiC, since it's the authentic comments that are inflammatory. In any case, the revelation costs us nothing at this point. We're done with it. And if they do disclose it, fears of faked calls will create an atmosphere of complete chaos throughout the law enforcement community. As it is, I have no doubt that the FBI is already second-guessing everything."

While Michael's face regained the relaxed look it had lacked for weeks, Pavel found himself drawn to the math like a dog to a meaty bone. With 625,000 potential payees and a $100,000 premium, Ivan's insurance scheme would bank $625 million if just one percent of people paid. "What percentage of people do you think will pay?"

"It's never been done before," Ivan said with a shrug unsuitably small for the circumstance. "Frankly, I have no idea."

The Suburban went silent.

Ironically, Pavel found himself experiencing the fear of loss.

Boris, apparently, was not so stunned. He asked Ivan, "What percentage of people pay for life insurance in the United States?"

Ivan held up four fingers on his left hand.

"Four percent?"

Ivan shook his head and raised his right hand as well, also with four fingers."

"Forty-four percent?"

Ivan smiled.

Forty-four times $625 million. Pavel couldn't manage the math during that magical moment—but then, when the numbers got that big, it really didn't matter.

88

Captcha

French Riviera

With Jo looking over his shoulder, Achilles navigated to fallingstars.info. The simple home page consisted of just four elements. At the top, a picture of the big black drone with its snaking snare backdropped by a stormy sky, dark and menacing. Beneath the photo, four bold words stated the question on every affluent mind: "Are you a target?" Below the text, the familiar 3-2-4-digit box arrangement with the instructions: "Enter your Social Security number." Finally, the Captcha, the Completely Automated Public Turing test to tell Computers and Humans Apart.

Achilles entered his SSN and then checked the box beside "I am not a robot." A collage of nine photos popped up with instructions beneath. *Select the edible items.* Achilles clicked on Chinese food, broccoli and a lollipop. The little arrow spun around, then stopped. The screen faded to white and words appeared center screen in bold black text: "You are NOT a target."

"That's surprising," Achilles said. "I'd think it would tell everyone they are a target. Just like everyone gets the 'You're a winner' notice."

"No, the press would point that out. Ivan's targeting the extremely affluent, not the especially gullible."

Achilles immediately understood that Jo's instincts were better than his when it came to cons. No surprise, given her background. "Of course. You're right. He wouldn't bother with anyone who couldn't afford a hundred grand. If I were him, I'd aim to target the wealthiest million Americans."

"A million people? How on earth would he identify that

many? And how would he get their Social Security numbers?" She gestured toward the computer screen where Achilles had just entered his nine digits.

"The credit agencies have that information. There are several of them, and they're large organizations. I'm sure he could find a clever employee at one of them willing to trade a covert data download for a million in cash."

"No doubt," Jo said. "That's got to be a good ten years' pay."

"At least, especially if you consider the fact that it's tax free. Plenty to tempt an ambitious geek with a case of the nine-to-five cubical confinement blues."

"I'm with you, but do you think people will pay Ivan's ask? Will they be motivated if their odds of being next are only one in a million?"

"Oh, they'll pay. It's insurance, plain and simple. Even poor people pay for that."

"Not when the odds are one in a million."

"They won't know the odds. I have no idea what the odds are that my house will burn down, but I buy fire insurance. No, when it comes to acquiring insurance, fear is the driver. We're hardwired to avoid loss."

"Won't someone do the analysis and point out the percentages?"

"I just passed through a complicated Captcha control. At the time, I wasn't sure why Ivan bothered, but now it's clear that he installed it to prevent that possibility. The Captcha will keep computers from learning the length of the list. Although even if someone does overcome it and calculate the individual odds, people won't look at their situation through that lens."

"How will they look at it?"

Achilles took a few seconds to convert his intuition into words. "Think of it this way: a million people is less than one-third of one percent of the U.S. population. Less than one in three hundred people. If fallingstars.info tells you you're a target, it's going to feel like having the red dot of a sniper scope on your chest. You'll rush to pay the premium, if you can afford it. And the top one percent of Americans can easily afford a hundred grand."

Achilles did the math while Jo nodded along. He felt his jaw go slack and had to double-check the zeroes. "A million times $100,000 is $100 billion."

Jo looked as stunned as he felt. "So even if only one in ten pay, Ivan still puts ten billion in the bank."

"Ten billion," Achilles repeated.

They both collapsed into their seats.

Achilles found himself repeating the sum. Ten billion dollars. Ten billion dollars. Enough to spend a million dollars a day for —the rest of your life.

Jo's expression changed.

"What?"

"Not me. You. You're smiling."

Achilles thought about it. "I guess I am."

"Why?"

"Ten billion dollars gives us what we were looking for."

She prodded him with a chin tilt.

"It gives us the big picture. An *Ivan the Ghost*-sized billboard of a picture."

"And what do you conclude from the big picture?"

"I conclude that Ivan is planning to retire."

"He was already retired. Kinda. Right? I mean, nobody heard from him for years."

"No, no," Achilles said with a jubilant shake of his head. "That's not the same. Before this, he was a beaten man. Out of business with a tarnished crown. If he pulls this off, he'll be the most successful master criminal of all time."

"Surely you're not forgetting Korovin?" Jo jibed, referencing Russia's notorious former president. A man with whom Achilles had tangled.

"I'd argue that corrupt politicians are a different category of crook."

Jo conceded that point with a nod. "So Ivan goes out with glory and retires as one of the richest men on earth—if we let him get away with it."

Achilles was pleased to see that Jo had her pluck back. She'd beaten the bug.

She continued thinking out loud. "I'm sure he's got a new identity arranged, complete with a detailed legend, greased government connections and appointments with top plastic surgeons."

"I'm sure he does too, but even that won't be enough for Ivan. Those things may provide satisfactory security, but they're insufficient for true peace of mind. Remember, this is Ivan we're talking about. The master of perfection. He won't risk a bad roll of the dice. He won't settle for just a high probability that he'll never be found."

"No?"

"No. Ivan will arrange things so that nobody ever looks."

"Are you kidding me? Half the world's law enforcement will be looking for him. Not to mention the million mad millionaires."

Achilles held up a finger. "They won't be looking if they think he's dead."

"You think he's going to fake his death? You think he'll be able to fool the world's best forensic scientists?"

"He won't need to fool forensic scientists. He won't need to fake his death either."

"You've lost me."

"If you look at the big picture, if you think like Ivan, you realize that he's been planning for this moment his entire criminal career. A clean exit with a huge payout has always been the ultimate goal. The culmination. The endgame."

"So?"

"So since the beginning, since the day The Ghost was born, he's been setting up his final con. Detail by detail. Year after year. With meticulous preparation."

"For what?"

"For leading law enforcement to reach the same conclusion you did. For guiding them to the right place at the right time— to convince them that Victor Vazov's playboy son is really Ivan the Ghost."

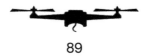

89

The Arrow

The Hoover Building, Washington D.C.

Rip's return to the Hoover Building's corner office was about as joyous as Louis XVI's walk to the guillotine. He had been summoned and the end was in sight. No explanation had been given, but none was necessary. One of his confidential calls with Director Brix had been recorded and leaked to the press. Rip had no idea how that had happened, but it was playing on every newscast from DC to San Francisco—and it was not flattering.

A beleaguered assistant ushered him into the power office with a polite nod, closing the door quickly behind him.

Rip found Brix standing before a pair of television monitors, hands on hips, back to the door. The focus of both broadcasts was the latest chapter of the *fallingstars* saga, the "No Hope" conversation the newscasters were calling it.

Brix let the shows run for thirty excruciating seconds before muting both screens and turning around. "Is that you talking?"

Rip found the question confusing. "I didn't pick up on anything that sounded edited, if that's what you mean?"

"Just answer the question," Brix pressed.

"Yes, it's me."

"Well, it isn't me."

"What do you mean?" Was Brix planning to deny the tape's authenticity? Rip glanced around the room, looking for video recording equipment.

"My calls aren't recorded. My phone can't be tapped. And I didn't have that conversation. You were talking to an imposter."

Rip felt his stomach fill with ice. He began to voice one question and then another, but obvious answers stilled his tongue, leaving him standing in stunned silence. A single word finally escaped. "Ivan."

"Of course it's Ivan. Are you any closer to catching him now than you were when you spoke those words?" Brix gestured toward the muted monitors.

It was over.

He had embarrassed the FBI.

He had committed a deadly sin.

The only road to redemption was bathing the Bureau in even greater glory, and he harbored little hope of that. Not after Ivan's ingenious impersonation made it clear that he was so thoroughly outwitted.

Rip owed Brix the truth. Bald wood, no varnish. "The website hasn't given us much. The domain name registration for fallingstars.info is with a trade attaché at the Saudi Arabian Embassy."

Brix bowed his head. "A Saudi spy? Ivan's just screwing with us."

"Yes, sir."

"What does the embassy say about that?"

"Nothing yet. It's closed for the weekend. I've got a call in to the State Department, but you know how it will go. They'll claim utter ignorance while obsequiously offering to check with their attaché. Then they'll eventually inform us that he's been back in Riyadh for weeks."

Brix grunted agreement. "What else have you learned about the website?"

"On the surface, there's not much to it. Not yet anyway. No hidden pages, embedded malware, or Easter eggs. The only notable feature is the Captcha, which is cutting edge. It's time consuming and beyond any existing automated workaround. It won't allow access from hidden IP addresses or permit open addresses to query more than once per hour."

"Your point?"

"We haven't been able to accurately estimate the target pool. It's a small percentage of the general population, that much is clear, but the end count could be twelve people or twelve million."

"That's not reassuring. Half our job—the half the White

House cares most about—is making America feel safe.
Regardless of their actual circumstances," Brix added.

Rip said nothing.

"Do you have anything we can use to reassure the people, or
relieve the President?"

"No, sir."

Brix fumed in silence for a second, then moved on. "What
are your thoughts on shutting down the website?"

"I've got a team assembling momentarily to tackle that very
question. You're welcome to join us."

Brix ignored the invitation. "I'm asking for your personal
opinion."

"I don't see any upside to shutting it down—beyond a
fleeting moment of feel-good. But the downside's obvious as a
beetle on a bed sheet."

"I'm not into linen. Why don't you enlighten me."

Rip took a deep breath. "Ivan undoubtedly has backup
domains he can activate with a finger snap. Before word gets
out that we've shut one down, he'll have a replacement running.
We'll end up playing whack-a-mole and look foolish doing so.
Worse yet, we'll force him to advertise each new domain."

Brix blinked. "Advertise... Huh... That means more high-
profile kidnappings, more media circuses."

"Exactly."

"So how close are you to catching him?"

"To catching Ivan the Ghost?" Rip used Ivan's full title to
emphasize the ask. "We're just one good tip away."

"That sounds familiar, but frankly not very reassuring." Brix
dropped into his chair. "Nothing more from Miss Ooh La La?"

"Not for a few days now. She'll call me if she has something."
Actually, Rip wasn't sure she would ever call him again. Their
last conversation had not ended well.

The Director shifted forward and brought cupped fists to
chin. "You've had a rough tenure as the San Francisco SAIC."

"The cards haven't been particularly kind."

"No, they haven't. It's clear now that I wasn't doing you a
favor after all, pulling you out of a regional role and handing
you the big ball."

More like a hot potato than a big ball, Rip thought. He saw where this was going, but was helpless to divert it. He had no countervailing force to present. No ace in his hole. He didn't have a blindfold and cigarette either, so he just sat steady in the saddle, waiting to take the inevitable arrow like a man.

90

Things to Come

French Riviera

Ivan grabbed a chilled bottle of Icelandic Glacial Water from the refrigerator and slumped into a lounger on his villa's balcony. Like everyone who worked at Silicon Hill, he lived there. It was part of his camouflage.

His villa used to belong to the billionaire's sommelier, a man with whom he conversed and in whom he confided, so it had an ocean view, which Ivan enjoyed, and a wine cellar, which Ivan converted into a secret workshop and storage facility. Otherwise, it was unremarkable. Camouflage.

He'd just returned from a meeting with Little V. A meeting that had yielded *good, better* and *best* news. The good news was that the steady flow of cash deposits had relieved Vlad's anxiety regarding the repayment of his loan. With his initial $300 million and then some repaid, Vlad was no longer belligerent. The better news was that Vlad had not connected the repayments with the K&R operations. The self-absorbed playboy continued to believe that they derived from legitimate business contracts. The best news was that Ivan had solved the mystery of the disappearing bodyguards. Now he was on Vlad's good side.

When the topic came up, Ivan offered to help think it through. They discussed the details over frosty mugs of Panaché. The capture. The fight. The zip ties. The departure for the marina. The failure to return. The yacht in its berth. The car at the heliport.

None of the storytelling yielded anything.

It wasn't until Ivan had him describe the plan to dispose of Achilles that he developed a provable hypothesis. And prove it he did, with a trip to the marina. Now Vlad knew that his missing bodyguards weren't working with Achilles, and he knew they weren't talking to the police. He knew that Achilles had somehow turned the tables and fed them to the fishes. Ivan assumed it was with the aid of Jo Monfort, but he didn't tell Vlad that. Ivan knew all of this because the *VaVaVoom* was missing its extra anchor chain.

That solved one of two questions bothering Ivan. By far the lesser of the two. He took a deep drink of the cool clear water, put his feet up on the balcony rail, and turned his focus to the other.

Achilles was alive. He was supposed to be dead, killed by Vazov's men while the FBI was on his tail—thereby leading the agents to Vazov. This was an integral part of Ivan's grand plan, and it was now off the rails.

Ivan had redundant measures in place, of course. He always established backups for the key elements of his plans. He had a backup for leading the FBI to Vazov, and he had a backup for killing Achilles. But those didn't kick in until the endgame. The question he had resolved to answer there on the balcony was: How much of a threat did Achilles pose in the meantime?

Staring out at an azure sea that merged seamlessly with a blue horizon, Ivan decided the answer depended on what Achilles knew. He didn't know Ivan's endgame. If Michael, Pavel and Boris couldn't guess it from the inside, an outsider surely couldn't. He also didn't know who Ivan was or where Ivan was. Nobody had ever been able to find Ivan the Ghost, and plenty had tried. Achilles did know that Vlad was not Ivan. Did that matter? Not at the moment, and Achilles would be dead before it did.

Achilles also knew that a drone killed Rider, but the FBI already had that information, and of course they were keeping it quiet. Did Achilles know anything else? Have any meaningful clues? Did Jo? Did her involvement change anything? Ivan stared blankly at the invisible horizon until he convinced himself that the answer on all accounts was *No.*

Satisfied that his magnum opus was still following the music and playing toward its inevitable, glorious conclusion, Ivan returned his attention to execution. The U.S. operation was nearly complete, and so far everything of significance had gone as planned. MiMiC and Raven were working flawlessly, and everyone from the FBI to the media to the actual and potential victims had acted predictably, like puppets on strings.

The endgame would be upon them before they knew it, so it was time to bring Team Raven into the loop. What a conversation that would be. Michael had been sensing something was up for months, but he still didn't have a clue what was coming—or his role in it.

91

Crazy

French Riviera

Jo slid into the tub of hot suds with a sense of relief she hadn't felt in weeks. Her health was back near one hundred percent and her life wasn't in immediate danger. Her mind was also oddly at ease. She found herself drawing deep satisfaction from uncovering Ivan's ultimate plan—even though she didn't know how to act on the information.

She did feel bad for Rip Zonder. He'd been crucified by the media for his "No Hope" discussion with Director Brix. The pundits made a sport of pouring scorn on the man and the agency in its aftermath. Of course, that cost him his position.

It was so unjust, being skewered for getting caught being honest. What did the public want? Lies? That was what they usually got, if they got anything at all. Most were just too stupid to realize it. They let the government get away with exaggerations, obfuscations, misdirections and lies of omission. They let politicians hide behind claims of committee work, confidentiality and national security. The truth was, the CIA and FBI and their European equivalents had all searched extensively for Ivan and none of them had found him.

Jo puffed her cheeks and exhaled, blowing suds. Maybe she was just projecting her own frustration. Rip's demise had reopened a wound, a wound she now realized had never quite healed. It wasn't that long ago that she had gone from the streets to the CIA and back again. For a few short months, she'd been at the pinnacle of global intelligence, part of a proud international brotherhood. It was undoubtedly the most special, unique and satisfying time of her life. Then she, like Rip, had been assigned to Ivan. Failing to capture The Ghost had ended her career before it really got started. Oh, how she wanted to bag that bastard.

Achilles' voice came from the balcony, disturbing her pity party. She'd left both the sliding glass door and the bathroom door open so she could enjoy the sound of slapping waves while soaking. Achilles was supposed to be off on one of his runs. "Jo?" he repeated.

"I'm in the tub." She checked the water and found it still sufficiently sudsy. A stuffed wash cloth and a slow trickle from the tap allowed her to keep it filled to the rim. "You can come in."

Achilles entered her room, but stopped at the bathroom doorway. He leaned against it, facing the wall so their eyes met in the mirror. "Before my run, I ran a fresh search on Vlad Vazov. His name popped up on a local blog. Google was nice enough to translate it for me. He's having two fortieth birthday bashes this weekend. One on Friday at the Monte Carlo Polo Club, and the second on Saturday at Silicon Hill."

"You in the mood to party?"

"That's when Ivan's going to off him. It totally fits his style."

"At which one?"

"Has to be Silicon Hill. It's got the connection to the drones. It's also the one he'll invite his family to attend, since his CEO face is the one he'll want to show his father. Ivan will want Big V dead too, to avoid comebacks."

"I can see that," Jo said with a nod. "Wait a minute. Ivan can't kill Vazov yet. The kidnappings are still going on."

"Yeah, but we've seen the big reveal. The insurance scheme. He's making his financial killing while you soak. It's time for him to vanish. If I'm right, between now and Saturday, the killings will stop."

"Sounds like you've thought it through."

"I've been thinking about little else."

"So what's your plan to catch him?"

Achilles gave her a wily look. "I want to team up with Vazov."

Jo couldn't believe her ears. "You're absolutely crazy."

"To the contrary, it's absolutely classic. The enemy of my enemy is my friend."

She couldn't help but roll her eyes. "Have you forgotten your last meeting with Vazov? Even if you're right about the big picture—even if Ivan has been setting up Vazov to take the fall—it's still a huge risk. Vazov's most likely reaction will be to say 'thanks for the tip' and put a bullet in your head. His second most likely reaction will be to skip the thanks."

"So it would be a crazy move?"

"Yes. I'm sure if we pulled in a few psychologists and told them about your recent boat trip and your intended course of action, the majority would declare you unequivocally insane."

"Does that mean you wouldn't consider going with me?"

"Now *I'm* starting to think you're insane."

"Not one chance in a thousand?"

"Not one."

"Excellent."

"Excellent?"

"Ivan won't have accounted for it."

"He will have in the sense that you end up dead."

"What if I can convince Vazov not to kill me?"

"How would you do that?"

"I don't know. I'm just brainstorming with you."

Jo swatted suds at him.

Achilles gave her a wink and a smile. "Seriously. How could I pull that off?"

92

All Inclusive

Chautauqua, New York

Michael was not enjoying the K&R operations anymore. Neither were Pavel or Boris. The novelty had worn off and the thrill of the hunt had given way to the fear of capture. While Ivan was back in France preparing for the *endgame* as he put it, they were stuck sweating in the heat of a thousand spotlights.

Ever since Ivan launched fallingstars.info and his insurance scam, he'd insisted on high-profile public operations. Maximum publicity was his mantra. *We can't sell 'em if we don't scare 'em. So let's keep 'em scared.*

It was working.

Not a night had passed without the latest drone attack leading the news. Morning talk shows covered little else. Even the President was playing second fiddle—and reportedly none too happy about it. Who was the latest victim? Who had dodged a bullet? The public was always eager to know.

Michael used express mail to send notes to those who allegedly would have been next, but were spared because they bought insurance. In reality, Ivan just picked people from his list who lived near the actual victim. His tactic added authenticity to the averted threat and facilitated side-by-side appearances on morning talk shows. The wise man and the rich fool. One counting his lucky stars and the other lamenting the skepticism that just cost him $10 million.

It was brilliant, but Michael wondered whether it was effective. He had no idea how many people were paying for the insurance—and Ivan was frustratingly tight-lipped about it. Getting people to act on anything was a challenge, even when they had the intention to do so. Throw in the $100,000 price tag and it was an uphill battle for sure.

Speaking of battles, they were about to begin the day's K&R. Ivan had sent them to Lake Chautauqua in upstate New York, a sparsely populated rural heartland destination with a 150-year-old intellectual hub known as the Chautauqua Institution. He figured it would be good for the insurance business to do a kidnapping that was nowhere near a major metropolitan area. Make sure that no one felt safe for geographical reasons.

Michael was studying the victim's lakefront estate through binoculars when Boris cried out from the passenger seat. "Whoa!"

"What?"

"Our victim. What do you know about her?"

"She's an heir to the Packard automobile fortune. She lives at Packard Manor. And she has a habit of meditating in her garden at sunset while Bach plays in the background."

"Yeah, well that omits a key piece of information. She's eighty years old."

"Eighty!" Michael dropped the binoculars and pulled up the photo supplied by Ivan's secret reconnaissance team. It was taken from where they were now parked—half a mile across the water on the opposite bank. It showed a woman sitting cross-legged on the grass with her palms upturned on her knees. The shot gave them everything they needed to identify their target, but it wasn't close-up enough to discern her age. "I guess Ivan's going for more than geographic diversity. He wants people to know that age isn't a disqualifier either."

"What if she has a heart attack?" Pavel asked. "What do I do then? Do I drop her or set her down or fly her to a hospital?"

Michael said, "She's a billionaire who has the discipline to meditate daily. She'll probably outlive you. That's why Ivan picked her."

"What's going to be next?" Pavel asked. "We've gone coast to coast, hitting major cities, posh suburbs and rural regions. We've kidnapped men and women, young and old, celebrities and nobodies, every race on the rainbow. What remains? Who's left to frighten?"

The question was a good one, and it stumped them all.

A phone call broke the silence. Ivan. "How's it going?"

"We're on location, waiting for the show to start. Shouldn't you be sleeping? It's what, 2:00 a.m. there?"

"I've been busy and my body clock hasn't adjusted. I wanted to let you know that this will be the last op."

"We're all done?"

"You will be within the hour."

"Night-shift flight?"

"Out of Buffalo Niagara International Airport. They know you'll be traveling with a crate containing four high-speed electrical fans with a battery pack and control unit. The paperwork is all filed."

"Nice." Michael was thrilled that the K&Rs were almost over, but something in Ivan's tone wasn't sitting right. He decided to ask the question so that he wouldn't spend the next twelve hours worrying about it. "Will there be champagne on the plane?"

"Pardon?"

"Mission accomplished?"

Ivan didn't answer immediately. When he did, Ivan made Michael wish he'd kept quiet. "We'll talk about the money when you get back."

93

Jack in the Box

Moscow, Russia

Her heels were impossibly high. Her legs were delightfully long. And her breasts had minds of their own. Both bouncing beauties appeared determined to break their silk bonds and breathe freely on that warm Moscow night. They dared any and all not to stare—but got no takers. At least not the driver of the Mercedes-Maybach parked on the sloping side street outside the Georgian restaurant *Aragvi*.

As the girl walked down the road toward Victor Vazov's car, Achilles walked up it—not in the street like her, but on the sidewalk. When she was about twenty paces from the car, her footfalls became less certain. A bit too much champagne? Or perhaps a date unwilling to risk rejection had spiked her drink? It was late enough that the possibilities plied the imagination.

When she was two paces from the Maybach, just a few feet from its driver, her luck ran out. Her heel slipped and her balance shifted, then her legs went up and her bottom went down. The impact was more than her button could bear, and her breasts broke free at last.

There were no onlookers at that late hour, but had there been any, they would have seen the driver's door to the Mercedes begin to open a split-second before its trunk. A few seconds later, he would then have seen both close simultaneously. In between, he'd have seen one man step out of the driver's seat, and another slip into the trunk.

Achilles was glad to find the trunk clean and empty. He'd gone with the odds, but it had been a gamble. The first of the night. By his count, he would be gambling six more times before dawn—and the odds would get worse with each.

He and Jo had spent hours discussing tactics by which he might approach Little V and get him to partner with them against Ivan. Their ultimate conclusion had been the same as Jo's initial one. Achilles would be crazy to try—not because Vlad wouldn't believe them, but because he'd likely kill Achilles all the same.

While the toilet was still flushing that brilliant idea, Achilles floated another. "What if I approach Big V instead? I bet he's coming here in a few days for Vlad's fortieth birthday bash. I could attempt to join him."

"Equally crazy."

"I think it might be different."

Jo's expression made her opinion clear, but she voiced it all the same. "Victor ordered his bodyguards to send us out in the trash. Vlad ordered his bodyguards to drown you. I don't think that's a difference we can work with."

"The difference is pride. I'd be telling Vlad something that damages his self-esteem. He'd lash out at me for that. I agree with you. But with Victor, I'd be warning him of an assault on his family—one for which he bears no personal blame. That's an entirely different pill to swallow."

Achilles eventually talked Jo around and they began brainstorming tactics. Both agreed that the time and place of the pitch would be critical to Victor's receptiveness. Ideally, it should be one-on-one and without forewarning, preferably under circumstances that allowed Achilles to escape if Victor gave him a bad vibe.

They decided that Achilles should visit Victor in his bedroom, preferably late at night so there would be no interruption. Then they set about figuring out how to make that happen. Once they had a plan, they discussed the option of Jo accompanying him, but it wasn't much of a debate. She had a ton of work to do in France preparing to catch Ivan.

Two days later, Achilles slipped into Victor Vazov's trunk, while a talented prostitute drew the driver's full and complete attention.

You don't need a key to get into a Mercedes trunk if the car's unlocked, and getting out is incredibly easy. Achilles had surprised a dealer by practicing the move. Turns out there's an *open* button that begins flashing green whenever the trunk is closed. It also serves as mood lighting, he was discovering.

Achilles worked himself into a comfortable position so that he wouldn't have to move when the driver returned from helping the damsel in distress. There weren't a lot of alternatives for a man of his size given the potential need to spring to action. That was the second gamble. He was gambling that nobody would open the trunk tonight. If someone did, he'd spring out locked and loaded, and hope that surprise gave him the opportunity to slip, shoot or smooth talk his way out of whatever situation presented.

Vazov was at a business dinner. That meant there would likely be multiple rounds of after-dinner drinks. Achilles didn't mind. Alcohol worked in his favor, and he'd be in the trunk for hours regardless—if nobody opened it.

The driver returned to the car a few short minutes after stepping out, removing the immediate threat of an opening trunk. Achilles allowed his mind to wander. It went to Katya, of course. He felt terrible that his past had come back to haunt her, and he missed her so much.

Achilles assumed that Katya was only about 250 miles from where he now lay, holed up in a rental cabin. When she described Lake Gryadetskoe that day in Napa, she told him it had been perfect for her purposes, boasting fresh air and a beautiful view and nothing else. No Internet or telephone or nosy neighbors. Just a few local villagers living like it was the 1800s and minding their own business.

He pictured her sitting on a picnic table covered in books and papers, scribbling away with a smile on her face. He wished he could visit. That was out of the question, of course. He couldn't see or speak to her until this was all over. Not without putting her in danger—given all the tracking tools at his antagonist's disposal. *Damn you, Ivan.*

On that thought, the Maybach's engine roared to life, a 463 horsepower biturbo V8. Two doors opened and closed, first the right rear and then the right front. Victor and a bodyguard.

As the car pulled from the curb, Achilles pulled up Waze on his cell phone. According to the driving app, he was 34 minutes from the Vazov residence. He hoped that was where they were headed. Gamble number three.

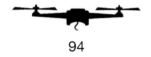

94

The Number

French Riviera

Butterflies fluttered in Michael's stomach as he entered Ivan's villa with Pavel and Boris. Despite foreknowledge of the people and place, it felt like he was stepping from an exploratory ship into a new land after a long and treacherous voyage. He was excited and relieved, but filled with trepidation about what they were about to learn.

Had they discovered gold? Or was the insurance scheme a flop?

What was Ivan planning to do next? And where did that leave Michael?

Ivan led them to the kitchen table rather than the soft seating. It was a round four-seater with a polished wooden top and off-white upholstered chairs. Spotless since nobody ever ate there. Off to the side, an ice bucket dripped condensation. A common sight in France, but the bottle within wasn't rosé or champagne, it was vodka. Belvedere. Was that a good sign, or bad? His ability to interpret Ivan's moves continued to flounder.

Ivan poured four shot glasses and raised his in a toast. "To Raven."

"To Raven," the three replied.

They drained their glasses and Ivan refilled them. This time he didn't raise his before speaking. "I won't be acquiring Silicon Hill."

Michael felt his stomach turn to ice despite the ethanol infusion. He couldn't believe the insurance scam had failed so completely.

"Why not?" Boris asked, his tone academic. The man had just lost one percent of $600 million but he still showed no emotion.

Pavel, also a one-percenter, drained his glass and immediately refilled it. "How much are we short?"

Ivan turned toward Pavel. "One dollar."

"I don't understand."

"I've paid back the loan. But I'm not exercising the option."

"You're not?" Pavel continued, his voice brimming with bottled rage.

"To be honest with you, I never intended to buy Silicon Hill."

Pavel clenched fist and chest. "But our options, our bonuses. That's what we've been working for."

"Oh, I've already made good on those—monetarily speaking." Ivan spoke with the nonchalance of an afterthought. "Each of you has a new Bitcoin account with a balance equal to your promised share of the $600 million."

"We do?" the three said in chorus.

Ivan raised his glass.

Relief washed over Michael like a warm wave on a cold night. He felt his shoulders turn to putty and his neck begin to tingle. Retirement was in the bank! His two-percent share was worth $12 million. Way more than he could ever have hoped to make as a boxer. And he didn't even get punched in the face.

After they drained their glasses, Boris again asked, "Why not? Why not buy Silicon Hill?"

Ivan turned to Pavel. "Do you know?" Then to Michael. "Do you?"

Michael couldn't care less at that moment. His payday beat what Ali and Foreman got for *The Rumble in the Jungle*, combined. He was certain Ivan had a sound strategic reason for his seemingly insane move, but then and there he couldn't fathom it. "Please tell us."

"I'm not buying Silicon Hill because stealing money is only half the battle."

"And the other half?" Boris asked.

"The other half is getting away with it."

"Unless I missed something, we've already gotten away with it," Pavel said.

"No, we haven't." Ivan paused to allow someone else to hop in, but nobody did. "You haven't gotten away with a crime until people stop looking for you."

Michael finally saw the light. He felt like he'd stepped out of a cave. "You're leading the authorities to Little V! You're going to get him arrested for what we've done."

Ivan shook his head, his expression more disappointed than contemptuous.

Boris jumped in as Michael's glow faded. "A minute ago, you told Pavel we were 'one dollar short.' But that's nonsensical."

"I answered his question," Ivan said, growing an approving grin.

"Let me rephrase," Pavel said. "How much did you make from insurance premiums? What percentage of people paid?"

Ivan broke into a full-faced smile. "About one in five. Twenty percent."

"Twenty percent?" Boris blurted back. "Of 625,000 people?"

"It's less than half the proportion that purchase standard life insurance, but it's a healthy number nonetheless."

"A healthy number? Twenty percent of 625,000 people paying a $100,000 is $12.5 billion." Boris did the math without breaking stride. "Are you telling us you banked $12.5 billion?"

Ivan raised his glass for a third time. "It's not enough to put me on the Forbes list, but it will do. The money is still coming in, of course. But the wise man knows when to stop rolling dice and walk away with the chips he's already got."

They drained and refilled their glasses, repeating "$12.5 billion" over and over as the staggering sum sunk in.

Thrilled though he was with the number, Michael knew Ivan didn't have them sitting around that table drinking vodka just so he could wow them with his wealth. The main revelation was yet to come, and he thought he knew what it would be. "So how do we get the police to stop looking for us?"

Ivan turned to him, and for a second he saw his old friend in those eyes. "You were partially right earlier. We will point the police at someone else."

"But?"

"But we won't get him arrested."

"We won't?"

"If he gets arrested, he can contradict the evidence against him. The smart move is to make sure that he can't do that." Ivan put both palms flat on the table and leaned in. "The really smart move is to make sure that nobody can provide contradictory evidence."

95

Hamburger Helper

Moscow, Russia

Achilles planned to pop the Maybach's trunk at 2:00 a.m. to begin making his way from Victor Vazov's garage to his bedroom. That was his timetable. Once he got to the garage, whenever that was, he would set an alarm, take a nap, and go into the assault fresh and rested.

His plan didn't last.

Not because someone else popped the trunk. They didn't. Not because Victor didn't drive straight home. He did. The driver took him straight from the restaurant on Tverskaya to his home in Krylatskoye. They arrived at 11:35 p.m., beating Waze's projected travel time by three minutes. Achilles suspected the navigation app failed to account for the flashing blue light used by elite snobs like Victor to push commoners from their path.

Achilles' plan didn't last because he had forgotten to account for the heat his 220 pounds of black-clad meat would generate when crammed into 12.3 cubic feet of insulated space. The inside of Mercedes' flagship ride might be as luxurious as anything on four run-flat tires, but the trunk felt like economy class on a commuter jet. And after an hour, the lack of ventilation made it as hot as a Phoenix runway.

He hit the flashing green trunk release button at 12:01 am.

He held the lid so that it wouldn't spring all the way open and attract eyes, then he peered through the crack while sucking fresh air. He couldn't see much more than the inside of a garage door, but the lights were out, which told him the only thing that really mattered: He was alone.

The garage was enormous and housed an impressive collection of automobiles, but otherwise was pretty normal looking. Six doors at the back, an entrance to the house at the front, and raised storage cabinets around the perimeter. Achilles recognized the doors as bulletproof and blast-resistant, although to most people they wouldn't appear extraordinary. The garage's checkered black-and-white floor pattern was a bit regal, but not over the top.

Once he confirmed his solitude, Achilles ignored the environment. He slid into the rear right seat of the Maybach, extended the footrest, reclined the seatback, and took his planned nap.

The starting bell sounded at 2:00 a.m., or rather it vibrated.

The house he was about to enter was French Baroque in style, with white and cream-colored stonework, plenty of symmetrical architectural flourish, and an ornate lead-toned mansard roof.

His investigation of the estate's exterior security quickly led to the conclusion that he didn't want to mess with it. Thus the stowaway infiltration tactic.

The mansion's most distinguishing feature was a semicircular portico. Online photos showed it opening into a circular foyer lit by an enormous crystal chandelier and featuring an elegant freestanding staircase. Beneath that chandelier, the depiction of an eagle holding a sword and scepter was emblazoned in onyx on the white marble floor. According to the article accompanying the picture, the Vazov family crest dated back to the 15th century. Achilles had his doubts.

Achilles didn't find much additional information online regarding the interior layout, and he didn't have time to access other resources such as building plans or past employees. But the garage was obviously connected, and the master bedroom appeared to be at the top of the circular stairs, so he was going in with most of what he needed. Hopefully.

Achilles was prepared to lock-pick his way out of the garage, but a twist of the wrist proved that unnecessary. Before slipping inside, however, he had one precaution to take. He pulled a quarter-kilo of double-bagged ketamine-soaked hamburger from his jacket pocket and broke both seals. Then he cracked the door just wide enough to slip it through at floor level and squeezed the contents onto the floor.

If Victor had dogs, the ketamine should knock them out, quickly and quietly. That was gamble number four. If he didn't have dogs, the maid would have a puzzle on her hands. Achilles listened to silence for a full twenty minutes, giving the scent time to circulate, then he slowly opened the door and stepped inside.

The house was dark. Electronic gadgets in various nooks provided points of dim illumination, but no lights were burning.

He heard nothing.

He smelled nothing but hamburger.

He sensed no one nearby.

If Victor stationed a guard inside his house at night for supplemental protection, that person would almost certainly be seated outside his bedroom door. Achilles considered circumventing the scene by slipping out a window and breaking into Victor's bedroom directly—but that would expose him to the exterior patrol. And to their dogs.

Risky though it was, Achilles' knew his best option was going through the bedroom guard.

But first he had to reach him.

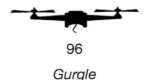

96

Gurgle

Moscow, Russia

Achilles didn't know what interior security measures were installed or if they were activated. All he could do was use best practices and hope the odds were in his favor. Gamble number five.

He low-crawled from the garage door to the entryway, slow and steady, hoping to avoid eyes of all kinds. Electronic eyes, if watching for motion, typically looked above pet level. Human eyes, if not new to the job, typically looked at books or movies. Only changes in lighting or rapid movements would draw attention to a monitor screen.

He reached the base of the staircase without provoking a reaction, and slowly rose to his feet. Rather than ascending by the normal route, which would put him dead-center in any waiting guard's field of vision, Achilles decided to climb.

He stood directly beneath the thirteenth freestanding tread, then reached his left hand overhead and grasped it by the edge. Slowly, oh so slowly, and silently, oh so silently, he worked his way up, grip by grip, rung by rung, with arms happily engaged and legs dangling over the 15th century crest.

Achilles had experience with sentry duty. He understood the psychology of men assigned to late-night watches. Certain universal truths applied. If a sentry was present, he would have his back to the boss's door. In theory, this was for the boss's protection. In practice, this was so the boss couldn't catch him napping. The sentry would also have his chair positioned to point directly at the top of the stairs. This put potential threats front and center of his field of vision, while allowing his focus to rest on a cell phone or book.

After nineteen vertical moves, Achilles' right hand took hold of the upper landing—some twenty-one feet above the marble floor. He didn't stop moving though, and he didn't peer over. Slowly, oh so slowly, he continued shuffling hand to hand toward the far end of the landing. He spent two full minutes covering the thirty-foot span from the top of the stairs to where the railing met the wall.

He paused there to listen—and detected a presence. A guard. It had to be a guard, dammit. With the stealth and patience of a stalking cougar, he brought an eye up to floor level.

The guard was immediately visible across the broad landing, not because he was moving or brightly dressed but because of the glowing screen in his hands. He was indeed seated with his back toward the master bedroom's large double doors, and his chest angled 45-degrees toward the top of the stairs.

Achilles was disappointed by the absence of an earphone cord trailing from the phone, but brightened when he spotted a white cordless earbud. The guard was probably just listening with his left ear, so he could hear the boss with his right.

To Achilles' surprise, he recognized his foe's features, although it took him a second to place the profile presented. The last time he'd seen the man, they'd been staring at each other face-to-face. It was the bodyguard from Vertical Vision. The one who left with Vazov and his party. The one who abandoned Jo to be raped and Achilles to die.

He was seated about twelve feet from Achilles on a stool. Not a folding chair or a recliner. A stool. Smart move on the boss's part. Much tougher to fall asleep on one of those.

Twelve feet is a tricky distance. It's close enough to put Achilles in his peripheral vision, but far enough that Achilles couldn't reach him in a single bound. But Achilles was five for five this evening, so he didn't hesitate with gamble number six.

Rather than attempting to slither over the rail without observation—a fundamentally risky tactic due to defenses our lizard brains developed against snakes—Achilles exploded into motion. Zero to sixty in the blink of an eye.

He began with a powerful double-armed jerk that brought his feet to the ledge and his shoulders level with the railing. Then he leveraged the jerk's upward momentum into a side vault that put him over the rail before the guard had fully turned his head. By the time the guard registered what was happening, Achilles had closed the gap between them.

Proximity was only half the battle, however. To win, Achilles had to silence the man. Instantly. He couldn't afford a fight. He couldn't afford a crash or a bang or a yelp or a shout. He couldn't afford anything louder than an exhale or a gurgle or the sound cartilage makes beneath a razor-sharp knife.

97

Serious Problems

French Riviera

Michael had known they'd be in for an interesting discussion when Ivan refused to answer the "Mission accomplished?" question over the phone. He'd expected that to mean Ivan wanted to finesse the answer. He'd expected bad news.

But the mission news had been unbelievably good.

The Raven program brought in the required $600 million—and $12 billion more. Ivan wasn't acquiring the company, but bonuses were being paid, so the guys didn't care. The thing was, Ivan could have told them that over the phone. Question: Mission accomplished? Answer: Bonuses will be paid. Details to follow. *Short and sweet.*

So what was the real reason for the meeting? Ivan had just clued them in. He wanted to discuss his plan for getting away free and clear. He wanted to sell them on a proposal for making the police believe Vazov was behind the K&Rs while ensuring that neither Vazov nor anyone else could "provide contradictory evidence."

Ivan continued leaning in over the table for a few seconds after dropping his bomb, adding weight to his words. Then he broke the tension by settling back in his chair and asking one of his big-picture questions. "If you look at the history of the human race, how have the rich typically come by their money? Inheritance aside."

"By gaining control of resources," Boris said. "Oil fields or gold mines. Ships or railroads. Patents or production equipment."

"I'm impressed. But you forgot one P word, the greatest wealth generator of all."

"People," Michael said.

Ivan leaned back in. "That's right. Pharaohs had slaves. Kings had knights. Noblemen had serfs. These days, the titles have changed, but the fundamentals remain the same. Even though business owners no longer legally own the laborers who make them their money, employers still control how employees spend the majority of their waking hours."

Ivan spoke without passion, more like an accountant than a demagogue. "Modern workers might be free to switch sweatshops or minimum-wage jobs, but that freedom is meaningless if it doesn't change their fundamental circumstances. In fact, today's laborers often receive no more now than slaves did then—just enough to keep them working. So you see, the rich have always been achieving or retaining their status by usurping other people's lives. It's the natural order of things."

Michael had heard Ivan go off on similar philosophical tangents many times before. His broad talks always had a specific purpose in mind. He was planting ideas, preparing minds to reach conclusions farther down the road. As Michael listened to the lecture on the plight of modern labor, he wondered what lay at the end of this road.

Michael wasn't the only one lacking insight at that moment. The other two were also staring at Ivan, trying to figure out where this history lesson was going.

"But back to getting away with our money. I've been planning and preparing since I first became The Ghost. I haven't always known when I would retire, or what my big score would be, but I always knew that I would need the police to believe Ivan the Ghost was someone else. So I picked the perfect patsy years ago, and began creating evidence."

"Vazov!" Michael said. "Like I said earlier."

"Earlier you indicated blaming him for Raven. Right direction, but only halfway there."

"He's perfect," Pavel said. "Right age, right build, right nationality, geography and facial features. He's wealthy, criminally connected and largely at leisure."

"And he's owner and chairman of the business that built Raven in a secret lab—secret from him too, but nobody will ever believe that," Michael added.

"I'm glad you approve," Ivan said. "There's other evidence that I'll plant around his property and on his computer when the time comes. Bits from other jobs and even my fake passports, all of which have his picture on them, but different names of course. The documentation puts him at the site of many of my crimes."

"How will you plant that evidence?" Pavel asked.

"I've had a spy in his camp for years. The head of his security. Unfortunately, Gleb recently passed, but I've still got all the access cards, keys and codes required."

Boris looked up from fiddling fingers. "There's a problem with your plan."

All eyes turned to him.

"The police investigation will go beyond the physical evidence. They're going to interview people. They're going to interview everyone at Silicon Hill. It will come out that Vazov was rarely there. They're going to say the four of us were really running the show."

"There's also the problem of Victor Vazov," Pavel said. "He'll know his son's not Ivan. While it's unlikely that he'll share his information with the authorities, it's highly likely that he'll use his considerable resources to conduct his own investigation. An investigation that's bound to get ugly for us."

The echo of those words congealed everything in Michael's mind, a mind that remembered Ivan's earlier comment about smart moves. This time the wave that washed over him was ice cold.

"You're absolutely right, on both accounts," Ivan said, meeting Boris's eye, then Pavel's. "Those are serious problems. And what do we do with serious problems?"

Michael answered, his voice barely above a whisper. "We eliminate them."

98

Strange Bedfellows

Moscow, Russia

Achilles didn't find a gun under Victor Vazov's pillow.

Or his wife Iveta's.

But she woke up while he was looking.

Victor jolted forward as his wife shrieked. In a fumbling flail, he smacked on the light but sent it to the floor, adding to the discord.

Achilles had experienced many scary scenarios, but he'd never woken in his own bed to find an intruder pointing a gun at his chest. It was the kind of experience that might make it hard to sleep soundly ever again.

The Vazovs both awoke to find guns pointed at their chests. Achilles was packing twin Glocks. "Quiet please. I'm here to help you, not hurt you."

Iveta began mumbling an incoherent stream of moans, pleas and prayers.

Achilles ignored her words but kept her hands in view, as he did Victor's. "There's a plan in place to kill you and your son. I came here to discuss it. To work with you to prevent Vlad's assassination."

Victor's eyes pulsed wider, but his wife spoke first. "I smell blood! Vitya, I smell blood!"

Victor glanced toward the bedroom door where the dark pool had leaked under. He quickly returned his focus to Achilles. "You're the man we caught breaking into the office the night of the investor reception. The man who killed Pasha."

Iveta's moaning got louder.

"I am. I visited Vertical Vision on the trail of the man who intends to murder you and your son. The man known by the global law enforcement community as Ivan the Ghost."

Victor's expression morphed from skepticism to scorn. "Ivan's not my enemy."

"Perhaps not. But he still intends to kill you, your wife and your son at Vlad's fortieth birthday party."

Victor considered that for a second. "Did Slava Gulin put a professional hit on us?"

"Good guess. That's exactly what Ivan wants the world to think."

"Why would Ivan want us dead? Or care what the world thinks? He and my son have a solid working relationship doing legitimate business."

Iveta finally stopped moaning. Decades by the side of a ruthless oligarch had toughened her nervous system and sharpened her mind. She was processing the revelation in parallel with her husband.

Achilles paused before answering the question as the unfairness struck him. He and Jo had repeatedly risked their lives, suffered traumas and toils, and nearly died while uncovering Ivan's plan. Now Victor Vazov was going to get spoon-fed most of what they'd learned. Breakfast in bed. "Ivan is active as The Ghost again. In fact, he's running the biggest illicit operation of his life."

Curiosity flickered. "So?"

"He plans to get away with it."

"Ivan always gets away with it."

"For good this time. He's going to convince the world that your, your dead son, is Ivan the Ghost. He's been setting Vlad up for years. Leaving clues. Planting evidence. Leading the authorities to his door." Achilles was only speculating on these latter points, but he was confident in his speculation, knowing Ivan.

"Go on."

"He needs you dead as well, so you won't refute the story— or go after him."

"It's an interesting theory. Why should I believe it?"

"I'm not asking you to believe me. I'm asking you to come with me—so you can witness Ivan's treachery with your own eyes. And prevent it, of course."

"You have a strange way of asking."

"After our last meeting, I doubted the wisdom of a conventional approach."

Victor was one of those guys who was charismatic despite being ugly. Hairless but fit, with taut skin, flat features and a neck two sizes too wide. His eyes were intelligent, but non-expressive. Hard to read. He gestured toward the gun Achilles was still pointing at his wife. "This isn't the kind of situation men like me are inclined to forgive or forget. What makes you think I won't kill you the first chance I get? "

"You're too smart to do that. By giving you the opportunity, I'll be proving that I'm an ally, not a threat. And to beat Ivan, you need every ally you can get. Furthermore, everything I've done tonight, I've done in the best interests of your family. And by getting here, into this room with you and your wife, I've proved that I'm better than any other weapon you have."

"What exactly are you proposing?"

Achilles lowered the Glocks. His seventh, final and most risky gamble. "First, we clean up the mess outside your door."

Iveta began blinking rapidly as her processor spun, but Victor immediately caught on. "You want to conceal your handiwork from my staff?"

"Ivan might have a spy within your organization. He did have one within your son's."

"How do I explain Pyotr's absence?"

"You inform the staff that you've decided to replace him."

Again Victor displayed the power of his oligarch brain. "With you, I presume?"

"With me."

99

Dread

French Riviera

To turn the wine cellar beneath his villa into a secret storage facility, Ivan had converted the stairway entrance into a coat closet. Michael watched him lead Team Raven there now. After opening the door, he leaned in, spread the hanging outerwear aside, and gave the rod on which they hung a twist. Had he been standing in the closet, nothing would have happened, but because there was no weight on the hardwood floor, it hinged upward from the back like a trapdoor, revealing the original stairway and activating a light.

They descended into a cool chamber hewn from bedrock and built with red brick. Solid, soundproof and stable in temperature. The size was a modest fifteen by twenty feet, the perimeter of which was still surrounded with wine racks. The middle of the room contained several large safes, but Ivan ignored them. He walked to the corner beneath the staircase and removed a specific bottle from the rack, a Bordeaux with artificially-adhered dust. He reached in to manipulate one of the supporting crosshatched struts, then put both hands on the side rails and pushed the whole rack including the brick wall behind it straight back. Rolling on concealed casters with perfectly balanced placement, it receded smoothly and silently under minimal effort.

The three men followed him into a room the same size as the one they'd just vacated. This one contained tool racks rather than wine racks, as well as workbenches that held large devices. "Recognize these?" Ivan asked with a sweep of his hand.

"The first two Raven prototypes," Boris said. "What's that you've added where the winch used to be?"

"It's the dock for these." Ivan pulled a tablecloth off a third workbench, revealing two black boxes roughly the size of large push lawnmowers, without the handles. "Anybody know what these are?"

Boris stepped forward and inspected one closely, paying special attention to the openings. He peered through them with the assistance of his phone's flashlight. The others watched in silence. "Is this a centrifugal gun?"

"It is. It's a DREAD gun. Don't ask me what the acronym means. I forgot."

"What's a centrifugal gun?" Pavel asked.

Boris was happy to answer. "They use centrifugal force rather than gunpowder to accelerate projectiles. Basically, they spin ball bearings around at tremendous speed and fling them out. Kinda like what happens when a lawnmower hits a rock, but a lot more organized. They can fire hundreds of rounds a second at speeds faster than bullets. They operate quietly and have no recoil or muzzle flash."

Michael could hardly believe his ears. "That's incredible! Why haven't I heard of them?"

"They've never been commercialized," Ivan said.

"Why not?"

"Accuracy," Boris said. "They're not much more accurate than lawnmowers kicking rocks."

"That's right," Ivan said. "But the DREAD will fire 6,000 7.62 mm rounds a minute at a speed of 8,000 feet per second."

"What about the accuracy issue? Doesn't the speed and power just compound that problem?" Pavel asked.

"Depends on the application. It's fine for blanketing an area at close range. Functions well in instances where you might otherwise want to detonate Claymore mines one after the other —like at Vazov's fortieth birthday party."

Boris skipped over the big reveal and asked."Why not just use Claymore mines, then?"

Truth be told, Ivan was loathe to use something so commonplace during his coronation. But he didn't want to share that glimpse into his soul—even though Michael had guessed as much, judging by the look in his eye—so Ivan voiced his secondary reason. "I need it to look like a mob did it. This will produce a scene similar to what you'd get if machine guns were fired on full auto. Not forensically, but in photos. And the low system weight and lack of recoil makes centrifugal guns much more suitable for deployment by drone."

Pavel jumped in. "Why do you need it to look like a mob hit?"

Ivan paused to up the tension before his dramatic revelation. "Because the Gulin family wants credit."

"They *want* credit?"

"It's analogous to ISIS claiming credit for a terrorist attack. Except in this case, they actually did contract with me to do it. It was the Gulins who did all that reconnaissance work for us in the States, the scouting and selecting of targets. They did it in exchange for my agreeing to wipe out the Vazovs."

"Their rivals."

"Exactly."

Once Michael's brain struggled past the shock and awe of the cool new weapon and the Gulin family twist, it thwacked back to the core of their conversation. He cleared his throat. It sounded a lot louder than usual there in the cave. "Are we really having this discussion this way? So nonchalantly? So matter of factly? We're talking about murdering everyone we worked with at Silicon Hill."

Ivan shook his head. "We did what it took to secure a fortune, and now we're doing what it takes to keep it. That's the theme of human history. The natural order. Why do you think Europe is covered with castles? First kings conquered, then they defended. Great men don't use knights and moats and boiling oil anymore, they use lobbyists and lawyers and spies, but they still do what they've always done. They do whatever it takes to defend their ill-gotten gains."

The clouds parted before Michael's eyes, but it wasn't sunshine that he saw. "That's why you gave us that speech about men getting rich by usurping other people's lives."

Ivan said nothing.

Michael kept going. "You've been preparing us for this all along. That's why you had us kill Gordon Sangster and Billy Burns. You were getting us ready for your endgame. Dirtying our hands and our consciences."

Ivan said nothing.

Michael said nothing.

Pavel broke the silence. "I see two drones and two DREAD guns. Who's going to fly the second?"

"Actually, Boris is going to fly one and Michael is going to fly the other. You'll be busy flying Raven. More on that later."

Michael felt the cold hand of harsh reality closing around his throat. "You want me to fly one of them? And pull the trigger?"

"It's up to you. But if the three of you all do your part in the final op, thereby ensuring that we'll get away with everything we've earned, I'll up your bonuses."

The unexpected twist left everyone dumbstruck, but Pavel eventually broke the silence with a telltale question. "How much?"

"The same percentage originally promised, but of the $12.5 billion, rather than the $600 million."

Ivan's ultimate revelation sent Michael's head reeling. His two-percent share was worth $250 million. Roughly $1 million for every person they were about to kill.

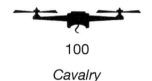

100

Cavalry

French Riviera

Jo had been too busy to worry about Achilles during his crazy quest to co-opt Victor Vazov. She had to prepare her side of the operation. The outside, so to speak. Over the last couple of days, she had successfully scouted Silicon Hill from the sea and procured the equipment their plan required. She'd checked off almost everything on her extensive list with time to spare. But now that she no longer had to dash and scrounge, haggle and negotiate, now that she had time to relax a bit before the big op, anxiety came calling.

Victor Vazov had beaten them once. He'd caught them. Vlad Vazov had also beaten Achilles once. He'd caught him. Both times, Jo had been the one to turn the tables—and she wasn't with Achilles now.

It wasn't that she felt superior to Achilles. He had the better operational brain and was far more physically capable. But she had tactical talents that complemented his, as well as a highly refined ability to manipulate objects and people. More importantly, Achilles was alone. Alone against a ruthless oligarch and his security forces.

There was nothing she could do to help him at the moment. No call she could make, no aid she could send. But she could help them both in the future. That was the final to-do item on her part of the preparatory plan.

She pulled up the TOR Fone app on her laptop and dialed a U.S. cell phone number. It rang six times before a familiar voice answered.

"Ripley Zonder."

"Have you missed me?"

"Like the desert misses the rain. Although I really wish you'd called a few days back."

Jo knew why. She'd seen the news. But she wanted him to say it. "Why is that?"

"Director Brix took me off the investigation, citing my lack of progress. He sent me on vacation without designating my next role. I'm supposed to do the honorable thing and resign."

"Tough break. I know exactly what it feels like. I lost my job at the CIA for the same reason—failing to catch Ivan. As did Achilles. We're three casualties of the same conflict."

"Well, spank me cross-eyed, I'd forgotten. I can't say that news makes me cheery, but it's mighty nice to have company. Do you want the number for my replacement?"

"Do you want redemption?"

"Pardon?"

"Do you want to help us solve the case?"

"I'm not in a position to do that anymore. As I said, I'm not in any position at all, unless you count purgatory."

"That's not what I asked."

"Am I interested in solving the case? Hell, yes!"

"Would you like to come to Europe and help me catch Ivan?"

"Me, personally?"

"You, personally."

"Hell, yes! I want to lasso that sumbitch with barbed wire and drag him all the way to Langley behind a slow horse. Show the sheriff that he was mistaken to lose faith in this cowboy."

"Well then get yourself to Paris. I'll meet you beneath the Arc de Triomphe at noon tomorrow. Wear boots and a cowboy hat." Jo had sourced the weapons for their big operation from an acquaintance in Paris, so she had to head north anyway.

Rip took a few seconds to respond, making Jo nervous. She was counting on his help. "You really think we can catch Ivan?"

"I have almost no doubt."

"Almost, huh? Well, that's good enough for me. I'll be there."

"Glad to hear it, partner. One more question."

"Fire away."

"Can you scuba dive?"

101

Opening Doors

French Riviera

Achilles stopped the limo at the entrance to Silicon Hill and lowered both left-side windows. "I've got Victor Vazov in the back."

In order to prove his outlandish assertion, Achilles had agreed with Victor to play the role of his driver and third bodyguard, while under the watchful eyes and loaded guns of the other two. The four had come to France a day earlier than Victor had planned. His wife would follow as originally scheduled.

Victor pressed him for details during the flight, but Achilles remained tight-lipped. He didn't want Victor deciding that he could prove Ivan's treachery without assistance.

The gate guard leaned forward to inspect the contents of the car. It wasn't the same guy who had admitted him when he visited with Jo. This one had a thick head of gray hair and a matching mustache. "And the rest of you?"

"Protection."

"All three of you?"

"All three of us."

"Our birthday party isn't until tomorrow. Today's celebration is at the polo club."

Vazov spoke up from the back seat. "I know what day my son's birthday party is. I was there for his birth. I came early for other business."

The guard queried his computer. "Your son's not here at the moment, Mr. Vazov. And you're not on today's visitor list. I'm sorry. Our security procedures are very strict."

Achilles jumped in. "Call Chantal. Ask her to authorize us.

Tell her Victor Vazov will be phoning her momentarily."

"I can do that. Just a moment please." The guard shut his sliding glass window and picked up his phone. He spoke for a few seconds, gave a thumbs-up and opened the gate.

Achilles called the number on the public relations manager's business card, using the hands-free phone.

"Bonjour, Chantal speaking."

"Chantal, this is Victor Vazov. Thank you for signing me in."

"My pleasure. Had I known you were coming, I would have made arrangements."

"I didn't want my son to know I was coming. Part of a surprise. On that note, I have a quick request. Would you kindly ask Mickey Leonov to meet me in the lobby?"

"Mickey Leonov. But of course. If there's anything I can do…"

"No, no. He's an old family friend. But I want it to be a surprise, so just tell him he has a visitor, please."

"My pleasure. You have my number if I can be of further assistance. Don't hesitate to use it."

Mickey was already waiting in the lobby when they arrived. The sight of four large men in suits walking straight for him with purposeful strides put a look of alarm on his face. "Can I help you?"

Victor held out a hand that looked capable of crushing ostrich eggs. "Victor Vazov."

"Mickey Leonov."

"We need to talk. Let's go to my son's office."

"Yes, sir. Absolutely. Follow me. It's a pleasure to meet you."

When Victor didn't reply, Mickey turned and led them up the stairs. He held the door open so they'd be the first to violate the boss's space. Victor entered like he owned the place and went straight for one of the soft leather chairs configured around a coffee table.

As the others followed suit, Achilles said, "Excuse me. Where's the restroom?"

Mickey motioned off to the right. "It's around the corner on the left."

Achilles wanted to be sure no witnesses were around for what was to come. It only took about thirty seconds to verify that the other three offices and the bathroom were vacant.

When he returned, Mickey was speaking in Russian. "Yes, it's really Mikhail. I was born in Saint Petersburg. My family immigrated to San Jose when I was eleven."

Achilles gave Victor a nod and remained standing by the door.

Victor said, "It's nice to meet someone who has made such good use of the opportunities his parents provided."

"Thank you."

"I'd like to provide you with an opportunity that may prove even more advantageous to your future."

Mickey scooted to the edge of his chair.

"I'd like you to give us a tour of the lower lab."

Again, Mickey's body language indicated that he wouldn't be skilled at poker. "Lower lab? I'm not sure what you're talking about."

102

Black and White

French Riviera

Mickey had faced a few tough decisions in his life, but nothing compared to the one confronting him now. The big boss's oligarch of a father and his three enormous bodyguards were asking him to betray a confidence he'd sworn at gunpoint never to reveal. For pure fear factor, the black eye of Michael's Sig was hard to trump, even by these big-knuckled Neanderthals.

The battle waged within him, while the four watched with steely stares. On the one hand, they already knew about the lab. On the other hand, if he allowed them to enter, they would no longer need him. The weird thing was, project Raven had been completed. The lab was likely empty. He was back at his old job, as were the other Raven engineers. But the triple-pay was still coming. Hush money.

He had every intention of hushing.

As awkward as it would be to turn these four down, they would be gone by Monday. Meanwhile, Mickey hoped to work for Michael for many years to come. He had half a mind to run, but he was seated in soft furniture and the bodyguards blocked the door. "I really don't know anything about a lower lab. I'm sure Chantal could arrange a tour of the East and West Wing Labs for you, sir. Shall I call her?"

Victor nodded at the bodyguard who had gone to the bathroom. That couldn't be a good sign. Then Victor stood and said, "Have it your way."

Mickey didn't know what to do. Could this all be a test? A loyalty test? "It was a pleasure to meet you." He stood and headed for the door like the room was on fire.

He never saw the punch coming. Didn't even feel it, really. He just found himself doubled over grasping his stomach while struggling to breathe.

The bellicose bodyguard scooped him up in a fireman's carry and walked him out of the room. When they turned right, he knew what was happening. It was a type of manual override. By the time Mickey caught his breath, he was back on his feet in the secret elevator.

"This jog your memory?" Victor asked.

Mickey kept quiet. He was pleased to have the traitorous decision taken from him, but far from relieved. He was disappearing underground with violent thugs. Malicious men who weren't happy with him.

As they descended, Mickey recalled his first morning on the job in the secret lab. He hadn't slept a wink the night before. His mind kept churning the exciting revelations and fantasies about what he'd do with all the extra pay. He'd finally given up on trying to sleep and had gone in early. Then he'd passed out in that very elevator. Mickey never told a soul about his embarrassing incident, and it hadn't happened again. He wished he would faint now, but his pulse was pumping way too fast.

The elevator door opened and Mickey turned on the lights. He'd expected to find the laboratory emptied, but everything looked exactly as it had the last day he worked there.

"Recognize it?" The bodyguard said to Victor as they walked side by side toward the one remaining Raven and its command console.

"The drone from the U.S. kidnappings. I don't know what I was expecting, but it definitely wasn't this."

The bodyguard said nothing while Victor walked around Raven, shaking his head. "You're telling me my son knows nothing about this?"

The bodyguard held up his hand in a stop sign.

Mickey hadn't thought about it, but now he realized that he hadn't ever seen Vlad Vazov in the lab.

"The other engineers who worked in this lab, are they all still employed here?" the bodyguard asked.

"There were only a few of us. Everyone's still here."

"Working in the regular labs?"

"Yes."

"What about the executives, are they in the labs too?"

"Now that you mention it, I haven't seen them there since they returned from the States."

"Where have you seen them?"

Mickey thought about it. "Just around. In the cafeteria. At the gym. This morning, I saw them heading down to the beach."

"What's at the beach?"

"Beach stuff. Chairs. Umbrellas. There's a fully stocked bar. Oh, and the company yacht."

The bodyguard nodded to himself, then gestured toward the Drone Command Module. "Show us how to use this."

"My pleasure. It's not that difficult. Have you ever flown a hobby drone?"

For the next two hours, they went over and over the controls, even hovering Raven in the lab. When Victor and his bodyguard were satisfied, Mickey stood and said, "I hope you don't hold it against me. My earlier reticence. Secrecy is a really big deal around here."

"No worries," Victor said. "We're big believers in that too."

Mickey didn't see the blow coming that time either. He just felt his jaw catch fire and saw a flash of light.

103

One Step Ahead

French Riviera

Thirty-four hours after landing in Paris, Rip bubbled to the surface behind Vazov's yacht. He studied the starlit sky as his new partner surfaced beside him. What a beautiful place to commit a crime.

Quietly, they laid their diver propulsion devices on the swim deck, followed by their gun bags. Then the two rolled out of the ocean and onto the *Bright Horizon.*

Jo brought a finger to her lips as they crouched over their weapons. Her precaution was unnecessary. He knew the plan. But he approved of the redundancy. When working with a new partner, he was doubly careful as well.

Her choice of meeting point had been the first sign that she took security seriously. The Arc de Triomphe was in the middle of the busiest roundabout in France, a monster with twelve feeder roads and more traffic lanes than you could easily count.

Yesterday, beneath the blazing sun, he had walked around that Paris landmark in his boots and cowboy hat, waiting for her to arrive. After an hour of pulling his roller bag back and forth amidst throngs of tourists, he began to wonder if Jo's summons was a bad joke. Then she appeared in a small white Peugeot and yelled for him to get in.

From the Arc de Triomphe, she drove wildly around the city until at last she pulled into an underground parking garage. There, she scanned him and his bag before changing cars and driving away, leaving his boots, hat and empty suitcase behind. She had lightened up after that, but still hadn't taken him to Achilles.

Achilles had reportedly scouted Vazov's yacht for them. He

had also formulated their game plan. But everything had been relayed through Jo.

Rip looked forward to finally meeting the Olympian later tonight.

While the stars twinkled brightly in the sky and the waves sloshed playfully against the yacht, Jo pulled two cell phones from her gun bag. She switched both on and handed him one. They'd be using them to talk and text each other during the operation. Next, she doled out their armaments, H&K MP7A1s and tranquilizer guns. Rip approved of the combination. It gave them options.

After an equipment check, Jo held both her barrels side by side, then spread them apart. One pointing left, the other right. Time to split up and search the yacht, confirming that it was indeed empty.

They'd agreed earlier that he would search deck two where the lounge and galley were located, and deck four, which had the secondary captain's chair and a dining area. She would clear the staterooms on deck one and deck three, which held primary navigation and a soft seating area.

He found nothing.

She joined him up top five minutes after they rolled out of the water. "All clear."

"So now we wait?"

"Now we wait." She pointed to three large backpacks resting under the dining table that ran down the middle of the deck. "Those are the Drone Command Modules. And those," she pointed toward the bow of the yacht, where white tarpaulins covered three mattress-sized objects, "those are the drones."

They couldn't risk going out on the bow for fear of being spotted by a partygoer looking down. "You said they're the same model used in the States, but two have centrifugal guns rather than winches?"

Jo nodded. "According to Achilles."

"How was he able to confirm that without being caught?"

"He was undercover."

"Is that where he is now, undercover?"

"No comment."

Rip gestured toward the terrace high overhead. "He's up there on the cliff, isn't he? Preparing to hop over the railing when the moment is right?"

"He's where he needs to be to get one step ahead of Ivan."

"And how does he know where that is? Nobody has ever gotten one step ahead of Ivan."

"It's just his best guess. But I think he's a good guesser."

"Seems to me, we're one step ahead of Ivan. It's pretty clear, right? The drones are here, so they have to be coming. The party is up there, so we know where they're going."

"I agree. But it's Ivan, so I know we're missing something."

A light flashed on shore. A rectangular light. The elevator. Three men were briefly visible before the door closed behind them.

Jo mumbled, "Michael."

"Who?"

"Ivan's right-hand man. I tangled with him once before. It didn't end well for me."

"Well, tonight's your chance to even the score."

"Yes, it is."

Jo pulled out her cell phone as they retreated to the hiding places Achilles had selected and prepared for them, storage compartments beneath the bench seats on the party deck. Rip noted that her screen was already active. He hadn't seen her dial. Then again, Jo was known to be exceptionally quick with her hands. She spoke into her phone. "Achilles, they're coming."

"Roger that."

"He's been listening all this time?" Rip asked.

Jo winked. "One step ahead."

104

Words Unspoken

French Riviera

Boris assumed a reporter's eye as he studied the scene before him. He did so because it struck him that before-and-after photos would be on the cover of every newspaper in Europe tomorrow morning—if cameras or cell phones had been allowed at Vazov's fortieth birthday party. The contrast would be breathtaking. Mind numbing. Heartbreaking.

One couldn't imagine a more opulent party. White ties and evening gowns, champagne and caviar, candlelight and crystal. Black tuxedoed waiters, gold linen tablecloths, silver place settings, vibrant bouquets of flowers. All set on the clifftop terrace of a billionaire's mansion overlooking the French Riviera. It was utterly spectacular. And it was about to become the most shocking murder scene of the century.

"It's time for cake and fireworks. Everybody outside!" Boris said with a swipe of his arm. He, Pavel and Michael were charged with getting people out of the building and onto the terrace. That included guests and caterers. Michael was busy emptying the kitchen under the pretext that the boss wanted all hands either pouring drinks or serving dessert. Pavel had locked the building's front doors and was now clearing the restrooms and lobby. Boris was manning the terrace doors. He was the one-way valve at the end of the funnel.

His was the least pleasant position. But he understood why Ivan had assigned it to him. Boris wasn't a people person.

Giselle from reception was walking his way. She wore a teal gown with slit sides that made her eyes pop and exposed lots of leg.

Boris held up a hand. "I'm sorry, we need everyone on the

terrace please."

"I need to use the restroom."

"Vazov wants everyone seated for the show."

"I'll just be a minute."

Boris used the line Ivan had fed him. "I'll lose my job if you miss the show or walk in after it starts. He has something special planned."

She backed off. "Okay. I'll hold it."

Pavel showed up with a handsome couple Boris didn't recognize. Both were a bit red in the face and disheveled. Pavel mouthed "closet" as he ushered them outside. "That's it. Let's lock the doors."

Boris took a last look around. He'd spent years here, but would never return.

They headed for the beach elevator. It was accessed via a dedicated stairway at the far right end of the lobby, near the kitchen entrance. Michael appeared as they approached the stairhead. The three descended together.

Nobody spoke.

Boris was certain he'd never experience a more somber moment, and undoubtedly the others felt the same. The elevator ride was a transition from their old lives to their new. From their old selves to their new. It wasn't an easy transition to process.

Before he met Ivan, Boris had been innocent. After he met Ivan, he lost that innocence bit by bit until all his compassion was gone. He hadn't really noticed while it happened. The moral descent had been so gradual. Meanwhile, the violence had slowly escalated to the point where he became an accessory to murder.

Initially, the lifestyle had stolen his focus, then the money took center stage. It had gone from good to great to a $6 million payout.

Now, over the course of the next few minutes, the transition would become complete. From comfortable to extremely wealthy. And from criminal to mass murderer. It was a leap he'd never have made from where he started. Had he seen it coming, he would have turned and run in the other direction. But now it was just the bottom of a slippery slope. Jumping was not required. Running was not an option.

The elevator pinged open, exposing the walkway that transitioned into the dock. The three stepped beneath the stars and eyed their getaway vehicle. The *Bright Horizon* was a beautiful yacht, 66-feet of luxury designed to be owner-operated.

They jogged to the gate that kept out the unauthorized. As Michael reached for his key, Boris remembered he had forgotten a job. "Crap. I have to go back to disable the elevator."

Without further word, they reversed course, stopping along the way to pull a sledgehammer and two steel wedges from beneath a mound of sand.

Pavel gave him a leg up onto the elevator roof, then Michael handed him the tools. Ivan had instructed him to cut the cable, but the cable wasn't exposed. Boris had agreed, then selected the simpler method of driving steel wedges between the lift and the rail it ran on. They would function like door stops. Plenty effective for preventing the elevator from operating this evening.

Three good whacks were enough to embed each. He tossed the hammer, slid to the ground, and returned to the gate double-time. Michael already had it unlocked and held open.

Time was tight.

They ran the rest of the way to the boat and out onto the bow, where each grabbed a tarp and pulled, exposing his assigned drone. With the Ravens free to fly, Ivan's three lieutenants climbed quickly to the top deck, where they removed the Drone Command Modules from their carrying cases.

Once the DCMs were set up on the table they'd been stored beneath, Michael typed a one word text for Ivan. He hit *send* and held out both fists. Boris and Pavel bumped them and nodded, but no words were spoken.

They launched all three drones at once. From the top deck of the *Bright Horizon* the sound was like a swarm of hornets. The gun drones flew to the left and right, with The Claw drone between them. All three flew toward the base of the cliff, then spread apart and began to rise.

105

Toast

French Riviera

Ivan watched Victor Vazov stand and take the mike, with vodka glass in hand. He was center stage, so to speak, with dozens of tables fanning out before him and his back to the guard wall. Stars above, sea below, ocean behind, and his birthday boy beside him.

As Victor Vazov toasted his son—*the visionary businessman, the accomplished athlete, the most-eligible bachelor*—Ivan studied the scene with a critical eye. Everyone was out on the terrace. By his count, not a soul was missing. As planned.

Ivan had seen his guys doing the jobs assigned—mopping up strays, herding guests, locking doors. Six minutes had passed since they closed the last latch. He should get the *Go* text any second.

Funny how whole lives hinged on a few select seconds. Catching the right girl's glance or getting hit by a car. Shaking the right hand or suffering a stroke. Dodging a bullet or catching one. Nobody on the terrace would be dodging bullets tonight. Not at 100 rounds per second.

His watch vibrated. He checked his wrist and read the text. Just two tiny letters, but a world of meaning: *Go.*

Ivan stood and turned to the stone wall a few feet behind his chair, the waist-high barrier that stood between terrace-goers and a 400-foot drop. He hopped up on it, stood with arms extended at shoulder height, and began walking toward Victor. He could sense the guests' attention shifting, but didn't dare to look in their direction. The ledge atop the wall was only a foot wide.

He could hear the drones now that he had one ear over the

ledge. Their hum was getting louder. A dozen steps took him to the spot directly behind the Vazovs. He stopped there and turned to face the crowd.

Victor completed his toast and raised his glass, but the crowd's response was lukewarm. All eyes were on Ivan. Victor drained his vodka, then turned. "Would you like the microphone?"

Ivan didn't answer. Instead, he stared into the oligarch's eyes while counting down in his mind. Five... Four... Three... Two...

Raven rose majestically behind him with a gust of wind and the hum of rotors. The crowd recoiled as if yanked by a common string. A few people screamed. Everyone stared. They all knew what they were seeing, but nobody expected to see it.

Almost nobody.

Victor looked oddly unwavering. Then again, he was known to be tough as a two-dollar steak. His bodyguards also remained unflinching.

Raven wrapped The Claw around Ivan the instant it reached the right height. He hadn't felt that cool constriction since the prototype-testing days. Tonight, he found it tougher and tighter than he remembered. It allowed him enough room to breathe but left no space to move.

The crowd gasped in unison.

More screams erupted.

His feet left the ground.

Raven took him up. Ten feet. Twenty. Thirty. Forty. Then it backed him away to optimize the view. Theirs, and his.

Every eye was on Ivan. Every mouth half open. The cameras would surely be out and rolling, if cell phones hadn't been confiscated.

The guests were transfixed on the scene in front of them and what was surely about to happen, so transfixed that nobody noticed the gun drones rising off to the left and right. Michael and Boris would start shooting the instant the guns cleared the wall. They'd calculated their flight paths in advance to optimize coverage and to avoid shooting each other. Distance and angle would also minimize the chances of ricochet, although even if a drone went down it wouldn't matter. The other could do the deed ten times over.

While Ivan watched, the gun drones froze. Why weren't they rising into firing position? Surely the guys weren't having second thoughts? Not both of them. Nobody walked away from $125 million. In the whole history of the world, that had never happened. Not once.

But they clearly weren't moving.

What was going on?

He looked up to signal Raven's camera—and saw the headset coming down.

106

Do it

French Riviera

Ivan grabbed the headset as soon as it came within reach and yelled "Fire! Everyone is in place up here. Raise the drones and fire!"

"The guns can't fire. Achilles disabled them."

The voice had a familiar accent, but Ivan couldn't place it under the circumstances. "Who is this?"

"It's Ripley Zonder here, Ivan."

"Agent Zonder," Ivan repeated. He looked down and back at the yacht but couldn't make out any details in the dark. He saw shadows behind the glow from the Drone Command Modules, but that was it. "Or should I say Former-Agent Zonder?"

"Why don't you just call me Rip. I'm feeling friendly. In fact, I'm feeling happier than a boardinghouse pup, knowing we're about to meet in person at long last."

"Don't count on it."

"Oh, I'm counting. Been counting for a while now. One, two, three. Boris, Pavel and Michael. Three collars clapped on, one to go."

Ivan wondered why they weren't bringing him back to the boat if they really had everything under control. Perhaps they just wanted to give him a taste of his own medicine, hanging there helpless in space, hundreds of feet above the ground while a crowd looked on like he was a float in a parade. Perhaps they were interrogating his men to see if he had explosives. Well, he had an explosive all right. "Put Achilles on the phone."

"He's not here at the moment."

Ivan guessed he was hidden among the crowd as part of a backup plan. Probably snuck in over the rail after climbing up the cliff. "Surely he can hear us?"

"I can hear you."

No background noise. No turning heads. Achilles wasn't in the crowd. "Why aren't you on the boat with your friends?"

"I figured you'd be down in your bunker of a lab when the bullets started flying. That's where the generals usually go. Figured I'd be waiting with a warm welcome. Apparently I underestimated your bravado."

"My bravado isn't all you've underestimated."

"This is no time for talking tough, Ivan. A man should know when he's been beaten."

Ivan pulled out his cell phone and typed in a dark web address from memory. "Why don't you come up to the terrace. We'll discuss this like men."

"I'll just meet you on the beach."

"I'm afraid you'll find the elevator is out of commission. You sure you won't consider the terrace? I'd really love for us to meet before I slip through your fingers again."

"No slipping this time. I've got you right where I want you."

Raven waggled violently in reaction to his words, almost causing Ivan to drop the phone. What a disaster that would be. He double-checked the screen, then held it up to Raven's camera. "It's not me you should be worried about. Don't you know by now, I'm always six steps ahead."

"That doesn't appear to be the case this time," Achilles said, his tone calm, cool and confident.

Ivan realized that Achilles couldn't see the camera image now playing on the DCM. He only had audio.

"He's got Katya," a woman said. Ivan recognized the French accent of Jo Monfort. "She appears healthy, but she's chained to a wall in a room with some books, a mattress, a bucket and nothing else. She clearly can't hear us. She's just lying on the mattress, reading."

Ivan was tiring of his dangling position. The Claw was digging into his ribs and every breath made it worse. Time to end this thing. "Before your petty little mind starts spinning and any silly little plans come out, you should know that the camera feed can't be traced and you can't beat her location out of my colleagues because they don't have it. You should also know that your precious professor has no food or water. She won't get either if I don't send explicit, coded instructions. And forget about trying to find her. You don't even know what time zone she's in. She'll be a dusty skeleton before you discover the body."

"How did you find her?" Achilles asked, obviously buying time to think.

Ivan ignored the question. "Here's what's going to happen. You're going to release my men and get off Vazov's yacht. You're going to let me and my men sail away. When we're where I want to be, I'll let you know where you can find Katya. End of negotiation. Now give the phone to Michael."

Ivan began counting to himself, "One billion dollars. Two billion dollars. Three billion dollars. Four—"

"Do it, Jo," Achilles said. "Do whatever he asks."

107

Disagreement

French Riviera

Rip savored the capture with the relish of the world's best whiskey. The slow and silent ascent up the stairs, armed to the teeth. The acceleration of the attack, fast and furious. The crestfallen faces of Ivan's lieutenants, helpless and bound. He lived for events like that.

But it got better.

The rush that followed the capture was more powerful than any he'd ever felt before. It was the rush of a revitalized career. Not just revitalized—reinvented. He would become a legend. The man who succeeded where hundreds had failed before him. The man who captured The Ghost.

He'd let Brix take the credit, of course. Brix would do the press conferences and talk shows and magnanimously mention "team" without ever saying Rip's name. Rip wouldn't mind. Well, not too much. His peers would know the truth, and more importantly, Brix would owe him. Rip would be able to name his next assignment. He'd pick San Antonio. Not the most powerful or prestigious SAIC post, but solid, rural and off the Washington radar.

It all vanished as quickly as it had come.

Fast as a finger snap, his rush faded and his career flushed and he was back where he'd been before Jo called.

When Ivan lifted the hostage video stream to the camera, Rip understood why the hundreds who came before him had failed. No matter how clever or competent you were, no matter how much you plotted, planned or innovated, that damn Ghost was always one step ahead.

Still, Rip had come closer than anyone before him. He *was*

closer. He actually had Ivan in his grasp. In his grasp.

He reached over Jo's shoulder and ended the call to Ivan while keeping Achilles on the line. As she turned to stare at him, he said, "We can't let Ivan go. We'll get the girl another way. The CIA and FBI will put their full resources into finding her."

They were standing in the middle of the top deck, in the open space at the top of the stairs they'd charged up minutes earlier. She was holding a tranquilizer gun in one hand and a phone in the other. He had an H&K MP7A1 in each hand. Both were leveled at the three men seated a couple of yards in front of them at the Drone Command Modules. Jo had duct taped their mouths and zip tied their ankles to each other, but she had left their hands free for now to operate the drones. Thus the raised weapons.

"You know that's not true," Achilles immediately interjected. "Once Ivan's in the can, all attention will shift to the next political priority."

Rip leapt on that. "I'll make Katya a priority. Not just a law enforcement priority, a public priority. We'll piggyback her story on the Ivan news. The media will eat it up. A ticking clock, a beautiful girl. It's the perfect human interest story. Within 24 hours the whole world will be searching."

"Where will they be searching? We don't even know what country she's in. Is it Russia? France? Or one of the two dozen countries in between? There's got to be half-a-billion basements between Moscow and Monaco."

"We'll put pressure on his three lieutenants. Offer a deal. The prisoner's dilemma. First one to talk, walks. One will talk. Guaranteed."

All three began shaking their heads.

"Ivan said he's the only one who knows," Achilles pressed.

All three began nodding.

Rip ignored them. "You believe him? You believe Ivan the Ghost, one of the greatest con men of all time?"

"I believe the three men before you have been too busy flying drones in the U.S. to be kidnapping Katya in Moscow. I believe Ivan would outsource the brute work to someone less critical. And yes, I believe he would keep that information strictly to himself because he plans for situations exactly like this. That's what he does."

"It's not your call, Achilles. I'm the only law enforcement officer here. It's my call." Rip was the only objective party on that boat. The only person with the detachment required to make the right decision. The decision that yielded the greatest good. Was he happy about sacrificing a life to put Ivan and his lieutenants behind bars? Of course not. Did commanders routinely make similar calls? They certainly did. Was it the right call? Absolutely.

"It's not your operation. You're a guest. And Katya's life is not yours to gamble."

"And yet here I am holding the guns."

Achilles tone changed. His voice cracked. "Talk to him, Jo. Make him see reason. This is Katya we're talking about. You may not know her, but you've been in her shoes."

Jo turned toward Rip and started to speak, but stopped herself. His look of determination must have halted her. She shook her head and handed over the phone, accepting one of the machine pistols in return. Then she pointed her tranq gun at his thigh and fired.

108

Suspicion

French Riviera

Michael took great pleasure in carrying Agent Zonder's limp body off the yacht and dumping him on the dock. There was something about turning the tables that tickled him to his core. Another reason he loved being part of Team Ivan.

He turned to Jo while reboarding the *Bright Horizon.* "I'm afraid the elevator's out of order, but I suspect Achilles will be climbing down momentarily to keep you company. Meanwhile, look on the bright side. Last time we parted company, you had a bullet in your chest. I'd say this is a marked improvement."

Jo raised one of her machine pistols. "I could still change my mind."

"Someone else could. You have too much heart."

He waved up to the navigation deck and Boris began backing the yacht away from the dock.

Jo lowered her weapon.

They sailed out far enough to fade into the dark, then stopped long enough for Pavel to land Ivan on the bow. The return of the king. He ran up top to join them. "Send the drones high up and far out, then hit their self-destructs. I'll meet you on deck three."

"Aye aye."

Deck three housed the main wheel and operating controls, the ones you would use during inclement weather or whenever you preferred to escape the sun. Ivan rose from the captain's chair as his lieutenants joined him and motioned toward the soft seating. "I've set course for Nice. We'll be there in an hour. Time to relax a bit."

"Relax?" Pavel said. "The CIA now knows who's behind the

drones. Victor Vazov now knows we intended to massacre his entire family. Vlad Vazov now knows we were framing him. And Kyle Achilles is still out there."

Ivan raised his left hand and flicked out a finger for each of Pavel's concerns. "Four problems." He raised his right hand. "$12 billion." He mimicked a balance with both hands, then landed on the right. "Granted, four problems is four more than I had hoped we'd have at this point. But I'm not blindsided by our predicament. I did plan for it."

"You planned for it?"

"Do you really doubt it?" Michael asked. "Look what he just did to Achilles and Co. Imagine the foresight that required."

"What is the plan?" Pavel asked.

Ivan dropped his hands. "There's a private plane waiting for us in Nice. It will take us to Bangkok, where we change both airports and planes before flying to Sydney."

"What happens in Sydney?"

"In Sydney, we'll be met by a man who has Australian passports ready and waiting for us. With new names of course. Anybody want a drink? I could really go for a vodka—on the rocks. Our time in the States warmed me to the American style."

"I'll pour," Michael said. Despite his confidence in Ivan, he was too anxious to stay seated. He wanted to look around.

There was a refrigerator between them and the captain's chair, right at the top of the stairs. Standing before it, he gave the horizon a 360-degree scan, spotting nothing but the lights of the distant shore. He glanced at the navigation console. They were headed toward the tip of Saint-Jean-Cap-Ferrat, en route to Nice.

Inside the fridge, Michael found ice and a bottle of Jean-Marc XO. He filled four tumblers with ice, grabbed the chilled vodka and returned to the table.

While Michael poured, Ivan said, "In Australia, I'll devise another plan to get our enemies off our backs. That will take time, but I promise you, we'll still enjoy a long and peaceful retirement."

Everyone drank deeply.

"How do we avoid capture in the meantime?" Pavel asked.

"Did you contingency-plan for that?"

All eyes turned back to Ivan.

"As a matter of fact, I did. It's not so much a contingency as another core part of my plan, a part I haven't yet revealed. But it will serve that purpose nicely."

Everyone waited for Ivan to elaborate. He let them stew for a minute while toying with his ice cubes.

"I've got two new pages prepared for fallingstars.info. I'll post them at the airport. My laptop's waiting on the jet. The first contains a link to the MiMiC program. Within hours it will become the most downloaded app in history. Mark my words."

Michael believed him. The ability to imitate anyone on the phone was a dream of every adolescent prankster, cheating adult and criminal mind. "And the second?"

"The second page delivers the blueprints for Raven and The Claw. Both of Boris's engineering packages. And since we didn't get the chance to use it, I'll also include what I have for the DREAD gun."

Everyone gasped, to the extent that men like them ever reacted that way. All three immediately understood the implications. Copycats would crop up like weeds after rain. The world would change overnight. Life on Earth would never be the same.

Ivan continued before anyone composed a suitable comment. "I think that will derail any pursuit plans for the foreseeable future. At the city, county, state and federal levels, law enforcement will be far too busy to bother looking for us."

"Won't they just disable the *fallingstars* website?" Pavel asked. "To date, they've been afraid to touch it for fear that you'll just put up another and advertise it. But as soon as they know you're out of commission, there's nothing to stop them."

Boris answered for Ivan, "It won't matter, once the genie is out of the bottle. And believe me, it will be out within seconds of the post going live."

Michael chimed in next. "Earlier you indicated that this action was part of your core plan. That means you planned on releasing MiMiC and Raven even if Vazov's party had gone as planned."

"I did say that," Ivan conceded.

"But why?"

Ivan set down his glass and stared into it for a few seconds before looking back up. "Vanity. I want the credit. I want to make a lasting global impact. I want my name in the history books. I want children to study me in seventh grade, and write about me in five-page reports."

"Like Nobel and Oppenheimer," Boris said.

"Like Nobel and Oppenheimer," Ivan repeated.

The room again went quiet as the four men drank and contemplated.

Ivan eventually broke the silence. "We will be parting company in Sydney. Where you go is entirely up to you, but I suggest you lose yourselves exploring the continent. Australia is the size of the United States, but its population is a mere 24 million. It's beautiful, modern, friendly and oh so easy to get lost in. There are beaches and rainforests and beachfront rainforests. There are mountains and deserts and lush green valleys. They've got cities big and small, and villages of every size. You name it, you got it, all first class." He raised his glass.

Michael and Boris raised theirs, but Pavel kept his vodka on the table. "If we split up, I don't see how your twelve billion helps us." Pavel held out his hands to simulate the scales, but after a bit of waggling, ended with them leaning left.

"Ah, yes. Thank you for reminding me. Your bonuses will be paid as if the executions went through. In fact, I've already made the transfers. In Bitcoin. Completely untraceable." Ivan pulled three slips of paper from his pocket, studied them for a second, and handed one to each man. "These are the numbers of accounts with the nine-figure balances promised. You need to switch the 1s and 7s, and the 0s and 8s—I didn't want to risk writing the real numbers down. I suggest you memorize them immediately. The passwords are your three initials in uppercase followed by your birthdays written DDMMMYY, like 11JAN77."

Boris raised his glass. The others immediately followed. "Thank you. Here's to your health, Ivan."

Everyone drained their glasses.

Ivan refilled them. "Any more questions? We've still got time."

"I have one," Michael said. "When are you going to call Achilles?"

"I'm sure you know the answer to that?"

"I have my suspicion."

Boris and Pavel looked on with mild curiosity. Visions of their new Australian lifestyles were sucking up the bulk of their attention, and the vodka was also taking effect.

Ivan leaned back and took another sip of his drink. "I'm not going to call Achilles. I want him spending the next few weeks looking for Katya, not us."

109

Leapfrog

French Riviera

Achilles pulled the listening device from his ear. He'd heard everything he needed to hear. His suspicion had been confirmed.

He slipped off the twin bunk of the *Bright Horizon*'s smaller guest stateroom, grabbed a Glock 19 with his right hand and a H&K MP7A1 with his left, and began climbing toward the third deck.

He moved as slowly and silently as a spider in sneakers until he reached the base of the second staircase. Then he paused to listen. The four were discussing plans for exploring Australia in style without attracting attention.

He cleared his mind the way he did before a complicated sequence on a climb, rehearsing each move. He'd pictured this exact scene while planning for tonight. Of course he'd pictured a dozen other scenes as well. As Ivan had taught him, he had prepared for them all, planting listening devices everywhere and practicing multiple moves.

He hadn't known that Ivan had captured Katya—and he still had no idea how Ivan had managed it—but he had known that Ivan would go into tonight with a trump card up his sleeve. So Achilles had come up with a blanket plan, a coverall ruse to put himself one step ahead.

Jo had been in on it, but Rip had been clueless. That was important for selling the scam to Ivan and company. He wasn't surprised by Rip's apparent heartlessness. It happened all the time. Commanders often knew there would be casualties when they ordered an operation, but they ordered it anyway. They told themselves they were serving the greater good. They told themselves the victims knew the rules when they signed up to serve. They'd say the same about Katya. "She knew what she was getting into when she got engaged to Achilles."

He finished his final visualization, opened his eyes, and charged. He took the stairs in three quick springs, landing in a shooters stance facing the table. Then he crouched and fired. Three bullets, three calves. Pop! Pop! Pop! Ivan. Pavel. Boris.

As they screamed and grabbed their legs, he holstered the Glock, swapped the H&K to his right hand, and leveled it on Michael. Holding the machine pistol rock steady, he pulled a pack of heavy duty zip ties from a cargo pocket and tossed it to Ivan's right-hand man. "Bind the uninjured ankles to the table leg, and wrists to wrists. Anything I don't find acceptably tight gets a bullet. We clear?"

The air was full of invectives, but Michael's affirmative came through clearly enough. He went to work.

When Michael finished with the zip ties, Achilles tossed him another pack. "Another round, just as tight. I want fingers and toes tingling."

Michael complied.

"Now the duct tape. You know the drill."

Michael ripped off six-inch strips and slapped them over his friends' mouths.

"Eyes too."

Michael gave him a nasty look, but obeyed. When he finished, he turned to face Achilles, with shoulders squared and head held high. He thought he knew what was coming, and apparently he was prepared to face it like a man.

Achilles pointed the machine pistol at Michael's center mass. "You shot Jo Monfort. You shot her in the chest and left her for dead."

Michael said nothing.

Achilles ejected the magazine. He put it in his pocket and tossed the H&K downstairs. Then he did the same with the Glock. Then he launched himself at Michael like a demon from Hell's door.

110

Shoulder to Shoulder

French Riviera

Achilles closed the gap to Michael in two quick bounds and ducked at the last second to come in low with a gut punch. Typically this would bend his opponent over, setting up a knee to the nose. Given Achilles' cross-country skier legs, that was usually the last blow required. Oomph! Crunch! Game over. Achilles was counting on that quick and clean takedown. The kind he'd dealt to Vazov's bodyguards. Revenge delivered, swift and sweet.

But history didn't repeat itself.

His punch did not connect with his opponent's gut.

Michael dodged like a professional boxer, then launched into a seven-punch combination, pummeling Achilles' head and torso with powerful blows. As Michael danced back and rolled his shoulders, Achilles found himself feeling dazed and experiencing blurred vision in his left eye. Although disoriented, he wasn't too confused to realize that he was likely to lose a punching match with this pro.

He couldn't let that happen.

He couldn't forfeit everything to one stupid move.

More importantly, he couldn't let Katya down.

Achilles, quite simply, refused to lose.

So, as Michael swooped in to deliver his next combination, Achilles dropped and swept his legs.

Michael fell, then both men began scrambling to gain a dominant position. They threw fists and elbows, pushed palms and jerked knees. Neither was doing decisive damage or making sustainable progress as they tumbled and rolled like wildcats in a cage.

Achilles punched and pulled, blocked and absorbed, grappled and strained.

Michael punched and pulled, blocked and absorbed, grappled and strained.

Neither could achieve a dominant position long enough to do anything decisive.

Achilles pictured Katya and punched harder. He pictured her in her cell, and clenched firmer. He heard her calling out to him, and he roared in response.

None of it moved the needle.

Was he destined to be the final falling star?

Michael had compelling motivations of his own. He'd just become rich beyond most people's wildest dreams, but had yet to spend a penny. And his team was right there, only inches away. Sending energy in his direction.

Achilles had known that the smart move was to treat Michael like the others. A shot to the calf, followed by zip ties and duct tape. But sometimes the shortcut was the wrong road to take. Sometimes you have to savor the moment, even if doing so might be a mistake.

He had been fantasizing about beating Michael to a pulp ever since the bastard shot Jo in the chest and pushed her from his moving car—while she was under Achilles' command. Looking down at her broken, comatose body in that Monaco hospital room, he had vowed that some day he would settle that score.

Today was that day.

On the surface, his decision didn't appear to be reckless. Achilles was younger and stronger than Michael. Unfortunately, as circumstances were now reminding him, luck could toss victory either way. In situations like this, you just never knew.

Achilles stopped second-guessing himself and began thinking like Ivan. One step ahead. What would victory look like? How could he achieve it? He pondered that picture as they punched and jabbed and grabbed and rolled.

At last, an image appeared in Achilles' mind. A wrestling move. It wasn't the flashiest, or the most complicated, but it was unparalleled for its efficacy and ability to inflict pain. The problem was the setup. It required a gamble. A gambit that could cost him his life.

Achilles went for it.

He flipped around, sacrificing his dominant position in a move that landed him on his back with his opponent positioned directly above, perfectly poised to slug or choke. Michael gleefully recognized the slip-up he'd been waiting for. He finally had room to move and options to exercise. He could punch Achilles into oblivion or choke him to death. In his excitement, Michael failed to notice that both of Achilles' legs were now locked around his waist.

Achilles brought his arms and elbows up like a face guard to block the blows he knew Michael was dying to deliver. In doing so, he exposed his neck.

Michael went for it.

As he reached out with both hands open and murder in his eyes, Achilles squeezed his legs and put his arms and shoulders into action. He twisted up to the right, wrapping his right arm all the way around Michael's upper left arm, while his left hand shot out and secured Michael's left wrist. Then Achilles slapped his right hand over his own left wrist, trapping Michael's entire left arm. He applied pressure, pushing the shoulder and elbow in unnatural ways. Painful ways. Debilitating ways. It was a Kimura lock, and it was one of the most dreaded in the mixed martial arts.

Michael flopped forward to ease the pain.

Achilles clenched and stretched his legs, then lifted his left arm higher, forcing Michael's face to the ground beside his own and leaving Michael completely helpless. Any move Michael made would put pressure on his shoulder and elbow joints, increasing the already considerable pain and threatening a crippling snap.

Achilles twisted his own neck and shoulders to look at Michael's head. It was awkward and painful, but important. "Look at me!"

"I can't," Michael grunted.

Achilles pressed his left arm a little higher, putting more pressure on Michael's locked joints. "Look at me!"

Michael groaned and bucked and twisted and strained until he could meet Achilles' eye. Sweat poured off his face and his jaw looked like it was trying to crush his teeth, but he didn't whimper or wail.

Achilles stared into Michael's eyes and began wriggling his wrist a little, increasing sensation without adding pressure. Priming his opponent's joints for things to come. When Achilles saw that Michael couldn't take any more pain, he asked the first question. "How did Ivan find Katya."

Michael blinked and exhaled. He was waging a mighty war in his own head—but in his heart, he knew that he'd been beaten.

Achilles pressed a little harder.

"He did what he always does. He planned ahead." Michael's words were labored and faint.

Achilles let a little pressure off. "What does that mean?"

"Before Ivan flew to the U.S. to frame you for killing Rider, he sent me to Moscow to plant tracking devices. I put them in her shoes. I put them in her purses. You called Katya within hours of Rider's death, as Ivan knew you would. When she fled to Lake Gryadetskoe, we still had twelve days of battery to spare—and a bulletproof insurance policy."

Achilles cursed himself. He'd been so focused on playing Ivan's game forward that he had neglected to play it backward.

Enough for the warmup.

Time for the big question.

Achilles waggled his wrist, priming Michael with even more pain. "Where is Katya?"

"I don't know. I really don't."

Achilles pictured Katya chained to a wall without food, without water, breathing air that reeked of feces and cursing the day she'd met him. He popped Michael's shoulder out of its socket.

Michael screamed and bucked, but Achilles didn't yield. He held fast. He held firm. All while Michael wriggled like a stuck worm. "Where is Katya?"

"I—don't—know." He was hyperventilating.

Achilles kept his eyes locked on Michael's and began grinding the arm in its socket. "Do I need to take your elbow?"

"I don't know where she is. I swear. I swear."

Achilles believed him.

111

The Choice

French Riviera

Ivan awoke to the scent of ammonia and the sight of a familiar setting. It took him a moment to place it, unexpected as it was. Pleasantly unexpected. He was back at Silicon Hill, seated in one of the glass conference rooms.

His left leg was screaming as if it had just been shot, which of course it had. Twice.

The last thing he remembered was listening—bound, gagged and blindfolded—to Achilles interrogate Michael. The prior fight had been both maddening and mesmerizing. Definitely the ten most anxious minutes of Ivan's life. He'd been confident in his boxing champ, and his hopes had surged as he heard the smacks of bone on flesh from what could only be Michael's signature seven-punch combination. But then the fight had gone to the floor where they'd flopped around like bobcats in a bag until the fight ended with the words, "Look at me!" spoken by Achilles.

The interrogation had been heart-wrenching, but ultimately fruitless, of course. The last thing Ivan heard was the pop of an air gun. It sounded three times, then he felt the fourth. This time in the thigh rather than the calf. A tranquilizer dart.

Ivan coughed from the smelling salts, but couldn't bring a hand to his face. They were cuffed behind his back.

Kyle Achilles and Jo Monfort were seated before him. Coughs made him aware that his team was seated behind him, but Ivan didn't look. His gaze was drawn to the table. It displayed his laptop. Retrieved from the jet. Jo was browsing files. She must have unlocked it with his fingerprint.

"You know the question," Achilles said. "Where's Katya?"

"You were on the yacht the whole time. Hidden not just from my team, but from your own." Ivan couldn't believe it. Achilles had anticipated his trump move, and he'd positioned himself one step ahead. One step ahead of Ivan the Ghost. That had never happened before.

Achilles was staring at him. Through him. He spoke to his soul. "You lost it all on the last roll."

"You going to break my arm now?"

Achilles tilted his head to the left.

Ivan looked left. The opaque floral design on the glass prevented casual glances into the neighboring conference room, but Ivan adjusted his focus and his mind filled in the unseen bits. Ripley Zonder was standing there, arms folded in front of his chest, grin plastered across his face. "So you're going to turn me over to the CIA? Let them try to pry the information from me in one of their infamous interrogation rooms? It won't work."

"Why not? What makes you so special?"

"I've already begun erasing the memory. Writing over it. You can do that, you know. Go over an alternative scenario enough times in your mind and you'll come to believe it. That's how most people manage to live with themselves after mistakes or drastic actions. It's routine really. A defense mechanism. Of course, I won't stop with one alternative scenario. I'll layer them on, one after the other. I'll create so many viable options that the original will become hopelessly lost."

"Your brain's going to be a bit too busy to imprint alternative images."

"I know how the CIA works, Achilles. And so do you. There are limits. Boundaries. If the bozos from al-Qaeda could beat Guantanamo's best, what do you think I can do? I might not last forever, but I can outlast Katya. Unless we make a deal."

Achilles held up two fingers.

"You offering a peace accord?"

"That's twice."

"Twice what?" Ivan did not like the look on Achilles' face.

"Two times I've been one step ahead."

"What are you talking about?"

Achilles tilted his head to the right.

Ivan turned to look into the other neighboring conference room. After adjusting his focus, he saw four men. Three were standing in similar poses, with arms clasped across chests, as if holding in aggression eager to escape. The fourth was swinging a polo mallet. The Vazovs and Victor's enforcers.

"We made a deal, Victor and I. He gets Katya's location out of you within 24 hours, and he gets to keep you and your boys for as long as he likes."

Ivan felt his hopes start circling the drain. The swirling sensation was making him dizzy. Winning was no longer an option. No matter what he did or threatened to do, no matter what story he spun or what scenario he invented, Victor wouldn't let him walk.

Ivan held his head high. "I've still got it, you know."

"Got what?" Achilles asked.

"The one thing that matters most."

"Something that matters more to you than your life?" Achilles nodded over Ivan's shoulder. "And the lives of your friends?"

"Reputation. I may not leave this world having won every round, but I can still go out never having lost." As Ivan spoke the words, the anguished look on Achilles' face told him he'd made the right move. The pained expression would feed him in the hours ahead. Ivan knew he would suffer, and suffer mightily, but Achilles would be tortured forever. "I choose the Vazovs."

112

Revelations

French Riviera

Achilles couldn't believe he was down to his last card and gambling for Katya's life. If the Vazovs couldn't beat her location out of Ivan. If they failed to get him to talk, to tell the truth, rather than sending them off to Smolensk on a wild goose chase, his odds of finding her in time were slim to none.

The Vazov party streamed into the central conference room. Ripley Zonder followed.

Vlad walked straight up to Ivan and kicked his bullet wound with the tip of his polo boot. Ivan roared, but quickly stifled himself. "I'm going to enjoy this," Vlad said. "More than you know."

"Oh, good," Ivan said. "I was afraid I'd get the good guy. The one with talent."

Achilles knew what Ivan was up to. He was trying to push Vlad's buttons and produce an extreme reaction. One that would end things quickly. But Vlad was not so easily played. He picked Ivan up in a fireman's carry and turned toward the door.

"Remember our agreement," Rip said. "I get the body, and it has to be identifiable. Face and fingerprints."

"Face and fingerprints," Vlad repeated. "We can leave most of those."

The other three members of the Vazov party moved in to pick up Ivan's lieutenants.

Boris blurted, "I know where she is!"

Everyone turned to face him.

"He doesn't know shit," Ivan said. "None of them do. But go ahead, figure it out the hard way if you must."

"I installed the surveillance system on the room she's in,"

Boris continued.

The look in Ivan's eyes sent a surge of hope to Achilles' heart.

"I can take you to her, right now. But after you have her, the three of us go with Agent Zonder—and Vazov gets Ivan. Agreed?"

Achilles bit his tongue and turned to face Rip.

To his relief, Rip nodded. "I'll still need the face and fingerprints."

Achilles turned to Victor.

"I can live with that."

Everyone turned back to Boris.

Achilles closed his eyes and bowed his head, and asked the crucial question. "How far away is she?"

"About 500 feet. She's in the hidden basement beneath Ivan's house. Michael knows how to access it—and he can still walk."

Achilles' heart leapt. He'd anticipated hours of tortured travel. But if Boris wasn't lying, Katya was only a minute away.

Wary of a trap, he, Jo and one of Victor's bodyguards followed Michael to Ivan's villa while the others stood watch. Michael led them to a closet. Achilles braced for a booby trap, but Michael's body language indicated there was none. A reassuring nod from Jo told him she concurred.

"Open the door, but don't step inside," Michael said.

Achilles complied.

"Now sweep aside the clothes and twist the rod."

Again Achilles complied.

The floor flipped up, exposing hidden stairs.

Achilles grabbed Michael by his bound wrists and, without regard for his swollen shoulder, guided him down the stairs. They ended up in a wine cellar.

"I recognize the bricks from Ivan's video," Jo said, excitedly.

"The next part is a bit tricky," Michael said. "Easier if you free my hands."

Achilles applied zip ties to Michael's ankles, then nodded at the bodyguard, who produced a knife and slit the ones binding his wrists.

Michael hopped to the rack beneath the stairs, removed a bottle, twisted a strut, and pushed with both hands. The wall gave way before him.

They walked into a hidden room containing workbenches, tools and the smell of grease. Katya wasn't there.

Achilles and Jo turned to Michael.

He looked flummoxed. "This is the hidden room. She's not here. That's all I know."

"This does look like the room," Jo said. "Except now it has workbenches and tools, while before it had nothing but books, a bucket and a cot."

Achilles got a sinking feeling. He didn't know if he could take much more of this roller-coaster ride without puking. He looked at Jo. Had they been duped?

"Oh, God," she said.

They ran back to the conference room, leaving the bodyguard to contend with Michael.

To their relief, they found everyone as they'd left them, with the Vazovs taunting Ivan and Rip looking blissfully satisfied.

"She's not there!" Achilles yelled.

Ivan grew a crooked smile despite his circumstances, but Boris looked dumbfounded. "No, I saw the same video stream you did. The underground brick room. The converted wine cellar. She was there."

Achilles turned to Jo. "I didn't see the video. Was it live, or could it have been a recording?"

Jo scrunched her face and twisted her neck. "It looked live, but I guess it could have been a recording. We didn't interact. She didn't know we were watching."

"Was the mattress still on the floor?"

"No mattress. Just workbenches and tools."

That drew a reaction from Boris. He turned to Michael. "You looked in the wrong room. There's another hidden room on the opposite side."

"I didn't know," Michael said.

This time Achilles threw Boris over his shoulder and ran. He ran to the villa and down the secret stairs. He placed Boris in front of a different wine rack, one kitty-corner from the one Michael had moved.

The bodyguard freed his bindings.

Boris performed a similar set of operations, then Achilles

pushed the rack inside.

Katya was waiting. She was chained so she couldn't run to him, but she was standing with a big, broad grin and open arms.

EPILOGUE

Palo Alto, California

Achilles thanked the Uber driver, ran up the driveway, and rang the bell of his own front door. He had not been home since the day before Director Rider died, so his keys were long gone. Katya opened the door and he walked into a wonderful embrace. This moment was what he'd been fighting for. Was there anything better than coming home to the woman you loved? Maybe if it also involved kids clinging to your waist. He wasn't sure, but he was ready to find out.

Six days earlier, they had flown from France to Virginia on Victor Vazov's jet. Victor had been eager to score a few preemptive points with law enforcement, and Rip had been happy to make a grand entrance. Given the reception they received upon landing at Marine Corps Air Facility Quantico, you'd have thought they were carrying nuclear ordinance. In a sense they were. Their cargo included Ivan the Ghost's three lieutenants and the sole surviving Raven drone—the one left in the secret lab to frame Vazov, along with its command module.

Achilles had been detained for five full days of questioning, quarantined no less. Katya, by contrast, had been released after two days. One for medical exams, and a second for debriefing. Their home smelled like she'd spent a good chunk of her three-day head start cooking.

"Achilles, I can't breathe."

He released the hug and followed his fiancée into the kitchen. Two plates and a chilled bottle of Twomey Sauvignon Blanc waited on the table. "Chili-glazed barramundi with coconut jasmine rice and sautéed summer vegetables from the farmer's market."

"It looks heavenly and smells divine."

Katya poured him a glass of wine, then raised her own. "They just made the big announcement while you were en route from the airport." She proceeded to repeat it with a news anchor's inflection. "Breaking news. The FBI has apprehended the man who was behind both the assassination of CIA Director Wiley Rider, and the drone kidnap and ransom attacks that terrorized our nation. The cunning culprit is none other than the world's most infamous architect of crime, Ivan the Ghost."

Achilles and Katya clinked and sipped. She said, "I was surprised they waited so long to announce it."

"Brix didn't want to go public before they had Ivan in custody."

"In custody or …?"

"The Vazov family worked Ivan over for a full 48 hours. I don't want to imagine what that was like. I heard veterinary stimulants and blood transfusions were involved. But when they dropped him off he was still alive. Apparently Victor decided that Ivan would suffer more from life in a maximum security prison than he would from another few hours of … his team's best work."

"I'm glad," Katya said. "I agree with Victor. Where did they turn him over?"

"Paris. The FBI has an office at the embassy. They had him delivered in a crate to the attention of Ripley Zonder and Robert Brix."

Katya met his eye and Achilles knew something serious was coming. "Now that we know that, let's never speak of him again."

"As you wish. Are you okay? How are you feeling? I'm sorry we didn't get nearly enough alone time before the quarantine at Quantico."

"We'll talk about me in a minute. Please finish your debrief first. I'm sick of being in the dark. I've had way too much of that. What's going on with Jo?"

"You're not going to believe this," he said with a lopsided smile.

"Tell me."

"She's back at the CIA."

"No way!"

"Apparently Rip Zonder got on Director Riddle's good side during the investigation, and he called in his chit to get Jo's job back. I heard there wasn't much resistance. Word has it that Riddle got a MiMiC call from Ivan too. It wasn't just Rip who got duped."

"She's happy to return to government service?"

"It's a great fit. She's really talented. Our country is lucky to have her. And now that she's in the good graces of the Director himself, she's golden. As is Rip, by the way. He got the assignment of his choice at the FBI: SAIC of San Antonio, Texas."

"You mentioned MiMiC. What will the FBI do with it and the drones?"

"The existence of gun-toting drones will be kept quiet. Same for MiMiC. They can't put the K&R drone idea back in the bag, but they can conceal the know-how to build it. Hopefully, they'll come up with countermeasures before the next guy figures out how to create one. If not, we'll be looking at a new world."

Katya raised her glass again. "A world that will need more people like you."

They dove into the fish and vegetables. Both were a bit cold, but they still tasted delicious. The secret to a great meal wasn't so much the food as who you ate it with.

Achilles cleaned his plate at embarrassing speed.

Katya put down her own fork when he finished. That was her habit. One of the ways she stayed so slim. He felt guilty for forgetting to pace himself. He was just so wrapped up in the rhythm of catharsis.

"What about the money?" Katya asked. "Any chance it will be recovered?"

"Already done. I gave Rip the Bitcoin accounts for Ivan's lieutenants. They were written down in code, but I overheard the key while on the yacht. Then Victor pried Ivan's personal account information out of him—once they were alone."

Katya shuddered as she pictured that conversation.

Achilles plowed on. "The FBI confiscated the $600 million Ivan forwarded to Vlad Vazov. Vlad also lost Silicon Hill, which was seized as a criminal enterprise. So Little V is broke, and Big

V is apoplectic. He's making Vlad move back to Russia, and putting him to work. No more polo for the playboy."

"Will people get their ransom and insurance payments back? Or will the money end up funding Homeland Security?"

"Good question. And not one I'm too concerned about. What I am concerned about is you. What did they say at Moscow State University?"

"The Mathematics Department Chair received a call from the U.S. Secretary of State. Professor Kushlinski was quite impressed, and called me to say so. I'm welcome back any time."

Achilles felt a rock roll off his shoulders. "Well, that's a relief. Director Brix must have spoken to the Secretary. I hadn't heard."

Katya didn't look relieved.

Again, Achilles asked the crucial question. "How are you feeling?"

She set down her wine glass and placed her hands in her lap. Her ebullience melted into a faraway expression.

He walked around the table, took her hand, and pulled her gently up into his arms. "What is it? What can I do? How can I help?"

She began to shake. Her tremors were barely perceptible, but enough to melt his heart.

He held her in silence, hoping she could feel the love bursting from him. Willing her soul to sense the security he would forever provide. No matter what, or when, or where. Always.

Katya's shakes grew stronger.

Achilles hugged her tighter.

He began stroking her hair. Long, slow strokes from the top of her head to the small of her back. Soft and tender.

She eventually stopped shaking. Shortly thereafter, he felt her muscles relax.

He waited another long minute before speaking softly. "Would you like to talk to a counselor, a therapist? I can get you into the best of the best. I've got an in. We'll go to her office in the morning."

"No, no. Thank you, but that's not it." She pulled back and met his eye. Her face was fraught with mixed emotions.

"Hawaii? How about a couple of weeks on the Garden Isle? I

know just the resort. Unbelievable beach, fantastic food and luxurious surroundings guaranteed to make you walk around with your mouth half open in wonder. Oh, and I hear the spa is amazing."

"This was *the third time*, Achilles."

He felt the muscles in his throat constricting. What Katya said was true. They hadn't even known each other for two years, but their association had put her life in grave danger three times. "I know."

"It was tough."

Should he have flown to her? Forgotten about chasing Ivan and taken care of his fiancée instead? Would that have been less risky? The CIA might have called ahead. Would have called ahead. They'd have been waiting. But he could have put his efforts into outwitting them, rather than Ivan. And he would have discovered the tracking devices. "I'm sorry. I'm so, so sorry."

"Ivan's goons grabbed me outside the tiny village grocery store. They picked me up and threw me in a van like I was livestock. Then they stuck a needle in my arm. I've never been more terrified than I was the moment that syringe punctured my flesh."

She paused to take a deep breath.

Achilles stayed silent.

"The next thing I knew I was chained to the wall in a room with nothing but some books, a mattress and a bucket. I had no idea where I was. It was silent as a tomb."

He was crying.

She was crying.

"But I knew you'd come for me. I knew it with all my heart. I knew you'd move heaven and earth and wade through the fires of hell. So I was all right. A bit hungry and a bit thirsty, but all right. Good even. Lying there on that moldy mattress in that solitary cell, I was good because one truth became crystal clear to me. A truth I'll carry with me forever. It's not what surrounds us that matters in this life, it's who. I love you, Kyle Achilles."

AUTHOR'S NOTE

Dear Reader,

THANK YOU for reading FALLING STARS. I hope you enjoyed it. If you would be so kind as to take a moment to leave a review on Amazon or elsewhere, I would be very grateful. Reviews and referrals are as vital to an author's success as a good GPA is to a student's.

You might be interested to know that the first few drafts of FALLING STARS had a significantly different ending. If you are curious about the road not taken, kindly email me at tim@timtigner.com and I will forward a copy to you.

Thanks again for your kind comments and precious attention. All my best,

Tim

NOTES ON FALLING STARS

The idea for FALLING STARS came from the conclusions described during the flashback scene where Ivan was on the beach in Cannes. In my case, I was talking to my brother on the phone rather than kicking sand, but in an instant I knew I had my next book.

There are drones that can carry people, although individual helicopters are getting more commercial attention. Here's a video of one: https://youtu.be/At3xcj-pTjg. And another video documenting multiple futuristic flying inventions: https://youtu.be/1juc7_7gnB0.

My novels all center around devices I invent. When creating them, I look for things that are near enough to the realm of possibility to be credible. A few times they've actually been invented while I'm writing the book. That was the case with MiMiC. You'll find a similar software program at lyrebird.ai.

The DREAD gun was a military project that died. I don't know why. You can buy a similar air gun which shoots BBs rather than ball bearings. Google Dread Gun to learn more.

Unfortunately, there already are drone-mounted guns. Here is one from Russia: https://youtu.be/SNPJMk2fgJU.

All these links and more can also be found on the Pinterest Board I used to store my research for FALLING STARS. www.pinterest.com/authortimtigner/research-for-falling-stars. (There's one for all the Kyle Achilles novels.)

WANT MORE ACHILLES?

CHASING IVAN, a 150-page novella, is the story of a pivotal mission in Achilles' career while he was still at the CIA. You can download it for free at timtigner.com. Kyle Achilles #1, PUSHING BRILLIANCE, and #2, THE LIES OF SPIES, are on sale now at Amazon and Audible.

ABOUT THE AUTHOR

Tim began his career in Soviet Counterintelligence with the US Army Special Forces, the Green Berets. With the fall of the Berlin Wall, Tim switched from espionage to arbitrage and moved to Moscow in the midst of Perestroika. In Russia, he led prominent multinational medical companies, worked with cosmonauts on the MIR Space Station (from Earth, alas), and chaired the Association of International Pharmaceutical Manufacturers.

Moving to Brussels during the formation of the EU, Tim ran Europe, Middle East, and Africa for a Johnson & Johnson company and traveled like a character in a Robert Ludlum novel. He eventually landed in Silicon Valley, where he launched new medical technologies as a startup CEO.

Tim began writing thrillers in 1996 from an apartment overlooking Moscow's Gorky Park. Twenty years later, he's still writing. His home office now overlooks a vineyard in Northern California, where he lives with his wife Elena and their two daughters.

Tim grew up in the Midwest. He earned a BA in Philosophy and Mathematics from Hanover College, and then an MBA in Finance and a MA in International Studies from the University of Pennsylvania's Wharton School and Lauder Institute.

CPSIA information can be obtained
at www.ICGtesting.com
Printed in the USA
LVHW04s1131260918
591411LV00018B/225/P

9 781979 259385